Sum

A Taste of Greek Summer

Mandy Baggot

First published in Great Britain in 2022 by

Bonnier Books UK Limited
4th Floor, Victoria House, Bloomsbury Square, London, WC1B 4DA
Owned by Bonnier Books
Sveavägen 56, Stockholm, Sweden

A CIP catalogue record for this book is available from the British Library.

eBook ISBN: 9781471411731
Print ISBN: 9781471412233

This book is typeset using Atomik ePublisher

Embla Books is an imprint of Bonnier Books UK
www.bonnierbooks.co.uk

Printed and bound in Great Britain by Clays Ltd, Elcograf S.p.A.

To all my Ready Steady Cook *friends!*
Thank you for the fun, laughter and an epic show
that turned out to be GREAT research for this book!

One

Obelisk 1, London, UK

Lydia Broom's hand was shaking as she put fork prongs to the intricately posed dish on the plate in front of her. What had they called it again? A *whisper* of salmon? Or was it a *ghost*? She was going to have to ask, maybe before she took a bite. And a bite was all it was, perhaps not even a *whole* bite. It was the smallest main dish she had ever been served. She raised her head to see if she could attract the attention of someone working at the upmarket eatery – Obelisk 1 – that they were guests at, for its soft opening.

Nice and pretentious, with the name suggesting both opulence and plans for other premises in the future. Very on trend, but personally she thought it sounded like a Russian submarine. Lydia looked to the open kitchen. She could actually see the head chef from their vantage point on a slightly raised plinth with mood lighting. He was pretending to be busy, but his eyes kept flicking up from the galley to survey the patrons, pristine white outfit somehow looking like it hadn't been near food, ever. And he seemed way too composed. In Lydia's experience, most chefs were always on his or her toes, energetic, slightly erratic, eager, a bit frazzled. His sous chef had no doubt done the real work here.

Opposite, Caroline, her colleague, slammed her mobile to the table and dived her fork straight into the salmon carpaccio with lemon aioli and a pork rind crumble. And then it was gone, just like that and Caroline was slugging it down with a great gulp of red wine. There was absolutely no chance she had tasted any of the highly nuanced flavours Lydia was reporting on for food and lifestyle magazine, *Luxe Living*. Where Lydia's expertise was culinary excellence, Caroline's was aspirational living. However, when it came to personal taste, Caroline's was far more Pukka pie than charcoal focaccia. Ordinarily, Caroline wouldn't be accompanying Lydia on a reviewing visit, but it had been decided at the magazine that as Obelisk 1 was paying a substantial sum to have its brand new restaurant splashed all over the front cover of the winter edition, all the stops needed to be pulled out. Caroline was all the stops, and she was going to write an article about starting a new business when the high street was dying ...

'Well, if that was a "tissue" of salmon then it was only the bloody one-ply kind!' Caroline announced *very* loudly.

A *tissue* of salmon! That was it. Lydia made a mental note.

'The wine's alright though. But I think I might need another.' Caroline was halfway towards putting her hand in the air to beckon a waiter when Lydia stopped her.

'You don't need another one yet.' She held on to Caroline's hand with her own, and then the fork dropped out of her other one, right on top of the food, bashing the salmon sliver and making the small stack fall over – plop – into the aioli sauce.

'Shit,' Lydia said, dropping her hold on Caroline and picking up her fork. 'Did we get sent pictures of these dishes?'

'No idea,' Caroline said. 'I did take some lovely pics of their light fittings though. Very on trend with the steampunk and industrial touches. Very regeneration!'

With sandstone and Sanskrit too, it was a melting pot of themes, that was for sure. Well, whether or not they had photos of the feat of engineering that was their minute, layered meal, Lydia did need to taste it. She pushed her light blonde hair back behind her ears and picked up the fork again. Scooping up the intricate shaving of salmon, she then used her knife to lick over the aioli and add a little of the crumb.

'While you're farting about playing with your food and I wait for inspiration for my article, I'll have a quick skim over Insta. I'm becoming obsessed with Greece in all its forms – sea, sky, scantily clad "actors". Oh and I've unfollowed Nigel BTW.'

Nigel was their line manager. Wasn't it obligatory to follow your boss? Particularly when everything they did at the magazine was about social media and optimum reach?

'He posted a picture of a car park,' Caroline continued, eyes already on her phone. 'A fucking car park. Not only that, he hashtagged it "my *favourite* car park". I'm sorry but anyone who has a favourite car park does not deserve a second of my attention on my downtime.'

Except this wasn't downtime, this was work. Yes, it might be half past seven at night, but that was the nature of reporting on restaurants. Lydia looked at the food on her fork and thought about how this would have been created with blood, sweat and a precision only the most steady-handed of chefs would be capable of. That had been her once. In charge of the food creation, leading the kitchen as head chef. She had been in her element back then, listening to every word her mentor, Mario, imparted – learning, growing, challenging herself every single day ... Now she was lucky if she could successfully open a tin of chopped tomatoes. And she wasn't sure if it was a total loss of skill, an incision into her muscle memory brought on by trauma, or whether everything was still intact and this was a case of the connections being broken through fear. She tried to quieten those thoughts.

Putting the forkful of food into her mouth, she waited for each morsel to invigorate her tastebuds. She tuned out Caroline's whining about being served advertisements for figure-of-eight exercise classes and focused on the food journey she should have been going on right now. Except nothing was happening. It was less of a journey and more a can't-even-get-the-car-started kind of feeling. The taste of the delicate salmon was gone before it was even there, the aioli seemed devoid of all trace of garlic, and the pork crumb tasted like a plain biscuit that had been neglected in the bottom of the barrel, possibly for months. This was not the 'flavour sensation' the website for this new venture was selling. And it certainly wasn't worth paying the extortionate price tag. But maybe it was just her. She had felt similarly two days ago at the new Colombian restaurant everyone was raving about being the best thing to come out of the country since Shakira. Maybe she was losing her complex palate the way she had lost her ability to julienne.

'How was the food for you?' Lydia asked Caroline.

'Miniscule,' Caroline answered without looking up from her phone. 'But it always is in these places, isn't it?'

Lydia was going to get nothing of use from her to help describe the tastes and textures. As she wondered what she could do apart from move on to the final course and hope it blew her mind, her eyes went across the sleek, maybe-slightly-too-bright dining room, to David Deacon, the lead writer from rival mag, *Note Cuisine*. He was tapping on his iPad like he was playing the piano and Lydia could see that he was only on his first course. She had been equally unexcited by that. The *ajo blanco* sounded fantastic on paper, a chilled almond soup that should have given 'sweet', 'light' and 'fragrant' but, in reality, it had tasted like a cross between milk gone past its use-by date and paint.

'I'm starving,' Caroline suddenly announced. 'What's for dessert?'

'It's a white chocolate mousse and sorbet with dill and cucumber,' Lydia informed.

'Ugh, so basically a bloody salad,' Caroline moaned. 'When did everyone stop serving chips? I bet they have sweet potato fries on the menu, don't they?'

'Celeriac ones actually,' Lydia answered.

'Christ, that's an ugly vegetable. If it was orange it would remind me of Vernon.'

Caroline talked about her ex-husband a lot considering they were long since divorced. Lydia couldn't remember a day of conversation without Vernon getting a mention in some way. Usually it would begin with an insult such as this and end up in some kind of reminiscence. Lydia was still unclear why the couple had separated in the first place …

'God, I need a holiday!' Caroline exclaimed. 'Did I tell you about the time Vernon took me to Mijas?'

'Yes. You did it in the *pueblo* and the *playa*,' Lydia responded.

It was a well-worn tale and told with way too much enthusiasm and sometimes even the mention of sand dune burns …

'Oh,' Caroline said, disappointment thick. 'Well, I obviously don't want to go there. But Greece would be idyllic, wouldn't it?'

Caroline had rolled the 'r' of Greece as if she was eating the country whole and it was the tastiest morsel she had ever had the pleasure of having in her mouth. And despite Lydia's protests, she had heard *a lot* about the kind of things Caroline had had in her mouth over the years.

'Beautiful little coves with turquoise water. Gorgeous, big strong Greeks wearing nothing but loin cloths …'

Abroad. She hadn't been out of the UK since Mario had taken her to Italy to meet his daughter, Antonia. Amongst all the *caffe* and *biscotti* and recipes handed down from *nonnas* of old, Lydia had felt a warm embrace from the Italian flair for cuisine in its natural habitat – if not from Mario's daughter …

'You don't have to say a thing,' Caroline said, plucking up the napkin and waving it as if in surrender. 'I am going to deep dive into travel trends again tonight – when I'm picking my way through a large portion of chips and a Spam fritter – and then I am going to come up with a plan to get us to Greece.' Caroline dropped the napkin. 'So, your choice, do I try and sell "glampervan" again or go down the more "hedonistic hideaways" route? I swear, if Gina tells me I'm only getting a minibreak in the Cotswolds this summer I'm going to have to find some blackmail fodder on the dark web about her.'

Gina was their top boss, one below the CEO of Escapade Publishing who put out *Luxe Living* and five other magazines. The buck and budgets stopped with Gina and the purse strings had been tighter than a Joel Dommett suit these days. Hence the importance of advertising revenue. No pressure for this review for Obelisk 1 … Lydia shook her head as a waiter brought them the white chocolate mousse.

Eyeing up the dessert, which was no bigger than a fifty pence piece, she mused on the idea of getting away. Travelling for work, writing reviews of European restaurants, might be exactly what she needed to reinvigorate her taste. And the quarterly could do with getting back to foreign hotspots. The only tapas Lydia had eaten recently had been as authentic as a bento box full of nothing but crisps.

Before Lydia could even pick up her spoon, Caroline had eaten the entire serving of pudding and was pulling a face.

'Christ! I think eating that has actually made me hungrier!'

Two

Lydia Broom's apartment, London, UK

'Come on, dig in!' Caroline urged, her mouth full of deep-fried tinned meat, the chip paper open on the coffee table of Lydia's apartment. 'You *can't* be fulfilled after that meal!'

Lydia had to admit the chips did smell good, but she almost felt she'd be personally insulting every beautiful restaurant she had ever got enthused over if she ate again after three courses – albeit small ones. But, in truth, they hadn't been nice ones either. It was going to be a struggle to find positive things to say in her article. Her writing style wasn't a full-on critique like some of her contemporaries, with star ratings and marks for presentation, flavour and value. She would, of course, give credit where credit was due, but she also didn't want to make or break someone's livelihood. She'd been on the receiving end of that herself and it wasn't a nice place to be. She took a chip and popped it into her mouth. Slathered in salt and vinegar, it tasted all kinds of simplistic divine.

'Thank God for that,' Caroline cackled. 'I was starting to think you'd mutated into David Deacon.'

'Did you see him?' Lydia gasped, sitting back into her sofa. 'He *loved* the food.'

'Of course he did.'

The way Caroline said 'of course he did' seemed to have an odd feeling wrapped around it. 'What d'you mean?'

'Oh, Lyds, David Deacon has zero integrity! You should know that, you've seen him at these things and you've read his pages! Not every bloody venue can be "irresistibly irresistible".'

He did use that annoying phrase quite a lot. It was like his catchphrase. Maybe *she* should have a catchphrase? A shiver ran through her. Were her reviews lacking? Nigel had never said so. But Nigel liked car parks. Were her articles as boring as car parks? *More* boring?!

'That restaurant will be paying him for a great write-up. That's the way he rolls,' Caroline said, dunking chips into a polystyrene vat of thick curry sauce.

'Well, I know the importance of advertising cash, but I can't let that affect what I write about the food.' She would always, *always* be honest. And if she couldn't be honest then she contacted the owner afterwards and said she really couldn't review.

'I'm not talking about advertising space, girlfriend,' Caroline said, chowing down on the Spam. 'I'm talking about under the table kind of dealings.' She touched her nose with a greasy forefinger as if she had morphed into a cheesy TV detective.

Lydia didn't respond straightaway. She mentally ground down on what Caroline might mean. Surely David Deacon wasn't accepting *cash* for five-star reviews?

'Little brown envelopes,' Caroline continued. Then she whispered. 'Like he's a *Line of Duty* CHIS.'

'You're kidding!' Lydia exclaimed. 'But that's ... that's ...'

Caroline shrugged. 'The geez has four kids. Two of them are still under whatever the Child Support Agency is called now. I get it.'

'You get it?!' Lydia stated. She was outraged. So outraged in fact that she got to her feet and flapped her arms. This was all kinds of wrong and the more she thought about it, the more she wondered if this had ever happened to her? Had some of the reviewers who had visited Maison Mario and written the most eloquent words about the dishes she had created been paid? She swallowed. Paid by *Mario*? No, Mario would never have done that. And not everyone was David Deacon, right?

'Oh, Lydia, you can't be naïve enough to think that it doesn't go on,' Caroline continued, drinking down some of a warm can of Heineken palmed onto them by 'Ashton' at the chip shop.

'I'm not naïve.' She hated that word. It tinged her lips with memories from the past as it left her mouth. That's what she'd been called the very last time she'd worked in a professional kitchen. And it wasn't true. She simply wanted to believe that not everyone was a complete arsehole on the take.

Lydia's eyes went to the framed photo on the wall. Mario Romano, dressed in his chef's whites, the most genuine smile on his face. His arm was around her shoulders, and Lydia, aged twenty, was also wearing the uniform of a professional cook. *That man. That uber-talented cook.* He had been both father-figure and mentor until he'd passed away too soon. He'd taken her right under his wing from the moment she had learned to bechamel like a boss and had brought a Tupperware container of lasagne to his restaurant aged thirteen. She reached out and touched the glass, her fingers grazing over that smile. He had made cooking come to life for her. Every dish he had made seemed to have soul, a *raison d'être*. That was what was missing in these meals she was consuming lately. They were all trying too hard to show off and completely missing the mark. She still missed Mario so much. And she mourned everything he had brought to her life that was no longer there. Was that naïvety? To believe that good things could last forever?

'But I want you to know that I've never taken anything in exchange for feature inches – well, not money, anyway,' Caroline stated somewhat proudly.

'What?!' Lydia exclaimed, looking back to her friend.

Caroline sighed and licked her fingers. 'You're making this sound seedy and it's not seedy, it's ... the way of the world.'

'Caroline!'

'Maybe a nice set of bronze candleholders,' Caroline said. 'A small weekend at a lovely hotel in Bath ... possibly my rattan garden furniture that you like ... absolutely not the keys to a townhouse in Malta. I earned those in an entirely different way.'

'I don't believe this!' Lydia said. 'It's not right. It's ... *corruption*.'

'Whoa there, Dominic Cummings. It is not the "c" word. And I have never asked any taxpayer to fund my home refurbs either.'

Lydia picked her drink up from the table and headed towards the kitchen for a refill. And now she was closer to that photo of Mario. He had always been honest, hadn't he? The wonderful, as-soft-as-he-was-strong person who led with integrity and honour …

'He *was* hot.'

Lydia jumped, suddenly realising that Caroline was at her shoulder and looking at the picture of Mario too. 'Don't say that.'

'What? Look at him. Olive-skinned perfection and that hair all long and sleek and Mediterranean.'

Caroline was at least twenty years Lydia's senior, but it was still a bit like her colleague saying she fancied her dad … Actually, Caroline probably *would* fancy her dad.

'He knew exactly how to make a mean paella,' Caroline added, nudging Lydia with her elbow. 'Fool proof, that recipe of his. Stopped me having to buy in the M&S stuff for the Latin-themed dinner parties Vernon and I used to have.'

'He could make anything,' Lydia admitted, nodding. There had been literally no food style Mario hadn't been able to tackle. He had been the maestro.

'And he definitely wouldn't want you moping in the hallway when you could be fixing your friend another drink.'

Caroline had never met Mario, but she *did* know how much the celebrated Italian chef had meant to Lydia. Not that Caroline knew the *whole* cooking backstory, just the parts she had been able to wind out of her under the influence of one too many craft beers at a restaurant inside an old railway station.

Caroline knew Lydia had once been the head chef at Maison Mario, a Michelin restaurant in London, taught from a young age by esteemed chef, Mario Romano. She knew that Lydia had adored the job as much as she had adored Mario. And she knew from the papers that Mario had died of a heart attack at the restaurant he loved so much. But what Caroline didn't know was that Mario had died in Lydia's arms. With the kitchen and its staff stunned into a silence that had never been witnessed before in this frenetic work environment, Lydia had dropped to the floor beside her boss, her beloved tutor, and tried to remember all the things you're supposed to remember if this kind of thing happens. She had loosened his shirt and listened for his breathing and then she had interlocked her fingers and tried to do *something*. *Anything*. But, as the ambulance was called and someone went running to find the nearest defibrillator, Lydia looked into Mario's soft brown eyes and she knew it was too late. Something had already departed.

The light, the spark that made Mario Mario. And as Lydia lay her head on his chest, tears streaming down her face, she also knew that a piece of her was leaving too. And there, amid the shock and grief and horror, Lydia could never have imagined what would happen in the weeks following Mario's passing. Caroline didn't know about that either, *no one* did, and Lydia wanted to keep it that way.

'You look better without the plaits,' Caroline said, sucking the very last drops of liquid out of her empty glass. 'And with your teeth done.'

'I haven't had my teeth done!'

'Well,' Caroline exclaimed, 'however the glow-up happened, it happened. Good for you.'

Lydia didn't know whether to feel complimented or appalled but her fingers went to her hair anyway. It was a little shorter and now she was a writer not a cook she didn't have any reason to braid it out of the way.

Caroline sighed and wandered forward, stepping into Lydia's kitchen that used to comprise almost every gadget and utensil ever invented and now housed little more than the hob, oven and fridge. 'Vernon had braids once. Some grungy woman did them on the beach in the Caribbean. Thank Christ he stopped short of a tattoo.' She turned back to face Lydia. 'Have you got any Sambuca?'

Three

Picking up her coffee mug – one Caroline had bought her in the not-so-Secret-Santa, that said 'warning, may start talking about food you've never heard of'– Lydia went to take a much-needed slurp. Empty. Again. This was her third, and another one she had finished in milliseconds and been left wanting. She screwed up her eyes and refocused on the screen ...

Like a brand new canvas, the bright white crockery was the perfect backdrop to this food portrait. An immediate delight for the eyes it ...

And that's where the review for Obelisk 1 stopped. Gina had told her she *had* to write it and when Gina said you *had* to do something it was akin to getting an order from the Queen. Except what could Lydia say about the tissue of salmon? That, after a light winter cold, she'd actually filled a Kleenex with more substance than made up any of the dishes? And it wasn't just the minute portions, it was the *taste*. As contemporary and on-point as the meal *looked*, there was something not quite there with the flavour. It was, at best, if she was being really *really* kind ... nothing short of bland. And it was going to be tricky for Lydia to write her true thoughts of 'below average' into a review that would get diners on seats at the new venture *and* keep her writing reputation intact.

She raised her fingers over the keyboard again until ... a bottle of wine landed on her desk with a bump and Lydia's pen pot slid sideways six inches as Caroline's backside slipped onto one wooden corner.

'I did it!' Caroline announced, picking the bottle back up, undoing the lid and moving her legs like she was a child on a swing needing momentum. 'I unlocked our future. Well, our summer anyhoo.'

'Oh?'

'Well, aren't you going to ask me what I've done that warrants me opening the good stuff at this hour?' Caroline asked, producing two plastic cups from out of her cleavage. 'And it *is* the good stuff. Vernon might have got the Audi, but I got the Naked Wines subscription paid for as an addition in the divorce settlement.'

Lydia knew that. For a while all the white wine they'd shared together had been called Penis Grigio. She also knew that Caroline was quick to open alcohol at work at whatever hour it was, to celebrate or commiserate or even once to honour Hug Your Cat Day. Not only did Caroline not have a cat, she didn't even like them much.

'What unlocking are we celebrating?' Lydia asked.

Caroline giggled and kicked her feet a little more. 'Guess who's going to Greece?'

This was a trick question, Lydia was sure of it. 'Vernon?' she offered tentatively.

'Is he?!' Caroline said, slapping a palm to her chest. 'Was it on his Facebook?'

Lydia furrowed her brow. She wasn't friends with Caroline's ex on Facebook. 'I don't follow Vernon on anything.' She didn't even know what Vernon looked like, unless he really did look like an orange version of a celeriac.

A breath of relief shot from her colleague's mouth. 'Ah, you're testing me. Good work. And forget the guessing, it's us BTW. *We* are going to Greece!'

What had she said? *They* were going to Greece?

'I know, you can put me forward for a damehood while we're lying on sun loungers overlooking the Ionian Sea.' Caroline looked over her shoulder before she poured out the pale liquid and continued talking. 'I mean, we are going to find all the hidden gems on the islands. From villas of princes, to tavernas fit for ... Julia Bradbury. No gorgeous white pebble will be left unturned in our mission to create a whole Greek edition of *Luxe Living*.'

What had Caroline said just now? A whole edition! No, she couldn't have meant that ... except a bendy beaker of wine was being pressed into Lydia's hand and that was Caroline's signature move when she wanted you to suddenly develop conversation amnesia. Or rather forget the crucial scary details amid the conversation, not the entire thing. Well, forgetting things wasn't a natural talent Lydia possessed.

'A whole edition.' Internally, Lydia had screamed the words like a battle cry, but they'd hit the air weak, wet and with a tremor. This was major. It took months of planning to shape and prepare an edition ... and did that mean Jonathan, who was in charge of the garden space and outdoor living – 'Outside In' – pages was coming with them?

'Lydia, don't do this,' Caroline ordered, slugging back the wine. 'I can sense "defeat" coming off you already and it's not a good fragrance.' She inhaled through her nose. 'Think of it more as a "supplement" rather than an "edition".'

'Well, which is it?' Lydia snapped, taking a meek sip of the alcohol. 'Because the last "supplement" we did was when Gina decided that our readers needed to fall in love with sorbet pastel tones for *everything*.'

'Focus on Greece and us being inside it!'

Caroline got down off the corner of the desk and trotted behind Lydia's chair, leaning right over her, arms encircling her tightly. 'Honestly, this is the most genius plan I've ever had. A few weeks on a Greek island, the supplement-style-edition will basically write itself.'

'A few weeks! How *many* weeks?' Lydia exclaimed. She couldn't go away for a few weeks. She had scores of restaurant reviews booking up her diary. She could shift a week's worth, maybe two, but that was her limit! She had never been on location working, or even been on holiday for longer than a fortnight before. Apart from that one long trip to Italy, when she had worked in the kitchen with Mario.

Caroline turned Lydia in her chair towards a desk on the far left of the open plan office. 'Well, we'll move as many reviews as we can and then ... give the rest to Bonnie.'

Now Lydia wanted to cry as her eyes stopped on the eighteen-year-old trainee who currently looked to be finding it difficult to put staples into a stapler. She came to work dressed in nothing short of anime cosplay most days and had more than ten pairs of Converse in all kinds of colours. 'Caroline,' Lydia began. 'I can't let someone who thinks pickled onion Monster Munch is a delicacy write reviews for my column!'

'She doesn't have to *write* them,' Caroline said, sighing with what sounded like frustration. 'Just, let her be here doing the eating and then she can report back to you and then you … work your magic on it.'

'While I'm visiting restaurants in Greece, enough for a whole edition?' And how hard would it be to write up someone else's experience of eating? She had never *ever* done that before. It felt like cheating. Her mind was back on David Deacon now.

'Not just reviews … but we can discuss that ON THE PLANE!'

Caroline stood up, but then, with a laugh like a manic supervillain, she suddenly sent Lydia's chair into a spin and Lydia revolved at high speed as the wine sloshed into her lap.

Four

Taverna Ilios, Benitses, Corfu, Greece

'Today's special!'

As Baptiste thwacked the enormous grey fish down on the countertop it spattered, sending juices of unknown origin up into the air and down onto the front of chef Thanos Nicolaidis's white T-shirt. He recoiled, but more from the sight of the gigantic tuna now resting on the board designated for vegetables than from the mess his boss had made on his clothes. The restaurant owner was turning to leave the kitchen, smoke rising from the cigarette that was permanently between his lips.

'Baptiste, we cannot have tuna as a special today,' Thanos told him.

Baptiste spun around, his lips already turning downwards into that sour expression he always wore when anyone said anything that opposed his way of thinking. He also stuck his rounded belly out a little more and, at the same time, tried to lengthen all five feet four inches of him. 'Why not?'

How many times had Thanos been through this? Every day since he had been let into the kitchen when he was eighteen. And Baptiste paid as much attention to him now – aged thirty-two and with all the experience – as he had then.

Thanos had worked at this taverna since he was fifteen years old, waiting tables, learning as many languages as he could pick up from the tourists, getting inside the kitchen as often as he could. But now that he *ran* the kitchen, this ritual dance around what made it on the daily specials board was exhausting. And

Baptiste never listened and always, *always* pulled the 'I am the owner' card. But still Thanos tried. Because if he gave up asking, he might as well be back carrying trays of food to customers instead of cooking them ...

'It is Tuesday,' Thanos told Baptiste, looking directly at him as the tuna fish continued to weep liquid onto the work surface.

'I realise,' Baptiste said, blowing out smoke. 'Tuna Tuesday. It has a nice sound to it. Like the Americans with their tacos.'

'And two other restaurants in the village have tuna as a special on a Tuesday,' Thanos reminded. 'Like some of them do *gemista* on a Thursday and roast lamb on a Sunday.' And he told him this almost as regularly as he begged him to stop smoking in the kitchen.

'What can I say?' Baptiste asked, throwing his hands up in the air, cigarette ash falling to the tiled floor. 'The gods of the sea bless the waters near Benitses with tuna on a Tuesday and we are grateful for that!' He pointed a finger at Thanos. 'And you should never disrespect the gods!'

This was another well-worn tale Baptiste used whenever he simply did not want to take on board a change to his routine. Baptiste went to church only because his mother threatened to leave her house entirely to his sister when she died if he didn't attend.

'Baptiste, please, if you want the tourists to choose Taverna Ilios when they come here, then we need to have something different on the specials board. Something no one else has.' Thanos held his breath, even though he knew he was wasting the effort as well as the words. He tucked his dark hair behind his ears and snapped at the elastic hairband on his wrist.

'Now you disrespect the fish!' Baptiste exclaimed. 'Look at it! It is a fine fish! The largest of the catch this morning, I made sure of it!' He looked at the creature like it might once have been a family friend. 'He will make some delicious steaks and perhaps a little left for salads?'

And now Baptiste was telling him the *exact* dishes he wanted Thanos to make out of the fish. The specials board was the only time he was allowed a little creativity yet that was being ripped from him too. He wanted to put his hands around the fish and grip it so tightly that its guts burst through its smooth skin and sprayed all over Baptiste.

'I will write it on the blackboard!' Baptiste announced, puffing on the cigarette again as he departed the space.

That damn blackboard! It was like something unearthed from an archaeological dig! Grey, not black, and almost unreadable. It was a wonder any of their customers got what they wanted.

Now, as Thanos looked out into the taverna at the bright white painted tables and chairs, the turquoise tablecloths moving a little with the breeze, the blue of the sea a few steps beyond the road that hugged the coast, he wondered what it would be like to have any sort of control in his life.

'Thaaannno!'

The voice full of age and gravel vibrated around the kitchen space, rattling the utensils hanging from hooks on a board Thanos had made himself. Before he could make a reply, the door that led to the small patio garden at the back of the restaurant creaked open and in trotted a scruffy ginger cat.

'Out!' Thanos yelled at it, grabbing the door and opening it wider. The cat stayed put, looking at him – with the eye that wasn't half-closed and filled with pus – as if it was a request and not an order.

'I hope you do not speak to me.'

And there was Ismēnē standing on the *plaka* stone. Her spine was so curved now that her chin almost touched her chest. Her wispy grey hair was loose and chaotic like it had never been tamed by a comb. A black cardigan covered a grey pinafore, her gold Adidas trainers were on her feet and her thick stick was in her hand – part to aid walking, part to use as a weapon as necessary. Thanos calmed a little. She was family. Not biologically so but in all the other ways that mattered.

The cat took a bold step towards his kitchen and Thanos quickly scooped it up in his hands, depositing it by an urn filled with tiny orange flowers as he closed the door behind him.

'I was talking to the cat,' Thanos told her.

'His name is Nuno. So, tell me, what did he say back to you?' she asked, grinning with all six of her teeth.

'He asked me what you are doing here when you should be at home for your chiropody appointment.' He checked his watch. He had made the appointment himself, made a week's worth of *pastitsio* to get the foot doctor to do a home visit.

'My feet are not Nuno's concern,' she said, taking a firm grip on his arm. 'And you need to come with me. See what is behind the sheets on the washing line.'

Thanos shielded his eyes from the sun as Ismēnē led him forward across the paved ground, her steps laboured and awkward. She really did need to see the chiropodist. 'Where are you taking me?' he asked.

'Sshh,' Ismēnē said. 'You need to look and you need to listen.' She stopped walking when they were directly opposite a large white sheet pegged up on the plastic-coated wire.

'Is this about the birds?' Thanos asked. 'Are they shitting on everything again? That cat needs to do his job or you should stop feeding it.'

'Thano! Quiet!' Ismēnē ordered.

He had no idea what this was all about, but if he got it over with and Ismēnē went back to her home in time to get her feet treated, then perhaps he could return to turning the tuna into something more than steak and salad for the lunch menu.

Just as he was about to ask what exactly he was supposed to be looking and listening for, a drumbeat pumped out, followed by tinny-sounding trumpets and a very weak synthesiser. Down fell the sheet from the line and there was the reveal. His fourteen-year-old brother, Onassis, and his three closest friends were all dressed up like would-be gangsters. Baggy jeans, baggy T-shirts, thick gold chains around their necks, sunglasses on their faces and attitude all over their expressions. Were they going to a fancy dress party? Was that a cigarette between Stamatis's lips? Then, all at once, they began pulsing in synch to the music as the vocals kicked in and so started a real dance routine ...

From knee slides through body-popping, to cartwheels and pelvic thrusts that were verging on disturbing, Thanos watched as his little brother and his companions put on a performance that had Ismēnē rocking on the spot and tapping her stick on the ground in rhythm to the song. It all ended with the boys making a tower out of their bodies with Onassis on the very top, standing on Stamatis's shoulders and wobbling very precariously as he held his position.

Ismēnē stabbed her stick at the floor in appreciation but Thanos was left wondering what part of his body Onassis was going to break when he fell off the shoulders of his friend.

'Onassis, get down!' Thanos ordered.

'Wait!' Onassis called. 'I can hold it better.'

Thanos watched as his brother stretched his arms out a little further, straightening up his body and attempting to morph into some kind of triangle shape. Thanos held his breath. This was exactly how things had been when Onassis had gone through a stage of wanting to be a circus performer. And then suddenly his brother began to lose his balance and the neat stack of boys started to quickly come apart …

Thanos rushed forward, arms outstretched, but Onassis was falling fast. In an instance that felt like an age, Thanos managed to break his brother's fall, but he knew he wasn't going to be quite so lucky. There was nothing he could do. His skin grazed against the sharp edge of the corner of the patio wall.

'Ismēnē!' Onassis wailed. 'Thanos bleeds!'

Thanos put a hand to his neck and yes, there was a little bright red liquid on his fingers. It wouldn't be a good look to have that on his white T-shirt. He pressed down on the skin and got to his feet. This was simply a distraction to the more important matter at hand.

'Onassis, why are you not at school?' Thanos barked as Ismēnē waved a handkerchief at him. Then, as she looked like she was going to leap in the air to get to his injury, he quickly took it from her.

'It is a saint's day,' one of Onassis's friends, Panos, answered quickly, doing something with his hands Thanos presumed he thought made him look tough.

'Do you think I am stupid?' Thanos roared then. 'It is not a saint's day and you should be in school. All of you!'

'Thano,' Ismēnē began. 'It is a day for the teachers of the school to train. The boys, they have been with me since early this morning.'

And as Onassis's brother and guardian he should know that. It was his sole responsibility, but he felt like his eye was not on the ball or rather his eye was not on the potential member of a boy band … and he could feel the blood oozing through the handkerchief. He pressed harder on his skin and bit down on his temper.

'Did you not like the performance?'

Onassis was hitting him with the soulful deep brown eyes of their mother now and every time his brother pulled that expression it beat at his heart. He still missed his mother and father every single day. Some days it was harder than others. Maybe Ismēnē would remind him of something his mother used to do – eat unripened olives from the tree, collect white pebbles from the beach – or Onassis would laugh a certain way and spark more memories. Whatever it was always provided a sharp prod to highlight the fact that this was his life now. He was the facilitator for Onassis's future. What else was there? He should be grateful he had any job at all, not constantly whine at the man who put money in his pocket every week.

Thanos smiled at his brother then. 'I did not like the performance.' He waited a beat. 'I loved it!' He removed the handkerchief and placed his palm in the air ready for the high-five he knew was coming. Onassis didn't disappoint and then the other boys, all jangling chains and jeans threatening to fall down around their knees, rushed forward to do the same. It was lollipop sticks in their mouths, not cigarettes, and Thanos had a brief thought that dancing with those was a potential choking hazard. Finally, Ismēnē slapped his hand with her own and then, drawing him close, she whispered, 'There is a competition in Corfu Town. Do not say anything now. We will make this work.'

Competition? What did Ismēnē mean? But before he could think any further about it, she was pulling at a leaf from the border of bushes in the garden and slapping it on his neck.

'Eucalyptus,' Ismēnē told him, fingers pressing hard. 'Clap the boys again.'

Thanos did as he was told. Just like he would end up doing with today's specials.

Five

Hotel Corfu Palace, Corfu Town, Corfu, Greece

'Now, make the most of this tonight,' Caroline began as she led the way from the taxi towards a rather impressive entrance. 'Because I might have blown quite a substantial part of the road trip budget on this one hotel.'

Part of Lydia's mind was still revolving around in that office chair with white wine dripping out of the plastic beaker. It had only been a week ago that Caroline had first mooted this idea and now, somehow, here they were, in Greece, on the island of Corfu. Lydia couldn't deny that from the minute her shoes hit the foreign tarmac, she had got a tiny bit goosebumpy.

Back home, she'd had to sort out her life priorities in a matter of days, from ensuring there was *some* hope that Bonnie would be able to pull off the visits to the restaurants she had made promises to, to telephoning her parents to let them know she wouldn't be there for their weekly FaceTime catch-up for at least the next fortnight. It was like everything had gone from nought to sixty: from Caroline bundling her onto a plane and moaning like hell that she couldn't be served nuts as someone on board had an allergy – *no one is wearing a hidden disability lanyard from what I can see, Milo* – to being here in Corfu Town. On their short ride from the airport the sunshine had lit up beautiful architecture down narrow streets, swallows divebombing as they flew from the eaves, glorious blooms of flowers amid stone piazzas, the buzz of café culture a sight to behold. And now, they were about to navigate these steps up to the arched doorways of the grand hotel. Hang on, had Caroline said 'road trip budget'? Lydia wasn't sure which bit intrigued her the most. But the thought that Caroline might be driving was actually a little bit terrifying. She still had minor whiplash from a trip they'd made to Southend. It had even made it to local news reports ...

'Christ, let's breathe it all in!'

Next, Caroline drew in an inhalation that would have had a reiki master passing out and then suddenly she let the breath go, as Lydia turned away to escape the backdraught. She didn't fancy the fragrance of second-hand sour cream and onion Pringles mixed with Bombay Sapphire.

'I can smell Greece,' Caroline announced. 'Can't you?'

And there was the country's name again, all the r's rolled. Lydia wasn't quite sure what she could smell – definitely heat, maybe the scent of orchids, perhaps a little citrus. She swallowed as the fragrance seemed to find its way down onto her palate. It felt unfamiliar and she suddenly felt the need to poke her tongue out like a lizard to rid herself of the sensation. It was too close of a reminder of all the time she had spent with Mario creating new dishes for the restaurant. *Light and shade in every meal, Lydia. Balance, like with life.* She couldn't seem to embrace these memories without sadness veiling everything.

'You're desperately thirsty!' Caroline remarked. 'I concur! Let's get to the bar. Before you turn into a gecko.' She heaved at the giant holdall on wheels she had been struggling with since London Luton airport and, when it didn't immediately comply, she gave it an almighty kick.

Lydia let Caroline take the lead while she stayed still, continuing to soak in the surroundings. Opposite the hotel entrance was nothing but shimmering sea, portions of it the darkest blue, other parts a glorious light turquoise. Boats sat atop it, some with towering masts and sails, others like the floating homes of billionaires all sleek lines and portholes. There was a concrete marina and then behind, grey sea walls bordered more rustic stone, and Lydia took in a structure that could only be the Old Fort she had read about when she'd googled their destination. Originally this island's defence, it was now a landmark visited by thousands of people every year. And she could see why. It was so atmospheric, solid and strong, jutting out in the ocean as a warning in bygone times to those who might want to invade, a large cross – perhaps a symbol of more peaceful times now – tethered at its highest point. It was different and unexplored. Perhaps the scent in the air was really *adventure*.

'Lydia! We need to brainstorm!' Caroline called, looking down from the steps she'd conquered, arms straining with the weight of her luggage. 'I said we'd have an email with a draft first article by five UK time!'

'What?!' Lydia shrieked. 'Five o'clock today? A whole article! Are you joking? We've just got here!'

Caroline's promises to their editor-in-chief felt a lot more achievable now Lydia had a cocktail in her hand. But even though Caroline had ordered a jug full of something called 'Aegean Fizz', Lydia was going to stop at one glass. Because someone had to decide what this first article was going to be about and writing it on the hotel they were staying in seemed like a cop-out. Their room *was* gorgeous though. A two-bedroomed suite. Lydia had never stayed in a suite before and when Caroline told her how much it had cost she realised she would probably never stay in one ever again. Particularly if they didn't get this piece written and were ordered on the very next plane back. She was surprised the magazine had approved something so grandiose though …

'We could just write about this hotel,' Caroline said. She had sunglasses on with bright white frames – very Audrey Hepburn – and was lying on a sun lounger in full-on sun-worshipping mode dressed in a bikini, a wrap under her head like a pillow.

Despite Caroline being the one who had made these writing promises, it was Lydia who was actually sitting at a table with her laptop out, changed into a light strappy dress, while feeling that they were never going to be productive if Caroline was wearing swimwear. Caroline was Caroline though, hugely distracting but an absolute queen at her job and the closest friend Lydia had. Being a chef was notoriously solitary despite the team you had working alongside you. And although Lydia might not have told Caroline everything about the end of her time at Maison Mario, she had told her more than anyone else, even her parents.

'Where's the itinerary?' Lydia asked. 'Perhaps we could go to one of the places you had earmarked for tomorrow now.'

'We don't pick up the car until the morning,' Caroline said lazily. And then Lydia watched her friend roll a little to her left, fixing her mouth to the straw dunked in her cocktail glass and sipping. She knew Caroline always came up with the goods when it came to deadlines but why was she acting like she didn't have a care in the world when *she* was the one who had signed them up for drafting something before the end of play today?! This wasn't a holiday and the getting-away-from-it-all sparkle was starting to fade like a cheap T-shirt.

'Caroline,' Lydia said sternly. 'This isn't fair.'

'I know,' Caroline sighed. 'Us in paradise and Nigel, probably as we speak, having a wank over a car park.' She tittered. 'That could be taken two ways. Oops. And that.'

'Caroline!' Lydia shouted. 'Please stop lounging around and help me!'

She hadn't meant to shout quite so loud. A waiter passing by, carrying all kinds of treats on a tray destined for the pool area, had actually jumped. But seriously, Caroline had orchestrated this, and lifestyle and trips were Caroline's speciality. Lydia had done a little foodie research and already earmarked a few eateries worth investigating, including a restaurant in Corfu Town to dine in tonight. And then Lydia realised that Caroline had sat bolt upright and was currently looking at her with a mixed expression somewhere between fear and awe.

'You have never raised your voice to me before,' Caroline said, her tone verging on admonishing but her look contradicting that.

Lydia went to apologise but stopped herself. She wasn't sorry. They needed to be a team on this. Whatever *this* was. 'Well—'

'I fucking love it!' Caroline exclaimed, standing up and slapping a hand to Lydia's shoulder. 'It almost brought me back to that time I had a girl crush on you when you first joined the mag. Now I can see *exactly* how you used to boss a kitchen. Like Gordon Ramsay.' She licked her lips. 'Maybe wearing chaps.'

There was so much information in that declaration that Lydia didn't know quite what to do with it. She decided to bluster on. 'Let's look at the guidebooks, maybe talk to the receptionist and then see where we can visit and commit to email before the deadline.'

'It's got to be super-chic,' Caroline mused.

'O-K.'

'But also very Greek.'

Did those two things cohabit? 'Chic and Greek,' Lydia wrote down as Caroline pulled up a chair. 'Are you thinking museum? Shopping? Something by the sea?'

Caroline wrinkled her nose. 'My readers wouldn't be seen dead in a museum unless they were buying it to knock down and turn into a Boxpark for mere mortals to exist in.'

Lydia didn't note that down. But she was beginning to think they both should have done a lot more planning before easyJet had got the wheels off the ground. Why had it been such a rush to get here *this* week?

'We need to find something with an exclusive,' Caroline said, reaching back for her cocktail glass. 'Like, I don't know, a … blind man who makes beautiful sarongs out of recycled glass.'

Lydia winced. That didn't sound comfortable. Or possible.

'Or maybe I'm thinking too hard. Gina said "draft". I mean that, to me, means "vague", right?' Caroline nodded as if giving herself validation. 'We'll walk to the centre of town, we'll make notes and take lots of photos and that will be plenty, won't it?'

'I don't know,' Lydia said, 'because I haven't seen Gina's email. Shall I message her and make sure she copies me in on everything? Just in case, you know, you go astray like you did at the exhibition in Norwich?'

'We said we weren't going to mention that again,' Caroline said through gritted teeth.

'I'm happy to not mention it again if you start including me more on this project. It's all a little too "loose" for me.'

'Fine,' Caroline said, swiping up her cocktail and sucking in the alcohol. 'We'll finish our drinks and then we'll get our reporting game on.' She sniffed. 'The sooner it's done the sooner we can forget about it and enjoy ourselves.'

It seemed like that was the most compliance Lydia was going to get right now.

Six

Thanos and Onassis's home, Benitses

'Ismēnē is going to make us costumes,' Onassis rushed out between forking pieces of aubergine, potatoes, peppers, carrots, onions and tomatoes into his mouth. *Briam* was one of Thanos's favourite dishes to make. It was easy, extremely nutritious and could be pepped up into something more exotic if required. This evening he hadn't had time to experiment. He had to be back at the taverna soon. He spooned a little more of the roasted mix into his brother's bowl. It was a week after his row with Baptiste about the tuna. Another week like the rest where his creativity wasn't allowed room to breathe and he was ordered to over salt everything.

'Thano, are you listening? You have to stop her!' Onassis continued. 'She will make us look like ... BTS. And not the cool-clothed version they used to be. The version wearing pastel and dyeing their hair pink.'

Thanos didn't really know what to say. 'Does it matter?'

Onassis opened his mouth like a 'shocked' emoji and a piece of pepper fell from his lips and into his bowl. 'Does our look matter?! Of course it matters! Do you not know anything about entertainment? First impressions count for everything.' He wiped at his mouth with the cloth napkin next to him.

Thanos put the tray back down on the worktop then dropped down into a seat opposite his brother at the table in the centre of the kitchen space. With the patio doors open, the whole room bled out into their small plot of land Thanos had done his best to make practical and relaxing. The patch of grass had enough room for a small game of football, the patio area held a wooden table that could seat six around it, and there was the vegetable garden his father had spent hours in that Thanos had almost let go when grief had threatened to swallow him up. One of the very first things he had learned about cooking was no matter what skills you had, you were only as good as your ingredients. And at the taverna that fact often held him back if Baptiste had made some purchases based on budget rather than quality.

'How is your maths coming on?' Thanos asked his brother.

'I need some new jeans,' Onassis replied. 'With chains on.'

'I asked you a question, Onassis.'

'I asked for new jeans.'

'Actually,' Thanos began, 'you did not ask. You said you needed them. Remember what Mama used to say about "wanting" and "needing".'

'No,' Onassis stated bluntly. 'I do not remember.' He blinked, his lids making them flutter over those dark, *dark* eyes. And Thanos felt immediately guilty. Sometimes he forgot exactly how young his brother had been when their parents had passed away. Thanos had been eighteen when their parents perished at sea. They had travelled to neighbouring island Paxos to visit his mother's ailing sister for the final time. On their return, the boat they were travelling in got caught in the most terrible storm and everyone on board that day was lost. There hadn't been time to absorb the news at first. There Thanos had been, waiting on the side of the harbour, Onassis squeezed into a carry pack on his back, not knowing how his life had just changed. Loss tearing at Thanos's own soul, he had focused on practicality back then, just as he did now. Onassis was the second child their parents never thought they would be blessed with. He might have arrived later than they had anticipated, but he had been very much wanted. Except fate had given with one hand and then taken away with the other ... With no other family still alive, the village had helped – mainly Ismēnē – but ultimately it had been down to him. Was *still* down to him. That dream to head to Athens and train at culinary school had been ripped apart, just like that first nappy he'd had to change.

'Onassis,' Thanos began. 'It is my job to look after you. To make sure you are doing well at school and—'

'I do not want to be Archimedes! I want to be ... Justin Timberlake.'

He sighed. Onassis had always liked to perform, but lately what Thanos had assumed was a fun hobby with his friends had turned into a bit of an obsession. Most nights, when he got home from the taverna, he knew his brother wasn't quite as asleep as he pretended to be. A tell-tale cell phone glow visible beneath the covers for a few seconds before it all went dark, the snake of a headphone cord trailing from under the pillow. He wanted something stable for Onassis. Something that was going to give him a good grounding no matter what career path he chose in the future. Something like business or finance, qualifications that could be put to good use in most jobs, except maybe entertainment ...

'Do I need to speak to your teacher? Do you need extra help?' Thanos asked.

Onassis looked a little sheepish then and focused on the food in front of him again. 'I do not need help at school. I need help to stop Ismēnē making matching costumes and I need new jeans.'

This wasn't the time. Onassis was closing up and when he got like that it was best to change tack and leave the battle for another day. Whether Onassis knew it or not, Thanos knew he got that trait from their mother. Compromise would only come after an interval to reassess.

Thanos's cell phone started to ring and he pulled it from his jeans and answered.

'*Ya*.'

'Is that my favourite chef?'

Usually Thanos would smile at the sound of his friend Dina's voice, but there was a hint of panic cutting through her tone. 'Dina,' he greeted.

'How are things?'

'Good,' he answered briefly, watching Onassis tear some bread from the loaf and use it to wipe around his bowl.

'You know, don't you?' Dina said, tutting. 'You can somehow smell my fear and panic down the line.'

He did smile now, taking a few steps from the kitchen to the outside where the sun was shining down on tomatoes, green beans, peppers, fennel, cucumbers, courgettes and artichokes in his well-maintained plot. There was also a stone-walled herb garden containing mint, parsley, rosemary, oregano and thyme that provided everything he needed for the kitchen here and at Taverna Ilios, as well as giving a sweet, aromatic fragrance to the air.

'What do you need?' Thanos asked her.

'You,' Dina answered and there was plenty of hidden meaning in there too.

He took a second before he answered, remembering the one time something romantic had almost happened between them. Somehow, amid far too much ouzo, he had been the one to call a halt. Dina was a friend. Friends had no strings attached. Friends didn't make demands that would interfere with his life as a guardian to Onassis. Lovers, he had found, always needed more than he had to give, despite what they might say at the outset. He wasn't a monk by any means, but Dina, well, he simply wouldn't want to destroy their friendship.

'What situation are you in this time?' he asked, checking the ripeness of a tomato not ready to be plucked from the plant quite yet.

'Can I have you for tonight?'

Again, her voice was laced with mischief. 'Dina, get to the point,' he said.

'I need you, Thano! Tonight! I have bookings, many of them, and no head chef!'

'Where is Ronaldo?'

'Who knows?' she shrieked and he could almost picture the raise of her shoulders, the shake of her long, curly, dark hair. 'He tells me that he has an appointment at the hospital. But seriously, Thano, I know that it is his sister's name day today and he knows I know so ... you know.'

What was he going to do? He would like to help Dina out – he loved nothing more than being in the far superior kitchen at her restaurant – but he couldn't simply abandon the job that paid him a regular wage. Plus, Corfu Town was a thirty-minute drive away. The long hours of being chef there weren't conducive to having an adolescent to look after. One of the reasons he was still at Taverna Ilios was because it was only a few steps away from this house. But inside of him, something was starting to waver, like a seed's first tiny movement on the road to germination. Could he accept this night of work, somehow be in two places at one time?

'Say yes. Say yes. Say yes.' Dina was whispering so quietly Thanos wondered if she knew she was speaking at all.

'You know I can hear you,' he told her.

'Good! My thoughts are coming out loud!'

'OK,' Thanos finally answered. 'I can give you tonight. But only four hours.'

Dina was shrieking now like Greece had won the European football championships for a second time. 'I love you! I love you! I love you!'

Thanos looked over to his brother. Onassis had picked up the empty bowl and was balancing it on his forearm while he danced. He guessed a night working for Dina would give a little spare cash for new jeans ...

'Thano, are you still there?' Dina wanted to know.

'*Ne*. I am here.'

'Can you wear black? The shorter the sleeves, the better.'

'What?'

'Come on, Thano, I might not have been able to get under there, but I know what will make my customers stay for dessert. And maybe ... when you have finished cooking, you could untie your hair. You know, shake it loose for whoever might like to see that.'

He shook his head. 'I will be there at seven. Make sure your sous chef is ready.'

'About that ...'

'Dina, I am ending the call before I change my mind.'

He took the phone away from his ear and slipped it back into the pocket of his jeans just as the *briam* bowl fell from Onassis's arm and smashed onto the *plaka* stone ground. He tempered the desire to yell when he saw the expression on his brother's face. Wide-eyed, with a little mix of terrified and repentant.

'I am sorry, Thano. I didn't mean to. I—'

He sighed. 'Perhaps you should leave the dancing to your feet instead of dancing with the crockery on your arm.' He bent down to pick up the pieces.

'Can I go to Zeus's house now? He has got this new speaker with lights that flash to the beat of the music and—'

'Not tonight, Onassis,' Thanos said, piling up the broken pieces into his hand and glad that his brother had mopped the bowl clean. 'I have to work.'

'You always have to work. What is new? Zeus's house is two minutes away on my bike.'

'I am not working at Taverna Ilios,' he said. 'I am working in Corfu Town.'

'So?' Onassis shrugged his shoulders almost like it was a dance move.

'So, I want you to stay here tonight, where Ismēnē can keep a close eye on you.' Thanos stood up, putting the pieces of bowl on the table.

'I am not a baby,' Onassis declared, grumpily. 'And Ismēnē, she falls asleep at one minute past seven o'clock anyway, even if she has had a full siesta.'

'Onassis, it is one night that I will not be a few metres away. Please do this for me.'

The second the words had passed Thanos's lips, he knew he had made a mistake. *Please*. *Asking* instead of telling? It was practically the first rule of parenting, so he had read countless times. Except not enough times to remember apparently. He had to retract and fast. He could already see 'opportunity' written in his brother's expression.

'Onassis—'

'How much is it worth?' Onassis broke in.

Too late. And now he was in a position of bartering unless he took a very firm stance. He was already going to have to work something out with Baptiste to free himself up to cook for Dina. He didn't really have time to enter negotiations here too.

'It is worth not having your phone taken away,' Thanos told him, fixing Onassis with a direct stare he hoped spoke of his authority.

But instead of being a little more understanding, his brother laughed out loud. 'You cannot.'

'Who pays the bill?' Thanos snapped. 'Perhaps I do not need to take the phone away. Perhaps I only need to stop the contract.'

He had raised his voice a whole lot more than he had intended to and he could feel his neck pulsing, his wound from earlier still a little sore. Onassis suddenly seemed as close to contrite as he had ever been.

'I am sorry, Thano,' his brother said, looking at him sheepishly from underneath his dark brown fringe. 'I will stay here. I will do as you say. I will poke Ismēnē with her stick if she falls asleep.'

'Do not do that,' Thanos told him. He took a breath before carrying on. 'I will not ask Ismēnē to sit with you all night. I will ask her only to look in until it is time for you to go to sleep. I will show you some trust. Do not abuse that.'

Onassis nodded.

'OK, well, I have to go to get ready now. No carbonated drinks after 7 p.m.' He picked up the pieces of the bowl then, before he made his way through the house, he ruffled his brother's hair knowing how much he disliked it.

'Is there more *briam*?' Onassis called after him.

'In the fridge,' he answered, still walking. 'Do not eat both portions. One is for your lunch tomorrow.'

Seven

Taverna Ampelia, Corfu Town

'I bet he was an ugly baby too.'

Caroline's statement sliced through Lydia's thoughts like the sharpest knife gliding through the very best fillet steak. Immediately it separated her from the gorgeous setting they had just been guided into by a very welcoming waitress. Taverna Ampelia – Restaurant Vines – was set at the bottom of one of the romantic alleyways there seemed to be a multitude of in this city. It was like a maze where every route led to a tiny hidden bar or coffee shop or a place where you could buy bread from a virtual hole in the wall. According to TripAdvisor this taverna was ranked in the top ten places to eat and once Lydia had seen the beautiful terrace area covered by a pergola around which spiralled lush green vines, she'd been completely sold. Her research prior to this trip had led her to a dish on the menu she couldn't wait to try. She looked at Caroline who was perusing the wine list. 'Who was an ugly baby?'

'Prince Philip. You know, Lizzie's husband. God rest his soul.' Caroline sighed noisily. 'I mean, he might have been born in Greece but that didn't gift him the Adonis looks, did it?'

Now Lydia knew what her colleague was talking about. Their search for something to write about for *Luxe Living* had led them to Mon Repos, the birthplace of the late Duke of Edinburgh. Once a royal residence, it was now owned by the state and was open to the public as a museum. It hadn't quite been the grandeur and opulence either of them had been expecting. On the exterior the thick stone columns still stood proud, but the balustrades were a little black with age or maybe neglect. It had taken a bit of imagination to think of royal family members sashaying around the balconies in their finery. Inside it was more modest mansion than grand palace but it had been interesting to find out a little bit more of its history. And, after walking a little through the extensive grounds, they had come up with an article entitled 'Destination Reinvention – could restoration be the new soul cleanser?'. Lydia hadn't completely been sold on how this all fitted together, but Caroline had suddenly got energised about it and when Caroline was firing like that it was best to roll with it.

'I don't think it works like that,' Lydia answered, pouring herself a glass of water from the bottle on the table. Even with heritage behind you, you weren't guaranteed physical finery. Her parents were Swedish and yet, because she had always lived in England, without the braids, she was as far from Zara Larsson as Boris Johnson was from, well, anyone else.

'Killed the article though, didn't I?'

Caroline made 'give me praise' motions with her fingers. Had she said 'I' and not 'we'? It had been Lydia's idea to go to Mon Repos in the first place. If it had been left up to Caroline, she would have tried to write a piece about the guy lying three sun loungers down from them at the hotel.

'Have we had a reply from Gina yet?' Lydia asked as she watched another couple be shown to a table on the edge of the terrace. They looked about her age. The man had to be Greek. It wasn't just the dark hair and the olive skin, it was that note of confidence underlining every nuance. What was it with Continental men? Mario had been exactly the same. He had been in control of every single situation in his life. From exuding confidence in the kitchen to effortlessly greeting diners and making them feel like the most important person in the restaurant. There had never been any second-guessing or extra thinking about consequences, he went at life almost like he knew his demise was in the calendar. And Caroline still hadn't answered her question.

'Caroline,' Lydia said, turning her attention back to her friend.

'Sorry, what?'

'Has Gina signed off on the article *we* wrote?' They might have thought it had hit the right note, but what if it was canned by their boss and they were on the next flight home? Lydia's eyes strayed from their table again, to the large urns spilling flowers the brightest colours on the spectrum – pink, orange, red. It was nice to be away. Despite the initial trepidation, this was different. And it felt good. She'd consider staying up all night to write something else if they really were in danger of being asked to download another boarding pass already.

Caroline poked two or possibly three large, slick green olives into her mouth and nodded. Was that a yes to her question or just her musing on the salty flavour hitting her tastebuds? No, Caroline was a gorger. She got pleasure from a full stomach rather than a food journey.

'So, when's our next deadline? Or is Gina going to keep us on our toes and surprise us with them every so often?' Lydia asked. She hoped not. Deadlines were OK as long as you knew when they were. Wasn't that kind of the point?

Caroline rolled her eyes as if she might be having some kind of synergy with the olives. And then they were interrupted by a smiling waitress.

'Welcome to Taverna Ampelia!'

Thanos could feel the sweat beading on his brow, but with his trusty blue and white bandana tied across his forehead, keeping his hair away from his face while a band took care of the rest of it, he was in his element. Dina's kitchen was very different to Baptiste's in so far as the appliances were at least twenty years newer. There was also much more space here and he could lay his things out in the methodical way he liked so everything ran as smoothly as possible. Back at the taverna in Benitses, there was a more scattergun approach caused by Baptiste not wanting to part with anything he had accumulated over his sixty years of being alive. He had blenders that were so rustic they looked like they had been crafted by the ancient Greeks.

'Thano!'

He shook the pan he was holding until the alcohol caught fire and started to flambé the steak. Flames licked up into the air, orange, blue and a tinge of pink that was gone in a flash. 'I will not speak now,' he replied firmly, eyes not moving from the pan as he set it back down and turned away to tend to another pot on the hob.

'That is OK,' Dina answered. 'I will do the speaking.' She squealed. '*This* order needs to be perfect.' She waved the ticket in the air.

'All my dishes are perfect.' And this steak needed to be timed completely accurately if it was going to meet with his own high standards. He turned to quickly rearrange a plate he wasn't completely happy with, before the sous chef took it for service.

'I know,' Dina continued. 'But please, for me, make this one *extra* special.'

His interest was sufficiently raised for him to finish with the plate, pass it off and then turn to look at Dina. 'Why?'

'They are from a magazine. English, I think. I would like them to write about my taverna. And only good things.'

Dina was always excitable and optimistic. It was one of the things he liked most about her. But there was a different vibe about her now. It wasn't simply enthusiasm for her business, it was tinged with desperation. They were still living in hard financial times and he knew all about that.

'You have been listening to customers' conversations again,' Thanos answered her. He needed to get this steak out and on a plate. He couldn't be having conversations in the middle of service.

'It is part of my job,' Dina answered with a shake of her dark curls. 'How will I find out the true needs of the customer if I do not pay attention?'

'The dishes will be perfect. What did they order?' He carefully placed the steak onto the platter and got ready to drizzle over the sauce and layer some thick chips.

'Bolognese—' Dina began.

Thanos laughed. 'The English! So obvious!'

'And the *yiouvetsi* with shrimp.'

Thanos raised an eyebrow as he sprinkled the steak with chives and black pepper. That was a good choice. Perhaps Dina was on to something, wanting to pay special attention.

'It will be done,' he answered.

Eight

'Christ! I mean it's not Dolmio, but it's a bloody good Bolognese, I'll give them that.'

Caroline was charged with a few too many glasses of the cold, sweet white they had ordered and was sporting an orange moustache, like a toddler who had chased the food around their lips with a plastic spoon. And Lydia wasn't going to tell her because she was currently trying to zone her friend's voice out and eat *her* meal as slowly as she could to savour every delicious second of it.

She put another forkful into her mouth and the shrimp popped, producing that unique slightly sweet, slightly salty taste she had always adored. But it wasn't just the fresh shrimp, it was the entire meal. She had chosen it to see how the chef cooked the orzo. She had always believed it should never be cooked in just water, like pasta, but always in a skillet with butter. She didn't know quite what he or she had done with *this* but it was absolutely divine. And as much as she wanted to make it last forever, she equally wanted to keep diving back into it.

'Did you hear what I said?' Caroline spoke loudly, phone now in her hand. 'Nigel has posted a picture of an egg mayonnaise sandwich! A fucking egg sandwich! How sad is that?!'

Lydia closed her eyes and tried to focus on the light Greek music drifting on the warm breeze, the gentle hum of conversation around them, this subtle yet overwhelmingly effective mix of tastes on her tongue.

'Are you having a seizure?' Caroline burst through her thoughts like a runaway express train. 'Can you lift your arms?'

'Caroline! Please!' Lydia yelled. 'Can you just be quiet for a few minutes?!'

Caroline's orange lips stopped moving until she shaped them into a kind of weird grin. 'I am liking feisty Lydia more and more.'

The food spell was temporarily broken so Lydia rested her fork on the dish and took a sip of her wine. 'Wait a minute,' she began. 'You told me you'd unfollowed Nigel on social media.'

'Why aren't you eating your food?' Caroline interrupted. 'Is there something wrong with it?'

Lydia shook her head. 'No.'

'Well, you've usually said something by now, in many words I don't understand the full meaning of. So, is it shit? Or is it sublime?'

Sublime. It was. That was absolutely what it was. And that was rare. It was like her tastebuds had been teased with something they hadn't experienced for some time and they were wriggling in anticipation of more of it to come. 'I ... don't have the words.'

'What?' Caroline asked. 'But you always have the words. And they're always far less vulgar than mine.'

Lydia composed herself, her eyes on what was left on her plate. 'Well ... this is the best orzo I've tasted ... ever.'

'*Ever?* It can't be *that* good? Where's its Michelin star? Where's Greg Wallace? Little Corfu can't do the crème de la crème surely.'

Was it even better than *Mario's* orzo? Was that what Lydia was saying here? It seemed unbelievable. Because Mario's orzo, the orzo he had made with 'That's Amore' singing in the air as he provided deft touches, sprinkling ingredients like every single grain mattered, had always been one of her favourite dishes. Perhaps she was overselling this. But she didn't do usually do that. Quite the opposite, in fact.

'Taste it.' She offered Caroline a spare fork and proffered towards her meal. 'See what *you* think.'

'God, no! You know I don't know the difference between a quince and a quail ... or Quorn actually.' She grinned again. 'I'll take your word for it. Well, *words* plural, as it's obviously going to make the cut for the magazine.'

It definitely *was* making the cut. But, apart from the food they had had at the hotel, this was their *very first* meal. Yes, she had researched, but surely this was some kind of blissful luck? This class of dinner so soon on their trip was a Greek miracle! Or perhaps it *was* going to be this easy. She couldn't hold off any longer; she put another scoop of the shrimp and grain into her mouth and savoured.

'I do not know what is happening! One of them finished their meal in around sixty seconds. The other one keeps closing her eyes. Is this good or bad?'

It was Dina bursting into the kitchen again, her energy even hotter than the burners Thanos was working with, which were driving the temperature of the room into the upper forties. This was how it was working in the heat of the summer. You changed your shirt several times a day and tried to drink as much fluid as you drained off. But the adrenaline always got him through. And Dina's taverna was far more exciting that Taverna Ilios. Her menu was good – not that he wouldn't make changes if he were in charge – but she wasn't afraid to experiment.

'It is good,' Thanos answered, concentrating on drizzling a little balsamic vinegar over the salad he had prepared. He wanted every dish he created to look delicious as well as taste that way too. After all, no matter how great the picture was to look at, it was only perfection if it satisfied *all* the senses and left the customer feeling fulfilled.

'How do you know?' Dina asked, picking up plates quite roughly and disturbing the lay of the ingredients a little. It irked him.

'Be careful!' he ordered, perhaps a little too loudly. He calmed his tone. 'You are tipping them!'

'Sorry! But I am nervous!' She sighed. 'I need an edge. This could be my edge.'

Thanos looked at her then, while gesturing to his sous chef that the preparation was needed for the next order. 'Those figs will be on the very edge of the plate if you do not stop shaking them.' He took a deep breath and tried to ignore the beads of sweat forming underneath his bandana. 'Why do you not ask them what they thought of the meal? Is that not what you do when you collect their plates?'

'Some of the time.' Dina sighed. 'When I am not terrified of the answer.'

'They are just people. You think because they write for a magazine it makes their opinion matter more?'

Dina huffed a sigh. 'I know that Mrs Adamos's opinion on my pork compared to that of her late grandmother is not going to get more tourists coming here. That is all.' She held the plates firm. 'But maybe ... *you* could ask them.'

Thanos spooned out some *gigantes* – giant beans – into a fresh white bowl he knew Dina thought wasn't fancy enough. The set she used was too busy in his opinion. It gave you no room for expression in the food décor. And had she really just asked him to ask customers what they thought of his food?

'I am not the front of house,' he responded swiftly, pushing the bowls along the sleek stainless-steel surface to the sous chef.

Dina balanced one of the plates on her forearm and pointed a finger. 'See! You are not so sure of how they feel about the food.'

Thanos looked away from the burners for a second, everything was under control. He had a minute to finish this conversation.

'I am confident of my food,' Thanos said, putting his hands on his hips. '*You* are confident of my food, or you would not keep asking me to cook for you. You want me to ask them if their meal was the best they have had since they have been here in Corfu? Fine. But I will do this as a waiter.' With that said, he took hold of the platters of figs in a sweet wine chocolate sauce and made his way out of the kitchen.

'Thano! Thano, wait!' he heard Dina call.

Nine

The shrimp and orzo had been delectable to the absolute last tiny mouthful and Lydia was both satisfied and completely buzzing from this food high. As she put down her fork she looked to her glass of wine. No, she didn't want anything to take the taste of the freshest seafood away from her just yet. Picking up her water glass, she took a sip. It was beautiful here, under the vines, a few bees gently floating in and out of the cups of flowers, cats seeking shade, bellies down on the stone cobbles ...

'Christ,' Caroline said, leaning over the table and peering at Lydia like she was a bug under a microscope. 'You look like you've just had mind-blowing sex.'

Lydia smiled, unusually not irritated by Caroline's statement. 'And how would you know how I look after mind-blowing sex?'

'Mmm, well, I have an imagination.'

Before Lydia could let that sink in, Caroline continued. 'Not that you could have had mind-blowing sex with Patrick.'

Suddenly Lydia's beautiful meal coma began to dissipate and reality rushed back in like an angry rodeo bull. She didn't talk about Patrick O'Shaugnessy. She tried not to even *think* of him. And sex with him had been about as good as his attempt at making choux pastry. Adequate but not exceptional, with no attention to the subtleties. When they had first met, at his interview for the position of sous chef at Maison Mario, he had come across as exactly the person they were looking for. He had worked at a very prestigious restaurant, he was calm and considered in his responses to their questions and he was thoroughly charming. After he got the job, and for the next three months, Patrick had worked hard. What he lacked in expertise he made up for with effort. And it was that commitment to Maison Mario, along with his good looks and silver tongue, that had managed to break through her self-imposed work-before-play rules until, somehow, before she even really realised it, they were in a relationship. She shuddered. If only she had had the benefit of hindsight. Mario had asked her on that interview day if she was sure Patrick was the one to join their team, when ultimately it was *his* decision. Why hadn't Lydia seen beneath the too perfect exterior back then? Even when Mario had spotted cracks in Patrick's perfect shell, Lydia hadn't listened. Because, by then, she was personally invested. And being personally invested had ultimately led to this non-cooking existence.

'Hasn't he got some silly little nickname when he's talking about his "laid-back lunch" in the Sunday supplements?'

Lydia felt her teeth connect of their own accord as another ripple of displeasure coursed through her. Yes, Patrick had a silly nickname. *The Griddler.* Lydia thought it sounded like a villain from Batman. And Patrick had never been skilled with a griddle when she had worked alongside him. One of the chinks in Patrick's cookery armour was needing to set an actual timer for everything. Mario had always taught her that the skill in being a chef was the sense of time as well as a sense of taste. You should be able to feel when three minutes had passed, not need a ringing alarm to tell you.

'Well, now, who is this luscious species coming towards us?' Caroline asked her. 'He hasn't been waiting tables until now. I bet *he* could do mind-blowing sex.'

Lydia looked up and had to admit the scenery had suddenly turned scorching. Dark hair tied into a small knot at the back of his neck, olive skin and – as he got closer – *really* nice hands. She sucked in a breath. She hadn't thought about anyone's hands for so long, thinking about them now was a little unexpected. She watched him deliver two plates of what looked like soft, moist figs, their insides slick with juice and a chocolate-looking sauce tumbling over them. She felt the need to lick her lips.

'I'd actually let him do anything he wanted to do to me,' Caroline said, sighing.

The man turned their way and within a few steps he was right by their table. The hands actually had *nothing* on his eyes. If there was an app to make your perfect eye colour, these would be top-rated. They weren't blue and they weren't green. They were just some crazy glorious mix of intense.

'Good evening,' the man greeted with a smile. 'Can I take your plates?'

'You can take anything you want,' Caroline purred, sitting a little upright in her chair and adjusting her rather flimsy top, which could really have done with tit tape.

He had tattoos. As he reached for their plates, she caught sight of a trailing vine peeking out from under the sleeve of his black top. Lydia had always had a little bit of a thing for tattoos. Especially well-thought-out ones. It was that seize-the-day attitude coupled with wanting something other than your football team's crest that she found attractive.

'May I ask ... how was your food tonight?'

His voice sent shivers up her body. The words were rolled out with that smoky Greek accent that somehow made you feel like you'd been smothered in honey and brought to orgasm. OK, maybe that was a little strong. But it had been a while. Back home she had started to find the guy who worked at the deli attractive simply because he said the word 'mortadella' like he had ancestors in Rome, not Romford.

'The Bolognese wasn't bad,' Caroline stated. 'Tell the chef a few chips on the side mightn't go amiss if he's looking for perfection.'

Oh God! Caroline was a nightmare! Lydia was glad the chef wasn't out here listening to this when he or she deserved all the praise in the world for *her* meal.

'I will tell the chef,' the man answered with a curt nod. He turned to leave.

'Wait,' Lydia said quickly. 'Could you please tell the chef something from me?'

He turned around and faced her. *God, those eyes!* She composed herself and continued before Caroline could ask for his phone number or tell him where they were staying and her room number.

'Could you tell the chef that the orzo was exquisite, and the touch of paprika just brought everything together so perfectly.'

Thanos found himself taken aback for a second. Paprika was never in Dina's original recipe. It was something only *he* added when he cooked here. And the amount he used was only enough to give the lightest of tastes. It was supposed to be so subtle it acted almost subliminally. Only someone who paid attention to detail would know it was there at all. Perhaps Dina was right about these customers being people of importance in the food world after all. One of them at least. *This one*. With hair the colour of sun-kissed honey and light blue eyes. *Sexy* eyes. And the sexy eyes were looking at him because he had made no response.

'You are a chef?' The words were out before he had analysed them. Why had he asked that? He had chosen the anonymity of coming out here as a waiter and now he was all but giving himself away.

'No,' she answered definitely. 'No,' she said for a second time. 'No, not at all.' *Three times*.

Thanos couldn't help but frown. It had been a 'no' that sounded a lot like a 'yes'.

'She—'

Suddenly, as the woman who had eaten the Bolognese began to talk, the carafe of wine on the table fell over and spilled right into her lap, continuing its gush onto the floor.

'Oh, Caroline!' the blonde woman said. 'I'm so sorry! Let me pass you some napkins.'

'No, don't worry,' the dark-haired woman said, getting to her feet. 'I'll suck the life out of it in the ladies' and it will be good as new. Won't be a tick.'

Thanos righted the jug as the dark-haired woman left the table, then collated the rest of the used plates and cutlery like a good waiter would. 'Listen,' he began. 'I will be straight with you.' He stopped moving condiments around then and looked at her. 'The owner of this taverna, she would like you to write good things about it. For your magazine.'

'Oh,' the blonde woman said in reply.

'She does not mean to listen to conversations of her customers, but she was blessed with the kind of hearing usually only superheroes possess. It is really more of an affliction for her than a deliberate intrusion.'

She smiled at him and it was warm, genuine and again, a little bit sexy ...

'But ...' he started again, resting the crockery on one muscular forearm. 'If the Bolognese was not to your friend's liking then—'

'No,' the woman interrupted quickly. 'Caroline, she has absolutely no clue about food. Honestly. She inhales it to fill a void and soak up alcohol. The Bolognese could have been cabbage and apricots and she would have moaned that there weren't chips on the side.'

Cabbage and apricots. For some reason his mind was already musing on the possibilities. And he was letting that show on his face. What was he doing? Waiters didn't muse on ingredients, they refreshed glasses and didn't dwell too long. He straightened his expression.

'So, can I tell my boss that you will write good things?' Thanos asked.

'Yes,' the woman answered with a firm nod. 'Very good things.' She smiled again. 'And please, tell your boss that she really needs to look after the chef. Because ... if they keep making food like this, everyone is going to want them in their kitchen. It was ... something really special.'

Now a real injection of adrenaline was shooting through him, like he was still standing in front of those kitchen burners and someone had turned the heat up to nuclear. *Something special.* His food was *something special* to a magazine writer from England. It was validation. He held on to that joyful thought for half a second until reality kicked in. He had told Dina that these kinds of opinions were unimportant. And what did it really change? Tonight was one night. Tomorrow he would be back in Benitses chopping up whatever Baptiste had secured for a bargain price ...

'The chef,' he began. 'He is called Thanos Nicolaidis. If you need to know. For your article.'

'Thank you. That's really helpful. I would ask to meet him, to thank him in person, but I can imagine how busy he is when he's creating perfection on a plate like this.'

Perfection on a plate. This was the best evening, even if he did have to go back to Tuna Tuesdays!

'And what is your name?' Thanos asked. 'For me to tell ... the chef.'

'Oh, well, I'm ... Lydia.'

She seemed a little off balance by his simple question, but her reticence only intrigued him more. There she had been, confidently telling him she could taste every intricacy of his dish, and now she was blushing about giving away her name. Who was this woman who said she wasn't a chef but had the refined palate of someone who perhaps should be? And, again, he was looking and not speaking.

'*Xero poli*,' Thanos said.

'Sorry,' Lydia said. 'I don't know what that means.'

'It is nice for me to meet you,' he translated.

'Oh, it is nice to meet you too. What—'

He knew what was coming. She was going to ask *his* name. But he wasn't going to blow his cover. He was going to take away these compliments incognito and pull them out of his mind whenever he needed reassurance that his cooking mattered.

'I am sorry,' he apologised. 'I must get back to work.' He gave her one last smile and, carrying the tableware like the waiter he had once been, he headed back into the taverna.

Lydia realised, as she watched the waiter go, that she had been holding her breath and she wasn't quite sure why. Except there had been *something* in the air, a fizz of almost anticipation, an unknown quantity that she hadn't felt with anyone for so long. He was so good-looking in all the archetypal Greek ways, perhaps it was simply that fact, the appreciation of his physical appearance, unexpected and long overdue in her life.

'The wine doesn't taste quite so good when sucked through linen,' Caroline announced, plumping back into her chair. 'I'm about ready to hit the top shelf. Shall we move on to a bar?'

Lydia found herself nodding. 'Why not,' she answered. Pulling together a whole edition of *Luxe Living* might be the biggest challenge she had faced in her role at the magazine, but could this trip be exactly what she needed in *all* areas of her life?

Ten

Corfu Palace Hotel, Corfu Town

'Lyddy!'

Lydia shifted her head on the pillow. The voice was familiar but it was too loud to be part of a dream. And, if it wasn't a dream, how was it fitting with this scenario? Because it sounded like ...

'Hello, Lydia's dad. This is Caroline, Lydia's much better-looking friend she's probably told you all about. I'm slightly longer in the tooth, but definitely playing with a full set of veneers. How are you? Looking very Morten Harket I have to say.'

That mad monologue had Lydia trying to force herself upwards and scrabbling for sense of this situation.

'Is Lyddy OK?' Per, Lydia's dad, shouted down the line.

Why did Caroline have the volume turned up so loud? And why couldn't she get out of this bed? It was like she'd been rolled and wrapped by staff members at Chiquito.

'Lyddy is fine. Cute nickname BTW. She kept that quiet.'

Lydia was now fighting the bed covers like they might be opponents in a wrestling ring. Who had done this to her?

'Lyddy called me last night and sounded very upset in the message she left for me. I wanted to check that ...'

Finally Lydia's legs were free enough to move and she bounced across the mattress, snatching her phone from Caroline.

'Dad, I'm here. I'm fine.' Apart from being completely out of breath. Had Caroline turned the air-conditioning down?

'Lyddy ... there is something stuck to your ear. Is it a creature?'

'What?!' Lydia exclaimed. 'What is it? Caroline! Get it off me!'

Caroline was laughing hysterically and then there was the release of a slight vacuum she hadn't realised was there and her colleague waved something in the air.

'My bad. This is a wrapper from the most delicious kebab I had last night,' Caroline cackled, crinkling the greasy paper up into the ball and throwing it towards the bin.

'*Gyros*,' Lydia interrupted. 'It was called *gyros*.'

Last night, after their gorgeous meal in Corfu Town, Caroline had ordered every bartender they encountered to ply them with a substance called *tsipouro* and then, when Caroline's stomach needed something to mop up the potency of it, she had insisted on purchasing late-night eats from a tiny grill room. Then followed over-the-top moaning, over thin pork pieces, thick tomatoes, red onion, chips and *tzatziki* all cosied up in a large pitta bread and secured with the wrapper that had somehow ended up attached to Lydia's face.

'Well,' Caroline breathed, 'it was mouth-watering whatever name it goes by.'

Now Lydia needed Caroline to give her some privacy so she could actually speak to her dad and put an end to this awkward three-way. *The balcony*.

'Give me a second, Dad. I'll turn the camera round and show you the view from the balcony.'

The scene really was breath-taking – a glistening sea stretched out before her, the sky a perfect cloudless blue, Corfu life buzzing around the sea wall: mopeds, vans, rusty Fiat Unos ... Lydia breathed in the scent of sun, sea salt and total escape. Despite her slight headache, she felt invigorated. Apparently not how she'd felt when she had left her dad a voicemail.

'It looks amazing there! Is it very hot? Are you wearing appropriate skin protection?'

Her dad always seemed to think she was twenty-eight going on seven. She turned the phone camera around so she could see him again.

'Yes, Dad,' Lydia answered.

'So,' Per said as Lydia settled herself in one of the two little chairs around a small mosaic table in the shade of the balcony. 'What happened last night to make you cry on the phone to your *pappa*?'

She had cried? God, that Greek spirit had a lot to answer for. She didn't remember crying. She had a vague recollection of needing to speak to him and little memory of the details. *That fantastic orzo dish*. Had that sparked something? Little bits and pieces were beginning to come back now ...

'You said you still hated Patrick and wished you had cut off his testicles with one of his blunt knives,' Per stated.

Oh God! She *had* been horribly drunk. And Patrick being back on her mind was Caroline's fault too. *The Griddler*. She rolled her eyes.

'I think I had a bit too much to drink,' she admitted. 'We had wine with our meal and then Caroline took me to many, *many* bars and that's obviously why I had a *gyros* wrapper on my face.'

'How is your time in Greece going? Are you inspired for your articles? Even if you are not inspired for ... cooking again?'

Cooking. This was a 'c' word that didn't readily appear in conversations with her parents anymore. There had been a point when if either of them brought it up, Lydia would either cry silently or turn into someone who was possessed by an evil spirit intent on sabotaging all good thoughts. And her dad wouldn't have brought it up now, unless somehow she had first. It was an unspoken rule that had been in place since her last service at Maison Mario.

'Did I ... say something ... about cooking last night?' She whispered the word 'cooking' like she was talking in code.

'You asked me if you were ever really any good,' Per said, blunt and to the point as always.

How self-indulgent had she got? What was the matter with her?

'You said you had tasted an exceptional meal last night that brought tears to your eyes in the best of ways and that you couldn't remember how that felt or if your cooking had ever moved people in that same way.'

God. Deep and slightly dark. Cooking was in her past. It didn't matter how or whether people had been moved by her food. And her dad had somehow memorised what must have been a very long message.

'Now you can see why I was worried,' Per stated, his soulful blue eyes – the ones she had inherited – looking into the camera with such concern. 'Your mother was worried too. I cannot lie, she was not going to put her *fika* on hold to speak to you, but she said you can always text her later if you need to ... after six o'clock.'

Lydia caught sight of a tiny pale gecko at the bottom of the table leg, deliberating whether or not to climb. That was the crossroads she was at with this conversation. Did she wait for answers to questions she couldn't recall asking? It seemed, subconsciously, they were still right there. Or did she blame everything on Caroline?

'I did have an incredible meal last night. The first really, *really* exceptional one I've had in possibly a year.' Despite the fur of alcohol left on her tongue, she could easily and delightfully remember the popping of the prawns, the perfect texture of the pasta ...

'It got you thinking?' Per asked. 'That it could have been you running a Greek kitchen?'

Immediately she was shaking her head. 'No.' And then firmer and more definite: 'No.'

Because she had run a kitchen before. Because the person she had loved most in the world, apart from her real father, had dropped dead when she was pan-frying a trout. Because just when she thought she could have a new beginning, keep Mario's memory alive by keeping his traditions at the restaurant, his daughter Antonia moved back to the UK and claimed her inheritance.

Except, in spite of all that, as she had been eating that meal last night, she had cooked it in her mind, seeing the preparation through the chef's eyes, imagining the buzz of the kitchen and the thrill of delivering excellence. Although that had happened many times in the past after she had downed her knives, it hadn't happened for quite some time. Was it regression? Acceptance? Or something else?

'Lyddy, for a while now, cooking has made you sad. I do not want you to be sad,' her dad said. 'But ... what is it you truly want?'

'Right now, a strong cup of coffee and two paracetamol.' And her dad's question was far too deep for this time in the morning. Particularly when she wasn't sure of the answer. Cooking had been her everything. She had been so completely set on that path from the youngest age, she hadn't ever thought she would have to deviate from it. *Misguided and stupid.*

'Remember when cooking made you so very happy? Like ... when you made your first omelette,' Per said, a smile spreading across his face.

'Dad! I've made you so many things over the years! Why do you always roll out the omelette story?'

'Because it is a great one. Come on, what other five-year-old takes the egg hot from the chicken's rear end, makes omelettes with grated parmesan and delivers breakfast to their parents at 5 a.m.?'

Lydia laughed. Other parents might have been a bit put out at being woken up that early but not hers. Per and Ulrika believed in freedom of spirit and independence – the heart wanting what the heart wants – whether that was a midnight swim or raiding the chicken coop before sunrise. They might live over in Sweden full-time now, but they were still very much part of her life, watching from a distance, never judging, always supportive. Sometimes Lydia had wished for a little more coddling, the hugs and closeness she had got from Mario, but her parents – her mother especially – had never practised that kind of love.

'That was passion, Lyddy,' Per continued. 'Wanting to rise with the sun and seek out adventures. Listen, maybe your future doesn't lie with cooking again. I do not know. But try not to plan too much. Breathe in the Greek air, give yourself time to relax, life is about enjoying the experience after all, not racing towards something you might never get to.'

She knew that was true. Like with Mario. Except he had achieved his goals before he passed away. She didn't feel like she had achieved anything. Perhaps this visit to Greece, pulling together a whole magazine, was going to allow her to shine in this role rather than just go through the motions. She swallowed. Was that what she was doing? Was there no passion behind her words on other people's recipes?

'*Was* I good, Dad?' she asked softly, scared for his answer as she directed her gaze across the top of the phone screen, towards the stone of the fortress.

'Lyddy! You know you were good! So good! Mario was forever telling you, was he not? He gave you a place in his kitchen, he taught you everything he knew, because you were the best student he ever had.'

She took a breath. Yes, Mario had told her that often and he had made her believe it. She *had* believed it. But it didn't matter how much confidence you had, if you were grieving, if you were weak and tired and feeling like your centre had been taken away, it didn't take much for someone intent on taking advantage of that fact to do damage.

'Oh, Lyddy, before I forget, your mother told me to tell you she has sent you some more angelica root. It is working wonders on my intestinal gas.'

Lydia smiled, hoping Caroline hadn't heard that snippet. 'Thanks, Dad.'

'No worries, and remember what I have said to you many times before, the words passed down from my great-grandpappa ...' Per stilled for a moment and Lydia knew what was coming. 'If you do not be-lieve, how can you be-living?'

It was and always had been their family mantra.

'Thanks, Dad.'

'OK,' Per replied. 'So, go have adventures! Send me photographs of you ... dancing through the olive groves ... or riding a dolphin or ... can you cook dolphin?'

'Dad! Absolutely not!'

'I know! I was joking! See, I still make you laugh!'

She smiled again. 'I'd better go. Caroline and I are picking up a car and heading off to our next destination this morning.'

'Is it very far to drive?'

'No, not too far. Around thirty minutes. It's a place called Benitses.'

'I will look it up. And I will tell your mother you are covered from head to foot in sunblock.'

'Bye, Dad.'

'Bye, Lyddy.'

Eleven

Taverna Ilios, Benitses

Thanos was late. After closing time at Dina's kitchen and driving back from Corfu Town, it had been almost 2 a.m. before he stepped into the shower and washed the night of cooking exertion off his skin and got into bed, the ceiling fan set to maximum. At some point, after early morning had got less dark, he remembered the ginger cat coming into his room and crying loudly and then Onassis arriving, backpack over his shoulders, a piece of bread in his mouth. Thanos remembered mumbling that he would make him some eggs but had fallen asleep again. And now here he was, late for Baptiste after leaving him at short notice last night.

He splashed a little water on his face and checked his watch again. He didn't have time to do anything else. If he wasn't there to prep for lunch, Baptiste would make service a misery. And he didn't want misery today. Today he wanted to maintain the high he had got last night when the customer from England – Lydia – had praised his food. Could it be that she would mention him by name in her magazine article?

He pushed out of the front door and stepped into the narrow alleyway that wound down from his house. He passed by three stray cats fighting for supremacy over a chicken bone, his neighbour Nikos's moped that only ever had one wheel on it, and blooming window boxes spilling colour from the concrete posts below the bedroom window of widow Maria's home before he finally reached Captain Octopus taverna and the collection of other eateries that sandwiched one another along the row opposite the main coast road and beyond that, the small beach and the sea. It had always been his home. He had known nothing but this village. And as much as he took comfort from that in some ways, there were other thoughts that took him away. What would somewhere else be like? How would his life be different? What if he worked permanently for Dina? Would the chance to excel in his craft be worth the getting in late and feeling beat?

He shook his head. No, he had been at this crossroads many times before and it all came down to Onassis and what was best for him. His school was close and there was Ismēnē to help. After his parents' death they had had the chance to move to Paxos, to live with his mother's brother and sister-in-law. It would have been easy to say yes at that time when things were raw and he knew almost nothing about the needs of a baby, but he had decided the best thing for them both was to cling on to what familiarity they had left. He had visited Paxos only once when he was six, his uncle and aunt next visited Corfu when he was thirteen. He felt more attached to Ismēnē and the spaces that had once held his mama and papa than he did to blood relatives he barely knew.

Now, as he looked through the taverna's covered outside eating area and into the body of the snug building – a combination of local stone and faded photos of yesteryear – he could see Baptiste was in the kitchen and someone else was standing at the preparation area. What was going on? He stepped on, emotions squealing like lobster in a boiling pot.

'Ah! Here he is!' Baptiste announced. Then the taverna owner looked at his watch. 'Almost lunchtime already.'

Thanos bit his tongue. Whatever was going on, he *was* late. He opened his mouth to say he was sorry. 'Baptiste, I—'

'You will show Giorgos around the kitchen and make sure he knows where everything is,' Baptiste interrupted.

Was he getting more help than Daphne, who, despite working here for years, still didn't know the difference between a filleting knife and a knife for peeling? Perhaps Baptiste had realised Thanos's worth and was concerned he might leave permanently if he wasn't treated a little better.

'Sure,' Thanos answered with a nod. He smiled at the new guy. 'It is good to meet you.'

'And as soon as Giorgos is happy he knows his way around, you can go,' Baptiste continued. He sparked up a cigarette, inhaled then puffed a big plume of smoke up into the air of the kitchen.

Go. Had Baptiste said 'go'? Go where?

'I will ... find the freezer,' Giorgos said a little stiffly, shuffling backwards from the space before disappearing faster than Nuno being booted from a restaurant.

'I do not understand,' Thanos said, looking directly at Baptiste.

'Have I not been clear, Thano?' Baptiste asked. 'Giorgos will be in charge here today.'

'In charge?' Thanos said through gritted teeth as realisation truly started to hit.

'Yes, in charge,' Baptiste reiterated. 'You decide to leave me shorthanded last night. For the rest of today you do not need to worry. You can do whatever you need to do that is more important than your job here at my *taverna*.'

This was payback. *Childish* payback. And he had not left Baptiste without thought. He had prepped everything he could before he had gone to Corfu Town. He had written instructions for Makis who he himself had called in to deputise. Makis was not a chef by any means, but he knew his way around a grill and could tell rosemary from oregano. Had there been a problem last night? If there was gossip to be had, it was unusual for Ismēnē not to burst in at 5 a.m. and be the first to tell the tale ...

'Baptiste, this is craziness,' Thanos began. 'Where is Giorgos from? He looked terrified to even be standing in a kitchen let alone taking control of it.'

'That is not your concern.'

'No, but it will be *your* concern when you have unhappy customers if he cannot cook.'

'That is also not your concern.'

Thanos was caught between really losing his temper now or backing out of this argument. Baptiste was answering everything with his mind already made up and he had a familiar unrelenting stance. It was a manner and pose he'd perfected when he was in a war with the local councillor about potholes in the road. It was completely unproductive and always ended up in a stand-off, sometimes for months.

'Fine,' Thanos said, pulling open one of the drawers and removing his sheath of knives.

'What are you doing?' Baptiste asked, cigarette bouncing up and down between his lips.

'I am taking my knives. *My* knives. Whatever Giorgos is making today, he will have to cut up with something your mother inherited.'

'You cannot do that,' Baptiste blustered, beginning to choke on his own smoke.

'Well, I did not think that you could give someone my job for the day,' Thanos responded. He opened another drawer and took out his high-heat tongs, his zester and his hand mixer. He had the same implements at home, but if Baptiste was going to try to play hardball then he needed to make a stand.

'You were the one that left to work somewhere else!' Baptiste exclaimed. 'And now you punish *me* and ... poor Giorgio by removing things so he will not be able to cook today?'

'I left you with extraordinary dishes to serve last night. And you have not told me that there were any complaints about the quality.' Thanos narrowed his eyes a little. 'I have completed my side of the contract as always.'

'You,' Baptiste said, pointing a finger at Thanos. 'You try to blackmail me now? Talk of contracts and taking things you say are yours?'

'They *are* mine!' Thanos insisted. 'And no one else in this taverna knows what a boning knife even is!'

'Are you calling me stupid?'

Thanos knew he had gone too far when Baptiste wrenched the cigarette from his mouth and ground it out on the kitchen floor. It was now a case of waiting for the explosion and then the impending fallout. Unless he apologised. He bit his bottom lip. He didn't want to apologise.

'In my own *taverna* you call me stupid?!' Baptiste blasted, slapping a hand to his own head.

OK, he might need to say something about that. 'I did not call you stupid, Baptiste.'

'You may not have said the words, but I felt it,' the restaurant owner said. 'Like a dart to my heart! After all the opportunity I have given you here.'

'Baptiste—'

'Fine! Have it your way! If my taverna is no longer good enough for you then let us not make this a temporary decision.' He drew in a long breath that somehow elongated his rotund figure. 'Let us instead make it permanent.'

Thanos's heart beat a little quicker.

'Take your chef things that no one here knows the names of ... and leave. For good. You are finished here!'

As Baptiste bustled out of the space muttering under his breath, Thanos's heart sank like it was a boat's anchor tossed out into the ocean. What was he going to do now?

Twelve

Benitses

The grey Renault hire car was actually held together by gaffer tape and cable ties on some sections. The bumper wasn't fully connected to the front of the car, the ceiling lining was sagging and coming down a little at the back, and you had to push the radio into its slot fully and hold it before it would change stations or allow you to decrease the volume. Lydia couldn't believe they had to pay money for this wreck and sign up to forfeit a deposit if they made it worse. However, seeing as the car hire guy had simply put a cross over the entire car on the damage sheet it was difficult to see how they could ruin it more.

'You know what I can smell?' Caroline asked, sniffing as she made to try and get round a moped on a rather narrow road.

'Please don't say a short circuit because there are bare, twisted-together wires coming out of the glove box and I'm afraid to touch them with my knees in case it sets off a chain of events,' Lydia answered.

'I smell opportunity in the air,' Caroline answered. 'And … jam. I nicked a few of those little tubs from breakfast in case we get peckish later. I hope they're not going to melt and ruin my handbag. It's new and I haven't Instagrammed it yet.' She made to blast the horn but all that came out was a very meek toot. 'Bloody tourists!'

Lydia looked across at Caroline, a little bemused. 'Aren't *we* tourists?'

'Yes, but it's a little trick Vernon taught me,' she replied as she drove the hire car up close and personal to a tanker omitting more fumes than an oil refinery. 'You drive like a local – plenty of horn and tight cornering – and you dismiss everyone else as tourists.'

Lydia couldn't wait for the tight cornering ... She perused Google Maps on her phone and made sure she was ready with directions should the voiceover stop working, or if the longest road names in the world became too much to comprehend. There didn't appear to be too long left of the drive – if the ropey car made it the distance. Benitses looked like a cute little resort when she had done some brief internet research last night. Once a haven for partygoers in the Eighties it was now apparently far more chilled out with numerous restaurants and bars and a brand new marina. Lots of the eateries had good reviews – Oi Oraises and Mr Spiros being two that had caught her eye – but the one she had chosen to eat at first was called Taverna Ilios. Ilios apparently was the Greek word for 'sun'. It had mainly good reviews on TripAdvisor – some said there weren't enough olives in the Greek salad, but a lot of others were praising the smooth service – however, the comments that had stood out for her were the ones where the customers had been adventurous in their choice of meal.

The Greek lentil soup was supposed to be just a starter, but it was the star of our amazing meal at Taverna Ilios.

The cheese flutes played a slow Greek melody on our tastebuds. Five stars.

Lydia was going to have both and perhaps also a Greek custard pie called *galaktoboureko*. She cast an eye at Caroline, who was baring teeth at the driver of a pick-up containing glass jars all stacked higgledy-piggledy and threatening to tumble from their confines with every sway. Caroline would probably ask if they could do a fried egg to go with chips.

'I still haven't had an email from Gina by the way,' Lydia said as Caroline navigated around yet another moped. 'You did ask her to copy me in on communications, didn't you?'

'I did,' Caroline replied. 'Of course I did. But you know what she's like. She's one of those people who never hits the "reply all" button for fear the Kremlin are going to somehow get hold of her personal information.'

That *was* true. 'So, did she *really* like the article we wrote? Does she want something else quickly?'

'Not at the moment,' Caroline answered. 'TBH I'm not sure she *really* needed that other article quickly. I think it was a test to check we weren't simply going to spend the next few weeks off our heads on ouzo.' Caroline grinned. 'She forgets what a beast I am at multitasking.'

'OK,' Lydia said. She took a deep breath of something close to relief. She used to love the stress of a deadline, particularly the shortest of timings on a night of kitchen service. When she had been working alongside Mario and the team he had carefully put together, the stress had only felt like 'energy'. You could feel it in the air almost. All these people wanting to produce beautiful-looking gourmet cuisine, knowing their roles were equally important if perfection was to be achieved. Mario had directed like he was the Martin Scorsese of the kitchen and made it harmonious but after he died, Lydia hadn't been able to get that feeling back again. It had felt like the pieces of the pie no longer fitted to make a whole dessert and that the filling was always one comment away from leaking out of the crust. Antonia might have been the one blow-torching everything in the end, but Lydia knew Patrick had been providing her with the butane for a lot longer than she had realised.

'Chill out already,' Caroline stated, giving another blast of the horn to a pedestrian who was straying a little into the road with a watermelon under each arm. 'This trip, it should be more than just business, you know.' She rotated her shoulders a little. 'Life's too short for regrets, right?'

Lydia turned to the passenger window then and took a moment to gaze at the mountainous terrain stretching up into the sky, a mixture of fierce rock, grass so dry it was straw-like and the odd hardy bush as a nod to greener and cooler times of year. *Regrets. Life being too short.* Why was Greece throwing up all these signposts? Why couldn't all her fears and insecurities stay mainly buried like they were in England?

'Time to set our sights on the next big things for our readers in Benitses. I've found someone who makes swimwear out of goat fur,' Caroline announced.

Ugh. That didn't sound appealing at all.

'Joking!' Caroline said with a loud laugh. 'But it would be a mood, right?' She rolled her shoulders again. 'That's the power we have, Lyds. This holiday is going to bring us up a level, give us the opportunity to influence so many more people.'

Lydia gazed out the window again as the scenery gradually changed and more of the sea came in to view. She wasn't sure she wanted to influence people in the same way Caroline did. Caroline's writing technique always teetered between 'power trip' and 'subliminal messaging'. It went alongside Caroline's personality: bossy and in control. Think Faye from *Love Island* without the ombre lip. It had been a while since Lydia had been assertive, but she had never been a fan of 'bossy'. 'Bossy' could very easily turn into 'bully', she had found.

Hang on, did Caroline just say 'holiday'?

'Caroline—'

Another blare of the horn broke in and Lydia found herself looking over the edge of a road that went from tarmac to crumbling stones in rather quick succession.

'Bloody tourists!' Caroline screamed in glee.

All joking aside, Lydia was rather looking forward to a bit of ouzo after this ride.

Thirteen

Thanos and Onassis's home, Benitses

Thanos thwacked the punchbag with his foot and relished the pain. He wanted it to hurt. It was punishment for his soul as well as his body. He repositioned and eyed up the heavy sack hanging from the steel-framed pergola at the bottom of the garden space, getting ready to repeat the move. He was a fool. He had taken a gamble last night leaving Taverna Ilios for Dina and Taverna Ampelia. It was one night and for what? A boost to his ego? A little bit more money? Now he was left without a job at the very worst time of year. Vacancies were already filled up for the summer; come wintertime, hospitality would all but stop here and he would be back to helping collect the olive harvest. And in a few weeks' time, school would break for the summer for Onassis and Thanos would need to keep an extra eye on his brother so he did not get into trouble.

He thumped the bag with his hand. That hurt too. He hit harder, the sweat seeping from his scalp and into his hair, strands loose from its bun. The scrape on his neck was still sore. Baptiste was stupid, the most self-absorbed person that Thanos knew, but he had been his boss. And he had employed him from the moment he was old enough to *be* employed! He should have been someone Thanos respected for that position alone, whether the man knew anything about running a restaurant or not. He hit the bag again and wondered if he should go back, take a chance at grovelling. It might cut a nick into his chef's gut instinct that working there was killing his flair but what was flair when Onassis needed food in his belly?

'Thaannno!'

He gritted his teeth. The last thing he wanted was an audience with Ismēnē right now. He ducked behind the bag and hid like he was five years old and had taken a handful of kumquats from her garden.

'Thaannno!' the throaty growl continued and Thanos heard the thud of the woman's stick draw closer.

He held still until something nipped at his calf and he inhaled loudly, swiping a hand at whatever it was. *Nuno.*

'There you are!' Ismēnē exclaimed, chuckling. 'You cannot hide from Nuno.'

The cat seemed to plump up at the compliment, its tail held high.

Thanos stood to his full height then and stepped out from behind the sack. 'I was not hiding.'

'Good,' Ismēnē stated briskly. 'Because we have much work to do.'

Work? What did she mean? 'I do not know—'

Ismēnē sighed, gold trainers shuffling across the *plaka* stone. 'Thano, it is over an hour since Baptiste fired you. Let us not pretend it has not happened. The news is all over the village. That stupid boy, Giorgos, who he is hailing as the next Greek *Masterchef* will ruin his restaurant and within a few days Baptiste will be begging for you to go back.'

Ismēnē pinched a fold of skin on Thanos's arm and tugged him out from under the pergola like she had done many times in the past. It shouldn't have still worked but somehow it always did.

'And that is why we have work to do,' Ismēnē stated. 'So that in a few days, when Baptiste comes to you full of apologies, you will be able to say that you do not need to go back to that place that does not deserve you.'

Thanos didn't quite know what to say or where this was going. He was eyeball to eyeball with the old woman who wore the look of a Titan. She had always been able to produce strength and resilience whenever it was needed. Like when his parents had died. There had been a very brief discussion about him leaving for Paxos with Onassis and then when he had made the decision to stay, Ismēnē had kicked into another gear, making sure the choice, with her help, had been the right one. Ismēnē's help had allowed him to finish school and Thanos knew there had been extra food on his and Onassis's table because his neighbour had made it happen. That was why he helped Ismēnē now – like with getting her feet checked – despite her insistence that she was perfectly self-reliant. In Greece, family was made up of many different pieces that created one beautiful picture. And Ismēnē was definitely a part of his and Onassis's life photograph.

'So, now you will come with me,' Ismēnē told him.

Thanos got the feeling it wasn't up for debate.

Ismēnē had her fingers around the metal door handle and was about to pull. This ancient old garage, with its rusty green door, was set behind Ismēnē's one-storey tiny studio of a house and it was more decay than it was bricks and tin. And Thanos knew how hard the door was to open. He was the one who had to shift it every December so the festive decorations could be fetched. It was full of junk that Ismēnē was sentimentally holding on to and would never use again, from her husband's collection of tractor parts off a vehicle that had long since been picked up by the scrap metal man, to bags of cement and broken sun loungers.

'Stand back,' Thanos ordered.

Ismēnē planted her gold trainers into the dirt and still tried to pull, soles not gaining any traction at all.

'Ismēnē!'

'Do not shout at me!' she snapped back. 'I am old, not deaf!' Her breath got raspy and she began to cough, reluctantly having to stop the exertion before finally letting him step in.

Thanos gave the door an almighty tug and it came open, forcing out dust and a heavy ancient aroma, plus two small brown lizards escaping from the darkness. Now it was Thanos who coughed. The years of damp and neglect crawled down his throat as he looked into the gloom. 'What are we looking for?'

'Hidden treasure,' Ismēnē answered, scuttling inside and propping her stick up against an old lawnmower.

Thanos shook his head. What was it with old people and their need for things around them? He swallowed then, suddenly struck by something as he watched Ismēnē fondly touching every antiquated seen-better-days item as she shuffled past. His father's *apotheke* – shed – had been hard to sort through after his death. There had been far more things inside that concrete cube than he had imagined. Amid the weed killer and the bamboo canes to prop up drooping plants were all the memories of his growing up. His tricycle with a wheel that had always squeaked so loudly it sounded like a tribe of mice were invading the village. Blankets his mother always had to repair every year when the moths had invaded. Baby photos of Onassis – so much thick black hair, which his brother still had to take time to tame. And a picture of the first meal he had cooked on his own. His mother had fashioned a tall white chef's hat out of paper and, when the photograph was taken, Thanos had juice from the stew all over the one eyebrow that wasn't covered by the hat, which had fallen down over his forehead. He'd made *revithia* – chickpea stew – and he remembered most of Benitses were ordered into the kitchen to taste it ...

'Thano!' Ismēnē's voice broke through his reverie. '*Ela*.' She beckoned as she pulled at a dust cover from the furthest corner of the garage.

He stepped around a wheelbarrow that had rusted right through and a painting of the saints Damian and Cosmas, before he joined her, helping tug at the sheets over something quite large.

'Come on,' Ismēnē said, pulling at material that was almost smothering her as she folded it up in her arms. 'There are many more to get out.'

Thanos started to reel off the covering Ismēnē had indicated, dragging it away from the corner of the garage until finally something was revealed. *Furniture.* Beautiful dark wood tables and chairs still somehow shining through the gloom and dripping with class.

Nuno let out a loud miaow and jumped up onto a chair, rubbing his neck glands against the armrest.

'Down, Nuno!' Ismēnē ordered. 'These are not for you.' She gently waved a hand at the cat's behind and it left the chair for the floor of the garage, where it began chasing a butterfly.

'Where did you get these? I have never seen them before,' Thanos said, running his hand along the back of the carver chair and loving the way the wood felt beneath his fingers.

'They were my mother's,' Ismēnē announced, continuing to unravel the sheets hiding the antique finery. 'And her mother's before that. It is beautiful, no?'

'It is beautiful,' Thanos agreed. 'You should use it. Not leave it here unseen.'

Ismēnē scoffed. 'And where would it go in my house? A chair in the shower? The table in-between the sofa and the front door? Thano, there is no room.'

He was puzzled. Perhaps she was selling it. There was no doubt it would most likely fetch a fine sum of money but, along with the rest of the contents of this garage, these items held memories for Ismēnē. There must be a desperate need for cash if she was about to part with this heirloom. Was that what this was? He had lost his job just when Ismēnē needed help?

'Why are you uncovering these if you are not going to use them?' He really hoped she didn't want him to move it because someone was coming to purchase it.

'*I* am not going to use them,' Ismēnē said, connecting their gaze. '*You* are.'

'I ... still do not understand,' Thanos answered. As nice as this furniture was, it wasn't exactly the style he had gone for in his and Onassis's home. When things broke or needed replacing, he bought cheap or patched things up with pallets for shelves until he could afford something better.

Ismēnē cuffed him around the ear and it stung. 'Ow!'

'I know you are not stupid so why do you pretend to be?' the woman asked. 'These tables and chairs ... they are for your first restaurant.'

Straightaway a chill ran over him, shrouding him like he had just dropped into an ice-cold pit of cobwebs and they were clinging like a second skin. He brushed at his arm, fingers pausing for a second on one of his tattoos – the waves and two hearts.

'What?' he found himself asking. It was like his brain couldn't compute the meaning of the word 'restaurant' any longer, as if it had fallen out of his inner dictionary.

'Do not tell me you have not thought about running your own restaurant.'

Thanos couldn't speak. Thought about it? He had *dreamed* about it for as long as he could remember. Where it would be. The style. The menu. His name above the door maybe. Everything his way. Success his to take. Except he knew it could never happen. It was as likely as Onassis being a member of an internationally successful boy band ...

'And now you are *over*thinking it,' Ismēnē stated. 'Stop that at once. That is always the cause of things *not* getting done. Come. Let us start moving the tables.'

Ismēnē was already picking up a chair that was way too heavy and unmanageable for her age and stooped stature. He swooped in and took it from her. 'Where are we taking them?' he asked her.

'I would say that you are to tell me, but I think the *drachma* has not dropped yet.'

Now Thanos was even more confused.

Fourteen

Benitses

Lydia took a long, slow deep breath and tried to still her mind in the way her mother did during her yoga. Ulrika's version of yoga was like normal yoga but if any of the moves felt too much you simply stopped and breathed instead. And if that still felt a stretch too close to straining, you got up, got yourself a coffee and a pastry, and hugged a cushion, calling it self-care. It was win/win. Except over the last few years, Lydia's Swedish genes seemed to have been waning in power. It took effort to relax now and that wasn't relaxing at all.

Trying to stop the whir of her mind, she focused on the rather magnificent view. The marina looked brand new – fresh paving, a terracotta, painted eatery with modern, light blue chairs outside in the sun – with luxurious vessels tied off but gently bobbing in the water. And the aquamarine water, so clear and inviting, made Lydia want to strip off down to her bikini and dive right in. That thought was *definitely* relaxing. With the sunshine kissing her skin and the scent of heat and salt water in the air, Lydia felt her shoulders take a welcome downward path.

'I smell money here,' Caroline breathed, eyes behind a pair of enormous sunglasses Lydia hadn't seen before.

And here *she* was enjoying the more natural fragrances …

'And you know what they say about men with big boats. Big—'

Lydia winced.

'Bank balance,' Caroline finished. 'And there's nothing more attractive to a woman my age than a big bank balance and if they have a big—'

'Boat,' Lydia broke in.

Caroline pulled a face. 'Yes, if they have a big boat it's a bonus. What did you think I was going to say?'

'I thought you were going to say it's time for an ouzo,' Lydia said quickly.

'Oh, it's been time for an ouzo since before your *pappa* called,' Caroline stated. 'Does he visit the UK often? Asking for a friend.'

'So, where are we staying here?' Lydia asked. They had parked the car on the roadside while they stretched their legs and looked around the marina.

'Sorry, what?' Caroline asked. 'Ooh, look at that little beach!' She pointed and Lydia's eyes followed. It was sand, loungers beneath fixed reed parasols, swimmers idling in the water, the mountainous terrain behind ... No, she had asked a question and Caroline hadn't answered. She wasn't going to fall for the distraction technique.

'Our hotel,' Lydia said again. 'Do we need to drive? Or leave the car where it is and get our cases?'

'I'm not sure yet,' Caroline answered. 'Just getting my bearings.' She licked a finger and held it up in the air like she might be a long-ago sea captain detecting weather and wind direction.

Lydia sighed. She knew this routine as well as the distraction technique. 'You haven't booked anywhere, have you?'

'Wellllll,' Caroline began. 'Sometimes it's better not to have anything tying you down, isn't it?'

'Like somewhere to sleep at night?'

Caroline pulled down the giant shades and winked. 'Come on, Lyds, with big boats in the harbour, two women like us are not going to be without a berth if we require one. Relax.'

Argh! That 'r' word was taunting her. But, how hard could it be to book a room for the night? This was Greece. Spontaneity was second nature to them if their driving was anything to go by.

'I can see your thoughts. Stop it!' Caroline ordered. 'When have I ever let you down?'

Lydia opened her mouth to answer but her colleague quickly continued.

'Hold those thoughts. They're going to breed negativity and negativity plays havoc with my digestion and ...' She looked at her watch. 'It's almost lunchtime. Where have you lined up for us to eat? Have *you* booked?'

Lydia hadn't booked but she did know where she wanted to eat. Taverna Ilios.

The heart of Benitses was a street full of *tavernas*. The way was lined with blackboards of hand-chalked specials or photos of traditional Greek treats – *sofrito*, *pastitsada*, *moussaka* – to lure customers in. And all of the eateries seemed to have a different style. There were those with plain tablecloths and menus inside glass-topped cabinets outside, others with brightly coloured dried gourds hanging from their ceilings and blooming urns of pretty flowers along the exterior. Trees spread their boughs out over the canopies, mopeds rested against flaking walls. And interspersed along the walk from beginning to end were wooden benches and more beautiful pots of colour, inviting bars and shops selling souvenirs from keychains to elaborate dreamcatchers in Grecian colours. From the rather cosmopolitan feel of the marina, this side of the village felt much more traditional. There was a buzz to it, but it was a gentle energy that came with a side order of tranquil too.

'It's taking rather a long time for someone to come to take our order,' Caroline said, pulling a small cork from the bottle of olive oil on the table and putting it back in again.

'I agree,' Lydia answered and made a note on her phone. There had been nothing about slow service in any of the reviews of Taverna Ilios she'd read.

'How long should we leave it before we, you know, loudly beckon someone?'

'I'm not sure what the etiquette is in Greece,' Lydia replied. Her eyes left the table where Caroline was fiddling with the condiments, and went to the patch of greenery just outside the taverna. There were more trees here, waving in the slight breeze, set back enough from the road that the noise wasn't disruptive and you could see the glistening slick of the sea. A ginger cat that looked like he only had one eye was sat on the grass, licking at his extended leg.

Caroline struck a hand in the air. 'Excuse me!'

It was so loud that patrons who *had* managed to get food looked up from their dishes as a large man, shirt straining against his Buddha belly, waddled up to their table, notepad in hand and an unlit cigarette resting behind his ear.

'Yes please,' he greeted, smiling, pen poised.

'We would like some bread,' Caroline began.

'Bread, yes,' the waiter repeated.

'And a large bottle of water. With ouzo. Enough to get the hardiest of drunken sailors very inebriated,' Caroline said.

'Eight ouzo, yes.'

'Wait! Not eight!' Lydia exclaimed.

'I'll drink seven of them,' Caroline said all smiles. 'Tell the now attentive man what you want to eat.'

'Oh,' Lydia began. 'I will have the Greek lentil soup and—'

'Not possible today,' the waiter answered.

'What's not possible?' Caroline wanted to know.

'The Greek lentil soup. It is finished.'

'Finished?' Caroline queried. 'You mean at not-quite-midday your customers have guzzled all the soup that my colleague here has travelled many miles to taste?'

'Today there is no soup. What can I say?' The waiter gave a shrug.

'Do you have the cheese flutes?' Lydia asked.

'This I have.'

'Well,' Caroline stated. 'I want a burger. Do you have that or should I hunt down my own livestock?'

'One burger. With fries?' the waiter queried.

Caroline smiled. 'Now I like you.'

'Very good,' the waiter answered, backing away.

Caroline snapped her menu shut. 'Let's hope he doesn't take as long with the drinks as he did coming to see us in the first place.' She sighed. 'What's up?'

'Nothing,' Lydia answered. 'I just had my heart set on the lentil soup that's all.'

Caroline shook her head. 'You foodies and your pulses. Honestly, the only pulse that would get me going belongs to Adrian Dunbar, but you must never repeat that in the office.'

Fifteen

The Roman Baths, Benitses

'It is perfect, no?'

It was the first time Thanos had ever been inside the gates that surrounded the Roman ruins in his village. But somehow Ismēnē had a key and they were now in the midst of all this time-eroded brickwork. There wasn't much of it, but what there was seemed to emanate its history.

Back when he was a child, his mother used to tell him stories based around the ruins. *Once upon a time it was a palace, the King of Benitses living here with all his servants. Roman emperors used to store all their gold here. It was a place for gladiators to rest after battle.* Back then he had believed every one of the tales, unable to wait each night for the next instalment. Now he didn't know whether any of them were true, but he did know what those stories and that time with his mama meant. He swallowed and kicked a foot at the grass.

'It is perfect for what?' he asked. Because that was the thing. He had moved at least twenty tables and four times as many chairs to the area just outside Ismēnē's garage and then, after letting him have a brief respite to drink a bottle of water, she had led him here.

'Don't continue to be dumb, Thano,' Ismēnē said with a shake of her head. 'It is for your restaurant tonight.'

Tonight. What was she talking about? But he barely had time to think any further before Ismēnē continued.

'I can see it all.' She inhaled. 'Imagine.' She splayed her hands out like she was an art teacher trying to inspire students with a vision of shape and form. 'Lanterns all around, lighting up the ruins, my tables and chairs amid the grass, candles on every table.' She took another breath. 'Haunting ... In a good way.'

Thanos began to see where they were standing in a different light and not just because of Ismēnē's talk of soft lamps and her beautiful furniture. His mind's cogs were clicking into place and he was getting that sensation inside him that required movement. He adjusted his feet in the grass and a cricket leapt into the air.

'I smell ... *kleftiko* and ... *fassolatha*,' Ismēnē began.

'*Fassolatha*?' Thanos baulked. 'I cannot cook *fassolatha* tonight. The beans are best soaked for over twenty-four hours.' There was a fast method, but it compromised the flavour. He hated to compromise when it came to his cooking.

'So, you are thinking about it.' Ismēnē was smiling now. 'You are seeing the possibilities.'

He had given himself away. But, really, even amid this unique setting with Ismēnē dragging out antique seating, it couldn't be done on such short notice ... and he didn't have the first idea about licences for this kind of thing. Surely he would have to have insurance or paperwork to play background music. Where would he even cook? Despite these internal revelations, he couldn't stop his eyes taking a tour of the site and his brain filling in the gaps.

'It is time, Thano,' Ismēnē said, suddenly right next to him, her elbow nudging his. 'It is overdue. Baptiste doing this is a good thing.'

'Is it?' he asked Ismēnē and possibly the universe too. 'Because it feels like this morning I had a job and now, at lunchtime, I do not.' And what was he going to say to Onassis? His brother had asked for new jeans, but he might not be able to afford new anything for a while.

Ismēnē nudged his elbow again as she raised her stick in the air. 'And now you have Roman ruins and the world waiting to taste your cuisine.'

The world. He wasn't sure that was true. And with only a few hours to decide on a menu, and obtain the highest-quality ingredients at the best price, he would be lucky to get even *some* of Benitses dining with him.

'We think too long,' Ismēnē said, moving forwards, skirt grazing the grass. 'We have much to do.'

'Ismēnē,' Thanos called. 'There is nowhere to cook.'

The old woman turned around and smiled, touching her nose with her finger. 'Thano, I have thought of everything. All you need to do is decide on the menu.'

He closed his eyes. His choices. *All* his choices. A night of cooking *absolutely* his way. The possibilities were endless. It was his first chance to showcase everything he had taught himself. He opened his eyes and took a deep breath, gazing out at the crumbling brickwork and letting his imagination wander. And it was then that he saw it, the bright blue flower, its petals glowing amid the yellowing grass. He smiled and as he stepped towards the plant, he found there were more nestled around this one standing a little higher than the rest. It had to be a sign.

'Thano! Come on!' Ismēnē shouted. 'I have use of a trailer until two o'clock and people ready to hand out leaflets. We need to make a start!'

It seemed like the decision had already been made. Plucking the blue flower out at the root, he headed after Ismēnē.

Sixteen

Taverna Ilios, Benitses

Lydia pursed her lips and attempted another bite of a second phyllo pastry flute. It should have been crisp, the pastry cracking and on the inside the menu had promised *metsovone* cheese. She had been excited to have the Greek smoked cheese on her palate as she had never tried it before. And the accompanying dip was meant to complement the flavours perfectly – tomato, yoghurt and orange zest. But this 'flute' was more like a disappointing recorder. The pastry was soggy and the cheese was definitely not *metsovone*, but halloumi. As for the dip, it tasted like garlic mayo straight from a squeezy bottle …

'Are you going to spit it out?!' Caroline exclaimed, hands around a big, fat burger that definitely looked more appealing than the plate in front of Lydia.

She shook her head. 'No, of course not.'

'You look like you want to,' Caroline said, still not focused on her *own* food.

'I would never do that.'

'What? Not even if you'd been served up a bucket of sick?'

Lydia had to swallow then and it wasn't pleasant, especially with Caroline's words ringing in her ears.

'I did that once at uni,' Caroline mused, eyes finally moving from gawping at Lydia and hitting the mid-distance. 'Perdy Rivers never forgave me. Blocked me on Facebook when I tried to reconnect.'

'You told me that before.' Lydia pushed her plate away, unable to eat any more. 'It's frozen too.'

'Frozen? In this heat?'

'No,' Lydia said, before taking a sip of ouzo and then a little water. 'No, I mean it's not freshly made today. It's been frozen and defrosted and refreshed. It's disappointing. It's not what I was expecting from this restaurant.'

'Bummer,' Caroline replied, sinking her teeth into the thick patty, lettuce, tomato and relish escaping out of the bottom of the bun and hitting her plate. 'So, are you going to have a confrontation about it?'

'No,' Lydia said. She didn't do confrontation anymore. It simply wasn't healthy. And she had only ever taken part in it in the first place when she had been forced into a corner. She was a naturally calm and collected person, but if she was slowly, methodically undermined, belittled and rinsed of confidence, she had the ability to change in a flash.

'So, you're not going to say anything?' Caroline asked, teeth full of beef. 'That's British politeness to the max, that is!'

'No, I *am* going to say something.' She might not ever write damning reviews or get paid for the right words like David Deacon but she wasn't going to let a bad meal go by without letting the waiter know it wasn't his chef's best work.

'Ooh, I can't wait! Shall I call him over now?'

Caroline looked like she might be about to put down her burger and beckon the waiter so Lydia poured another ouzo shot into her long mixer glass that contained the dregs of her last measure, some water and ice.

'Excuse me!'

It wasn't Caroline calling but a man at another table. Lydia had already noted that he had ordered *moussaka* and it had looked slightly too perfectly square to have been freshly baked and straight out of hot ovenware.

The waiter bustled over, cigarette still behind his ear. 'Yes, sir.'

'This *moussaka* is cold,' the man announced. He held up the plate. 'And it's actually solid in the middle.'

'You do not like?' the waiter asked.

'No, I do not like.'

'That is sad for you,' the waiter replied. 'I will bring you more bread.'

'Christ!' Caroline exclaimed as agitation ensued across the restaurant. 'Maybe we *do* need to write about this restaurant. Perhaps *I* should do a feature. Service with a side of savage – what are your restaurant rights?' She licked slaw off her fingers. 'Have you got a notepad in your bag?'

Lydia watched the waiter depart for the building across the road from its seating area, heading into the kitchen. Something wasn't right here. Everyone had a bad day, but a taverna praised so highly in most reviews wasn't the kind of eatery that dished up frozen food still frozen and didn't care.

'What *are* your rights if you don't like what they've served up?' Caroline asked, pen poised over a napkin.

'You can ask for an exchange or you don't have to pay for it. In England anyway,' Lydia told her. 'I'm just going to pop to the loo.'

'I knew it wasn't just "offer them bread",' Caroline said with a scoff.

Lydia left the table and stepped through the restaurant, its overhead fans working hard to try to bring down the outside heat, and headed out into the sunshine. While holidaymakers were browsing for somewhere to eat or looking at merchandise outside shops, Lydia headed into Taverna Ilios's small inside section that seemed to house a tiny area with a till and some stools, the kitchen and the toilets. There was frenzied talking coming from the direction of the kitchen so, while she was alone, she looked at the eclectic collection of ornaments and photographs arranged on shelves and hanging from the stonework.

There were a variety of seashells stuck into a glass box frame with scrawly writing that seemed to say they were originally from the Corfu Seashell Museum here in Benitses. Lydia didn't remember that being in her guidebook. Her eyes moved across to some rather nice earthenware pots and then to the photographs. Their waiter looked a little younger in this pic but still had a cigarette resting behind his ear. *Baptiste Bouras – owner*. That title explained a lot. She read along the names, Daphne Aetos, Marietta Cirillo, then ... *Thanos Nicolaidis*.

For some reason Lydia was holding her breath as she shifted a little closer to the faded photograph behind a very dusty frame. Was this really going to be the chef who had cooked her the magnificent orzo dish last night? She squinted. This person in the picture looked young but undoubtably it was ... *the waiter from the taverna in Corfu Town!* There was no mistaking the eyes, or the hands. But a few things didn't make sense. This man with the delicious eyes had told her the *chef's* name was Thanos Nicolaidis.

So, was this guy both waiter and chef from last night? And if that was the case, did he also work *here*? Was he guilty of serving up soggy flutes and stone-cold *moussaka*? The picture was old though, perhaps ten years or more judging on the fading and the clothes people were wearing. But if he hadn't moved on, how could he possibly be serving up dishes so in opposition to what he had made the night before? And then, last night, why had he not wanted to take the credit she'd been handing out for the meal? Why had he all but pretended he wasn't the one who had created it?

'You need pee?'

It was Baptiste Bouras. Lydia shook her head. 'No, thank you, I was just coming to ask you for the bill and to suggest that the chef might like to freshly cook some of the dishes instead of serving up things that have been frozen, possibly for months.'

She let that statement sink in for a moment before she continued. 'And my cheese flutes didn't contain the cheese as specified on the menu – *metsovone*. Instead they were full of halloumi. It's false advertising.'

Lydia watched Baptiste open his mouth to reply but then he seemed to think better of it, so she carried on. 'We will pay for the burger and the ouzos.'

Baptiste seemed to wind his shoulders up in protest so Lydia forged on again.

'And we won't put our thoughts on TripAdvisor.'

He looked grateful then and gave a small nod. 'As you wish.' He made to leave.

'Just one more thing,' she said, indicating the photo on the wall. 'This person here, this Thanos Nicolaidis, is he still around?'

'No,' Baptiste stabbed out the reply. 'He is not. He is unreliable to me and he does not follow the rules of my taverna.'

So, he *hadn't* concocted this awful food. That was something. She didn't know why she felt so invested after eating one meal but it had been so good she wanted to believe that it hadn't been a fluke, to know that meals like that were going to go on pleasing customers all summer long and her review in *Luxe Living* was going to send more people there to experience the same dining excellence. With a hot chef who didn't seem to be an egotistical arsehole ...

'I fire Thano this morning,' Baptiste informed. 'My new chef, he is still learning ... but he is cheap.'

Lydia couldn't believe that he had just told her any of those things. And then she regrouped her thoughts and knew exactly what to say.

'Well,' she began, 'I'm sorry to say that you've made a grave mistake. If I were you, I'd get on my hands and knees and beg Mr Nicolaidis to come back.'

And with those words imparted, she made her way back across the tarmac to their table. When she got there Caroline had nearly finished the burger and was still scribbling on the napkin.

'I know most of my readers all have money to throw around, but they hate bad service and TBH they start winding up those Apple Pay purse strings as tight as a Jack Grealish hairband if they feel they haven't had a beautiful experience.'

'We won't be paying for my meal,' Lydia informed her as she sat back down on her chair.

'Oh, bravo. Did you want a bit of my burger bun? I've kind of devoured the rest like a bear fresh from a winter sleep. Oh, but look, I've got us an exclusive invitation to something tonight.'

Caroline was waving what looked like one of Willy Wonka's golden tickets in the air.

'What is it?' Lydia had been away from the table for a few minutes tops, it wasn't probable that anything had dropped into her colleague's lap except maybe a greasy battered onion ring from that burger.

'It says ...' Caroline began. She cleared her throat and peered at the letters on the foil paper. 'One night only. A dining experience at the Roman ruins. Four courses for twenty-five euro. Gates open at 7 p.m. Limited capacity. Actually "capacity" is spelled with two "p's" and a double "e" on the end but, you know, cooks are better at cooking than writing.' She gasped. 'Oh, except you, of course, who is good at both.'

Lydia took hold of the 'ticket' and re-read everything Caroline had already told her. 'Who gave you this?'

'Oh, he was about fourteen, wearing jeans that were two inches too short and lots of visible sock. Quite insistent that I took the ticket though, in that persuasive way these Greeks have.'

She hadn't known there were Roman ruins here – another missing point of interest from a guidebook. She was beginning to wonder if the writer had even visited this island. *Dining experience. One night only*. Nothing could be worse than the dire halloumi-stuffed pastry fingers. And she did love a pop-up restaurant. Perhaps a Greek one would be twice as intriguing.

'So,' Caroline said with a yawn and a stretch. 'After this, I suppose we ought to see if there's somewhere here for us to stay.'

Lydia felt her stress levels creep up a few notches. 'You really *haven't* booked anywhere?'

'Spontaneity, remember? I would say let's ask the waiter but seeing as his shirt looks at least forty-eight hours worn I'm not sure I'd trust the bed sheets of any establishment he would recommend.'

Lydia sighed and pulled out her phone. 'I'll check Google.'

Seventeen

Thanos and Onassis's home, Benitses

This is joyful. This is what I love the most in the whole world. This is easy. And ... Thanos was pretending.

With his music on loud and the heat from outside penetrating the shutters, he was trying to immerse himself in the preparation and completely shut out the fact that his crazy cat lady friend had somehow established him an outdoor restaurant that was going to be serving people *tonight*. Yes, the word 'tonight' was enough to transmit terror into every part of him. Cooking didn't scare him. But cooking with such *expectation* apparently did. He put down the knife he was holding and rested his hands against the worktop of the kitchen, dropping his head. This was what he wanted. This was what he had *always* said he wanted for as long as he could remember – the kitchen to be his realm. And now he had the opportunity. Except even though he had been mentally preparing for this for so long, he didn't feel ready. His eyes went to the fine tentacles of the octopus tattooed on his forearm. A reminder of his mother's favourite dish ...

'*Ya!*'

Thanos quickly stood up straight and picked the knife back up as Onassis entered the kitchen. There wasn't a lot of food prep to do as they were still a few hours away from opening the restaurant in the ruins. But he wanted to do a trial run of the lentil soup he'd decided on for the starter. When he made it at Taverna Ilios, Baptiste always insisted he created it without celery and with a little too much salt in Thanos's opinion. Now it was his chance to make it fully his way.

'*Ya*,' he answered, mind back on the task in hand.

'What do you make?' Onassis asked, picking up a handful of carrot pieces and pouring them into his mouth.

'Hey!' Thanos complained.

'I am hungry! No one made me eggs this morning.' Onassis held his belly like it hadn't been filled for weeks.

'I'm sorry,' Thanos answered. 'I will make them tomorrow.'

'What are we eating tonight at the ruins?' Onassis plucked a stick of celery from the counter and simultaneously hoisted himself to sit up alongside the hob where pots were bubbling.

Thanos was torn between telling Onassis to get out of the way of the flames and asking how he knew about the cooking evening. And if his brother knew about the dinner tonight, did he also know Thanos had lost his job?

'Well?' Onassis asked when Thanos didn't immediately answer.

'It is a surprise,' Thanos answered. The truth was he still didn't know what he was going to cook for the main course. He had three options and was waiting to hear from the local farmer and one of his fisherman friends. Whatever his final choice it was definitely going to be fresh.

'You are scared!' Onassis announced, laughing as he kicked his legs against the cabinets.

'Do not do that,' Thanos ordered. 'And I am not scared.' He drew in a breath. 'I do not get scared.'

'Everybody gets scared,' Onassis answered, the humour suddenly departing.

'Not me,' Thanos said with a determined nod. He swept the celery into the pot and stirred it with a wooden spoon.

'You were not a little bit scared when Baptiste fired you?' Onassis asked, blinking those dark eyes.

Thanos let out a sigh and faced his brother. He *did* know. *How* did he know?

'Onassis, who told you I was fired?'

'Were you not fired?'

'No ... I mean ... yes. But—'

'Ismēnē texted me. She told me not to worry that you had been fired because you were going to make money cooking for tourists in an extravaganza for the tastebuds tonight at the ruins.'

Thanos didn't know what he was more worried about: Ismēnē texting or the pressure of having to make an 'extravaganza for the tastebuds'. But the overriding feeling was that he didn't want his brother to have to worry about anything.

'Onassis, there is nothing to worry about, OK? If tonight does not go well, I will find another job. I will ... work at a bar or I will ... get a job at the airport. I will find *something*.' He would find *anything*. Because when it came down to it, a job was more of a necessity than a career ambition.

'Why would tonight not go well? Panos has given out one hundred golden leaflets already.'

'What?!' *One hundred*. He didn't have room to serve one hundred people. Simply because they were setting up tables amid ancient arches did not mean this could turn into a loaves and fishes scenario. Divine intervention had already come into play when he had found money in a drawer that he thought he had already spent. The best ingredients did not come cheap – but he would also be using what nature had delivered him for free alongside that. The vegetables he carried on growing to remind him of the times he had watched his mother and father, fingers poking holes in the earth, filling the soil with seeds and covering them back up again. They had bickered good-naturedly, the way couples did when they knew each other by heart, deciding what plants would be best. A tightness grew in his shoulders.

'Ismēnē said that you should always work in thirds,' Onassis carried on. 'A third of the people will be interested. A third of the people will not. A third of the people will not know what they are doing. You should expect thirty-three and a third people to come on one hundred leaflets.'

And Ismēnē is now teaching maths. He took a breath. Maybe thirty-three people. It wasn't the scary drama of one hundred people but was it enough? How much was he going to charge each person? He needed to cover the cost of his outlay, plus make enough to tide them over before he found different employment.

'Do not worry,' Onassis said, jumping down from his perch on the counter. 'Stamatis is also giving out leaflets and he must be busy because he has not messaged me back yet.' Onassis grinned. 'I think he had two hundred.'

Now Thanos's core was shaking a little, along with his self-confidence. Was he really up to this?

'I know what you are thinking,' Onassis started, his fingers around more of the vegetables on the wooden board. 'In this I-am-not-scared place you are in. You are thinking that you wish Mama and Papa were here to tell you what to do.'

Straight off, Thanos shook his head. 'No.'

'I know you talk to them,' Onassis said, putting a piece of onion in his mouth. 'When you are in the garden you pretend you are talking to the vegetables, but I know you are speaking to Mama and Papa. No one looks for advice from a zucchini.'

Thanos swallowed. He had had some dark and desperate times on that allotment patch when Onassis had been unwell, or when they had *no* money and he was having to consider what to sell. He hoped his brother had not heard any of *those* tear-filled one-way conversations.

'But you can always talk to me,' Onassis said softly. 'I know I am not Mama or Papa and I might not give the same kind of advice ... but I can listen and I can guarantee I will listen better than a tomato.'

'Onassis,' Thanos began. 'I do talk to you.'

Onassis shook his head. 'No, you keep things inside. Ismēnē says that is what Papa used to do. If he had any worries he would hold them all in so Mama did not have to think about them. Ismēnē says he would likely have died from a stroke if he had not died in the accident.'

Ismēnē talked to Onassis about their parents! Now Thanos was bristling, the fine hairs on his arms standing to attention. Despite all her help, it wasn't the woman's place to talk like this to Onassis. Thanos was grown, an adult, he alone called the shots for his brother, particularly when it came to sharing memories of their parents. Yet here Thanos was letting Ismēnē in even further. She was in charge of this event tonight, controlling what happened when, deciding it was time for him to cook this way. Maybe this was a mistake. Perhaps all this was more about Ismēnē's need to feel included than it was about not taking his dismissal lying down ...

'Ismēnē should not be saying these things,' Thanos said. He swiped up the wooden spoon, realising that his vegetables had sauteed too long. He quickly added bay leaves, garlic, chilli flakes and cumin.

'Ismēnē says them because you do not,' Onassis said bluntly. 'Because you keep things in exactly like Papa.'

Thanos kept his face over the large pot, the steam hitting his cheeks, the scents of the spices filling his nose. Greek lentil soup was one of his comfort foods but he didn't feel very comfortable in this moment. The problem was, he didn't know how to let anyone in. He did strong and capable. He silently moved obstacles that stood in the way of their getting through life. *Getting through life.* Was that what he was doing? The thought shocked him a little and he looked up at his brother.

'You want to help me tonight?' he asked him.

'Of course,' Onassis replied, still chewing. 'Ismēnē is paying us in Milka chocolate. Did you know she stockpiles it?'

'I didn't mean help Ismēnē,' he clarified. 'I meant help *me*. In the kitchen. I have Makis but I will need someone else. Someone who I trust to get things right.'

Thanos watched his brother's demeanour puff up just a little, but then he relaxed his shoulders again and tried to pull off nonchalance.

'I will help you,' Onassis agreed. 'On one condition.'

'I am not agreeing to conditions.'

Onassis folded his arms across his chest and narrowed his eyes. 'Then I will require a contract to work tonight. And it should be overseen by my lawyer.'

Thanos sighed as he added the lentils, the chopped tomatoes and the stock. He really didn't have time for this. There was so much still to organise. Unless ... he backed out. No one had paid any money yet. No one knew it was him who was supposed to be cooking. Although he had no idea what was written on these 'tickets'. He took a deep breath. No, he didn't do letting people down. Even unknown tourists who would just find themselves another taverna if the gates were locked when they arrived ...

'What is the condition?' he asked his brother.

When he looked up there was the beginnings of a smile on Onassis's face. 'New jeans ... and for you to sign a form for a dance competition in Corfu Town.'

'Onassis, your maths is not that bad. That is two conditions.' He put the lid on the pot.

The boy groaned and pulled a face.

'You need to decide what is more important to you,' Thanos told him.

Onassis's expression changed quickly to a smile. 'That is easy. Please sign the form for the dance competition. Ismēnē is making adjustments to the outfits. When we win the prize money I can buy myself new jeans.'

Dreams. They were something to aim for, thoughts that made you happy during the waiting process ... but if they never happened they could tear your heart apart. Perhaps he had to let Onassis have ownership of what happened next with regard to this contest. It was likely, if he did not give consent, that his brother would find a way around it.

'I will sign the form,' Thanos told him.

He watched the boy's face light up and then Onassis leapt at him, throwing his arms around him and thumping his back with his fists, as was their way. 'You mean it?! You *really* mean it?'

'One thing I do not do is break a promise,' Thanos said, letting his brother go and looking at him seriously. 'Now, go and find your best clothes. Black trousers, white shirt. Make sure they are ironed. In forty-five minutes I will need you to taste this soup. And, I have not decided yet, but we might need to go to collect a pig.'

Eighteen

Argo Hotel and Apartments, Benitses

Lydia had had visions of there either being no room at any of the 'inns' or the 'inn' being the equivalent of a Greek stable – but this was blissful. Their apartment was simply decorated, but beautifully clean, with the most amazing views of the pool. It also had a corner bath she hoped to have time to dip into later before they headed out.

Now shoulder-deep in the glistening pool water, she pulled a few gentle strokes towards completing her fifth length. It was exactly what she needed to properly decompress from Caroline's parking outside the hotel – four three-point-turns and an almost-coming-together with a large bin on wheels. Her empty stomach was telling her this food at the 'dining experience' later was going to have to be significantly larger than her meal at Obelisk 1 to hit the spot.

As she reached the end of the pool, Caroline sat up from her lounger and lowered her sunglasses. 'I'm planning.'

'Good,' Lydia replied, dipping her head back into the water. But, with Caroline the planning could be anything from who she was going to stalk on social media to what she was going to eat after she had eaten. It was never usually further ahead than the next twenty-four hours. Except there was that one time ... Lydia smiled, remembering the first time they had branched out into the friendship arena and met up outside of a work assignment. Caroline had texted her asking if she was a cinema person or a theatre person. When Lydia had replied 'theatre' there had been emojis of the two masks, a regal building and music notes followed by an 'are you free on Friday'. It turned out that Caroline was less of a theatre fan, more a fan of Abba. They started with Italian food, then spent a fun evening at *Mamma Mia!*, followed by riotous drinks with some of the cast of the ensemble. By the time the night – early morning – was over, Lydia realised that Caroline was perhaps the only person she had met since leaving Maison Mario who hadn't ever questioned her on it. And that decision, to put fun and laughter first and getting to know one another with no prerequisites, meant that, as time went on, Caroline was the shoulder she had started to turn to a little.

'Tomorrow we're going to head out to an olive mill. It looks all the kinds of luxury my readers love,' Caroline said excitedly. 'Well, the bottles look expensive and I have *you* to tell me what it tastes like. Definitely aspirational.'

So, Caroline was doing *feature* planning. This *was* good.

'And there's ruins of a Byzantine castle not too far away that might be a good photo op.' She put her pen-grasping hand in the air and gasped. 'I wonder if they've ever done weddings there. I could do a whole section on weddings in Greece! Why did I not think of that before?'

'Because you hate weddings,' Lydia called, watching a dragonfly land at the very edge of the pool, taking in some water.

The sunglasses came off completely now, thrown to the lounger, and Caroline ditched the pen for her phone, finger tapping on Safari no doubt. 'I don't hate weddings.'

'Caroline,' Lydia said. 'You once told me that you would rather seek employment as an undertaker than go to another wedding.'

Caroline didn't look up. 'Well, I was probably going through my hating Vernon stage and trying not to think about my own wedding.'

She wasn't *still* going through her hating Vernon stage? Although Caroline mentioned him every second second – like now – there was usually a caveat of animosity dropped in somewhere. Caroline and Vernon had been married for eleven years and eleven days and the fact that Caroline knew that and had told Lydia over a battered sausage on the night bus back from singles bingo spoke volumes.

Loud and heavy volumes. Lydia had never really been sure why they had split up in the first place. Caroline had given her very sketchy details that had involved key phrases like 'trust issues' and 'irreconcilable incompatibility'. As much as Lydia liked Caroline she could see that there were sharp edges to her, a portcullis ready to drop if needed and she did wonder if this version of Caroline was different to her pre-divorce character.

'It was beautiful, my wedding.' Caroline looked up, a faraway expression on her face. 'Like Las Vegas meets Hawaii.' She sighed. 'Rhinestones and grass skirts – and that was just Vernon. Texas barbecue for the wedding breakfast.'

The wedding breakfast. That all important meal when you found someone special. The first thing you ate together as man and wife. Lydia fanned her hands through the water. She had planned her wedding breakfast once, when she thought things were serious between her and Patrick. Devilled eggs for the starter followed by a main course of beef fillet with a watercress mousse and dauphinoise potatoes and for dessert a trio of deliciousness – a ball of salted caramel chocolate mousse, strawberry and clotted cream pannacotta and a conch shell filled with champagne ice cream. She swallowed as hunger pangs hit. Patrick hadn't been Mr Right. If she hadn't let herself get swept along by him and his charm, if she had been more astute to his way of controlling without appearing to control, they might not ever have shared more than a kitchen. But she *hadn't* known. Not had an inkling that her slight uncertainty about being in *any* relationship, was a spot-on warning sign. She was in the relationship, had *committed* to it and so, after Mario's death, she assumed Patrick would be there for her. She'd expected the comfort of his arms, some softly spoken words about how missed Mario would be but how loved he would have known he was. She had needed Patrick to just hold her and tell her everything would be OK. But what she had actually got was the complete opposite. He hadn't held her. He had pushed her away like an unsatisfactory meal he didn't care for. He'd seen her grief as weakness. And he had used that against her.

'My mother dressed as Dolly Parton,' Caroline continued. Then she shook herself. 'I digress. But I can write about weddings. I'll prove it to you.'

'You don't need to prove it to me,' Lydia said, enjoying making ripples in the water. 'I know better than most that you can do something without being at the absolute centre of it.' She sighed. 'Otherwise I wouldn't be able to still write about food when I don't really cook with it anymore.'

'But you're thinking about cooking with it, aren't you?' Caroline said, putting her phone down and gathering her legs into a crossed position.

'No ... I ... what makes you think that?'

'Well, as plush as that room at the Corfu Palace was, the balcony doors weren't exactly soundproof. I heard your conversation with *Pappa*. Plus, you were talking ingredients in your sleep. Something about wild heather. I didn't really know whether that was a plant or a person.'

Lydia shook her head. 'That was nothing.' It wasn't nothing but she wasn't ready to discuss that with Caroline now, possibly not ever. As much as she had confided in her friend about the loss of Mario and her break-up with Patrick, there were still a few things she didn't want to impart. It was all like raw dough around a stuffed crust pizza, unnatural, best kept flat ...

'Well,' Caroline said. 'If you ever want to pick up the utensils again you can always cook for me. No judgement.'

Lydia laughed. 'No judgement? If I make anything other than chips and a fish finger sandwich you'd be disappointed.' And already her heart rate was picking up a little at the thought of preparing food for someone. She might have said 'fish finger sandwich' but her brain was firing off suggestions for other more complicated fish dishes, delivering a step-by-step guide to bring them to delicious fruition. She swallowed, tried not to let the feelings grow to engulfing proportions ...

Caroline nodded. 'I can't lie. That does sound good.' And then she settled her gaze on Lydia. 'But you *do* miss it, don't you? Because careers like that, passions, they're a vocation, aren't they? They're written in your DNA somehow. Like Vernon being interested in giraffes. I don't know whether it's because he's tall, I used to think it was weird but ... well, it still is weird, but it's something that can't be explained and why should it? We don't always know why we like what we like or do what we do.'

Was being a chef written in Lydia's DNA somehow? She knew her desire to create in the kitchen hadn't come from her parents. Ulrika would pay extortionate amounts of money for anyone to make her an outlandish coffee and Per was all about simplicity in all things. His eggs were cracked raw into his Swedish-style morning drink. What had made her want to experiment with food in the beginning? What was still there, deep inside, refusing to let go?

'Why not start small?' Caroline said. 'And don't start until you get home. Because we have work to do and I need your expertise on the eating not the prep.'

'Noted,' Lydia said, hauling her body out of the pool and shaking her arms a little to dispel the water. And Caroline was right. Writing about good food in Greece was her only mission right now. 'So, how far are these Roman ruins from here for the meal tonight. Can we walk?'

'We can,' Caroline said. 'A couple of minutes. So, lots of time left for sun!'

Nineteen

The Roman Baths, Benitses

If the site had looked small before, it looked even smaller now with Ismēnē's tables and chairs dotted about in every tiny available space. They had even had to put some tables outside the boundary fence in order to make thirty.

Thanos surveyed the scene. Ismēnē was ordering around a troupe of people – some he knew, others he did not – placing lanterns ready to light up the ruins as night fell, making sure the tables did not wobble – no easy task on grassland. Helpers were wiping surfaces, clipping down cloths, setting up cutlery and condiments that had been procured from somewhere by Ismēnē. And he had a tent across the pathway, pitched on the land belonging to another of Ismēnē's friends that incorporated a four-ring gas burner and a preparation area fashioned out of two wardrobe doors – that had been sanitised to within an inch of their lives – standing on concrete blocks. It was rustic. It was the bare minimum you needed to cook, but he was supposed to be producing food to set alight the tastebuds. At the moment, he was worried about setting light to the canvas.

Makis drew up to him. 'There is no grill in the tent.'

'I know,' Thanos replied.

'I am not sure what to do.'

Thanos put a hand on his shoulder. 'Do not worry, my friend. You only need to assist. This will be a little preparation when it comes to the main course and plating up, making sure everything is perfect. My brother will be here to help also.'

'I have not heard of many of the things on the menu,' Makis admitted, worry lines creasing his forehead.

'Relax,' Thanos said. 'You do not need to know how they work together. That is my job. Now, the soup is prepared. It will arrive and we will plate this up. It is vegetarian, it is vegan, it is dairy-free and gluten-free. It is also egg-free, nut-free and suitable for those on a low-sugar diet.'

'Do I need to remember this?'

Thanos shook his head. 'Everything is written down. But if someone asks then ...'

The main course was also all of those things. He had dropped the idea of meat. It was a risk, to make the menu vegetarian and as allergen-free as possible, but if he had cooked meat or fish he would need to provide an alternative and there just wasn't time to have choices tonight. He only hoped the lack of options would not put people off from coming to dine.

'*Ela*,' Thanos said, leading Makis across the pathway to the tent. 'Let me remind you how this is going to work.'

With Makis off familiarising himself with the route from Thanos's kitchen at home, where the most difficult parts of the preparation had already taken place, to the ruins, Thanos could really take stock of what he was doing. And that was when he started to shake. Internally and externally. He was about to run a restaurant for a night, almost single-handedly. Customers, if they turned up, were going to pay money for three courses that he was mainly cooking from a tent whose last event was possibly before the Second World War. What was he doing? His hands trembled and he grabbed one with the other. This could not happen. This wasn't about him, not really. Yes, this might be a long-held career aspiration – maybe not the tent part – but it was still all about providing for Onassis. Twenty-five euro per person, Ismēnē had said. So, after tonight, unless he had to return everyone's money if everything turned inedible, he would have enough funds to regroup, think properly about what to do next.

'Thano!'

He took a sharp breath inward at the sound of his brother's voice. It didn't sound like good news.

Stepping out of the tent, he almost collided with an animal.

'It was not my fault!' Onassis bleated.

'Onassis, why is there a pig here?' He made a grab for the animal but it gave a loud snort and trotted off into the tent.

'I went to collect it. I thought I would save you some work. But when I got there it was not dead. It was *this!* Living! Running! I did not know what to do. He made me take it.'

Thanos closed his eyes and willed the universe to give him some kind of break from madness in his life. A clattering inside the canvas woke his priorities and he rushed back into his 'kitchen'.

'You have to take it back,' Thanos ordered, trying to corral the animal into one space as it ran around sniffing at everything and drooling.

'I cannot!' Onassis exclaimed. 'That man was scary. He had no teeth.'

'He is not scary! George has known you since you were a baby. He would not have expected you to keep the pig like this. This is a misunderstanding.' He had told George he no longer needed the pig! But Thanos had zero time to sort out this issue. And having a pig inside a restaurant kitchen – even a temporary one – was contravening all kinds of health standards. He did not want to start this being like Baptiste with his ashtrays and coughing.

'I'm sorry, Thano,' Onassis said, his eyes tearing up.

Thanos bit his lip. This wasn't the place to start apportioning blame. He had to do what he always did. Solve this problem and quickly.

'I am going to throw him a little bit of pepper,' Thanos told his brother. It was getting hot in the tent already and nothing was switched on yet. He fanned his vest away from his body and wondered if he would have time to wash himself down before he began service. The rear door of Mrs Kastellanos's house had been left open for handwashing purposes and to provide a toilet. It was four or five steps away from the tent but Thanos was very aware that the woman was enjoying his presence a little too much.

The last time he had nipped in to rid his fingers of garlic she had taken a photograph. Mrs Bakirtzis was in charge of washing up. And he had no idea how he was meant to repay these people for their help or why they were offering it. The only thing he could think of was that they all owed Ismēnē a favour or a debt from a card game ... He refocused on the pig.

'Do pigs like pepper?' Onassis asked.

'Pigs eat anything,' Thanos told him. 'He would eat one of your socks if I threw that. Ready?'

'Wait, what do I do when you throw the pepper?'

'Be ready to help me catch him.'

Thanos didn't let any more time pass for his brother to ask any further questions. He threw a portion of the vegetable towards the pig and as it moved to devour it, Thanos pounced, jerking forward and grabbing hold of it. This wasn't as easy as he thought.

'Take off your belt,' Thanos ordered as the pig, now finished eating, started to shake off this hand shackle.

'What?' Onassis asked.

'We are improvising on a collar. Be quick!'

He knew he could if he had to, but picking up a pig of this size when it would be reluctant and angry was not what he needed right before the biggest evening of his life. 'Strap it around his neck. Tight enough so you can steer him.'

'*Me* to steer him!' Onassis exclaimed, holding out the worn pleather belt.

Thanos took it and, using his hand and one knee to steady the pig, he managed to get it around his neck with just enough material left to hold on to. The pig was not happy though. It squealed and began to drool at an even faster rate.

'You will have to take him,' Thanos told his brother. 'I have a restaurant to run.'

'But ...' Onassis started as Thanos pushed the belt into his hands. 'Where do I take him?'

'I do not know,' Thanos stated. 'I do not care. He just cannot be here.' He took a deep breath and, in doing so, he had a sudden thought. 'Actually, take it to Baptiste. He might pay you good money for it.'

'I'm sorry, Thanos,' Onassis said, struggling to keep hold of the animal. He tightened his grip and then stood a little taller. 'I will deal with the pig and then I will be back here to help you make tonight your biggest success.'

The fabric of the tent parted and Ismēnē appeared wearing a green patterned dress Thanos had never seen before. He could barely recall a time when she did not wear black or grey.

'What is this?' Ismēnē asked, bending a little to look at the pig. 'You have finally bought Onassis a pet?' She tickled the pig under its chin and it seemed suddenly transfixed.

'Onassis is taking it out of my kitchen. There is barely any time left for me to prepare three courses.' He checked his watch for what felt like the millionth time that day. It was like the minutes were evaporating.

'Three courses?' Ismēnē asked, standing up as straight as she ever was able to get. 'What do you mean three courses? The golden invitations my team have been giving out all said *four* courses. I told you!'

Now Thanos felt the heat as his body flooded with white hot dread. He had to create another course! With no time! He eyed the pig again, fighting against the strain of Onassis. Maybe this was a hidden opportunity after all. And then he shook himself. That was insane. And it definitely wasn't keeping his menu as meat-free as possible. He looked to his brother.

'Onassis,' Thanos said seriously. 'When you have got rid of the pig, I want you to pick me as many figs as you can get your hands on.' He put fingers to the bridge of his nose. 'And bring the cheese I tell you not to eat.'

Twenty

'Can you smell anything?' Caroline asked as they took a slow meander along the narrow footpath that led the way from the main eating street towards the Roman ruins. It was stone walls outside, paving on the ground with white lines marking the edges. Then, turning a corner, there would be a yellow-painted home, bougainvillea spilling over its gates, small terraces housing washing lines, plastic tables and chairs and flagons of unknown liquid. They had gone for a drink at the Sunshine Café Bar prior to taking the stroll up here and it had been nice to relax, watch the world go by and not think too deeply about anything.

Lydia breathed deeply. There were many scents in the air in Greece she was finding and this night was no different. Humidity. Grapevines. She was about to make comment when Caroline beat her to it.

'I'm hoping to detect essence of lamb shank in the air. That's what I want from my eating experience.'

'Well,' Lydia began, watching a white cat chase after a pale butterfly, 'if it's really only twenty-five euro a person, I wouldn't get your hopes too high.'

'As you know, my hopes usually involve the takeaway still being open once the meal has been finished and I'm at least three glasses of wine down.'

The path began to wind upwards a little and the humidity of the evening made Lydia have to pause for a second and catch her breath. 'Have you always been this way? Since you were little?'

'Naturally beautiful?' Caroline asked. 'Yes.' She laughed.

'I meant picky about your food.'

'What?!' Caroline admonished. 'I'm not picky!'

'Caroline, you wince at literally everything that hasn't been deep-fried.'

'I don't!'

'You really do.'

'OK, well, how about I show you,' Caroline said, a stubborn edge to her tone. 'Tonight, whatever we're served up, I will promise to give it a go.'

Lydia snorted out a laugh. 'Give it a go? Already it sounds like you think dinner is a challenge. People say "give it a go" if they're about to do something they consider not pleasurable.'

'Are you food shaming me?' Caroline asked, bolshy now. 'Because that is not OK on Twitter and it is definitely not OK IRL.'

Lydia linked their arms. 'Sorry, I didn't mean for it to come across that way. I just want you to enjoy food like I do, that's all.'

Caroline pouted. 'Not all of us came out of the womb somehow fully prepared for fennel.'

'I'll admit, it's not everyone's favourite. But, trust me, it is good for blood pressure and it can help lower your cholesterol.'

'Noted. But I'd much rather find some tablets from Holland & Barrett that aren't green and don't look like they could take your eye out.'

They rounded the corner and that's when the ruins came into view. Arches of worn stone, greenery growing from the cracks, all lit up with lanterns and flickering candles in pots casting everything in a romantic glow. They had followed a few small groups up the pathway here and now, as they were arriving, Lydia could see there were quite a number of people already seated at tables. The tables were dark wood, antique maybe, some of them seeming like they were perched overhanging what must be the actual Roman bath. But it was a scene like no other. *Special.*

'Well,' Caroline breathed. 'This might be worth the entrance fee alone.'

Lydia couldn't disagree and she quickened her steps slightly, not wanting to miss out on dining here, no matter what the food was like.

'Welcome! Welcome! Here is your menu for tonight. It is twenty-five euro for every person including a glass of homemade wine. You want more wine, it will cost extra.'

'Hello,' Lydia greeted the little old lady at the gate. 'Two people please.' She took out her wallet and extracted some money.

'Very good. Very good. Please, this is Stamatis, he will be your waiter for tonight. Stamatis, show the good ladies to our very best table.'

The waiter was possibly no more than fourteen wearing trousers that were two sizes too small and a white shirt that was far too large.

'That's him,' Caroline whispered. 'That's the child who gave me the golden ticket. What are the working age limits in Greece? I don't want to get caught up in a child labour ring. That's definitely not the kind of article *Luxe Living* needs.' She gasped. 'Unless we *expose* it. You can be Ross Kemp and I'll be Stacey Dooley.'

'I am fifteen,' Stamatis answered with a bow. 'And I speak very good English.'

'Yes, you do,' Caroline agreed. 'Well done you. Note to self. Don't teach you any more swear words than you already know.'

'Please, this way,' Stamatis directed.

Lydia wasn't looking where she was going, her full attention on the menu. It was handwritten in Greek and English.

Amuse-bouche
Anthotyro cheese and honeyed figs

Appetiser
Greek lentil soup with olives

Entrée
Artichoke paella with saffron and lemon

Dessert
Edible flower cookies with a champagne sorbet

'Lydia! Christ! Watch where you're going!'

Lydia finally looked up from the paper to Caroline's warning as she narrowly avoided coming off the edge of a mound and certain bumps and bruises at the very least. She skirted around her mistake, feet following Caroline's tread now until Stamatis drew them all to a halt at a table on the edge of the area, a view straight down over the houses, cypress trees towering up above the site.

'Thank you,' Caroline said as Stamatis pulled her seat out.

'I will bring you some wine and some water and of course, some Greek bread. The food will start arriving very soon.'

Lydia took her seat, the paper menu still gripped in her hand. The way she was feeling was unexpected. Usually it would be unwelcome, but in this gorgeous setting, tables all packed together under arches from bygone times, the candlelight, it felt like some kind of epiphany.

'What's the matter? You've not got sunstroke, have you? I did say to be careful in that pool,' Caroline said, phone immediately coming out of her bag.

'There's no lamb shank,' Lydia whispered, a smile growing on her lips.

'Oh bloody hell! Well, hit me with it.' And then a look of real fear crossed her colleague's face. 'It's not fennel, is it?'

'No,' Lydia answered. 'But if this is cooked right, it might just be the best food you've ever tasted.'

And she couldn't wait.

Twenty-One

People had come. And people were still coming. Ismēnē had started handing out cards with times to come back, such was the interest in the event. And Thanos really couldn't believe it. He was doing this! Whether it was all above board or not, he was cooking in his own restaurant and surely nothing could go wrong when they were virtually on consecrated ground.

But it was hot in the tent, the steam circulating and not seeming to find any way out despite the flaps being open. But, even from inside, with the burners roaring and the waiters and waitresses buzzing in and out collecting dishes, he could hear the sound of gentle conversation, light music in the air, the occasional hum of a passing bumblebee ...

'I think we will need more rice,' Makis announced.

Thanos turned his head from where he was assembling figs for the next tables expecting the *amuse-bouche*. Makis was ladling paella into bowls like each customer had the appetite of Shrek.

'Makis, not so much,' he told him. He took a breath and stood up straight, every muscle in his back already calling out for rest. He knew it wasn't the standing up – he was used to that working for Baptiste – it was the stress. His spine was locked with nervousness and tension, every part of him willing this to go well.

'Not much?' Makis exclaimed. 'Are you even Greek?'

Thanos gave a smile. 'I am Greek. But there is a difference between feeling satisfied and feeling like you will burst.' Meals needed to fulfil their primary purpose. To nourish. He took the ladle from Makis.

'Imagine the bowl like your jeans,' he said, putting a careful large spoon of the food into the centre of the dish. 'You want them to fit perfectly, but you do not want any of you spilling over the sides, right?'

He saw Makis look at his own waistline now. Perhaps the reference was too distracting. Thanos had never been a fan of some of the tiny meals some of the famous chefs served up. He knew the flavours would be excellent combinations, but they were plates for show. He wanted his food to be pleasing on the eye and an embrace for the inside – like an enthusiastic hug from your *yiayia* but not suffocation.

'Makis,' Thanos said sharply. 'Fill the bowls, but do not *overfill* the bowls.'

'Thano!' Onassis called. 'The onions are making me cry!'

'Do not drip tears onto the food,' he replied. *Focus*. He had to remain focused. Perhaps it was time to turn up the music in here …

'Smile!' Caroline ordered, mobile phone raised and ready.

Lydia did smile. There was nothing not to smile about here in this atmospheric setting amid all the history. However, the highlight was already the absolutely *wonderful* food. The honeyed figs with the cheese she had never heard of had been the perfect pre-starter. Amid the juice of the fruit had been subtleties to the honey she had never tasted before – it was oak and berry and maybe even wildflowers. And the cheese on top with such a simple milky, lemony taste really brought the dish together.

'Wow,' Caroline said, looking at her photo on her screen. 'I don't think I've ever seen you look so relaxed.'

'Let me see,' Lydia said, reaching a hand out for the phone.

'Nope,' Caroline reacted, snatching it back. 'You'll delete it.'

'I won't. I promise.'

'No. I don't give my phone to anyone now. Not after the Newquay incident.'

'The what?'

'I can't go into it,' Caroline said, putting her phone back in her bag and flapping a serviette at her face. 'It's too upsetting. It involved Vernon and a giant seagull and I've never been able to eat a Cornish pasty since. And I really, *really* like Cornish pasties.'

'And what did you think of the lentil soup?' Lydia asked.

The lentil soup. As Lydia said it, the flavours were back on her tastebuds. It had been everything she had hoped for when she had set her mind on it for lunch and been disappointed. This soup had the capability to go spectacularly wrong. Lentils could go hard if the salt was added too early. This chef had not made that mistake. And the vegetables were perfectly cooked. The thing Lydia disliked the most in stews and big pot dishes was when vegetables were overdone and lost all their colour. In this meal the colour had actually been vibrant, calling to her, painting a picture …

'It wasn't chips,' Caroline stated.

'No.'

'But it wasn't fennel either.'

That was about as big a compliment as Caroline had ever given.

'It was actually not bad,' Caroline concluded. 'For something that had no meat in it and wasn't deep-fried.'

Not bad. That really was the highest of praise. Lydia got to her feet. 'I'm just going to find the toilet before the main course arrives.'

'See if you can find our very young waiter and get some more wine,' Caroline said, raising her glass.

'OK,' Lydia said.

Picking up her bag, she stepped away from the table and began making her way up the grassy rise where they'd entered. She took a moment to look at the other customers, chatting, eating, relaxing amid the rustic stone arches and two large lights on wheels that had switched on as soon as night started to fall. It was buzzing, diners waiting outside the gates, tables all filled up now.

A handwritten sign staked into the grass with an arrow had letters that were foreign to her but underneath was the English alphabet – W.C. – and she followed it out onto the path beyond the fence.

The rock music cranked up, Thanos was completely in the zone now, managing this canvas kitchen and his inexperienced staff the best he could. Onassis was wearing sunglasses over his eyes so nothing could irritate them and Makis just about knew what a tablespoon was without needing an actual measure.

'Clean plates,' Ismēnē yelled, bustling into the space with her hands full. 'And this music is too loud. The customers outside are enjoying the light songs of Nikos Portokaloglou. They do not want Jimi Hendrix.'

Thanos couldn't help but smile. Jimi Hendrix was Ismēnē's reference for anything she did not like that involved loud guitar. He could correct her, but it wouldn't make a difference the next time.

'I am surprised you can hear anything in here,' Ismēnē continued.

'We can hear the music,' Onassis offered with a grin.

'I can hear the faint thud of my heartbeat as I worry about portion size,' Makis said.

'Everything is under control,' Thanos assured. He felt strangely composed. From beginning the day without a job, to thinking Ismēnē's idea of doing this was insane, to now, running a restaurant in Roman ruins ... Well, it was like something from a storybook.

'That is good to know,' Ismēnē said all smiles. 'Because I have just taken bookings for two tables of ten in an hour.'

'What?' Thanos exclaimed. Now his relaxed demeanour was stress-stretching into unpliable panic. She couldn't mean that. He had told her he only had enough paella for the tables they currently had plus the bookings at nine o'clock. Yet now she wanted him to find food for another twenty people?

'Ismēnē, we do not have enough paella.'

'You cannot make more?'

Did he have extra ingredients to make another batch? And did he have the time to make it? It took forty minutes from start to finish but that was only if that was the one dish he was concentrating on. Some tables would soon be on their dessert ... He looked to Makis and Onassis. They both thought this busy-ness was high-pressure enough. But what was his alternative? To not try? To tell people they would not be able to eat here?

'I can make more,' Thanos decided with a nod. 'Onassis, you will need to go back to the house and harvest the artichokes and the peppers from our garden. I will tell you how many.'

'OK,' his brother agreed.

'Makis, can you take ownership of the soup?'

'I do not understand.'

'Here,' he passed over a spoon. 'Keep it simmering very gently. Do not let it boil.' Thanos took a deep breath and nodded at Ismēnē. 'It will be done. But no more bookings, OK.'

'For tonight,' Ismēnē said, grinning. 'But I think there are many possibilities for the future, no?' She pulled a face then. 'If we are not all deaf from Jimi Hendrix.'

Thanos adjusted his bandana a little then washed his fingers with bottled water. He didn't have time to leave the tent now. He was going to have to create another paella here and hope it was as good as the first ones. He closed his eyes and felt his way to his favourite chef's knife. It was going to be fine. He had this.

And then, just like that, the music stopped and all the lights went out.

Twenty-Two

Lydia gasped as she was plunged into darkness in the middle of washing her hands in this tiny toilet at the back of someone's house. It had already been a little disconcerting having a little Greek lady sitting in a beach chair and doing crochet watching her go into the small shed-like building, but now she couldn't see a thing. Fumbling for the lock she somehow navigated her way out and began feeling her way out of the garden – she hoped there weren't any snakes in the bushes.

There wasn't a light to be seen and, although the moon was full and beautiful, it definitely wasn't enough to light the path. Then she remembered her phone. The torch app. One of the greatest things about modern technology was packing a calculator, clock, diary, payment method and all kinds of literal life-saving stuff in something so small you could carry it around all the time. She slipped her hand into her bag and drew the phone out.

With one press she had light to guide her, but then her other senses kicked in and she was suddenly drawn to a canvas structure a short way up the path. Steam or smoke was escaping through the entrance way, as well as the scent of sizzling vegetables and stock and an underlining leathery, hay-like fragrance that Lydia knew well. *Saffron*. This was where the cooking was taking place. An outside kitchen putting together the most incredible food. Now, she was really intrigued ... particularly as it looked like the whole thing was in complete darkness except for a tinge of blue flame coming from the burners.

'This is Jimi Hendrix!' a woman screamed. 'He has overloaded the power with his music of fury!'

'I cannot see!'

'I have put too much in this serving dish!'

'QUIET!'

Lydia held still, her breath catching in her throat. She was right at the door of the tent now, and she could just make out a few figures of people inside. She hurriedly focused her torchlight on her shoes.

'Please!' the male voice continued. 'Let us all take a second for our eyes to adjust to the darkness.'

'I have not eaten enough carrots,' a teenage voice mumbled. 'I will not be able to see if we wait an hour.'

'Ismēnē,' the man who had shouted 'quiet' said. 'You will take my phone and use the torch. Make sure that the customers have light enough to see what they are eating and to not fall into the Roman bath.'

'A lot of the lanterns are solar-powered,' the woman answered. 'If I need to, I can activate the donkeys with head torches.'

'Good. Then reassure everyone that we are working to restore the power. Makis, you will go with Onassis to collect the vegetables.'

'I do not need help!'

'You say you have not eaten enough carrots. It is very dark.'

'But you will be on your own,' the woman remarked.

'The gods have answered my prayers,' came the reply.

It was then that the familiarity hit Lydia. She had heard this voice before. She recognised the low sexy timbre and immediately she was reminded of those olive-coloured eyes ... It was Thanos Nicolaidis. The waiter. The chef. The maker of every exquisite meal she had tasted so far on the island. Before she had really thought it through she was stepping into the tent, her torchlight leading the way.

'Hello,' Lydia greeted. 'Is there ... anything I can do to help?'

What had she just said?!

Thrown off by the sound of another voice in his kitchen – a female voice – Thanos turned his phone torch in the direction of the door and it bathed the new arrival in light that had the person reeling back a little and waving hands in a bid to cover their eyes.

'Ow! Wow! Too bright.'

'Sorry,' he said, dropping the beam from the woman's face.

But even in the shadow he felt recognition. It was *her*. The writer who was going to put Dina's restaurant in her English magazine. The woman he had thought was pure understated beautiful. *Lydia*. Here in Benitses.

'Dinner is coming,' Ismēnē butted in. 'You should be sitting at your table.'

'I was ... using the toilet and then the lights went out and—'

'Ismēnē,' Thanos said. 'Please, make sure the customers are not alarmed. Onassis, Makis, please go to get the vegetables. Artichokes and peppers. Bring them all.'

There was some scurrying, some knocking into the worktop and then quiet. Only the two of them now. And no one was taking care of the soup. He picked up the spoon and began to tend to it. He needed to get his head back in this night. His good fortune could very easily reverse if he didn't keep up with orders.

'*You're* Thanos Nicolaides.'

It wasn't a question but a statement and never had his name sounded so big, nearly filling the space in the tent. And from her lips his name didn't just sound like something he was called, it sounded like a title. *Important*.

'Yes,' he answered. 'And I am sorry if you have not yet had your paella.'

'Well, the soup was the best I've tasted.' She paused for a moment, then: 'Ever.'

He looked up from the simmering pot and even in the darkness he found her eyes. He was looking for extra validation to her words. *Sincerity*. And it was there, her whole expression was loaded with it.

'So, is there anything I can do?' Lydia asked. 'I could ... take plates for washing or—'

'No,' he answered quickly, eyes back down. He was only sharing his kitchen with Makis and Onassis because he had had little time to organise the way he would like. He wasn't naïve enough to think he could *never* have help – all the best chefs had a team behind them – but not here, not now.

'But ... you can't see,' she clarified.

He looked up again. 'I do not need to see as well as you might think.'

He sensed her draw closer, heard her feet step forward on the grass until she was right there by the burners, gazing at him with curiosity. 'This is not my first time cooking in the dark,' he told her. 'In Corfu we have many power cuts.'

'That might be the case,' she answered. 'But to produce meals of the highest quality means complete diligence.'

'You think you cannot be diligent unless you have light?'

He could hear his own breath in the still air and the atmosphere seemed to thicken. He checked his watch; his servers should be here with the cookies and sorbet for dessert by now. If they were dwelling too long on the track up from his home, things would begin to melt.

'I think,' she began, 'that there are some things that are better in the dark ... but cooking isn't one of them.'

'Unless you are prepared.' He came around the wardrobe doors and put his hands on her shoulders drawing her into his workspace. '*Ela*. Look.'

Lydia didn't know whether she was internally fizzing because of the lack of clarity of her vision, this man's hands on her shoulders – warm, firm and a little bit sensual somehow – or the stupidness of suggesting she help. Despite the lighting situation, this man knew *exactly* how to cook. He didn't need some washed-up, could-have-been-but-never-was chef sticking her baster in. She let out a breath as he flicked on a large, obviously battery-powered lantern and her gaze travelled across the countertop.

It might have been made up of what looked like a pair of wooden doors, but what was set out on there was meticulously arranged. Neat, tidy, clean and a set place for everything. It was perhaps the tidiest working area she had ever seen. It spoke not only of diligence, but real care about the small stuff. And he was still holding her shoulders ...

'Really,' he said, warm breath dissipating over the back of her neck. 'The only thing that can ever go wrong in the kitchen is poor preparation.'

Lydia's eyes moved along the selection of knives laid out, pristine, ready for the next use. There were three Santoku knives. She had always favoured those herself. It wasn't just the way they cut things so cleanly, it was the way they felt in her hand and the texture of the blade when you ran your fingers along it.

'This is like an operating theatre.' The words were out of her mouth before she had thought about it.

'I like it,' he answered, finally removing his hands from her shoulders. 'I have never thought of it that way before.'

'You did it like this in case the power went off?'

He smiled. 'I *always* do it like this in case the power goes off. Or to help if I suddenly lose my sight between courses.'

'But it can't always stay like this,' Lydia said. 'I mean, when you're rushing between pans and plating up, you're just going to put things down anywhere.'

'Really?' he answered, raising an eyebrow. 'Anywhere?'

Suddenly she felt under scrutiny and it was a sensation that quickly began to grow and multiply. Someone questioning her methods. Someone telling her her way was the wrong way. Not the wise, soft and reassuring words from Mario, advising alternatives, suggesting a different approach. The accusing, condescending, acid lines that attacked from the inside. This was a mistake. She didn't do kitchens – even ones under canvas – the scent of caramelisation in the air. What had she been thinking walking in here? *If you do not be-lieve, you cannot be-living.* Her dad's words were echoing in her ears as her body decided between 'fight' and 'flight'. And then there was that vision of Mario swimming in her sight. He'd been humming to himself, keeping an eye on a simmering consommé, and then he'd dropped ...

'Lydia,' Thanos said. 'Is everything OK?'

His tone was somewhere between firm enough to jog her attention but gentle so it didn't sound accusatory. And he had remembered her name ...

'Absolutely,' she answered quickly, making sure her lips moved into as confident a smile as she could manage. 'But, seeing this …' She indicated the general well-ordered production line. 'Well, you clearly don't need any help.' She took a step back.

'Lydia,' he said again. And then he stopped talking, looking like he might be caught still deciding what he wanted to say next. 'Thank you. For what you say about the soup.'

She nodded, her body telling her in no uncertain terms that she could not stay here any longer. Saying nothing further, she turned her back on him and made her escape.

Twenty-Three

'Cor! I have to admit, this champagne sorbet is something else! Is it going to get me drunk?'

'I think the white wine is doing that all on its own.'

Lydia put another tiny spoonful of the sorbet into her mouth and let it fizz over her tastebuds. It was clean and crisp and the perfect accompaniment to the moist, buttery cookies baked with a bright blue flower embedded into the dough. Not only were the two cookies beautiful on the plate – like an edible miniature – they were perfect on the palate too. It was substantial enough to be a full dessert but not too heavy to overfill the stomach. This chef didn't only know food, he also put thought into the bigger picture. He had fitted all the pieces together in his menu choices and created a flawless dining experience.

'It's sensually atmospheric with the lights out, isn't it?' Caroline remarked. 'With these rustic lanterns I can almost visualise the hulking horny Romans running around here in nothing but loin cloths.'

What would Lydia have come up with to cook if she had a tent, Roman ruins and customers to feed? Might she have started with a little sushi – perhaps making it Greek – cucumber rolled up with *tzatziki*, feta cheese, red pepper and a little fresh dill. For the main? Lamb with tarragon cream?

'Now what is *he* doing here? These waiters must have so many jobs. Not that I'm complaining. Forget ancient Romans. I wouldn't mind seeing *him* in a loin cloth.'

Lydia woke from thoughts she knew better than to be having and set her gaze to where Caroline was staring. It was Thanos. Out of the tent, bandana removed from his forehead, he weaved amongst the tables, helping to collect plates and ensuring the flaming torches a didn't-really-look-fifteen-year-old had set light to some forty-five minutes or so ago were not going to set fire to tablecloths or scorch arm hair … He was so broad in stature, but he moved with graceful confidence that was so very attractive. She swallowed. And Caroline had no idea he was the cook tonight …

'He isn't a waiter,' Lydia said. 'He's the chef.'

'*Another* job?! Christ, things must be desperate over here. When does he sleep?' Caroline exclaimed. 'Hmm, never mind that, when does he have sex?'

And with that thought implanted in Lydia's brain she held her breath as Thanos approached their table …

He had been thinking about Lydia as he cooked that extra paella. She had an attachment to food because of her job, but he was sensing, just from their two brief interchanges, that she definitely had cooking in her soul. Except when she went to accept it – like she had when she had offered him her assistance – something else kicked in to stop her. It made him curious for her story. He wanted to know why she was here now in Benitses.

'Hello again,' Thanos spoke. 'How was the food for you tonight?'

'Nearly as delicious as you,' Caroline replied straightaway.

'You will make my cheeks blush,' Thanos answered.

'I could make other things blush given ten minutes of alone time.'

'Caroline!' Lydia exclaimed.

Caroline rolled her eyes. 'Is the "men aren't pieces of meat" lecture coming on again?' She gasped. 'Speaking of meat, I think this is my very first vegetarian meal and … I liked it.'

'Believe me, that is a real compliment coming from Caroline,' Lydia assured him.

'Thank you for your words,' he answered. 'It would have been my choice to welcome you to a restaurant where the tables did not move with the terrain, but this was the only location available tonight.'

'Do you do this often then?' Caroline asked, elbow on the table, seeming to study him closer.

'Cook?'

'Pop up!' Caroline said. 'You know, create a culinary night from scratch and then roam like a wandering Greek gypsy to another town the next day.'

'This is my first time,' Thanos answered.

Caroline let out a long, slow, guttural sound.

'Please ignore her,' Lydia jumped in. 'And the location here, it is so beautiful. I've never dined anywhere quite like it before.'

She seemed a little more relaxed now. Altered from the half-terrified person running from his tent. Still the same kind of beautiful. He realised he was staring at her. He wet his lips and tried to hold on to professionalism.

'It is a small piece of history,' he replied. 'Some people, they come here to Benitses expecting to see a grand palace and they are disappointed there is not more.'

'I'm not disappointed,' Lydia told him.

'*I* won't be disappointed if you take off your shirt.'

Thanos smiled at the older woman. 'You should come to the beach in the morning. Every day, before sunrise, a local man called Spiros takes a swim naked.'

'Mmm,' Caroline said. 'I'm not quite sure where my readers stand on nudity at the moment. It's a fifty-fifty split between thinking anything involving getting naked is a kind of therapy or thinking it's a big no-no because of "the children".' She got her to feet. 'Anyway, I am going to navigate my way to the toilets and then I'll be back.' She rested a hand on Thanos's shoulder. 'Wait until I return to remove clothing.'

As embarrassing as Caroline was with her lewd comments, Thanos shirtless *was* an attractive prospect. The shape of him hadn't passed Lydia by and she really did want to know where that tattoo on his wrist led to.

'Sorry about Caroline,' Lydia ventured. 'She's a long time divorced.'

'And are you?' Thanos asked. 'Divorced?'

Lydia shook her head and smiled. 'No.'

'You are married?'

She laughed. 'No, I'm not married either.'

'Good,' Thanos answered, plucking up Caroline's dessert plate.

'Is it?' Lydia asked.

'Yes.' He nodded, leaning a little closer and putting his perfect hands around her plate. 'Because ... I would like to have breakfast with you tomorrow.'

There was so much in that sentence Lydia wasn't sure she had grasped anything other than the word 'breakfast'. And as the rest of the words formed a detailed picture in her head Thanos spoke again.

'I ... did not mean that in the way that breakfast might come after a night. I mean ...' He stopped talking and seemed to mentally regroup. 'I could blame my English. But really I can only blame my lack of thought.' He took a breath. 'Breakfast. Tomorrow morning. At the beach.'

The words were direct now. No 'if you can make it' or 'if you want to'. Not one question mark. Was that arrogance? Was he super-confident that she would not refuse an invitation from him? Lydia didn't think it was that. Because the way he was looking at her gave off a touch of nervousness, perhaps even a hint that he was stepping into unfamiliar territory ...

'Does a man called Spiros really swim naked?' Lydia found herself asking.

It broke the tension and Thanos smiled, a definite glint in those to-die-for eyes. 'Six a.m.,' he said as he removed the used serviettes.

'Well, what should I bring?' Lydia called as he stepped away from the table.

'Not your friend.'

Lydia laughed. 'She hasn't ever started anywhere at 6 a.m. I meant, the food.'

He turned back to her with a shrug. 'Whatever you like. *You* will be cooking.'

Twenty-Four

Benitses Beach

What was she doing? Lydia was standing inside a bus shelter on the edge of the beach with a carrier bag containing bread, potatoes, sausage, eggs and her favourite herb, thyme. It was almost 6 a.m. and everywhere was quiet, the sun not yet risen. It wasn't cold though, the air simply a little less humid. But she was shivering, quaking in fact. From the tips of her toes through to the very ends of her hair and all the internal pieces in between. This was *exactly* what she didn't do anymore. This was what she hadn't done since the day she had left Maison Mario. She closed her eyes as the restaurant came to mind. The classic styling, curved-back chairs and soft tablecloths, Italian sculptures and artwork on the walls, uplighters like sconces from Rome providing subtle lighting. It had always felt much more than a restaurant. It was a beautiful piece of Italy in London, exuding cosmopolitan class and cool effervescence as well as cosy chic. It had felt like home.

She slapped a fly away from her arm and dragged her thoughts back to the present. Was she actually going to go through with this? Meeting a guy. Cooking. Two pursuits that seemed equally foreign to her. And, really, what was she going to make with potatoes, sausage and eggs when she didn't even have a pan? *Why* hadn't she brought a pan? Because there *were* basic cooking things in their room – two rings of a hob and knives and forks. There was probably a pan. Maybe she hadn't looked so they could just eat the bread and no cooking could take place ...

But, despite her trepidation, it was lovely here on the beach with no one else sharing it with her. Sun loungers were perfectly straight underneath natural reed shades, the sand not littered by floaties or bags or people playing beach tennis. The sea was calm and the gentle in and out motion would have been soothing to her nerves if it hadn't been for the whole inner turmoil thing she had going on.

And that's when she noticed Thanos. Over to the left, near the rocks and the concrete wall to the marina, he was tending to something perched on the sand. Was that a barbecue?

There was a chance she would not come. A big chance. And Thanos almost felt stupid for being so blunt about his invitation the night before. He could not remember the last time he had asked someone out. And breakfast ... he had always felt that breakfast was a lot more intimate than dinner. It was the very first meal of the day, a new beginning, a chance to make over and start without any regrets ... He had no regrets this morning. Last night had gone well despite the inconvenience of the power cut. Between them they had pulled it off and, as well as the profit they had made, there had been a large pot of tips for the waiters that Thanos felt sure would be spent quickly on App Store games or *gyros*. Ismēnē had been exhausted when they had finally cleared the site at close to 2 a.m. – not that she had admitted it. But, by the time Thanos had escorted her home, her eyes were closing and despite her reluctance, he had helped her to bed and pulled over her covers. He also didn't make Nuno climb down from his nest at the bottom of the bed, the cat's head resting protectively on the old woman's feet. Ismēnē had worked so hard for him yesterday and all last night. But what came next, he still really didn't know.

'Hello.'

He looked up from the barbecue and Lydia was right there in the half-light, some of her blonde hair tied back from her face, the rest loose. It was a good look for her. And he needed to say something instead of staring. '*Kalimera*. Good morning.' He stepped up to her and leaned in, kissing first one cheek then the other. He did it, as was the Greek way, before he had thought too hard about it.

'*Signomi*. Sorry. We Greeks start the day as we mean to go on. With the hugging and the kissing.' He smiled. 'And it is not even light.'

Lydia smiled back, putting a bag down on the rocks. 'I actually like it. Because it feels genuine. In the UK we seem to spend a lot of time hugging and kissing people we don't really like much.'

'Really?' Thanos said. 'I do not understand this.'

Lydia laughed, stepping closer to the grill. 'So, you are barbecuing.'

He shook his head. 'No. *You* are barbecuing. What did you bring?'

'Well,' Lydia said. 'I didn't bring a pan.' And he noticed her hands were shaking a little.

'Wait,' Thanos said, moving across the sand to his big black rucksack he had propped up against the wall. He dipped his hands in and brought out his favourite pan. He banged a hand against the base. '*Edho!* Here!'

She looked so nervous. He didn't want her to feel that way. He took something else from the bag and he came back across the sand. 'You would like some tea? It is green tea, my way, with apple peel and cinnamon.'

'I ... have never had that before.'

He put the flask down on his cool box that was next to the barbecue and took off the lid. Quickly pouring, he then handed Lydia the cup before she could do any more of the deep thinking he sensed was going on.

He watched her first take a smell of the tea and then slowly sip the liquid. It was considered, careful, respectful to a new flavour. He liked that. A lot.

'Oh! This is ... lovely. Really lovely,' Lydia said, bringing the cup down from her mouth. 'And you made it this morning? What time did you get up?'

'Well ... I did not really go to sleep,' he admitted. 'When I finished at the ruins it was late, or perhaps early, so I cleared and cleaned, I fed a pig I should not have and then I made tea.'

His mother had taught him how to make all different kinds of tea from leftovers – the very things that people would put in the bin or on the pile for compost. His father had been the grower of things and his mother had made sure they used up every scrap. It was as much about saving money as it was about not being wasteful.

'What did you bring for breakfast?' he asked her.

'Oh, well, I didn't really know, although perhaps, given last night, I should have guessed that ... we would have actual cooking facilities here on the beach.'

He smiled, shaking his head. 'You English people, always with so many words to say a simple thing.'

'But at least our words are short, even if we might elongate the sentences. Greek words have so many letters. Like ... the word for "bill" – "*logariasmo*".'

Thanos held his hands up in surrender. 'You make an excellent point.' He picked up her bag from the rocks as the sky began to lighten a little. '*Psomi*. Hmm. *Patatas*. *Avga*. Ah, *loukaniko*. Very good.' He held up the thyme. 'Why did you pick this herb?'

Now it felt a little like she was a contestant on *Ready Steady Cook* and her choice of items for a fiver were being closely examined by Rylan. Simply going to the supermarket and putting these things into a basket, thinking about creating something, it had been a leap. At home she didn't consider anymore, she bought for necessity, often mismatched because she did not care ...

She swallowed. 'Thyme is my favourite herb,' Lydia answered. And she hadn't used herbs at all for so long. Now it was up to the chefs who cooked for her to remind her how effective they could be.

'Why?'

'Well,' she began, 'I like how versatile it is. You know, depending on what you're cooking it can help produce many flavours. With chicken it can make the dish more earthy and peppery. In desserts it gives lemon and mint and floral undertones. I like what it does to sausage.' She stopped talking then as her face flamed. Who was she channelling? Caroline after too many white wines and not enough carbs? And Thanos was an excellent chef. He would know what thyme did.

'I like what it does to sausage too,' Thanos replied, grinning. '*Kai etsi*. So, cook for us. I have extra virgin Greek olive oil, salt, pepper, oregano – *my* favourite herb – and I have sardines. Fresh off the boat.'

Cook for us. It sounded so simple when Thanos said it. Because it was what he did. He had thought nothing of creating dinner perfection last night, in a tent, under extreme lighting circumstances, and here he was, before the sun had risen, setting up a barbecue on the sand. She hadn't even done so much as made a from-scratch curry in months. She could probably plead loyalty and ask for a stake in Patak's. But that really wasn't what she wanted. And there was a big difference between making an effort here or at home and reconsidering her cooking career ... wasn't there? Or was cooking just cooking no matter what environment it took place in. The minute she began, would her mind push her all those memories of Mario, on the tiles of the kitchen, work going on around them for a moment like nothing had happened, then the realisation that he was so horribly still ... or would Patrick's snarling face come into view? Those words of spite peppering her subconscious as she tried to regroup and regain her confidence after her mentor's death, Antonia watching on, saying nothing, looking a little too indifferent ...

'I brought your favourite knife,' Thanos told her, his voice bringing her back to the beach. He had put the pan on the hot grill and now held out the medium-sized Santoku.

Lydia swallowed. 'How did you know it was my favourite knife?'

'I told you, my kitchen is organised. I saw exactly where your eyes lingered longest, even in the dark.'

She shivered. Goodness, she hoped she hadn't given eye-lingering clues to other things in his kitchen that might have held her attention for the longest time ... OK, this was a bit better. Perhaps honing in on his attractiveness would take the pressure off thinking about what it would mean to cook here. What it would mean to cook *at all*.

'I am stepping back now. And sitting down.' He plumped into

one of the two beach chairs that were set up with a view of the sea. 'In a few minutes I will prepare the sardines.'

She had a Japanese knife in her hand and ingredients that needed her attention. But it was almost like starting over again. Being the new recruit, the youngest recruit, on her very first day. She had been so full of enthusiasm and passion then, so self-assured, so hungry to learn. That's why this was even harder. Back then she had only had natural talent, but now she had years of experience in the bag. Except she was too afraid to use it anymore. She closed her eyes and let her fingertips graze the wood of the chopping board, trying to bring back the Lydia Broom who feared nothing from food, the person who worked *with* it, the chef who wasn't afraid to try something and fail. What would Mario think if he could see her now? His protégée eyeing up a sausage like it might suddenly come alive and club her over the head. What about Patrick? Would he be pleased that *still* his words made her second guess her intuition? She opened her eyes, breathing in the calm and serenity. She was safe. This was nothing like the fiery galley on a Friday night. Taking another deep breath, she gripped the handle of the blade and sliced into a potato.

Twenty-Five

Thanos had watched her work in silent awe. Her technique was different to his, but it was good. *Very* good. Despite an initial hesitancy, there was now absolutely no doubt in his mind that Lydia was a cook. Whether she had done it professionally, running a working kitchen, or was just an amateur who paid attention to detail, he did not yet know, but he was intrigued to find out. And he was still looking at her as they sat eating the breakfast of eggs, potatoes, sausages and thyme she had prepared, alongside the sardines he had grilled with some asparagus. The sun was up, but it was still quiet, a few cars passing on the road, the gentle rolling of the sea the overriding sound.

'The sardines.' Lydia spoke suddenly. 'I've never tasted anything so fresh. They just melt in your mouth.'

'The fish accept the compliment,' Thanos answered, biting into another one of them. 'Really, there is not a lot to do to something that pure of taste.' He swallowed his mouthful. 'But you already know that.' He paused a little longer. 'You are a chef, no?'

'No,' Lydia answered.

He heard the slight hitch in her tone. It was as if he had discovered a secret she had locked away. He raised an eyebrow at her reply and shook his head a little. 'Diagonal cuts. A solid rocking technique. Your choice of ingredients. You can *say* you are not a chef, but you cannot fail to show that you are.'

He watched her bury her mouth into her second cup of apple peel tea. *Buying time.* He was guilty of that exact move when he didn't want to answer someone. He said no more. If he waited long enough then perhaps ...

'I ... used to be a chef.' She paused. 'It was ... ages ago. And ... now I write about food instead of cooking with it.'

He felt himself smile. 'Cooking *with* it. I like it.'

'What?'

'Most people they simply cook the food. Like *they* are the most important thing in the situation. But, for me, I feel the *food* should always be the star.'

He caught himself. He had never said that aloud before and it reminded him of moments in the kitchen with his mother. *We thank the food, Thano. The way we thank the people who grew it or fished for it. It gives itself to us so we may thrive. The very least it deserves is our gratitude.*

'That's why you're so good with it,' Lydia replied. 'Your attention to how the ingredients work together is what makes the meals so special.'

Special. She thought his food was special. Was she going to write about last night in her magazine? Were people in the UK going to read about a chef from a small village in Greece? And then he realised what she had done.

'You have changed the subject,' he stated, forking up another piece of the breakfast combination. 'Who taught you to cook?'

'Just ... someone I really, *really* admired.'

'Your mother?'

She laughed then and the sound was somehow warm and light and he liked it. The movement had also relaxed her face a little. It was good to see.

'No,' she said, shaking her head. 'My mother doesn't cook. She barely ever makes a coffee. She doesn't enjoy food like other people either. For her, eating is either a necessity to keep her healthy or something she does to indulge her friends' needs for expensive pastries with their chatting.'

'Then who? Your father?'

Lydia took a breath. The cooking hadn't been easy in the slightest here, despite the huge difference between the sand and the fiery galley on a Friday night. But she had tried to make herself be in the moment, the way she had at the very beginnings of her food journey. It was all about the ingredients, the way they felt as she prepared them, the way they complemented each other. It wasn't about her. She was simply the vessel. And the sky hadn't fallen in. It was a *huge* step.

'He wasn't my father,' Lydia said. 'But he was like one. And then he ... died. And, when he left ... some of my love for cooking, it died with him.'

She had never fully admitted that, even to herself, before. Things had felt different, less fluid and kind of empty after Mario had passed. She had taken a little time out, a week to try and somehow make sense of it all, but Mario's absence was heightened by the unfamiliarity of her apartment she never usually spent that much time in. She had decided the show had to go on because that's what she thought Mario would have wanted. She had tried to throw herself back into the breach to keep Maison Mario the way it always had been, but not working through her loss had left her weak and vulnerable. Unprepared for Antonia's arrival and Patrick's behaviour.

And then, as she attempted to mentally reassess, Thanos reached out and took hold of her hand, squeezing it so gently, but with firm reassurance. It was the simplest of actions yet everything he did, everything he said, seemed so genuine.

'I am so very sorry, Lydia,' he whispered.

His voice so quiet, his face so close, her eyes began to well up with tears. She didn't remember anyone ever saying they were sorry to her before. Her mother didn't believe that the death of someone was the end. Her dad always found tears a little awkward. And Patrick had only taken three days to make Mario's mandoline slicer his own.

'Thank you,' she answered.

He squeezed her hand again and she realised then she was enjoying the contact perhaps a little too much. She had thought he had incredible hands on first sight but *feeling* them was altogether even better. His skin was smooth, a little flecked with the oregano he had finely chopped and sprinkled liberally over the sardines with nothing else but olive oil. There was strength and masculinity there, the feeling that his hands were capable of hard tasks as well as finesse. She swallowed and, perhaps sensing a shift, he took his hand away and went back to eating.

'Would your like-a-father be happy that you were not cooking any longer?' Thanos asked.

He said the sentence so matter-of-factly it caught Lydia by surprise and she needed a second to catch on. 'I ... don't know.' It was true. If Mario was looking down right now she didn't know if he would be furious that she had turned her back on the kitchen or whether he would understand that having his own daughter and the man Lydia herself had put into that restaurant crushing her entire existence was too much for anyone to stand.

'Let me ask a more important question,' Thanos said. 'Are *you* happy to not be cooking any longer?'

She let a light laugh leave her lips but there was nothing really weightless about it on the inside. These were tough asks she didn't remember anyone had called her on before. And they were coming from someone she barely knew, on a beach ...

She slipped off her flipflops then and sank her toes into the sand that was already beginning to get warm. Forgetting the panic she still had recalling the night Mario had died, dismissing what had happened with Patrick, how did abandoning something that had used to make her so incredibly happy make her feel?

She took a deep breath and then began speaking. 'Some days I miss it so badly I get this aching feeling like someone very roughly cut that love out of me.' The depth of that statement triggered a little stomach flutter. 'But there are other days I don't miss the intensity at all.'

'The intensity?' he queried, shifting his beach chair even closer to hers.

'The madness, the yelling, the stress ... everything but the food.'

'That is how all kitchens work in England?' he queried. For a second, she thought he was going to snort hot air from his nose like a furious bull. 'I cannot believe it.'

'Well ...' Lydia started. 'Everything is time-challenged in the UK. You rush to work, you rush *at* work, you rush home from work and you try to squeeze in as many light-hearted TV shows as you can before you rush off to sleep.'

'And you rush when you are cooking?' Thanos asked, one eyebrow raising as he licked fish from his fingers.

Lydia's thoughts went back to The Griddler and his need for a timer ... but it wasn't only that when it came to Patrick. From the very beginning he had seemed to thrive on stress. Even as a sous chef his work had been fast and furious. And then, when he had charmed his way into Antonia's affections – and most probably her bed – he had taken charge and brought that vibe right the way through Maison Mario. But, like it or not, perhaps that was how things were in the industry now. She shook her head. 'People never have enough time. There are expectations as to how long a meal should take to be prepared. *Any* meal.'

'I know that,' Thanos answered. 'But it is sad, no? That people live their lives around the expectations of others.' He seemed to muse on his own point for a second, turning his head a little to the sea and watching the waves.

'Sometimes it's good to have something to aim for,' Lydia said. 'It can help with focus.'

'But what if you were eating food in a restaurant and someone kept telling you how long you had to eat it?'

And that was an excellent point. Lydia had never been a fan of the double or sometimes triple covers. A 6 p.m. booking had to be done by seven-thirty. A seven-thirty had to be done by nine. How could you relax and enjoy if you had a stop-clock running? And that's exactly how Patrick's kitchen had worked.

'They do that in England?!' he exclaimed in horror as if he had read her mind.

'Well, if a restaurant is popular and has bookings months in advance then people don't usually mind if the visit is brief.'

Even as she said the words, she was thinking about what most people loved the best about going to restaurants apart from having someone cook for them. It was the whole experience, the having a drink somewhere, heading to the restaurant, taking time to choose from the menu, lingering a little, not being rushed ...

She looked up from the specks of sand rushing between her toes. 'It's the opposite of Greece, isn't it?'

Thanos nodded. 'Eating for Greeks is all about switching off, relaxing, savouring every moment as well as every mouthful. We eat late, when all work is done, when it is time to wind down and there are no other demands on us for the day.'

This was a perfect moment to savour, Lydia thought to herself. The warm sun on her skin, the delicious combination of fish, eggs, meat, vegetables and herbs with the sweet apple tea to wash it all down with, this gorgeous man next to her. Perhaps any second now she was going to wake up ...

Her phone began to sound. Loudly.

'Oh! Sorry,' she said, wriggling in her seat and trying to balance the plate on her knee while getting her phone out of her pocket.

'Is that an alarm?' Thanos asked. 'To tell you that your time for breakfast is over and you must rush to another place?'

She recognised the humour in his tone before she saw the grin spread across his lips. 'Very amusing. No, it's Caroline. We're going on a road trip today. An olive oil tour and then to a castle.'

He nodded. 'Do not hurry the time. Corfu has many interesting places, but they are better enjoyed slowly.' He took her plate from her.

'Thank you,' she said, getting to her feet. 'For breakfast.'

He smiled. 'You did it, remember?'

She *did* remember. And, despite her heartbeat pumping in her throat as she tried to bring back even the merest basics of cooking, when the pan was sizzling hot and the knife was in her hand it had been harder to stop the muscle memory from kicking in than it had been to let it run free. And that was thanks to Thanos.

'Would you be ... up for an interview?' Lydia asked him.

'An interview?'

'Yes, for the magazine. I usually only write food reviews and Caroline does the feature pieces but ...' She took a deep breath. What was she trying to say? That she wanted to branch out into her colleague's area of expertise? Or that there was something about the way Thanos thought about food, *was* with food, that was reminding her of her own passion for it?

'But?' he asked.

'I want to see you eat,' she said bluntly.

He laughed. 'What?'

'I ... want you to tell me what food means to you and ... I want to ... see you eat something that someone else has cooked. And I mean more than my pitiful mess of a hybrid omelette you've been too polite to pick apart. Verbally at least.'

'OK,' he answered. 'I have not had this request before.'

'Well, you don't have to accept but—'

'Where do you stay?' he asked. 'In Benitses.'

'At the Argo Studios. For tonight at least. Then we are heading somewhere I can't pronounce.'

He nodded. 'OK. I will pick you and Caroline up at seven tonight.'

'O-K. Well, where are we going?'

He smiled again. 'We will go somewhere where we can all take our time. You can ask me your questions and we will eat like Greeks.'

Twenty-Six

The Governor's Olive Mill, Agios Mathiaos

'Remind me why I booked the early tour again?'

Caroline was wearing sunglasses that almost covered her whole face. They were currently waiting outside for their tour guide with rich, dark Greek coffee and water that they had guzzled quickly due to the stress from the terrain they had navigated on the way here.

Lydia had been in the driving seat, to this renowned place for olive oil production, because Caroline was blaming additives in the rustic wine for her monstrous hangover. Driving in Greece seemed to be a bit of an extreme sport and there were three very distinct types of Greek driver.

The first type drove like they had a death wish, the second type drove so slowly they could possibly actually be asleep at the wheel and the third type drove at a moderate pace but had overloaded their vehicle either with livestock, or a large wooden cupboard held on with a tied scarf, or both. It was a miracle the women had arrived on time. And the main road Google Maps had been trying to take them down had been closed.

Following the diversion, the way had led them up into the mountain where small roads had turned quickly into little more than alleyways the car was only just able to pass. At one point, Caroline had had to open the window and push in a wing mirror before they had a coming together with the awning of a *cafeneon*. But, as they passed through, it was quite obvious that life was going on there amid *espressos*, crepes, cigarettes and dogs scratching their ears in the sunshine. And it was an altogether different busy-ness to back home. Here, in the middle of terraces that clung to the rock, there was still a sense of relaxation, like it did not matter if things were achieved today or tomorrow or maybe even next week. And the feeling Lydia had been left with was something akin to envy. How nice to be able to feel that way, to be content simply *being*.

Lydia smiled at Caroline. 'You booked the early tour because you're a professional and we have a magazine to write.' She swatted away a wasp.

Their guide arrived and ushered the group under cover. There were large, cream-coloured millstones that once were used to grind the olives and, under a glass section of floor there were ancient tools and different types of barrels – wood, stainless steel and porcelain. Stainless steel was best to keep the oil in tip-top condition they were told and apparently there were twenty-two ingredients to an olive. Who knew?

'Honestly, my readers will only want to know if this stuff is going to make them live longer and can they put it all over their face as a skin treatment,' Caroline said as someone in their group was asked to pretend they were a tree.

'Sshh,' Lydia ordered. 'I want to hear the details. Aren't you taking notes?'

Caroline tapped her head and then made a face as if the light touch could bring on an aneurysm. 'All up here.'

Lydia was already reaching into her bag for something to jot down on because the last time Caroline had said she was making notes on a circus-themed dining night, all she had remembered was the size of the juggler's balls ...

It was lovely here though. This stone building with arches and beams, a cool fragrance in the air, the enthusiastic guide imparting all his knowledge on how this island had gone from somewhere with the very worst reputation for olive oil to now one of the best. Here, on Corfu, they had already been informed, was the variety of olive called the *Lianolia*. And this type of olive tree was in absolute abundance here. There were approximately four million on this island alone, some cultivated, some not and many of them hundreds of years old.

Their guide had shown them photographs of the aged trees, the years written in those dark knotted trunks that gave the appearance of wise old women. A solid backbone, strong roots and branches still providing nurture. She thought about Thanos and the way he spoke about cooking, like it should always be as natural as breathing. That pulled hard at her. The restaurant had been chaos after Mario's death, as if everyone had suddenly lost their way now its founder was no longer there. The energy had turned spoiled, the dynamic altered, a new boss in charge of the company, a new chef in charge of the kitchen. There had been no timings and new dishes and how Patrick wanted everyone to work seemed at odds with the whole previous ethos of the brand. If you were making food to please, how *could* it give off pleasure and relaxation and gentle contentment if it had been furiously plated up with the countdown ticking? What Thanos said, it was all beginning to make perfect sense.

'So, are you going to tell me where you went this morning before the sun came up?' Caroline asked as they walked over to the production machines. 'I'm at that age where the bathroom calls around 5 a.m. so I notice these things. Not sorry.'

'I … went for an early breakfast. On the beach.' All the memories of having the sand to themselves, the delicious fragrance of all the ingredients combining in the pan along with Thanos's fresh from the water sardines grilling. 'And …' She paused, as her body's reaction to what she was going to admit next gathered pace. 'I cooked.'

Two words. It was far more momentous than that. It had been like the first time she had made something properly complicated she had seen on *The Great British Bake Off*. Like that first lasagne she had given Mario. Like Mario's mother's secret meatball recipe he had finally shared with her and allowed her to attempt. It was a mark in time.

'You cooked.'

'I did.'

'On a beach.'

She nodded. 'Yes.'

'OK, so you just sparked a couple of rocks together, knocked up a fire and used driftwood sticks to skewer fish straight from the water in a kind of Hugh Fearnley-Whittingstall meets the *Famous Five* fusion?'

'Well, not exactly. Thanos had a barbecue and—'

'Oh, I see,' Caroline said *very* loudly. 'And is "barbecue" a euphemism?'

'Caroline,' Lydia said as their tour guide's gaze moved to them. 'Your *inside* voice.'

'But we're basically in a factory,' Caroline continued. 'So, was there naked swimming?'

'No.'

'So, you just cooked.'

'Just' cooking sounded Naked Noodle meets boiling water. This had been so much more than that. But perhaps it was better not to go into the portentous emotions it had brought out in her with Caroline.

'And ... we talked.' Lydia swallowed. It had been good to talk with Thanos. It had been so easy, like they understood each other a little, even though their encounters had been brief and by chance. Dropped into each other's recipe like an unexpected ingredient ...

'And are you seeing him again?' Caroline asked as they followed the group towards another room where long wooden tables and benches were set up with glasses, plates and bottles of olive oil stood proud at each side. It was another fabulously rustic room with a silvery leafed olive tree at its heart.

'Tonight,' Lydia stated. 'I forgot to mention, he's going to pick us up.'

'Well, where is he taking us? We need elegance and culture and ... maybe something like a fortune-telling donkey.'

'I'm not sure,' Lydia admitted. 'But he said we will eat like true Greeks.'

Caroline's face fell. 'With our fingers?'

'Hold on. You love eating with your fingers! You always refuse those little wooden chip forks in the takeaway *and* you're forever telling me that cocktail sticks are ridiculous because after you've eaten the thing you've prodded you have nowhere to put them.'

'There's always a plant pot,' Caroline began as they took their seats. 'However, my readers definitely do not eat with their fingers. Unless it's something artsy like they're gorging on burgeoning bunches of grapes in Botticelli poses for an out-there exhibition.'

'Well,' Lydia said, 'if it will make you feel better we can take some cutlery with us. That way, if it's all finger food, we can put knives and forks in any photos we take for the article.'

Caroline nodded, seemingly satisfied. 'You think of everything. Very organised. That's why you're so good at your job.'

Was she good at her job? Writing about meals didn't feel the same as cooking them. But was it enough to still have that association with food? She took a breath; this trip was making her do more thinking than she had done in months. And here, as the guide gave them a step-by-step account of how to taste the olive oil – gently rotate your glass, take all of it into your mouth and swill it around, swallow and then make a sound from the back of your throat like a cat about to cough up a fur ball – it seemed like there were a lot of questions that needed addressing. But none were more pressing than noting down the techniques and procedures for getting these plump fruits from the branches and transforming them into the finest oil. And Caroline still didn't even have a notebook out …

'So,' Caroline began again. 'We can go, but perhaps you could research the nearest grill room for the trip back, just in case there's no meat again.'

'You said you liked the menu last night.'

'But I still won't be dreaming of artichokes any time soon.'

'Please, a fork for you,' the tour guide said, pushing a tiny little bowl towards Caroline with the exact kind of 'chip' fork they had been discussing, balanced upon it.

From inside her across-body bag, Lydia felt her phone vibrate with an incoming email. 'Give me a second,' she said to Caroline. 'I'll be back.'

'I can't promise I won't eat all the bread or this ... ooh this yoghurt is nice. Is there actual olive oil in this? And ... is that wine? Can I drink that as well as the olive oil? And do I have to make the cat noise again?'

As Caroline continued to chat up their guide, Lydia strolled into the gift shop – dark wood display cabinets containing olive oil, kumquat liqueur and limoncello bottles, plus remedies for the skin and treats for the stomachs in glass jars – and checked her phone. It was an email from Bonnie the trainee. And the title was in bold and italics.

The Griddler – Get Chips and Grill. A brand-new cooking show! Coming soon to Channel 54!

Lydia blinked and blinked again. Was this ... Patrick ... getting his own TV show? Suddenly she felt a little bit queasy.

Twenty-Seven

Thanos and Onassis's home, Benitses

'Last night, you were the stars of the show. Truly, I was humbled.'

Thanos gave a bow towards what was left of his rather decimated vegetable patch as he held the hosepipe over the remaining plants and watered. There was something about the solitude he found in his back garden, when he was here alone with nothing but the sunshine and the produce he and Onassis had started to grow from seeds and cuttings. It wasn't just the memories he had of his parents, it was the calm it brought. These were brief moments where no demands were being put on him – as a brother-cum-guardian, as a chef. Back to nature and food in its very purest form.

'But I do not know if it was enough. To make a living from.' He sighed. 'Perhaps I should start to ask about other work. To guarantee money each week. Maybe at the olive press.'

As he said the words, he almost sensed an inhalation from his vegetables and, was it his imagination or did their leaves curl a little? And then the pig gave a snort from the makeshift enclosure it was housed in. He really needed to get rid of it. He would have to call George. He furrowed his brow and eyed the animal. 'And you, you do not be this way and judge,' he told him. 'I have promised Onassis new jeans and I cannot pay for those with you or these cucumbers.'

'There you are!'

Thanos almost dropped the hosepipe at the sound of Ismēnē's voice so close in his space. He turned around and there she was, only a few metres away, the ginger cat under one arm, her other hand on the knot of her stick. She still looked tired.

'Where else would I be? I do not have a job, remember?' Thanos said, moving to turn off the outside tap and stop the water flow.

'Nonsense! After last night you are the talk of the town,' Ismēnē stated, putting the cat on the outside table. It immediately leapt down and went to investigate the pig.

'Really?' he asked, coming over to her.

'The mayor wants to speak with you about catering for his wedding. He was dining with us last night.'

'What?! The mayor was there at the ruins?!' He'd had no idea the mayor had been one of the guests he was feeding. Why had no one told him?

'And that reaction is the exact reason I did not tell you he was there,' Ismēnē answered. 'You would have ... second guessed your choice of menu or ... maybe sent the pig to look for truffles.'

She was right of course. 'His wedding. Are you sure he said that?' Thanos said, unable to keep the smile from his face. 'There was a rumour he was going to have five hundred guests and set up marquees along the marina.'

'His fiancée is trying to cut it down to four hundred,' Ismēnē said with a chuckle. 'I wish her luck. She has trouble wearing the same pair of shoes for a second time.'

'When is the wedding?' Thanos asked, pulling a chair out for his friend and urging her to sit down.

'Next spring.'

He felt his heart sink. He needed something sooner than next spring. Unless they all ate pork for the entire winter. However, he was not sure the pig was even big enough to see the season out should he have the guts to make meals of him.

'It is good,' Ismēnē said, still not sitting down. 'Because you are going to be busy for the rest of the summer. In a few days' time you are going to be show-cooking.'

'Show-cooking?' he queried.

'At the food festival in Agios Stefanos. It is new this year. There are many people selling different kinds of food all through the day and then there is the entertainment at night.' Ismēnē grinned. 'I have a friend on the committee and a chef had to drop out at the last moment so ... I have managed to get you on the bill.'

'I ... do not know what you are talking about. I am a cook. I am not someone who can do acrobatics and eat fire.'

'You worry all the time,' Ismēnē said with a sigh as she picked at plants to deadhead them. 'Just like your father used to.'

'He had the same responsibilities as I do,' Thanos told her.

'And where did all the worrying get him in the end, huh?' Ismēnē said, pinching another brown flower between thumb and forefinger.

'Will you stop doing that and sit down?' Thanos ordered.

'Why do you shout at me?'

'Because you should be resting. It was a late night last night and you did far too much. Come on, sit down.' Thanos pulled at the chair again, bringing it nearer to Ismēnē.

'Stop,' Ismēnē yelled. 'I cannot sit down.'

'What?'

'My back hurts to sit down today. I am better to stand.'

He could see she was unbalanced a little, stiffer than normal on her feet. 'Have you seen the doctor?'

'Yes,' Ismēnē answered. 'I saw him this morning, outside the coffee shop. He was having all the things he tells his patients not to have ... with extra cream.'

'Ismēnē—'

'Do not!' she said in such a tone that Thanos knew she was serious. 'Every day I grow a little older, a little weaker and a little less happy about all of that.' She put her hands on her hips and rolled her lower body around. 'I should get Onassis to teach me some of his dance moves.' The pig gave a squeal and Thanos watched as Nuno struck through the bamboo 'bars' and slapped its face with a strong paw.

Thanos shook his head. 'I wish that he would spend as much time learning his maths as he does on making sure his moves look good.'

'Thano,' Ismēnē said, a disapproving eyebrow dipping. 'Do not make him grow up any faster than he already is.'

'Is that what I am doing? Wanting him to do well at school so he has as many opportunities as possible?'

'I am simply saying … he will not be young for long. Let him have these moments where he makes his own innocent choices.'

Thanos swallowed, his gaze going to the ripening tomatoes on his plants. He had not had the chance for innocent choices. All choice he might have had had sunk to the bottom of the sea with the boat his parents perished on. And he did not wish that weight of responsibility for his brother. *Normality*. Wasn't that what he had always tried to provide?

'Let him think for a while longer that the type of jeans he wears will determine his life path,' Ismēnē said.

'You think he has a chance in this competition?' Thanos asked, plucking some red tomatoes from the plants.

'You do not?'

Thanos shrugged. 'What do I know about dance?'

'Thano! So modest! You were the one all the girls in the village wanted to dance with when you were younger.'

'Before I became the one who would amount to nothing because I had to look after my brother.'

Ismēnē made a hissing noise through the gaps in her teeth. 'You expect me to say "Poor Thano, he has had such a hard life". Life *is* hard. I lose a husband, you lose your parents, but, believe me, the real disaster is when you lose yourself.'

It was a talent Ismēnē had. She always managed to make him feel the age of Onassis again and leaning heavily towards the pool of self-pity. She had suffered. She was still suffering. Yet every day she got up and started all over again. It was the way of stoic Greek women. And he needed to take a lesson from that.

'If you amount to nothing there is only one person to blame. *You*. You have the skills and now you are free of Baptiste, we are going to use them. We begin last night and next we have the food festival.' She took some of the tomatoes from his hands. 'Let Onassis have his dream of dance. Maths will catch up. You want to give him a little responsibility? Make him take care of the pig.' She drew in a sharp breath that made her tap her feet on the stone floor a little.

'You are OK?' Thanos asked, putting a hand to her elbow.

'Yes, stop trying to *yiayia* me,' Ismēnē ordered. 'Instead ... you tell me ... who is the girl who came into the tent last night. The one with hair the colour of sunshine and eyes like jewels?'

Thanos's insides were already waking up to the thought of Lydia before Ismēnē had even got to the end of the sentence. Physically she was oh-so-attractive to him but it went deeper than that. Food had brought them together but after spending a little more time with her, finding out how she experienced it, how it made her feel, he wanted to know more. And this morning on the beach, when *she* had cooked, he had been mesmerised. She had talent too, although she was going to great lengths to hide it for some reason. There was one point where he hadn't been sure she was even going to cut into the potato. But he had kept quiet, given her time and space and then, when she got into her stride, it had been a pleasure to watch, almost feeling like a performance. *Show-cooking*.

'She is ...' Thanos began. He stopped, unable to explain any further. He didn't even know what it was himself. How could he put it into words?

'Thano,' Ismēnē said. 'Do you blush?'

'No.'

'You like her,' Ismēnē said, grinning.

'You make me sound the age of Onassis again.'

'You like her,' Ismēnē repeated.

'I do not know her very well. And I do not have time for knowing her.' But the things she had said to him had resonated. Their conversation had somehow felt more intimate than any words he had shared with anyone else before.

'You like her.'

'Will you please stop saying that.' He had to swallow to drive some moisture into his mouth. It might be true that he liked her. It *was* true. But Lydia was here for her work and then she would be gone. And he had to focus on his life here with his brother. With no job, it was the worst timing. But, nevertheless, it could be an opportunity.

'She writes for a magazine in England,' Thanos told Ismēnē. 'She said she will write about my food. But—'

'Oh! That is amazing!' Ismēnē exclaimed, slapping Thanos hard on the back with the hand that did not contain tomatoes. 'Your name in an English magazine! English people reading about your cooking! Soon you will have your own television show like Akis Petretzikis. We will think of a different name to *Kitchen Lab*. Give me a moment.'

What it sounded like was a dream and he needed not to get caught up in it. It was OK to reach a little, but he had to keep his feet on the ground. More importantly, he did not want Ismēnē floating away on the idea. It was probably best not to tell her he was taking Lydia out tonight. Because he hadn't thought hard enough about that invite until it had been made. He'd selfishly wanted to spend more time with her and he'd jumped right in. He took a breath and smiled at Ismēnē. 'Let me make us some coffee. Then you can tell me more about this food festival.'

Twenty-Eight

Gardiki Castle

Lydia wasn't listening to Caroline and she wasn't really taking in the sight before them either. *Focus, Lydia.* She drew in a breath and aimed her phone camera at the stone remains of bygone times, crumbling like the best panko, loose rocks amid the grass. No, her thoughts were still very much on that email from Bonnie. *Luxe Living* have been invited to a pre-launch party for Patrick's new television show, which included a tasting menu. And it was the tasting menu that had really made her blood boil. It was *her* menu. *The* menu that she had told Patrick would be the core of Maison Mario when *she* took over the kitchen.

It wasn't a coincidence that *Luxe Living* had been invited. Yes, they might be one of the leading lifestyle magazines, but this, she knew, was all about her. This was Patrick having taken her career from her and now wanting to rub her face in it. The only flaw to his plan was the fact that she was currently in Greece and Bonnie was going to be eating the food. It would almost be funny – instant-noodle-fan Bonnie eating his 'delicacies' – if it wasn't such an almighty heart-punch.

'There's not much here, is there?' Caroline sniffed. 'No gift shop. Not even a *floor*!'

The approach had been very rocky and Caroline was wearing inappropriate shoes for navigating the chunks of stone sticking out where they had been laid since the Byzantine era. Inside the castle walls – some of which had been restored or were being held up by wood and metal props – there were merely remnants of what had gone before. Mounds of green interspersed with unrecognisable clumps of rock that once would have stood firm as the walls of elaborate rooms.

'I'm not sure my readers would bother coming here,' Caroline stated.

'It's ruins,' Lydia snapped. 'This is what ruins are.'

'Alright, *Time Team*. Keep your trowel on. What's happened to the smiling Lyds who cooked on a beach with a Greek hunk and bought beeswax and lavender olive oil cream to calm her strawberry legs?'

Lydia sighed. Should she share this info with Caroline? Was it ridiculous to get so het up over it? It had been two years since she had left Maison Mario and two and a half years since Patrick had ended their personal relationship. He had traded her in for Antonia and manoeuvred himself into her job before Mario's ashes had even been taken back to Italy to be scattered. Patrick was an absolute git. Nothing had changed in that respect. Except he seemed to feel the need to keep pouring salt all over her wounds like he was curing pork.

'I had an email,' Lydia began. She stepped down into one of the towers and looked up to admire the arrow slits, imagining Patrick on the wrong end of a longbow for a second.

'You had an email,' Caroline repeated, feet slipping a little on the dry, gritty ground as she came to join her.

Lydia looked at her friend. Was it her imagination or had her voice come out a little shaky? Maybe it was all the walking they had done already today. Caroline's step count usually only involved walking to and from the coffee machine at the office or padding her feet on the floor to make her chair spin around.

'From Bonnie,' Lydia stated.

Caroline closed her eyes and suddenly started to hum the theme tune to *The Apprentice*.

'Caroline, what are you doing?'

Caroline opened her eyes. 'Now I want you to know, first of all, that everything is going to be absolutely fine.'

Oh God. Caroline already knew about Patrick. How did she already know? Lydia couldn't remember Caroline being copied in on the email. And, if she knew, why hadn't she said anything? Caroline must have realised how this would get under Lydia's skin.

'You knew?'

'Don't say anything else,' Caroline said, taking hold of her arm. 'Not yet. Because I think this conversation requires ouzo and things that had been heavily deep-fried, not archways that could fall on us at any moment and … lizards.' She pointed to a little green creature who looked desperate to get back into a wall now it had discovered people.

'I'm not going to disagree with that but, Caroline, why didn't you tell me?' Lydia drew back her arm.

'Why didn't I tell you.'

There was the repetition again and Caroline hadn't really phrased it like a question. It was more like a stalling action as if she was biding time before giving her answer. Caroline started to lead the way back up the bank.

'How long have you known?' Lydia asked. 'Before Bonnie's email today?'

'I thought we were waiting for ouzo and fried foods,' Caroline said, reaching back and offering Lydia a hand. 'Come on, there was that nice-looking café place where we parked the car. They definitely serve frappés and I'll eat whatever they have and not make a fuss.' She started walking upwards again, pulling Lydia towards the way they had come in.

'Am I overreacting?' Lydia said, wrenching her arm away and giving a heavy sigh. 'Just tell me that.'

'Yes,' Caroline said immediately. 'Yes, because, as I just said, there is absolutely nothing to worry about. *Nothing*. I am going to make sure of it.'

Lydia frowned. Why did it sound like Caroline had some sort of plan? Should there *be* a plan? What was she going to make sure of? Shouldn't Lydia be taking the high road and pretending she really didn't want to score his testicles like she used to score the outside of fish …

'We just need to stick together. Two becoming one. You know what I mean,' Caroline stated.

'No,' Lydia breathed. 'No, I don't really know what you mean.' She sighed again. 'Because Patrick is my problem, not yours. Although I don't *want* him to be my problem. I don't want to think about him at all. But now he's done this! Well, I don't know what to think. Or even if I should think anything.' But in the back of her mind she wondered if this was some sort of reverse karma at work. She had reclaimed a little piece of herself this morning when she cooked with Thanos. And now the universe was serving her up a slice of retribution because she had enjoyed herself. Why couldn't she just enjoy *being* for a moment, sucking olive oil through her teeth and pouring it all over ice cream with walnuts?

'Patrick,' Caroline said, shaking her head.

'I refuse to call him The *bloody* Griddler.'

'Oh, yes,' Caroline said. 'Absolutely. Awful name.'

'So, if we're in this together, what are we going to do?'

'Well,' Caroline said, slinging an arm around Lydia's shoulders as they tentatively made their way back down the craggy pathway to the road. 'We do what I originally suggested. Ouzo for a starter – for you, because I am going to drive – and you can explain ... I mean, get me fully up to speed, with what Bonnie's told you.'

Lydia took another deep breath and felt herself settle a little. It was good to share. Whether Caroline could really help or not, it was going to make everything a little lighter, surely.

'OK,' Lydia said. 'But let's take some more photos of the outside of the ruins first. This could actually be a nice location for a wedding if you were still keen on that feature. The bride and groom might have to wear trainers but that's very in these days, isn't it?'

'You're right,' Caroline said, nodding. 'As always. Phew. Nothing we can't overcome. Yes, photos.'

As she watched Caroline pull out her phone and capture more images of the stone perimeter oozing with Byzantine history, Lydia breathed in the quiet and the heat of the day. She needed to do more believing in herself. That was at the root of all this. It was time to rediscover her self-confidence. And maybe that began with going out with Thanos tonight ...

Twenty-Nine

Ismēnē's house, Benitses

'You are wearing scent,' Ismēnē announced.

Thanos had only set one foot inside the doorway of Ismēnē's little studio and now he wondered if his aftershave was too powerful. He held his loose white shirt away from his body and sniffed.

'Ah! You are concerned about this like it has to be right! Where do you go?' Ismēnē was shifting Nuno from her lap and trying to get to her feet without the aid of her stick but failing badly. 'Nuno! You have made me stick into the chair!'

Thanos stepped further into the room and held his arm out for her to grab. She took it and as she raised from her seat she gasped. 'That is a new tattoo.' She made a disapproving noise that came from the back of her throat. 'Why another one, Thano?'

His eyes went to the depiction of a set of worry beads he had had inked a week ago. It was healed now and was an accurate representation of the set his father used to carry and count between his fingers. He would recite prayers sometimes or maybe a shopping list or sometimes he would be sitting still and not be mouthing anything. Those were the times Thanos hadn't known what concerns his father might have had as he moved the spheres up and down the thin string, but it always appeared to give his father comfort. It was another memory to add to most of the other tattoos that played out his loss.

'I know you do not like them,' Thanos answered. 'But, my body, my choice.'

Ismēnē snorted. 'I do not know where you find the money for body graffiti.'

‘I do not pay,’ Thanos said. ‘Gianni, he likes my sweet tahini pies.’

‘That is still payment,’ Ismēnē fussed. ‘Your food is your wealth. Never forget that.’ She pulled him forward. ‘Your collar is up.’ She began to fold it down with her crooked fingers.

‘It is meant to be up!’ He took ownership of it and stepped back a little. ‘Ismēnē, I am going out tonight. Onassis is at home working on some History and English. I suspect he will last thirty minutes doing that before he is bored. Could you please just listen out for him? Make sure he does not head off to Panos’s house.’

‘You would like me to go over there to babysit? I can work on his costume for the dance competition. I can watch your films with the army soldiers.’

‘You do not need to do that,’ Thanos said. ‘Please, take some time to rest.’

‘Resting is for the weak or the dead. I am neither of those things,’ Ismēnē reminded him. ‘The first I can control with willpower and the other I control with *horta*, olive oil and lemons.’ She grinned. ‘Do you drive somewhere?’

‘I am not telling you where I am going.’

‘But do you drive there? With someone?’

Ismēnē was fishing and he wasn’t about to take the bait.

‘I am driving. I will be careful.’

‘You are not taking a passenger in that car with the door that is held on with string.’

‘It is not string, it is rope.’

‘Thano! No,’ Ismēnē said, shaking her head as she shuffled into her kitchen area. ‘You are a chef. A very talented chef who is going to be the star of the food festival. You need to drive a car of a professional.’ She began rummaging around the detritus on her worktop – magazines, pens, tin foil, lids from jars, jars that did not fit the lids – until she found what she was looking for. A set of keys. She held them aloft.

‘You will take Spiros’s car.’

‘Ismēnē, no,’ Thanos said immediately.

'Why not?' She narrowed her eyes. 'Because it is old? Do they not call old things "classics" now?'

'It is not because it is old,' Thanos answered. It was not the age of the vehicle, it was the sentiment attached to it. The car in question was a dark blue 1960s Mercedes with a fin tail. Apparently, Ismēnē's husband Spiros used to drive it when he was alive, but Thanos had always had trouble believing it had ever been on a Corfiot road. It was pristine, not a scratch on its bodywork and waxed to within an inch of its life. This was something he *did* know Ismēnē owned and, along with the antique furniture, it was another something she should think of auctioning so she could live more comfortably.

'Then take the car, Thano. If it will start.' She jangled the keys.

'I would be nervous the entire evening,' he told her.

'Mmm,' Ismēnē said, closing her eyes and swaying a little. 'I remember feeling exactly the same way so many times when Spiros would take me out.' She had a faraway look in her eyes, gazing out of her small window and into her tiny front courtyard filled with urns of flowers she kept well-tended. 'I had the bats in my stomach every time Spiros would look my way, even after we were married.' She sighed. 'I still sit in the car sometimes. I feel that I am close to him there.'

'Ismēnē—'

'No,' she interrupted. 'The car needs to live! It must miss the excitement of a date night, the potholes beneath its wheels, to sound its horn, perhaps parking at a nice vista for a little action in the back seat.' Ismēnē grinned and jingled the keys a bit more furiously.

'I did not say it was a date night,' Thanos told her.

Ismēnē laughed. 'You did not need to say this with words. You said this with your cologne.'

Thanos shook his head. 'I will take the car. If only to escape from this crazy talk.' He reached for the keys, but this time Ismēnē closed her hand around them.

'I know the car is in the best condition,' she began. 'But really, it is a car to have fun in, Thano. Spiros and I, we had the kind of fun that lasts forever in the memories.' She unfurled her fingers. 'The time is not later, it is now. Tomorrow will always come, but it does not come for everybody.'

Thanos swallowed, this life lesson hitting hard. He nodded and then the keys were plonked into his hand.

'On the way back from wherever you are going with your date with the pretty girl, you should go to Cape Drastis,' Ismēnē imparted as Thanos pushed at the door. 'There is a blanket in the boot.'

'Goodnight, Ismēnē.'

'Be very late,' she replied. 'Onassis and the pig, they will be fine.'

Thirty

Sokraki

'We need photos of this car,' Caroline announced. 'And is there a big vintage car clique on Corfu? Don't worry if you don't know, I can google. A vintage angle and Greek weddings are going to tie nicely together with your foody bits for our aspirational edition.'

Foody *bits*. Lydia shook her head as Caroline slammed the door of this lovely old car Thanos had picked them up in. Inside it was all perfect cream leather and a polished dashboard but the treat for the nostrils was coming from Thanos himself. A heavenly scent of citrus and sandalwood had been in the air from the moment she got in the passenger seat. And he looked good too. Jeans that were neither too tight nor too loose and a white shirt that was a little bit snug on his upper arms in all the best ways ... His hair was loose, swept back, ending a little before his shoulders.

'I do not mean to be rude but does your friend ever stop talking?' Thanos asked.

Lydia smiled. 'No. And the really bad news is she talks even more after she's had alcohol.'

'Should we lie and say there is none here?'

'Oh no,' Lydia said immediately. 'She will get very cranky if she *doesn't* have alcohol and, believe me, she will find it by any means possible.' She laughed until she realised that Thanos was looking at her. 'Sorry, we shouldn't still be sitting here. We should get out.' She reached for the door handle.

'No, it is OK,' he said, putting a hand on her arm. 'I was just ... taking a moment to ... listen to you laugh.'

‘Oh,’ Lydia replied. ‘Was it weird?’

‘No. Not at all. It was ... very nice.’

She suddenly felt warm, the temperature rising in the car’s interior from the closed windows, lack of air-conditioning and perhaps her body’s reaction to being in close proximity to this hot guy.

Next there was a rapping on the window and Lydia jumped in her seat. It was Caroline, knuckles on the glass, mouthing something and then pointing. Lydia smiled at Thanos. ‘We should probably get out now.’

Why had he said her laugh was nice? What was the matter with him? This was Ismēnē and her talk about dating and Cape Drastis ... Although Thanos couldn’t deny that when he had seen Lydia approaching the car back in Benitses every part of him reacted. Her hair was tied back from her face in one neat plait, highlighting her delicate features and she was wearing a simple peach-coloured dress that somehow brought out the blue of her eyes.

He took a second now as she got out and joined Caroline. Was it OK for him to pursue this evening? Get to know someone a little? Or should he keep closing off and holding back? The trouble was he had never met someone with an ethos that matched his so well, particularly when it came to his feelings about food. Dina, as much as they laughed together, did not understand the way he felt about cooking. She was not in the restaurant business because it was a passion. She was in it for the money alone. Her taverna had been inherited from her parents and it could have been any type of business and she would have taken it on and tried to make a success of it.

He took a breath as he watched Lydia looking around at one of his favourite villages with narrow streets that seemed to get smaller every time he visited. Maybe he was thinking too deeply about everything, perhaps he should live in this moment and have fun. *Damn Ismēnē!* How was it that she was always right?

*

'This place reminds me of one of the little dioramas that Vernon used to make when he was designing gated communities,' Caroline stated, whipping her sunglasses off her face and putting the arm into her mouth, sucking like it might be a cigarette. 'I'm pretty sure some of them have appeared on creepy thriller book covers. You know the kind, "you think they have the perfect marriage, but one of them is lying and one of them might be dying".'

Lydia wasn't finding Sokraki like that at all. She thought it was another fine example of tiny stone homes all nestled close together in long strings of streets with pathways appearing out of nowhere, leading to secluded corners or back doors of houses open and full of Greek life – pots on the stove, radios playing, loud conversations.

'So, where are we eating like Greeks?' Caroline asked, nudging Lydia's arm.

'I'm not sure,' she answered.

'The view's pretty impressive I have to admit. You wouldn't want to fall down there in a hurry.'

Sokraki was on the mountain and peeling away from it, were hundreds of green trees – cypress, olive, oak – rolling downwards in complete contrast to the undulating harsh rock line of the mountain. This was true, simple, Greek life, carved out, or perhaps carved *into* this landscape.

'Everyone is OK?' Thanos's voice cut through Lydia's thoughts and he was there by her side, smelling divine.

'Everyone is OK,' Caroline stated. 'I'm glad I'm not in charge of the driving and I can't wait to drink like a Greek.'

'Drink like a Greek?' Thanos said, furrowing his brow. 'We do not drink very much here in Corfu. Mostly simple olive oil.'

Lydia couldn't keep a straight face but it was fun, just for a second, to see Caroline's expression drop.

'I thought our guide at the olive oil place was joking about that,' Caroline stated.

'Relax!' Thanos said, laughing. 'There will be wine. Come, the eating and drinking takes place not far away.'

They had parked at what seemed like the village perimeter and, as they walked closer, the number of houses crammed into the space seemed to increase. There were also many people out and about – ladies with sticks carrying trays covered in foil, groups of men gathered together talking at volume – all somehow looking integral to the make-up of this place.

Then, finally, Lydia could see why Thanos had decided to bring them here. The road widened only slightly and there was the hub, a centre, set around a tree, its branches extending over a pond with a stone surround. Café Cherry the sign said. And opposite there was another eating place with an awning overhanging tables and benches covered in multicoloured mats – Emily's Café. Then, on their left was a beautiful, pale yellow building with all manner of items made from olive wood hanging from hooks or nestled in baskets outside. They looked so beautiful, like sculptures, Lydia wanted to touch them all. She stopped, trailing a finger over salad spoons, chopping boards and then what looked like wooden necklaces. She held the beads of one in her hand, smoothing her thumb over the miniature balls.

'These are worry beads,' Thanos told her, at her shoulder.

'Oh, I thought they were prayer beads,' she answered.

'Yes, you can use them to pray, but they have many purposes.' He pointed a finger to his arm and a tattoo just below his bicep. 'For Greeks to pass them between their fingers is a form of mindfulness. A chance to rid yourself of whatever is taking up room in your brain and focus on what is important. It is nice to count blessings as well as ask for forgiveness, no?'

She liked this tattoo of his. It was beautifully drawn, the beads trailing down from a circular loop. It looked good on him. But then *everything* seemed to look good on him. She gave an involuntary shiver and let go of the beads.

'Come,' Thanos said. 'Meet my friends.'

Thirty-One

It was a party atmosphere, Greek-style. Everyone was sitting close together around possibly every table every villager owned, talking and laughing and listening to the music from those who had brought along an instrument. The air was alive with joy here – you could sense it seeping slowly into you as any stress or strain seemed to evaporate.

It was close to *medicinal*, like time here should be given out as a prescription to cure all ills. And the food so far had been as mountainous as the landscape surrounding them, a sumptuous feast that never seemed to stop coming. Lydia wasn't quite sure this was the kind of event Caroline would want to write about – only one set of cutlery, plastic glasses, animals on spits – but it was this generosity, not only of food but of spirit, that Lydia had always hoped might form the basis of any kitchen she was in control of. Giving people more than they expected, from an extra side serving to complement the main meal, to blankets for outside dining or a small token when they left in the hope they would come back. Mario had always given out a small decorative pebble to his customers at Maison Mario, each one unique, each one signed by him on the back. If you went a little bit above and beyond, customers, friends, they could never be disappointed.

'Come on, up!' Thanos said suddenly, taking her hand and urging her from her seat.

'What? Well, where are we going?' Lydia looked to Caroline, but her friend seemed to be having an animated conversation with someone who had been introduced as 'the bee man'.

'Everyone takes a turn to cook here, Lydia,' Thanos told her, holding onto her hand in a way that was not altogether unpleasant. 'O-K,' she said. Now she felt nervousness creeping back in.

'You do not want to deny the people of Sokraki your skills in cooking when they have been so welcoming to you, do you?'

His tone was serious and Lydia swallowed, suddenly feeling like the relaxed night might completely turn on its head and change to full-on pressure cooker.

'No,' she answered but she knew her reticence was obvious.

'Hey,' he said softly. 'Breathe. It is OK. We will cook together.' He gently squeezed her hand in his. 'Nothing tastes good if you cannot relax. Do you not find that?'

Cooking and relaxing. Those two things had not gone together for so long. When exactly had cooking changed from being something she took so much pleasure in – creating new fusions for her parents, wowing Mario with something even a chef of his calibre had not already thought about – to something about being better than anyone else. The shock of that last thought chilled her. Was that how it had been at the end? Was that still why she was feeling so bitter about Patrick? Could this all be about wanting to triumph?

'Lydia,' Thanos said, and this time he clicked his fingers in front of her face. 'Come back to me from wherever you are right now. Be in Sokraki. Be *only* in Sokraki.'

She internally refocused and outwardly her attention took a happy diversion from contemplation to the arrival of a herd of goats, each with a very loud bell hanging from their neck. Perfection came in all shapes and forms. And she sensed no one here was going to make a complaint.

She took a deep breath. 'What are we making?'

'That is the spirit,' Thanos said, smiling. 'We are making *lalagia*.'

'What is that?' *It sounds complicated* was her first thought. She tried to shut that side of her brain down and quieten the negative voices. She could do this! She *wanted* to do this! It was basically therapy!

'You are a chef? And you have never made *lalagia*?' He shook his head in mock shock before his face broke into that beautiful smile again. 'OK, I understand. Unfortunately, the whole world is not Greek.' He led the way behind the table with a two-ring gas hob on it, rusted and dented but apparently still working.

'The most difficult part,' Thanos began, 'is making the dough.'

'We have to make dough? Here?'

She used to love making dough, but dough needed a good mixer – and all she could see here was something that looked like it had been unearthed from Roman times and had to be turned with a handle. The dough also needed a good deal of refrigeration before it was ready to do anything with. There would never be the time. Hello, Panic, my old friend ...

'I see fear rearing up like an angry stallion in your eyes,' Thanos said, looking closely at her.

'No,' Lydia reacted quickly. 'Not at all.' She folded her arms across her chest and tried to keep the anxiety down like she was calming a behaviourally challenged jumping puppy ... or foal. She had nothing to prove. This was her on a working holiday, cooking for pleasure. No one was about to write an article about *her*.

He laughed then and put one of those strong, beautiful hands on her shoulder. 'I have made the dough.' He produced it from a bowl under the counter, a large quantity wrapped in clingfilm. Like everything with this man, it looked faultless. 'It has been refrigerating in Eleni's kitchen since we arrive.'

'What ingredients did you use?'

'Sugar, water, flour, the yeast, then cinnamon, cloves, salt and extra virgin Greek olive oil, of course.'

'Of course,' Lydia said with a smile. Olive oil was the elixir of this island, and she was finding it went hand in hand with life here.

'You laugh again,' Thanos said. 'Why do you laugh?'

'Did I laugh?' Was she really doing it without realising it now? That was new. Usually she was so tightly wound she tried to stifle yawns in case they were an inconvenience to anyone.

'You do not believe in the magical qualities of extra virgin Greek olive oil?' he asked, studying her with those intense eyes just as the musicians got going with a slow, haunting melody.

'Oh, I want to, really,' she answered. 'And we were told this morning, at our tour, it is basically all you need to regrow hair, soothe sore skin and act like ibuprofen.'

'Then why do you not yet believe? Why do you think it is at the heart of Greece if it does not act in this way?'

Lydia didn't really have an answer. Until suddenly it came to her. 'Because it's simple. It's something so readily available here. It's not too expensive. You don't have to do anything complicated to it ...' She stopped talking, realising the absolute magnitude of what she had just said. It really rocked her. It was like she had just found out that the sky was blue ...

'Lydia,' Thanos whispered. 'You are getting it. Simple. Humble. The little things making a big difference. And *that* is my cooking.'

Tears were welling up in her eyes as Thanos busied himself setting out pans and cleaning down the area for preparation. He was lining up spoons and plates and tools in a certain order as if the beautiful lanterns hanging from these old stone houses could be extinguished at any moment. They weren't sad tears though, they were tears of recognition. Thanos was pure in his approach to everything, nothing was overthought. Yes, there was planning, but she was certain if things did not turn out the way he expected them to, he would be ready to improvise at the drop of an olive. It was like cooking with Mario had been before his world-renowned success and the frenzy of evening service and food reviewers from all over the world, but upped ten-fold, or rather, downplayed, so stripped back you didn't know whether it was simplicity or skill in charge. And Lydia yearned to see more of it, be part of it, perhaps redefining her own ideas about cuisine along the way. Except they were leaving Benitses tomorrow ...

'Lydia,' Thanos said, his voice breaking through her thoughts. 'You want to get dough on your hands?'

She nodded, miming rolling up sleeves that weren't there. 'I absolutely do.'

People were watching them and Thanos had been worried that Lydia would find this difficult. Usually he would not like the concept of *this* open a kitchen, people sticking their fingers into pots beside them, swiping up spoons, breathing close to their creations, but with the music a sweet rhythm to their making of *lalagia*, he was as relaxed as he could be. And so, it seemed, was his sous chef.

'What is that?' he asked as she neatly twisted a long strip of dough into a shape.

'What do you mean what is it?' Lydia exclaimed. 'Can you not tell?'

He moved to her, leaning close, shoulder to shoulder, watching her hands at work. 'It is ... an elephant?'

She laughed hard yet light. It was not controlled, it just *was*. She was as calm and relaxed as he had seen her since they'd met and he knew, whether she had realised it or not, it was being with food again. That was the power cooking could have. It had the ability to mend the heart and restore the soul, if you were open to it.

'Thanos! It looks nothing like an elephant ... does it?'

He nudged her with his shoulder. It was cute the way she had confidence and then very quickly it turned into insecurity. He wondered if someone in her life had made her second guess herself a lot of the time and he did not like that thought.

'I see now,' he said. 'It is a butterfly.'

'What's yours?' Lydia asked, eyes going to his board, next to the pans where other shapes were being fried until they were golden brown.

'You do not know?!'

'Well ... if Caroline was over here and not drinking retsina with the bee man, she would say that it looks a bit like a penis.'

'And what would you say?' he asked, fingers shaping the dough a little more.

'I ...'

He couldn't help but look at her lips, watching her cheeks pink a little, feeling the rising heat in himself at the turn in conversation. He didn't do this. It was friendship *or* attraction. It wasn't this dangerous mix of both that was the perfect recipe for something altogether different ...

He flicked the dough into the air, turning it as he had done many times before when he was making something for Onassis. Onassis in his high-chair, thumping his little fists on the tray as

Thanos made almost every food he produced into shapes of things he could recognise – a car, the sun, a figure with long hair like their mother. He mentally batted away the reverie and slapped his creation down on the board, doing rapid final finger work to bring it to its conclusion.

'Oh my word,' Lydia said. 'It's an owl.'

'It is a scops owl,' Thanos elaborated. 'We have many of these on Corfu. It is small, their feathers are like soft fluff and they camouflage themselves against the trees. The ears of this one are a little big and his eyes are scaring me.' He made slight adjustments then popped two black olives into place for the pupils. 'There.'

'It's a work of art compared to my butterfly,' Lydia remarked.

'With *lalagia*, like with every food, looks, they can deceive. It is the tasting that counts the most. Let us put our creations into the pan and see how they feel to our tongues.'

He took another glance at Lydia as the connotation of the word 'tongue' hit him hard.

'I may have added something else to my dough,' Lydia said as she carefully placed her butterfly into a bubbling pan of oil.

'What?!' he exclaimed. 'You changed my age-old recipe of a famous Greek dish?!'

'Will I be cursed?' Lydia asked.

When he did not immediately reply, she let out an anxious sound. He kept going with the deadpan. 'If you change recipes that have been the same for hundreds of years, people will find where you stay and fill your bed with grasshoppers in the night.'

She pointed a spatula at him. 'These lovely people who have fed me all evening would not do that. *You* would not do that.'

'Well, there is much for you to know about Greeks. I hope I have not parked the car one centimetre on someone's land. We might never be able to leave.'

'Thanos, stop it!'

Thanos reached over and plucked a section of dough from Lydia's board. Before she had time to react, he had put it into his mouth. He began to chew taking time to try to isolate each one of the tastes.

'Hey! That was going to be shaped into the look of a takeaway pizza for Caroline!' Lydia told him.

Ginger. She had put ginger into this. That was a twist that could have gone spectacularly wrong if she had added too much. But she hadn't. It was *nostimo*. Delicious.

'I do not like it,' he said, using his finger to tear off then scoop up another piece. 'A recipe from long ago should not be adapted.'

'Then why are you eating more of it?' Lydia asked.

He sucked the remaining dough from his finger as he looked at her expression. She knew it was good. She was delighting in the fact it was good and her pride was radiating out of her. It was so transparent to him and so, *so* sexy. He moved quickly, taking the cooked *lalagia* from the pan and resting them on paper towels then setting their others to start bubbling.

'Come with me,' he told her, reaching for her hand.

'Well ... where are we going?' she asked.

'Come, I will teach you *sirtaki* in Sokraki,' he replied.

Thirty-Two

'This is so much more difficult than cooking!' Lydia said over the music drifting through the night air.

They were halfway between the three eateries in the square and the main road through the village, dancing in a circular formation and navigating chairs and mopeds, dogs and cats, performing a routine that was currently getting Lydia's heart rate going more than a good session on a Peloton. And no one really seemed to be out of breath except her, although Caroline had already retired, citing that the steps were more difficult than a Week Ten *Strictly* routine. Old, young, babes in arms, each person was swaying back and forth and then side to side as the stringed instruments of mandolin, guitar, bouzouki were played at a furious rate and an old man with a small drum kept the solid beat. It was hot and humid but her body being so close to Thanos was the best kind of temperature raiser …

Thanos laughed then, his arm still snug across her shoulders. It was both pleasurable and helped to keep her in line and on track with her steps.

'In Greece,' he said, 'we are brought up with the most important things. Food, music, dance, coffee and, of course, *ouzo*.'

'What about olive oil?'

'It is a food, Lydia. A magical food, but still food.'

'Well, I don't believe that every Greek can dance!'

'Every Greek *can* dance!' Thanos insisted. 'It is as natural as breathing.'

'If you're Greek or … BTS,' Lydia said, still getting her left mixed up with her right.

'You like BTS?' Thanos asked suddenly.

'I … have been known not to skip them if they slip into my

boyband radio on Spotify.' She looked up at him. 'Do you like them?'

'No ... well, I guess they are OK. I ... have a ... friend who says they do not dress as they used to.'

Suddenly he broke the circle, ducking out and taking her with him to the edge of the dance space that had been created.

'What are we doing?' Lydia asked. 'I hope we don't get cursed for breaking the circle or anything.'

'You said you wanted to interview me,' he reminded her. 'We are taking *taramasalata* and limoncello and you can ask me the questions.'

Lydia watched him pick up a large earthenware bowl filled with the creamy-coloured dip from one of the tables, then lift up an almost full bottle of the yellow spirit and tuck it under his arm.

'*Ela*,' he said. 'Come.'

Lydia looked over to where Caroline was sitting, a spoon in her hand and open jars of honey on the table in front of her. She caught her gaze and mouthed an 'are you OK'. Holding up a full glass of wine, Caroline pointed towards the retreating figure of Thanos and made shooing motions to Lydia. Content her friend was content, Lydia followed Thanos's lead.

Was it coincidence that Lydia had mentioned Onassis's favourite pop group, the one his brother was trying to emulate with his friends? Or was it the universe reminding Thanos of his responsibilities. And, in the moment, put on the spot, he had lied. *A friend*. Why had he not said *a brother*? Perhaps because for one night he wanted to act like he was a little bit free and able to make his own choices based on only him. Except his get-out had been to suggest she asked him questions ... He was an idiot.

'Here we are,' Thanos announced, stepping into the wooden shelter that was set up with multicoloured rugs and cushions on the bench. There was a small table, a candle burning inside a glass lantern and some books on a shelf.

'Oh, this is so sweet,' Lydia exclaimed, coming in after him. 'What is it?'

'It is the bus shelter,' Thanos answered, sitting down and opening the bottle.

'Oh.'

'You sound disappointed.'

'No, I ... wasn't expecting you to say that but, looking at it now, I can see that.' She smiled. 'There aren't many wooden bus shelters in England now. I think people set them on fire too often.'

'They set them on fire?' Thanos exclaimed.

'I know,' Lydia said, sighing. 'Madness. Don't ask me to explain it.'

'Here the bus comes only twice a day so, the villagers decided to make something more of the shelter.' He picked up one of the books and opened it. 'Here is a meeting point. You can talk with someone if you wish. You can be alone with your thoughts if you wish. You can read a book or look at the view.'

'It does have a lovely view,' Lydia said.

The view was the valley dropping away from the heights of Sokraki down into the bowl of green olive and cypress and then over to the right, the mountain soared onwards and upwards again, touching a turning-peach sky.

'I always think the view here is a perfect reminder that life, like Sokraki, is always a little in the middle.' He pointed down towards the blanket of trees. 'There are the lows.' Then he pointed to the mountain line. 'And there are the highs.' He took a swig of the drink. 'But all anybody really needs is something halfway.'

He wiped around the mouth of the bottle with the bottom of his shirt and held it out to her.

'But ...' Lydia said. 'You always seek perfection with your cooking.'

'I am not really the judge. The judge is whoever is eating the food. I can only do my best.' He shrugged.

'Do you really mean that?' she asked.

He lifted his eyes to hers. From her expression it seemed the answer he gave now was going to be of huge importance. 'Yes,' he breathed. 'I can put my heart and soul and skill into creating what I think is the ultimate meal, but if the customer does not like it, if it is not to *their* taste, then there is nothing I can do.'

'Oh my God!' Lydia announced. She took a long swig from the bottle of limoncello then passed it back to him. 'I mean, Thanos, honestly, that is a *revelation. You* are a revelation to me!'

'I am a revelation?' He didn't quite understand but she sounded so vibrant, so alive, he didn't want to say anything that might destroy that.

'I have never thought about what we do like that before,' Lydia said, picking up one of the cushions and settling it behind her back. 'All the time, sweating over cooking dishes to try to make history or get into the pages of magazines or to impress Jamie Oliver and it comes down to one person's palate.'

'You did not realise this?' Thanos asked, giving an eyebrow raise.

'And it's stupid, isn't it? It's so stupid! It's showing off! It's like people putting food colouring in *taramasalata* to make it pink! Why?'

She took the limoncello back from him and drank again before he had the chance to even have another drop.

'All that stress. The stress that basically killed Mario. And none of it actually really matters because the whole thing could fall down like a poorly stacked, five-tier wedding cake at any moment.'

'Mario?' Thanos queried, but Lydia did not hear.

'And I have gone from being at the centre of this whisking up a frenzy over high-end plates to writing about them.' She gasped. 'What if the food at Obelisk 1 wasn't terrible to anyone else but me? Oh my God! What if *all* the food I've reviewed and said is delicious is actually dire?!'

'Lydia, stop,' Thanos ordered. 'You are taking it too far away.'

'Am I?' Lydia gasped again. 'What if, after all this time, it's Caroline who has the right idea about good taste and not me?'

'I saw her dip *saganaki* into chocolate sauce. Believe me, she does not have the right idea about good taste.'

He could see she was twitching a little with all the thoughts that were sparking inside her. He didn't want her to start second guessing every decision she had ever made. He took hold of her hand and held it in his. It was warm, but shaking a little. He smoothed the flat of her palm with his.

'I think it is time for an experiment,' he said.

'What kind of an experiment?' she asked, voice a little ragged.

'One that will put both our palates to the test,' Thanos said. He squeezed her hand and then let go, sitting forward a little on the bench and reaching for the bowl.

'Give me a second.' He slipped his hand into the pocket of his jeans and drew out his Swiss army knife.

'You always carry that around with you?' Lydia asked him.

'Of course,' he answered. 'You never know when you might need to ... look through a magnifying glass.' He released the small blade. 'Give me your hand.'

'When you're holding a knife?' Lydia asked with a nervous laugh.

'You do not trust me?' He held her gaze, enjoying looking into her eyes a little too much. 'Because you did make *lalagia* with me so I thought ...'

She laughed and held out her hand. Scooping up a small knife-tip's worth of *taramasalata* on the blade, Thanos carefully pasted it onto her index finger.

'Now, take a taste and tell me what you find.'

Lydia looked at the little beige splodge on her finger and wondered why she had lived her life thus far with no one having ever delivered a dip to her that way before. She couldn't help but inhale first and then she put the cream on her tongue and waited for the flavours to hit.

'The fish and ... the garlic and—'

'Try to not let your knowledge of the recipe lead your senses,' Thanos suggested.

'A tiny bit of lemon,' Lydia added.

Thanos sighed. 'Why are fingers so disappointing? It is what we usually use to taste, no?'

'Well, you can't do that in kitchens in the UK. It's a clean tablespoon for every tasting.'

'But when you are at home, when you are trying something new, we use our fingers. And, really, they are so bad.' He dipped the knife into the bowl again. 'Here.'

Lydia flinched a little at the cold of the dip hitting the inside of her wrist. *A pulse point.* She could feel the slight vibration underneath her skin and it was giving her all kinds of sensations.

'Try it from here,' he encouraged. 'It will taste a little different.'

Would it? Would it *really*? It seemed insane. Or was this what other chefs were doing and it had completely passed her by? She thought the reason behind some restaurants serving their food up on slates, wooden boards or even on top of garden shovels was a gimmick, but could it be that what the food was served on changed the taste?

She kissed the *taramasalata* off her wrist and let her tastebuds go to work. There was still the taste of roe, lemon and garlic but this time she could isolate pepper, thyme and ...

'Star anise,' she breathed, looking at Thanos. 'There's star anise in this.'

He looked confused for a second before dipping his knife into the bowl, putting some dip on his own wrist and tasting for himself.

He nodded. 'Wow. I did not know. Mrs Argyros, she has been making this recipe for as long as she has been alive and, one day, I suggested to her that star anise might take it up to another level. She told me I was crazy.'

'But she listened,' Lydia said.

'It is so.'

Lydia shifted in her seat, leaning forward to pick the limoncello bottle off the table. A moth buzzed up from beside the candle then flew into the darkening skies. 'Where did you learn to cook, Thanos?'

He smiled. 'Is this my interview?'

'Did you train?'

'I train every single day,' he told her. 'Each meal is a lesson. You get an official qualification and perhaps you stop really learning.'

Suddenly the limoncello bottle was tumbling from her hands and Lydia rushed to catch it. But not before her left arm got covered in the sticky alcohol and began to drip. Before she realised what was happening, Thanos had taken her arm and was using his mouth to stop the spill from reaching her clothes. And the heat from his lips moving up the skin of her arm was giving her all kinds of sensations she wasn't used to. But before she could close her eyes and enjoy the feeling some more, it stopped.

'I am ... so sorry ... I saw it fall and ...'

He looked so apologetic, as if not knowing what to do with himself. But all Lydia could focus on was how acutely she had felt every tiny subtle action of his tongue, each gentle roll of his lips, and the citrus scent was hanging in the air between them.

'How did it taste?' she whispered, reaching for his hand. *His beautiful hands.* So smooth yet strong, that trickle of a tattoo creeping onto his wrist but not invading the clean skin of the back of his hand.

'Pure,' he said, his tone thick. 'Sweet.' His eyes held hers again. 'Sexy.'

Now Lydia wanted nothing more than his lips on her skin again. She ran a fingertip down the limoncello still on her arm and then slowly she brought it to his mouth, painting the liquid onto the flesh.

'Lydia,' he breathed, lips moist.

'I think I'd like to test my palate a little more,' she told him.

'Is that so?'

They were leaning towards each other on the bench, the tiniest bit closer, perhaps invisible to the naked eye, but Lydia could feel her own intention almost rattling her bones. As for Thanos's intention, if the heat coming from him and the intensity in those delicious eyes was anything to go by, he was feeling this moment as much as she was.

And then, before she had time to take another breath, he had scooped her up, effortlessly drawing her body into his and sliding them both down the bench a little until her back nestled against the furthest cushion.

His lips found hers, lightly to begin with, and it was a limoncello hit of epic magnitude with the added taste of masculinity and a hint of olive oil, oregano and woodland ...

It was then her libido was done for and she drew him closer

to her, hands in his hair, wanting to taste more deeply, feel more keenly and explore their attraction as thoroughly as she dared in this bus shelter ... As Thanos moved his mouth from hers, lips grazing her neck, then her collarbone, Lydia realised she had never been kissed this way before. It was organic, raw, so incredibly hot and like nothing she had tasted in her life. She shifted her weight a little and Thanos drew back.

'You are OK?' he asked, looking concerned.

'Yes,' she answered, palming his face. 'Yes I am.'

'Lydia,' he breathed, resting his forehead on hers. 'What are we doing?'

'Experimenting with taste,' she whispered, hands on his shoulders. 'Just like you said.' She kissed his lips gently, loving the way the hint of stubble tickled her skin. 'And it's a sweet treat.'

As his mouth moved onto hers once more, Lydia closed her eyes and let all her senses enjoy every single second, unhurried.

Thirty-Three

Benitses

'What am I going to do with all these jars of honey?'

It could have been a cry from a produce manager at Waitrose but it was Caroline trying to squeeze the pots into her small cabin case. And there seemed to be about twenty-five of them …

'Are they different flavours?' Lydia asked, re-rolling the few outfits she had got out of her case and put into the wardrobe. They were leaving Benitses today for somewhere in the north of the island. She really should try to get on top of the itinerary as Caroline still wasn't sharing full details. Lydia knew her colleague ran on power as much as she ran on items covered in thick and greasy batter, but she was keen this magazine edition should be equally apportioned.

'Many flavours,' Caroline stated. 'Wildflowers and cherry. Oak and rosemary. Olive and cornflakes.'

Lydia whipped her head around. 'Olive and cornflakes?'

'OK,' Caroline said. 'I might have made that one up to check if you were listening or not.'

She had been listening, but Lydia couldn't deny she had also been indulging in glorious memories of last night in the mountain village. Sokraki had been like another world. It was community at its finest. From the turn-taking cooking to the shared eating, the dancing and games, all in this idyllic, quaint and oldy-worldly setting. And then there was the action in the bus shelter … On unbuttoning Thanos's shirt she had discovered a number of tattoos that lay across those tight pecs and continued a pattern over a washboard midriff. Greek letters, circular symbols, creatures, waves ... She had wanted to run her tongue over each and every one of them, but caressing them with her fingers was as far as she had got until Thanos had slowed things down. *Thanos* had slowed things down. What would have happened if he hadn't? Because she had been fizzing with more desire than Mel kissing Jack on *Virgin River*. Would she have bared all and got down to business in a bus shelter? That was definitely not UK Lydia but *Greece* Lydia ... who knew?

'That one sounds nice, doesn't it?' Caroline said very loudly. So loudly Lydia gave a jolt, knees knocking into the bed, and she realised that this time she *had* actually zoned out.

'I ... missed what that flavour was. Remind me,' Lydia said, smiling.

'Fig and onion,' Caroline stated.

Lydia wasn't sure whether this one was real or not. 'Wow.'

'Might go well with chips,' Caroline said. 'After we've done a photoshoot with them. I did take some photos of the beehives and the village so I have the traditional bent, but I also want to get some pictures with a contemporary twist.' She touched the side of her head with her index finger. 'Make sure every single target market is covered.' She sniffed. 'Vernon taught me that.'

Ah, another Vernon day today.

'So, what did Thanos teach *you* last night?' Caroline blurted out, shutting the lid of her case and manually pushing a pot beyond the zip.

Suddenly Lydia felt *very* seen and an all over body flush rippled over her. 'We made *lalagia*.'

'I know,' Caroline said, leaning on her case with full force. 'I didn't taste it, but don't apply for a job presenting crafts on children's TV because some of those dough shapes were literal porn.'

'I told Thanos you would say that.'

'And what else did you share with Thanos?' Caroline asked. 'Because don't think I didn't notice the vibe when we were travelling back in the car.'

'The vibe?' Lydia said. But even the word 'vibe' was somehow giving her goosebumps and flashbacks to Thanos's mouth and the limoncello ...

'After I shooed you off and I did a dance with goats, his shirt was buttoned up wrong when you reappeared.'

'Oh ... I ... well ...' She was ridiculously flustered for someone her age who was usually extraordinarily capable.

'So, have you broken the curse?' Suddenly Caroline completely mounted her case, plumping her bum on top and grinding down like she was doing a dirty move in a rap video.

'Curse?' Lydia asked, frowning as she put a T-shirt into her case.

'Not having had sex since The Griddler! You know, when he fell asleep despite you wearing your fruitiest undies.'

Lydia closed her eyes. She had forgotten she had told Caroline that. She blamed the night at the Lebanese restaurant. It had been an excellent Jordanian fish tagine but also there had been far too many *araks*. And after that night with Patrick perhaps she should have realised that if your partner could fall asleep when you were wearing something from Boux Avenue then the relationship probably wasn't destined for the long term.

'No,' Lydia said. 'We didn't do that.'

'But you did *something*! I knew it! His buttons weren't misaligned, BTW, but you had that flushed look that either says "spent too long confined on a Tube" or "got vigorously amorous". As there's no underground here in Corfu, I made the correct assumption.'

And now Lydia felt stupid for being duped into giving Caroline food for thought. But, then again, what was there to hide? She was single. Thanos was ... Well, he had to be single, didn't he? Suddenly her stomach went into a fast spin cycle. She hadn't asked. Should she have asked? She looked to the patio doors and the view down over the pool so Caroline couldn't read anything else from her expression. There was that rippling cooling water and the blue sky giving off all the relaxation vibes ... *Breathe!*

'Well,' Caroline said. 'What was it? A long slow snog to the sweet melody of the mandolin? Or a quick hand job under the stars?'

It was exactly like Caroline to cheapen everything. That's what she did for every life situation except when it came to *Luxe Living* readers. The best thing to do was ignore her, not add fuel to her fire, change the subject …

'Where are we heading to next?'

'Oh, so we're moving on from Thanos and looking for new meat! Excellent! I'm game!' Caroline reached between her legs and managed to make the zip circumnavigate the perimeter of the case to close.

'I thought you were talking very intently to the bee man last night,' Lydia said, dropping her wash bag into her luggage. 'Not sweet enough for you?'

'His priority was the yellow and black buzzy things he takes care of. Four generations of his family. It would make a lovely backstory if I was writing a heartfelt piece for the *Guardian* but all my readers want to know is "is it organic?" and "can I get it before anyone else?".' Caroline sniffed. 'And truthfully … he backed away so fast when I leaned in for a kiss he almost fell into the pond.' She jumped down from the bed and brushed her hands together. 'You win some. You don't.'

'Oh, Caroline, I—'

'No. No morning-after pity, please. He wasn't really my type. He was just … there. A bit like Thanos for you, except the bee man had slightly less fantastic hair and was more … Jason Manford than … Brian Cox.'

Lydia didn't know what to do with any part of that sentence. But when it came to Thanos, for her, their time in the cosy bus shelter hadn't been because he was *there*. It wasn't convenience, it was *connection*. And not just when it came to food, but when it came to *thinking* and *feeling*. Or was she simply caught up in the warm, holiday romance bubble and that was heightening her reality? Except she wasn't on holiday … Now her mind was back with that email from Bonnie she hadn't replied to yet. Bonnie had asked what she could do to prepare for the tasting for Patrick's TV show, and whether she send back the RSVP with a list of her allergies. That had been the only section of the email that had made Lydia smile a little. Patrick hated customers with allergies or intolerances. She remembered, one time, he had suggested that instead of eating real food perhaps they could take supplements and not grace his restaurant before they killed cuisine completely. Mario had once called him a *cogliona* which roughly translated as 'arsehole'. Despite employing him, Mario had never really warmed to Patrick as a chef or as a partner for her and oh, how Lydia had wished she'd listened ...

'But onwards and upwards to Arillas! There's a holistic retreat, a brewery, a lovely sandy beach and there's bound to be men who won't run from a powerful woman,' Caroline announced. 'The bad news is it's an hour and a half's drive.' She sighed. 'Have you noticed literally everywhere on this island is an hour and a half's drive?'

And with Caroline at the wheel, it really would feel like an eternity. Lydia closed her case and took it off the bed. 'So, how far away from somewhere called Agios Stefanos are we?'

'Christ, I don't know. Do I look like I work for what3words?'

As Lydia took one final look out of the window, at the village of Benitses which had given her so many highlights, she wondered what Thanos was doing right now.

Thirty-Four

Thanos and Onassis's home, Benitses

He was playing Greek music through his Bluetooth speaker, not the rock he usually favoured and he could only assume this need for something more traditional, something more emotional, was down to the atmosphere last night.

It had felt good to introduce people to Greek village life and the customs still upheld … and it had felt *more* than good to hold Lydia in his arms and taste her lips. He shivered then and refocused on the cookery books laid out on his worktop. She was leaving today.

They had kept it casual. He had told her about the food festival. They had exchanged phone numbers and she had said she would try to come along. Food was what she was in Corfu to write about, so it made sense. And he really wasn't worrying that she might eat another meal that moved her like his cooking had and decide to write about that chef instead …

He felt nervous all over again, despite all his big talk about only being able to do your best and what came next being down to the customer. He really should come up with something other chefs wouldn't be making at the festival, so he was drawing inspiration from his mother's old books. Inside these tomes were not just the bones of traditional cooking, there were insights into the reality of cooking them. Thanos turned a page and there was a face his mother had drawn. It was a crude circle with dots for eyes and a frowny face. Next to it was written the word '*kakos*'. Bad.

'What was so bad about this time you cooked this apple cake, Mama?' he asked into the air.

'She put the oven on too high and used orange juice from a carton. The type with the bits.'

Thanos jumped. Ismēnē was in his kitchen, Nuno inside a handbag on her shoulder, his ginger face peeking out, silently judging. Thanos put a hand to his chest to check his heart was still in the right place.

'But I do not want to talk about apple cake. I want to hear all about last night. Did you go to Cape Drastis and use the blanket?' Ismēnē plumped the handbag on the countertop.

'No,' Thanos answered firmly. 'But we had a good time in Sokraki.' He swallowed. 'You know how it is there when people get together.' It was Ismēnē who had taken him to Sokraki the very first time. It was shortly after his parents had died and, after they had all looked for ways to make sense of it and had come up empty, Ismēnē had made it her mission to bring some kind of joy back to his life. With Onassis strapped to her back in a sling made up of old tights and bed sheets, she had introduced him to her friends and the community in this village a long drive away from Benitses where her grandparents had hailed from. He wasn't too young to know that it was a distraction technique, to surround him with music and laughter and life so there was no room to think about the sadness and the emptiness and the quiet. And it had been a night he had never forgotten. The people he had met there as an eighteen-year-old were his friends for life.

'Sokraki,' Ismēnē said, a crackle to her voice as she walked around the kitchen table and pulled up a stool. 'You took Lydia there?'

Thanos shrugged and instantly regretted it. It was worth nothing. By taking Lydia to that village, Ismēnē already knew that Lydia was not like any of the very few other girlfriends he had had. Because Sokraki meant something to him, the people there had helped him come to terms with his loss, had shaped who he was, had welcomed him without question.

'You are seeing her again,' Ismēnē said, holding on to the table and trying to boost herself up onto the seat. The sentence hadn't been phrased as if there was doubt.

'She is leaving Benitses today,' Thanos said.

'To go back to the UK?'

'No. To stay in another part of the island.'

'What part?' With a big push, Ismēnē arrived on the padded seat and listed a little to the side. 'Oof! Why are these seats so high?'

Thanos had already put an arm out to stop her from toppling right back over.

As soon as she had her balance, she shrugged him off. 'What part of the island?'

'I do not know,' he admitted.

'You did not ask?'

'I ... told her about the food festival. I thought she could write about it.'

'Thano! If you like this girl then ...'

The sentence was left hanging there, the letters spiralling with the beams of sunlight coming through the bi-fold doors from the garden outside. He *did* like Lydia. He would love to know more about her. But ... where could it go? Probably not as far as he would be satisfied with if he spent any more time with her.

'Thano, Onassis is carving out his own life like it is a pumpkin at Halloween.' Ismēnē picked up on the recipe books. 'It might not be the interests you wanted for him, but he is making plans, being independent. It is not so long and he will not need you at all.'

Thanos shook his head. His brother was naïve. He hardly knew one end of a pencil from the other. His gaze went to the only non-painted door frame in the entire house. There were tiny marks and dates, the initial 'T' in both his mama and papa's writing. And then, in his less neat scrawl, large 'O's and more lines and years.

'You said I should let him have his innocence. Not to let him grow up too quickly. Now you speak like he is ready to pay rent on his own apartment and ... drive a car.'

'It is all about balance, Thano. And that is often what you are missing in your life and, sometimes, in your cooking.'

'What?' So, Ismēnē was here to not only tell him he was failing in his role as guardian but also to make comment on his cooking? When she was the one pushing him to join food festivals and cook inside ruins and take a chance with Lydia ...

'We need something else for the food festival. Something that will make people realise that cooking is *like* life. Sometimes it can be challenging but there is always, *always* excitement around the corner.'

He bit his lip and drew a new tattoo in his mind. Perhaps it would be a puzzle, one of those mazes with no straightforward path. Or a wild river, bubbling and hissing, powerful and unending.

'But we can talk about this later,' Ismēnē said, turning her handbag towards her and stroking the cat under its chin. 'Is Onassis ready?'

It was like his blood had suddenly been siphoned from him and ice was now running through his veins. 'What?'

'There is a school trip today. A coach is picking up the children from Benitses at the bus stop. I said I would walk with him.'

Ismēnē was still talking as he began to move, his elbow knocking into the cat bag as he rushed from the kitchen and headed towards the bedrooms. Last night, when he arrived home, he had assumed Onassis was in bed. This morning, with his brother's backpack gone from the hook where it usually resided and no pastries left from the batch he had made the day before, Thanos had assumed they'd been taken for breakfast on the walk to be picked up. But now ... had the pastries and the bag been there last night? Or were they already gone? Why had he not looked in on Onassis last night? Why had he not taken a second to watch his gentle breathing as he slept or admonish him for still being awake and on his phone?

Throwing open his brother's bedroom door he expelled a sigh of relief. But it only lasted momentarily. There was a mound in the bed but the covers were pulled up a little too far, unnaturally so.

Ismēnē was at his heel now, the cat hissing from its confines. 'He is still asleep! Onassis! Come on! We do not have long! Get up! Get dressed! The day is being wasted!'

'He is not here,' Thanos said, his voice uneven, caught between terror and anger. He wrenched back the covers and revealed what was making the shape. Two pillows and a large watermelon.

Ismēnē gasped and Thanos put his hands into his hair as he realised the seriousness of the situation. Onassis was missing.

Thirty-Five

Arillas

Lydia inhaled long and slow and rolled her shoulders as she stepped out into one of the garden areas at their new lodgings in the north-west of the island. It had taken almost two hours to get here. After taking a few wrong turns that had led to frankly spine-tinglingly close encounters with precipices, Caroline shouting 'bloody tourists' even though *Lydia* was the one in the driving seat, and her phone pinging every second minute with a new notification, they were finally here.

It turned out, when they had briefly stopped so Caroline could purchase baked goods, that Patrick had tagged her in a post on Instagram about the new TV show. Tagged her *personal* account as well as *Luxe Living* and as many other publications as he could fit within the limitations. Her blood had briefly boiled as she'd sunk her teeth into some sweet and sticky *baklava*, until it had calmed to a low simmer and she took time to consider what Patrick tagging her actually meant.

Either he desperately wanted her to know about his TV show, or he had someone managing his social accounts now he had his own TV show and they were just throwing everything at this new venture and not thinking too hard about it. Perhaps there had been no intent with the invitation sent to *Luxe Living*. Maybe she was just a name with a little influence in the reviewing arena like David Deacon.

Whatever it was, she needed to show indifference. Because what Patrick did with the rest of his life had absolutely no bearing on what she did with hers. And, after spending last night with Thanos in that vibrant little village where simple pleasures ran their world, it had never felt more inconsequential. Except they had left each other with nothing more than a mention that their paths might cross at the food festival …

With her phone pressed against her ear as she lowered herself to sit on a painted green bench, Lydia waited for the call to connect.

'Hello.'

'Hi, Dad,' she said. 'I'm … just letting you know that Caroline and I are in the north of Corfu now and I drove a car across the mountain and made it to the other side and all wildlife was preserved. Oh, except one grasshopper that got caught under the wiper blades.'

'Oh, Lyddy,' Per began. 'You sound so much more together.'

She stretched her legs out towards the sunshine and leaned into the back of the bench. 'I feel together.' She let out a sigh of contentment. 'The edition Caroline and I are working on is really coming on. Caroline says Gina loved what we've put together so far and to just keep it coming. We've already visited so many interesting places in such a short space of time and Corfu is packed full of culture and fantastic food and …' And there was a memory of Thanos last night, frying the *lalagia* and then heating her up with his kiss. 'And … the fantastic food.'

Her dad laughed at her repetition. 'I have envy about the food. Your mother has taken to cooking things in the sauna.'

'What?'

'She has three steamers for the kitchen but no, she has read a Finnish book of things that can be cooked while she sweats out her impurities.' Per sighed. 'Sometimes she comes in smelling of our evening meal. It is fine when it is something like corn on the cob but not so fragrant if it is fish.'

'Aren't you pleased that Mum is cooking at all? It happens so rarely.'

Per scoffed. 'This is simply practice. We have new neighbours, moved in across the street. You know how your mum likes to impress everyone with full effort if only once. It will not last.'

Lydia smiled. It was good to know that things with her parents hadn't altered. She knew her dad would make the most of quiet time when Ulrika was out 'evolving' with her friends, then accept any evolution that wove its way into their home afterward. Perhaps now was the time to confess a little change of her own.

'Dad,' Lydia said, voice a little weaker than she had hoped for.

'Yes, Lyddy.'

'I ... I've been cooking ... a bit ... while I've been here.'

The line went quiet and all Lydia could hear was the rhythmic croaking coming from what could only be *cicadas* camouflaged in the nearby trees. Or maybe it was her dad's end of the line and it was the hissing of sauna rocks as water was poured over them ...

'Dad?' Lydia asked. 'Are you still there?'

'Yes,' Per answered. 'Yes, I am here.'

She couldn't help but feel a bit miffed that he hadn't immediately said something uplifting ... and still wasn't saying anything. Perhaps he didn't understand. Given her lack of cooking action, maybe he thought she had just buttered some toast ...

'I made a kind of breakfast omelette with sausage and potatoes and thyme and ... then last night, I helped to make *lalagia*. It's Greek. It's a dough with cinnamon and—'

'Lyddy, what has made you happiest about being in Greece so far?' Per asked suddenly. 'Is it the relaxation? The chance to take a breath and inwardly evaluate? Is food more fun there? Less frantic than cooking for a kitchen?'

'It's most of those things,' she answered truthfully. 'And realising that no matter what I might tell myself, no matter how many times I get reminded that Mario isn't here anymore, cooking is such a large part of who I am.' It might have been the very first time she had admitted this to herself. Who was she without those recipes in her mind? That compulsion to constantly create, the need to be half-coated in flour eighty per cent of the time, it was inbuilt, a lattice formed around her soul.

'But you can't want to go back to working in a busy kitchen. You found it so stressful at the end. You were pale and so angry all the time and ...'

Her dad's sentence tailed off as perhaps he realised the depth of what he was saying.

'And?' Lydia asked, her tone angry. 'Why don't you tell me how you really feel? Because you were the one who encouraged me to *believe* and *be-living* last time we spoke, and now I am and I have been and you don't sound as supportive as I was hoping for.'

'Oh, Lyddy,' Per breathed. 'Part of me was hoping that you would get back to cooking, but perhaps see it as a hobby like you used to.'

She wrinkled her nose, drawing her legs in and sitting up a little straighter. There was a green lizard poking its head out of one of the biscuit-coloured urns as if it was listening in to her side of the conversation at least.

'Cooking was never just a hobby for me,' Lydia told him firmly. 'It was all about making it my whole existence from way before even that first meal I made for Mario. You know how I looked for opportunities. I made cakes for the soroptimists, I cooked for your clients and let them think Mum had done it, I lived and breathed the art of cuisine.'

'I do know that,' Per answered. 'But, Lyddy, my priority is your well-being and your mum, she obviously feels the same.'

'I know but you can't protect me from the world anymore. And I'm older now, I'm not going to get my wellington boot stuck in the grate of a cattle grid.'

There was no laughter for her childhood anecdote, usually one of her dad's favourites. Instead, Per gave a very heavy sigh. 'Lyddy, there's something you should know before you say any more and before you make any firm decisions about your future.'

Lydia sighed. 'I'm not making any firm decisions about my future. I'm just exploring and—'

'Lyddy,' Per interrupted quite forcefully. 'Your mother and I have been invited to the preview evening for Patrick's new TV show.'

All those joyous feelings simmering under the surface as she recounted all the meals she had eaten here in Corfu and the ones she had had a hand in preparing suddenly stopped their dance and her stomach transformed to the consistency of a weak Hollandaise sauce whose butter had been added too hot. Now she was sure this was personal …

'What?' Lydia asked, getting to her feet and scaring the green lizard back to the sanctuary of his bush hideout.

'Your mother wants to go. You know how she dislikes to show weakness and—'

'Mum wants to go!' She was outraged. 'Why? Why would she want to go?!' She could feel her emotions setting off on a path all of their own now, her psyche flipping back to that time when Patrick decided to end their relationship right before he wormed his way into her role in the kitchen at Maison Mario.

'Well,' Per began, sounding a little tentative. 'Your mother feels it is either a threat or an olive branch. The thing is, we cannot seem to agree on which.' He sighed. 'We would both die if this was *Squid Game*.'

Lydia swallowed, turning a circle in the grass, her mind desperately trying to find missing details. 'Why would it be either?'

'Well, Lyddy, you must understand that at the time we were extremely worried about you. You know how it was. The not getting out of bed. The not washing. The crying.'

She closed her eyes to the beautiful surroundings and the humidity began to get suddenly oppressive. She didn't want to think back to how awful things had been after Mario's death. She did her best never to revisit those memories and feelings. She had done a lot of work to rebuild herself as best she could. 'Dad … we don't talk about this.'

'I know, Lyddy. But sometimes you have to go back and evaluate the whole picture, from its origins, and then strike at the root of the cause.'

'Dad, I don't know what you're talking about!'

She was almost shrieking now and she hated that feeling of control slipping away from her. She had always clung to stability. Things slid if she couldn't own her own mind and be the mistress of her actions and decisions. Mario had guided and advised but he had never ordered or told. It was that change in direction at Maison Mario that had hurt her more than Patrick ending their relationship. With the executive chef dead, with Lydia not at all herself when she got back to the helm, Patrick had savaged *her*, playing on her insecurities, whispering them into the ear of Antonia until there was nothing left for Lydia. Until she was so sickened with them both, until she was so enraged, so pushed to the limit, so fragile, that something snapped.

'Your mother and I could not let him ruin you. He had already made you so sick, so destroyed,' Per announced. 'So, before he could fire you, before he could make your reputation black ... we spoke to Patrick and ... we helped with the severance package.' He took a breath. 'Lyddy, after you were driven to attack him, we had no choice but to step in. We did not want you hurt anymore.'

Lydia couldn't catch her breath. She opened her eyes and the sunlight was blinding. What was her dad saying? That what she thought was the whole truth about her ending at Maison Mario wasn't the whole truth? Everything felt like it was slowly being upended and mixed about like ingredients in a KitchenAid. 'Dad,' she said hoarsely as tears began to leak from her eyes. 'What have you done?'

'Lyddy, we did this for your own good. So you could still be *involved* with cooking, just like you are right now with the magazine.'

'*What* did you do?' She had gritted her teeth and the words came out rough and accusing.

There was a sigh of something like resignation and then Per spoke again. 'Patrick promised not to go to the police about you attacking him, or to the press and we promised ... that you would never work in a competing kitchen again.'

Thirty-Six

Benitses

Thanos had phoned every parent of Onassis's friends that he knew. He had also phoned the school and every taverna and shop in the village to see if anyone had seen his brother. He had even phoned Baptiste. And it was during that rather awkward conversation, interspersed with what sounded like screams from the Taverna Ilios kitchen, Thanos realised Onassis wasn't the only one who was missing. The pig was gone too.

With George at the farm not answering his phone, Thanos had headed over there and left Ismēnē and a sleeping Nuno back at his house in case Onassis returned or someone else called back with an update.

Usually he would be shot with a dart of nostalgia as he walked from his parked car towards the large shed where George would always be found in the middle of mending something or taking an ouzo and cigarette break. So many times he had been here with his father to collect meat or eggs or to play a game of cards with the farmer.

His father and George had been school friends and whether their family needed food or not, Christos Nicolaidis had made sure to visit. Thanos scuffed his trainer at the ground, kicking up a little dust. He had visited more often when the loss of his parents had been fresh. Onassis had needed to get out and see the island and the people who had mattered to his parents. Thanos had hoped, new to being a guardian, that he could somehow make his brother absorb the essence of them if he surrounded him with all that had been familiar. He sighed now, his stomach coiled in tight knots. He was here because he had lost the person he was supposed to be in charge of. The person he loved the most.

'George!' he called. 'George, it is Thanos!'

He only made it as far as the bales of straw at the entrance to the main barn before a tall, slim, twenty-something appeared from behind the tractor. 'Can I help you?'

'You are not George,' Thanos said stupidly.

'No, I am his second cousin, Manos. George is on Othoni today with a delivery.'

Thanos shook his head. This was not the news he wanted. Othoni was a small island off the coast of Corfu. It meant that if the pig was involved, Onassis was somewhere else, somewhere perhaps a lot more dangerous than George's farm trying to sell it.

'You are OK?' Manos asked. 'There is something I can do for you?'

Thanos shook his head again. 'Not unless you have seen a fourteen-year-old boy and a pig today.'

The look on Manos's face didn't need to be translated into words.

'He said he was fifteen,' Manos said with a groan. 'Are you an undercover policeman? Am I going to get a fine? George will kill me.'

A whole stack of emotions toppled inside Thanos like a pile of books knocked from the shelf to the floor. Onassis was here! He was safe! And now he was going to ground him until he was twenty-one.

'Where is he?' Thanos asked.

Thanos slowed his walk across the field of fruit trees watching his brother at work. Even from this far away he could see Onassis had earbuds in and, as he plucked apricots with one hand, he was using the other to match his feet as he danced along the rows. *Always moving to music*. He remembered their mother commenting that Onassis moved a great deal more in the womb than Thanos had.

Perhaps that was where it had all began, before he had arrived and made every kitchen item a musical instrument to bang or put into his mouth and try to make a sound with ...

'Onassis,' he called.

The dancing stopped and Thanos watched his brother turn statuesque like this was suddenly a game of Red Light, Green Light. And then Onassis spoke.

'I can explain.'

'Excellent,' Thanos said. 'I am so glad.'

'Do not be angry.'

His brother still was not facing him but Thanos could see there was a nervousness to his disposition, a slight tremor to his arms, his hands gripping two apricots a little too tightly.

'Turn around,' Thanos ordered.

'Not until you say you will not be angry.'

'Onassis, if you want to be treated like an adult you need to begin to act like one.'

Very gently, like he might be dancing a slow-motion segment of a routine, Onassis rotated until he was face forward, although his face remained tipped a little downward as he dropped the fruit into his baskets.

'Onassis,' Thanos began. 'You went out last night when I said that you could not. Then you did not come home at all and I only discovered that this morning. Next, Ismēnē came to collect you for a school trip I did not know about and you have not gone to that. What is going on with you?'

'Let me explain,' Onassis said, finally looking up and meeting him eye to eye.

'I am waiting for it.'

Onassis sighed. 'I had to go out last night for my homework. Ismēnē's cat, it peed all over my worksheet and so I needed to get a copy from Stamatis so—'

Thanos held up a hand. 'Onassis, you are in no position to try to lie to me. You have a phone that can receive photos.'

'But Stamatis does not.'

'But he has a photocopier?' This story was already so far-fetched.

'No, but I took a photograph of his worksheet so I could draw a copy.'

Thanos frowned. 'How does the cat's pee stop you from drawing a copy of that one?'

'Why do you not believe it?!' Onassis threw his hands up in the air. 'If you would like to see how much the colours ran to make it unable to read, it is in the kitchen bin!'

'OK, OK,' Thanos said. 'So how do you go from Stamatis's house to being here?' And why had Stamatis's mother not said that Onassis had been there last night when he phoned her this morning? And where was the pig?

Onassis sighed. 'We finished the homework together. We did not cheat, I swear. And then, as I was already there, we did some dance practice and ...'

'And?'

'And ... I fell asleep.'

'Onassis, I telephoned every mother or father of every friend I know you have. If you were asleep at Stamatis's house then—'

'I woke up early, at 5 a.m., and I came home. But then I remembered the trip and I did not want to go. I wanted instead to do something to help you. It was my fault that the pig was there so I decided to get rid of it. To give it back to George.'

'Onassis, how did you get a pig here without a car?'

'I tied a basket to the front of my bike and I sat him inside it,' Onassis said.

'And the watermelon in your bed?'

'There is a watermelon in my bed?!'

Thanos shook his head. It hurt. He still didn't know if he actually believed any of this tale or not. And he was angry that Onassis had left without telling him where he was going or leaving a note.

'Onassis, this behaviour is unacceptable. To sneak out, to fill your bed with a watermelon, to come here and work instead of going to school. I cannot even—'

'George was not here. His cousin said he would take back the pig and he said if I wanted to earn some money I could work here for the day.'

'Well, your fruit-picking day is over. And you are grounded.'

'What for?!'

'For all the lies, Onassis! For scaring me and Ismēnē half to death, for putting yourself at risk, for not going on your school trip, for being selfish.'

Onassis threw the apricots into his basket. 'I am not selfish. I am trying to make up for my mistakes. I am trying to get us some money.'

'I told you I will take care of our finances,' Thanos said.

'I cannot do anything right!' Onassis said, stamping his foot on the floor.

'We will talk about this when we get home,' Thanos told him.

'You can't ground me,' Onassis wailed. 'I have to practise for the dance competition!'

'Well,' Thanos said. 'You should have thought about that before you turned into a farm worker.'

'Well, you are trying to turn into my father! And you are not!'

It felt like shards of ice had pierced Thanos's heart as he looked at his brother. Onassis appeared both grown yet also five years old with his eyes fiery and his trainers pushed into the earth. They stood there, facing each other almost as opponents in the bullring, both waiting for the move of the other. And, right now, Thanos knew only one thing. He was going to have to get on his knees and beg Baptiste for his job back.

Thirty-Seven

Arillas

'I had an email from Gina. She wants us to really get down deep into the heart of Greece now. Dig for more of those buried treasure places no one else will have ever reported on. I tried web searching using my top keywords "aspirational", "adventure", "pleasure-seeker".' Caroline laughed like she was gargling sewer water. 'That last one usually throws up more than a curveball or three but … nothing feels quite right yet, so we need to talk to the people.'

Lydia was listening but internally she was still reeling from the phone call with her dad. She was also reliving every conversation they'd had after she'd left Maison Mario. Why hadn't she caught on to what they had done? Were there signposts she had missed? She knew, at the time, and for a few months after, she hadn't been fully aware of much, but for her parents to have kept this information from her this long … and if Patrick hadn't reared his rather too-large-head now, how long would they have continued to keep it from her? Forever?

'Talk to the people,' Lydia parroted, realising she had left replying to Caroline a little too long. It was early evening now and they had come into the village for food. The taverna was small and homely with thick green vines tracking the metal framework over their heads. She had ordered *kleftiko* – lamb, potatoes and vegetables wrapped in parchment and cooked in the oven for hours. It should be pure comfort food and she was hoping it hit the spot as far as settling her stomach went. Caroline had ordered *saganaki* – fried cheese and two portions of chips.

‘Something’s off with you,’ Caroline said suddenly, pointing with a crust of bread she was holding between thumb and forefinger. ‘Share.’

‘I’m fine,’ Lydia said, trying to brighten her expression. She wasn’t up for sharing at the moment and Caroline would promptly give her a battle plan.

‘Are you missing Thanos?’

Lydia swallowed. You couldn’t miss someone you had only just met, could you? Except, after the phone call with her dad, when the initial foundation-shaking shock was more tremor than full-blown earthquake, she had thought of Thanos. She wanted to tell him the context of the issue, if not the full details of Patrick yet. She wanted to know his opinion, his thoughts on the situation.

‘You don’t need to answer that. I can tell from your face. You’ve gone peach.’

Could you go peach? Lydia put her hands to her cheeks anyway, as if she would be able to feel the colour change.

‘Did you swap numbers?’

‘Yes.’ But was she going to use it? Or was she going to play it cool and professional, and see if they crossed paths again at the food festival?

‘Don’t call it,’ Caroline said straightaway. ‘You need to act like you’re not bothered one way or the other if you see each other again.’

‘O-K,’ Lydia said, unsure of that as a tactic.

‘You know where he’s going to be. We are going to be there too. Just see what happens.’

‘Yes,’ Lydia said, nodding.

‘That’s my sitch with Vernon right now,’ Caroline said, pouring vinegar on her plate and dipping her bread into it. ‘He’s posting pictures of women-who-look-like-Black-Widow on Insta and I am ignoring every single one of them and definitely not revenging it out with photos of me with the bee man, the Greek dancers and the best-looking guy from Sokraki.’

‘Right.’ So, Caroline definitely *did* still have feelings for her ex-husband. They had been divorced for three years now and, in that time, neither of them had moved on with anyone else. But was Vernon moving on with someone else now and Caroline really didn't like it? Perhaps her friend wasn't looking for free love here in Corfu as happily as she was making out.

Then Lydia furrowed her brow. 'But ... wasn't Thanos the best-looking guy in Sokraki?'

Caroline laughed hysterically. 'And now I know that you are smitten. Hit me.' She held her hand out for a high-five. Lydia felt compelled to follow through.

She wasn't smitten. She was in a full-on quandary, questioning every tiny corner of her life and the people who were closest to her. How could she start to have any form of romantic dalliance with someone when all those memories of the last man she had shared anything with were being stirred up like a red-hot Szechuan stir-fry. This Greek edition of the magazine. That was what she should put all her focus on now. She was going to make sure it was the best copy of *Luxe Living* that had ever been put out and it was going to help her with the decision process regarding what came next. And she was going to ignore the curdling in her gut that was trying to taint the feeling of being ready to embrace cooking again.

'But while we remain aloof because we are strong and independent women of the twenty-first century, I've booked us into a yoga retreat tomorrow. It's *perfect* for my readers. It's spirituality meets a little bit whacky meets something Gwyneth Paltrow might approve of ... with colourful robes.' Caroline's eyes were lit up like she could power the Blackpool lights.

'What food do they have? Because *my* readers usually want more than a juice cleanse.' And so did Lydia. It was her opinion that good food shouldn't feel like some kind of medieval punishment.

'Ah, well, you are going to be pleasantly surprised,' Caroline said, shaking salt over her vinegar bread as a black cat looked on at her feet. 'Because according to Buddhist beliefs, food should be for the body as well as the soul and guests need to be fully nourished before they enter a deep meditative state.' She sighed like nirvana was suddenly within reach. 'They mention the food being vegetarian but there's nothing you can't add a Peperami to, is there?'

Lydia smiled. No matter what was going on, no matter where they were, Caroline never changed. Perhaps that was the solid foundation she should hang on to for now. Caroline was consistently consistent in her opinions on all things and was never shy about voicing them. And she was always there, always brutally honest, never failing to pull things together when they needed to.

'Did you really bring Peperamis in your carry-on?' Lydia asked her.

'Do you even know me at all?' Caroline said with a wink.

Thirty-Eight

Taverna Ilios, Benitses

'No.'

'But—'

'What do you not understand, Thano? I said no.'

Thanos couldn't believe this. Baptiste was not giving him a second chance no matter what he offered to try to persuade him to change his mind. Well, he wasn't done yet. This was about Onassis, and giving him the stability Thanos had always provided until recently when he had let his dumb ambition take over. He needed to rectify the situation and fast.

'I will take a ten per cent pay cut,' Thanos said, the words hurting a little as they flew out. A guaranteed income was better than no income at all. And Taverna Ilios was as quiet as he had ever seen it. There were only half a dozen tables occupied. Compared to the other restaurants on 'eat street' this was sparse. And there was a very strange aroma coming from the kitchen ...

Baptiste was polishing glasses with a cloth, something he only usually had time to do when they were winding down for the end of the season. And he didn't seem to be paying Thanos any attention at all. In fact, was he humming?

'Baptiste!' Thanos said, trying not to sound impatient as the man moved to search another cupboard. 'Are you even listening to me?'

'No, I am not,' Baptiste answered, getting the unlit cigarette from behind his ear and putting it between his lips. 'Because it does not matter how many times you ask me, or how low a price you are willing to bargain to work for ... the answer will still be no.'

Thanos put his hands on his hips. He hadn't anticipated this outcome and he really did not know what to do next. So much for his cooking being 'the talk of the town'. So much for Baptiste being the one to come begging. *Begging*. He swallowed and had a quick internal tussle with that idea. It was to keep his brother in school, to be there to stop him falling off the tracks …

'I will work for free. For a week. Nothing to pay me for a whole seven days. If you still do not want to take me back on then—'

'Thanos! Stop! Can you not see I have glasses to polish?' Baptiste asked, cigarette waggling as he talked.

'I do not understand! Giorgos's cooking is terrible. Mine is …' He stopped talking. He had been about to say something complimentary but in this moment his confidence was about as low as it could get. 'Mine is …' he began again.

'Worthy of running a kitchen catering for kings so I am told,' Baptiste commented.

'What?'

Baptiste took the cigarette from his mouth and put it back behind his ear. 'I would have you back in charge of the kitchen. Giorgos was a mistake and the girl I have now makes everything with herbs I have not heard of. *Stifado* tastes like mustard. *Sofrito* tastes like mustard. *Moussaka* … well, you have the idea.' He sighed. 'But sadly, it is not my decision to make.'

Now Thanos really did not understand. Had Baptiste sold the taverna? Who had bought it? Could he ask the new owner for a job? All these thoughts were swimming in his mind as Baptiste went to speak again.

'It has been decreed that you will not come back to work here until I am told otherwise.' Baptiste sniffed and picked up another glass to polish.

'What is going on here? Who has decreed that I cannot work here?' But, as Thanos finished the sentence, his brain put the pieces together and he already knew …

'Ismēnē,' Baptiste said.

'She is not my mother,' Thanos said immediately, anger building like a huge burning bubble in his chest. 'And even if she was, it does not give her the right to govern my future.'

'But *I* cannot go against *her* wishes,' Baptiste stated. 'It is a pact I made with Spiros before he passed away.'

Thanos closed his eyes. *This island!* This was the downside of the Greek community – everyone thinking they could mind your business. Well, he was going to have a few choice words with Ismēnē. He might have rolled with her idea of striking out on his own and being independent to begin with, but it was ludicrous when he was faced with a rebellious Onassis.

'Please, Baptiste, if you do not do it for me, do it for Onassis.' He swallowed. He hated doing this. He had pride, but sometimes you had to admit things were difficult and take a temporary hit.

'I cannot help you,' Baptiste said, finally lighting his cigarette and puffing smoke into the air. 'Not even if it would be for all the needy children in Greece.'

'Ismēnē has that much of a hold over you?' Thanos asked. 'And you, so well-thought-of here, such a leader ... practically Mr Benitses.'

Baptiste laughed. 'It does not matter what you say, Thano. As I said, the answer is no.'

Thirty-Nine

Retrace and Retreat, Arillas

The following morning, Lydia had more missed calls from her dad and one from her mother. *That* meant the situation was serious. Her mother would usually distance herself from any kind of involvement with conflict unless forced into a corner. But Lydia wasn't ready to discuss it with them yet. She still felt so incredibly hurt that they had made decisions about her future without consulting her and kept it under wraps.

'Ah, it's beautiful here,' Caroline said, extending her arms to the sky as they stood in the gardens of the yoga-cum-wellness centre. 'I feel more Buddhist already.'

They had been shown around the retreat building by a very tall man called Frederick who only spoke when he felt it was completely necessary. Luckily, Caroline had spoken enough for all of them as they were taken through into the main spiritual room where they would be taking part in the mindfulness and meditation seminar later. It was shaped like a yurt – with cross-hatched wooden beams over the ceiling and large windows around the circular perimeter that were opened wide revealing the view of cypress trees, mountains and the glistening sea. It was another warm day and Lydia was glad she'd opted for her lightest summer dress. She looked back to her phone as it erupted again. *Dad*. She still wasn't going to answer it.

'Who's phoning you?' Caroline asked, nudging closer. 'Because if it's the office I would ignore it. I've told them that we need to be left undisturbed so we can immerse ourselves. I mean they can't expect this edition to be completely authentic if they don't give us room to breathe, can they?'

'It's not the office,' Lydia told her. 'It's ... nothing important.' She dropped her phone into her bag and tried to switch off from the hurt and switch on to their upcoming experience. And, just like that, someone arrived. It was a man with a very similar build to Frederick, but his hair was long, silver in colour and tied back into a large braid.

'Greetings, newcomers,' he said, bowing a little.

'Well, hello,' Caroline said, suddenly seeming to unfurl like a slinky cat desperate to show off its best attributes. 'What's *your* name?'

'My name is Brightness,' he answered with another bow.

'Did your mother hate you?' Caroline asked with a cackle. 'So, now tell me your real name.'

The man smiled. 'Here at Retrace and Retreat we leave our earth names at the door and adopt names that will cultivate a more balanced, positive lifestyle.'

'O-K then,' Caroline said. 'I will be Moana and Lydia here will be Princess Fiona.'

Brightness smiled again as Lydia felt a tiny bit aggrieved that Caroline had pegged her balanced, positive lifestyle as someone green who lived in a swamp ...

'I am afraid you do not choose your own name,' Brightness explained. 'Your name chooses you.'

'Ooh!' Caroline exclaimed, arms flying out and her hands colliding with a cactus plant bearing bright red fruit on top of its flat spiky body. 'Ouch!' She rubbed the back of her hand. 'So, you mean it's like the sorting hat from *Harry Potter*.'

Brightness smiled again. Did he do anything else *but* smile? Perhaps that was testament to his inner peace?

He continued. 'Once you are dressed in your robes, we will bring you into the circle with the other new guests and the earth will decide your Retrace and Retreat name.' Brightness held out two large reams of cloth that looked like they could completely reupholster two L-shaped corner sofas.

'So, do we drop everything and put these on here? Or do they go on over our clothes?'

Another smile. 'The day's course is all about leaving your old life behind and anything that is going to stop you from moving forward must be liberated here and now.'

'So, we *do* have to drop everything here and now?' Caroline quizzed, already reaching for the strap of her top.

'There are screens,' Brightness said. 'In the Garden of Neutralisation.'

Garden of Neutralisation. That sounded ever so slightly on the verge of creepy. Lydia knew she might be going through a few issues at the moment, but she wasn't sure there were parts of her she wanted neutralising. Looking now at the flowers, the wooden arbour with wind chimes dangling from it and the screens that you could probably see everything through if you stared hard enough, it seemed only relaxing. And Caroline was right about one thing, this was exactly the type of thing readers of *Luxe Living* would lap up. She took the robe Brightness was offering and, for some reason, gave a bow.

Lydia's robe had actually morphed into pantaloons and she was struggling not to take flight every time a welcome sea breeze drifted through the open glass into the main hall. There were maybe fifteen people in the room wearing outfits in a similar style, plus 'gurus' who were all dressed in orange.

'Make mental notes,' Caroline said through the corner of her mouth. 'My leaving behind my past life meant my notebook as well as my phone.'

'OK,' Lydia replied, nodding. She might not remember all the names of moves or techniques but she was sure there would be a pamphlet they could have when they left. Or they could ask Frederick or Brightness any questions they might have.

'Welcome everyone and welcome to our new joiners for the day,' Brightness began. 'I know some of you who have been here for a few days now are becoming accustomed to our way of life and I hope if our newcomers have any questions you will be able to catch them up and help them along their new life journey.'

They were here for one day. Lydia was wondering just how much of a life journey they were going to be able to get through. And Caroline had assured her that this was much more about yoga than it was about soul-cleansing …

'Now, as you know, this is a harmonising couples' course so …'

Brightness's commanding voice continued but Lydia's body just froze. What had he just said? Couples' course?

'Caroline,' Lydia said, her lips shaking a little. 'Did you hear what Brightness said?'

'Sshh!' Caroline ordered. 'I won't be able to hear anything he says if you keep talking.'

'But, Caroline, he said this was a couples' course.' Surely Caroline couldn't have known this. After all, they weren't a couple! Lydia began to scan the room, looking at the other participants. Some of them were holding hands, others were stood close together, male/female mainly, but there were two male/male and one other female/female pairing besides her and Caroline. This was unbelievable. And if they were here under false pretences then they might be cursed or something. Perhaps the ornamental arbour turned into a guillotine if you were found out.

'Together we are going to help you reinvigorate your relationship and teach you how to be more understanding and intuitive yet also powerful and in complete control of your own needs.'

'Caroline,' Lydia hissed. 'Did you know about this?'

'Do you trust me?' Caroline asked, not turning her head to engage.

'That was not an answer to my question!' Lydia's pantaloons suddenly blew up and out like someone had inflated them with a pump. How intimate was this couples' course going to get? And how intimate was she going to have to get with Caroline dressed like a clown and completely naked underneath?!

'Listen,' Caroline whispered, finally casting an eye in her direction. 'You know my readers don't buy our magazine for themselves, the last survey we did said it's enjoyed mainly by couples. It inspires them towards growth and new opportunities. They are going to eat up this tantric pathway!'

'I don't want you within a Peperami's width of my tantric anything! Is that understood?'

'I'll imagine you're Vernon if it helps,' Caroline suggested.

Lydia wasn't sure it *did* help and with Brightness saying phrases like 'foresight before foreplay' and 'Uranus and the rest of the relationship galaxy', she was wondering how soon she could get out of the ridiculous trouser robes and get back to their apartment.

'Think of the lunch,' Caroline whispered, closing her eyes and joining in a low moan with the group. Then she stopped with the guttural pregnant heifer noise and grinned. 'Epiphany.'

Lydia sighed. Yes, that was her Retreat and Retrace name. 'Epiphany' to Caroline's 'Embers'. They almost sounded like a female detective agency ...

'Right, well, to compensate me for this, you are going to let me spend however much time I like at the Agios Stefanos food festival. I don't want any moaning about how I'm taking longer to browse artisan goods than Bonnie takes over a Müller Corner. Or any comments about how everything would taste better if it was covered in batter.'

Caroline closed her eyes again. 'You're trampling on my inner deity now.'

'You're lucky that's all I'm trampling on, Embers!'

'Fine! No moaning! No comments! Now look at me like you want to rip my robes off.'

Forty

Ismēnē's house, Benitses

'Ismēnē! I need your help! I have become entangled in your washing line!'

After his shouted declaration, Onassis looked to Thanos as they both stood in Ismēnē's small courtyard garden. It was early evening, bees buzzing around the urns spilling waterfalls of deep colour. 'Why are we doing this? She does not wake this early from siesta. And I thought I was supposed to be grounded yet here I am, out of the house.'

Thanos shot him a glare. 'You are here because this is an intervention,' Thanos reminded him. 'People cannot know about interventions until the last moment. If she knows she will not want to take part and ...'

'And what?' Onassis queried.

'She just needs to not be prepared.' Ismēnē was excellent at using memories to steer her propaganda. And it was too easy to fall into that trap. He could shout. He could get angry like he had been with Baptiste at Taverna Ilios, but the best way with Ismēnē was to catch her off guard, to not give her time to formulate her own plan. But there was no movement from the house, not even any sound ...

They were stood there in front of her old wooden door with the ornate metal framework that was always a little ajar no matter how many times Thanos had told her she should keep it closed. And nothing was happening. The only sound was the light hum from the insects.

'What should we do now?' Onassis asked in a whisper. 'Should I shout again?'

Thanos shook his head and pushed the door with a fingertip. It was dark in the house, the shutters were all closed to keep out the heat, there was nothing unusual in that but ... was that a flickering light coming from inside? And the scent of ... smoke?

'Do you smell that, Onassis?' Thanos asked, his body spiking with concern.

'Smell what?' Onassis said, putting his nose in the air and giving a sniff.

Thanos hesitated no longer. 'I think it's smoke. Stay here.' He pushed the door wide and headed in.

'Stay here?!' Onassis exclaimed. 'I cannot stay here if you are going in.'

It was so dark Thanos had to feel his way forward. It took effort to negotiate even the tiny entrance way. And he could definitely smell smoke. Then, as he took a tentative step ahead, lights flashed on and he almost walked straight into a large table that was right in the middle of the entire living space. It was set for three people with tablemats, knives and forks and glasses and in the centre were many candles and some large porcelain urns, lids on with steam rising from the gaps at the side of the lids. What was going on? He didn't have time to think because there was Ismēnē, her hair loose for the first time in a long time, a grey floor-length dress almost covering up the gold trainers on her feet.

'Please, sit down,' she addressed them. 'I've been expecting you.'

Thanos could feel the weight of his brother's eyes on him. *This* was an intervention. Planned. Instigated a lot longer ago than his. Ismēnē had cooked and from the scent in the air that wasn't the burning wicks of the candles he knew it was some of his favourites: *spanakopita* – spinach and feta cheese pie and *yuvarlakia* – chicken meatball soup. And the very worst thing was, he did not know what to do. Sit down? Leave? Push his own agenda from the outset? Onassis was already pulling out a chair and inhaling the fragrances like he had not eaten in a month.

'What is wrong, Thano?' Ismēnē asked firmly. 'You look a little surprised. Were you expecting me to still be asleep? Or perhaps dead?'

'No,' Thanos said immediately. 'No, of course not.'

'Which one?' Ismēnē asked, shuffling around the table and squeezing her body out of the smallest of gaps to get to the stove where another large pot seemed to be simmering.

'I said you would still be asleep,' Onassis answered proudly.

'I have instead been busy,' Ismēnē told them both. 'I have finished your costumes for the dance competition. They just need a final fitting to make sure that everything is perfect. And I have made food for us to eat together.'

'Ismēnē,' Thanos began.

'Hush,' she said with authority. 'You do not need to tell me why you are here.' She began serving up greens with a large ladle. Of course she knew why he was here. Because Thanos could not have an original thought without Ismēnē knowing about it, even before he had established the idea.

'Sit down, Thano,' Ismēnē ordered.

Onassis already had his knife and fork poised. Thanos literally had no choice. But, perhaps, even though he had not instigated this exact scenario, he could make sure that Ismēnē knew how he felt about things. He dropped into a seat feeling suddenly very tired.

'You went to Baptiste,' Ismēnē said, serving up the exquisite-smelling food. 'And you,' she began again, turning to Onassis. 'You should not have missed out on a school trip and disappeared without telling anyone where you are going. Thanos is right to ground you.'

Thanos frowned at the exact same time that Onassis did. How did Ismēnē know that Thanos had grounded Onassis? Did she really have some kind of sixth sense? Or were the walls of their homes not quite as thick stone as they appeared?

'Onassis, you know that to have the best chance in life you need to finish school.'

'I will finish school,' he answered nodding.

'Then why would you go to pick fruit?'

His brother had no answer. But then he responded. 'Sorry, Ismēnē.'

Sorry, Ismēnē? The one thing Onassis had not done since the pig and the fruit-picking incident was apologise. Thanos was about to make a comment when Ismēnē beat him to it.

'And as for you,' she said, spooning a large portion of meatball soup into a bowl and handing it to Thanos. 'Why would you go back to Baptiste and grovel for your job when you have no need for it?'

Thanos sighed. 'I do have need for it. *We* have need for it. It is a regular income and it provides me with stability. I will work in Benitses, *only* in Benitses and I can be here for Onassis and—'

'And waste your talents as we talked about before.' She placed the plate down in front of him. 'What has changed, Thano? Where has your drive and ambition disappeared to? Do you not remember the feeling of exhilaration when you made a restaurant out of the ruins? The power of bringing your food, the way you want to cook it to the people?'

Ismēnē was making him sound like some revolutionary again. He needed not to let this filtrate into his psyche. Because it didn't last and many other things were much more important.

'Did you do the interview?' Ismēnē wanted to know, producing fresh bread from under a tea towel and simultaneously pouring wine into a jug.

'What interview?' Onassis asked, his mouth already spilling food.

'It is nothing,' Thanos answered.

'It is not nothing,' Ismēnē insisted. 'There is a girl from England. She is a famous writer. For a magazine about food. And she wants to write about your brother's cooking.'

'Is this true, Thano?' Onassis wanted to know.

Thanos could already see the pride shining in Onassis's eyes. It was misplaced. It was hope that had no foundation. It was not the reality of the every day.

'Yes, it is true. And I hear that she and her friend are staying in Arillas right now,' Ismēnē continued.

Thanos's heart beat a little quicker then. Lydia was in Arillas. That was not far at all from Agios Stefanos. Maybe she would come to the food festival. But, again, how did Ismēnē know this information? And was the way he had felt with Lydia when they were on the beach here in Benitses and again in Sokraki another case of more hope than reality?

'She is the one who came into the tent! When the lights went out!' Onassis erupted, pointing his fork, greens falling back down onto the plate. 'She is very pretty!'

Yes, she was very pretty. *More* than pretty. She was beautiful and intelligent and passionate. The memory of their kisses in the little wooden shelter started to blend in his mind …

'You like her!' Onassis exclaimed, mouth full of food.

Thanos realised then how transparent his expression must be, but he was not about to confirm anything. In fact, he needed to get this conversation under control and not let Ismēnē lead all the proceedings. 'Ismēnē, the night at the ruins, the food festival, the ideas are good, but let us be real. Even if I was mentioned in a magazine in England, it is not going to lead to things so great I can turn down work that is regular, that is here for Onassis.'

'Oh no,' Onassis said, dropping his cutlery and folding his arms across his chest. 'I will not be the reason you go back to work for Baptiste.'

'Onassis, it is not your decision to make.'

'Because I am not allowed to make any decisions, am I? Because I am a stupid dumb kid!'

'Onassis, you cannot understand,' Thanos told him.

'Because you think I am a stupid dumb kid!'

'Enough!' Ismēnē roared.

It was rough and piercing all at the same time and seemed to sap the energy from the small woman. She put her hands on her hips and drew in a deep breath. 'What would your mother and father say if they could see you now, fighting with each other, working against each other.'

Thanos bit his tongue. If words turned heated between him and his father, it was his mother who had always been the first to suggest both of them going away and cooling down, reflecting on the situation before regrouping again once tempers had died down. It hurt him that neither of his parents could see Onassis as he was now, trying to be so strong and independent. He was as proud of that as he was frustrated by it.

'From now on, you are going to work together as a family. Because that is what you are,' Ismēnē reminded. 'No more, "I decide to do this for him" or "I am going to go to this place with a pig and not tell anyone". Everything in the open. Everything together.' She recommenced serving the food. 'Now, we will eat. And then you will listen to my ideas about the food festival ... and then you will make a plan.' She sniffed. 'I will only make suggestions. It is up to you what you decide to do. The only thing I will say is this ...'

Thanos watched as she lifted a framed photo of her husband from a shelf. Spiros looked smart in a suit, perhaps a Sunday long ago, before morning worship. Ismēnē lightly traced a finger over the glass, smoothing the image lovingly.

'You only have one life on this earth,' Ismēnē said, her eyes on the photo. 'Is it not better to take chances ... rather than miss them?'

The sentiment was heavy and the very second Thanos caught his brother's gaze he knew Ismēnē was right. She was always, annoyingly, right. He gave Onassis a half smile and watched his brother return the gesture.

'Right,' Ismēnē said, putting the photo down and clapping her hands together. 'Let us put on the music of anyone but Jimi Hendrix and I will open some *retsina*.'

Forty-One

Arillas

'I cannot wait to get this bloody robe off!'

It was the morning after the day before at Retrace and Retreat and what had started out being a full day of soulmate-searching had turned into an evening and a night too. Lydia still wasn't sure if Caroline had known all along that they would be overnighting – in a double bed in a room with everyone else – or whether she really had been as oblivious as she had acted.

'And I never, ever, want to wear anything like it again,' Caroline continued. 'It's rougher than those Fairtrade bags they sell in Oxfam.'

They were back at their apartment and the next stop on their agenda was the Corfu Beer brewery. They were certainly ticking all the boxes when it came to lifestyle, going from food that was meant to reach parts of you you didn't know you had – even after your partner had elongated your cosmic aura – to alcohol. And alcohol would go down quite nicely now as Lydia's robe was itching too and there were several text messages from her dad including one that was begging meaningfully in English and Swedish. This was an absolute mess and the fact that she had had no idea her parents were wrapped like the two ends of a ribbon around the money she'd been given to leave Maison Mario was ripping into her. It was one thing to finally realise that the only person Patrick cared about was himself, but it was quite another to be shown that your own parents thought you were too mentally unstable to go forward in life without their interference. They had picked up the pieces of something she didn't really know she had smashed quite so completely. And for that reason, because she still couldn't think about their secrecy without feeling a little bit nauseous, she wasn't going to answer her phone or reply to the messages yet.

'Argh!' Caroline screamed. 'Get me out of this thing! I can feel myself coming out in hives.'

Lydia looked at Caroline now and stifled a laugh. She looked like a magician trying to perform escapology. But before Lydia could aid with loosening the robe there was a knock at the door.

'Christ!' Caroline yelled. 'If that Brightness has followed us back here I'm going to have to throw ouzo at him and hope he melts down like the witch in the *Wizard of Oz*.'

'Why would he follow us back here?' Lydia wanted to know. 'He was full of smiles when we left him, giving us enough literature to write a whole edition on the retreat alone.'

'He was full of smiles the whole time we were there,' Caroline reminded, voice muffled from being trapped under the clothing. 'It's not natural. A bit like this material!'

Lydia headed to the door then pulled it open. It was the lady from reception and she was smiling too. It must be something in the Arillas air.

'Hello,' Lydia greeted.

'*Kalimera sas*,' the woman replied and then she looked past Lydia to Caroline whose head was still stuck in her robe. 'Who is Lydia?'

'That's me,' Lydia answered.

'That is good,' the woman said. 'You do not have your head stuck under clothing. Come with me.'

The woman was already edging the door to the room to a close and Lydia was coming right along with it as if she didn't have any say in the matter.

'Lydia! Don't you leave me! I can barely breathe! And you and me, we are earth partners remember?'

With Caroline's pleas ringing in her ears, Lydia was suddenly glad she was being escorted from the apartment. But she wasn't about to be marched up the corridor without knowing where they were going. 'Is something wrong?' she asked the woman as she strode ahead. Maybe Caroline hadn't paid their bill …

'There is man,' the woman replied. 'Waiting for you.'

Thanos was nervous. As he stood in the sunshine outside the apartments, he wondered if this was a mistake on every level. He wasn't even sure why he was here. The potential to have his cooking highlighted in a magazine, to prepare for the food festival or just to see Lydia again. What he did know though, after Ismēnē's intervention dinner, was that trying to hide things from his brother wasn't working. Pretending that the garden was as red and rosy as their crop of tomatoes, painting a fairy-tale dream where there was only success and no struggle, would do Onassis no good in the long run. In his head he talked about reality and the importance of that over wishes and aims, yet all that did was tell his brother it was OK to have low expectations for life. How would that stand him in good stead when it was his time to make decisions? He didn't want Onassis to have limited dreams. So it *was* time to be brave. Even if it meant making cutbacks and sacrifices at home for a while. And that step forward started here.

He heard the door open and turned around, shielding his eyes from the sun. And there Lydia was, looking amazing, her blonde hair loose, wearing a baggy outfit and sandals on her feet. Straightaway, his heart began to beat a different rhythm.

'Thanos,' she greeted, sounding a little surprised.

'I hope this is not a little bit weird,' he said, stepping forward. 'That I did not call first but—'

'How did you find me?' she asked.

'I had to use the Corfu underground network.' He smiled. 'It is like if you had a tracking device fitted inside you, except you don't.' He was nervous and he hoped she didn't think he was talking nonsense. 'Everyone on the island knows everyone on the island. A beautiful woman from England who writes about food. It did not take long.'

She smiled. 'I was going to call you. But Caroline got us involved with this very odd activity and I've only just got back here.'

'You do not need to explain,' he said. He found himself wondering if she would have called him. Did she feel they had a connection like he did? It scared him a little that she might not. When he had held her in his arms in Sokraki, it had been different than anything he'd shared with anyone before. Somehow it had felt far more significant. That it could perhaps be more than a moment. He swallowed, pushing his hair back from his face. 'I wondered … if you might like to come to Agios Stefanos with me. They are setting up for the food festival and, well, I would value your opinion on what I should think of making.'

He valued her opinion. With everything going on behind the scenes in her life – Patrick, her parents – it was a sentence that filled her with the purest joy. Something simple, yet it meant the world. And she couldn't deny that Thanos being here – dressed like he'd stepped off the cover of *Men's Fitness* with dark, skinny jeans and an oversized vest that was split all the way up the sides revealing tattoos and torso in equally glorious measure – was almost as appealing as his request.

'Give me two minutes,' Lydia said. 'I need to rescue Caroline and get out of this awful outfit.'

He smiled, all full lips she wanted to taste all over again. 'I will be here.'

Forty-Two

Agios Stefanos Avliotes

Signage and stands were being set up all over one end of the golden sandy beach. It was a little windswept, the waves rolling hard towards the shore, people in the water leaping up to jump over the foaming surf. But the breeze was keeping the heat down a little as they walked close together across the sand. Thanos stole a glance at her at the very same time her eyes met his and he smiled. He wanted to hold her hand. But this wasn't dancing in the village streets or cooking *lalagia*, this was like being back at the beginning again. So, instead, he slipped his hands into the pockets of his jeans and started conversation.

'Have you cooked at a food festival before?' Thanos asked her.

Lydia nodded. 'I have. Mario was always getting asked to cook at them. Some places would pay him extortionate amounts of money for only a thirty-minute appearance. One little fete wanted to pay him ten thousand pounds just to cut a ribbon and start the day. He refused. Told them to give the money to charity and he would open the event for free if they gave him a room at an inn for the night and kept him in limoncello.'

'You talked of Mario before. He is important to you?'

His question had come out a little tight because he was worried for her reply. Was Mario going to be someone she had loved? Someone she *still* loved?

Lydia's expression changed immediately, her eyes dimming, her mouth tightening a little. It was like she had said something wrong or let out a secret. And then, finally, she answered him.

'I worked with Mario Romano.'

He stopped walking. *Mario Romano*. Thanos's breath was suddenly trapped in his chest and it was getting tighter and tighter like an overfilled airbed running out of space. She had cooked with Mario Romano, one of the best Italian chefs in the entire world! One of his cooking heroes! He literally had no words.

'And that's why I didn't tell you,' Lydia said, her mouth forming a smile now as she carried on moving, slipping off her shoes and sinking her toes into the warm sand. 'That's the expression on everyone's face the minute I say his full name.'

'Sorry,' Thanos said. 'I didn't mean to stop ... breathing. It's ... well ... he was the best chef.'

Lydia nodded. 'Yes, he was.'

And then Thanos really caught on. 'Mario. He was the man like a father to you.'

She nodded again. 'Yes.'

Now, she looked so incredibly sad he couldn't stop himself from reaching out. He gently palmed her face and drew her in towards his body, wrapping her up in a soft embrace. 'I am sorry. To lose him as someone you were so close to. I cannot imagine.'

Her body was trembling ever so slightly and he held her until she had stilled again. Then she raised her head and stepped back a little.

'He would have enjoyed your food,' she told him. And then she smiled. 'Actually, he might not have enjoyed it because you would have been a rival to him.'

'No. Mario, he was trained at a cooking school. I have learned what I know from YouTube and experiments.'

'And Mario hated cooking school. Did you know he was thrown out of one of them for disobedience?' She giggled. 'Mario always told me that genius cannot be controlled. He felt that way about food too. The more precision, the more chance for things to fail. And if things always go the way you plan, how do you ever discover those happy accidents? Like, the reason you add paprika to your orzo.'

He shook his head. 'How did you know that began as an accident?'

She laughed. 'I didn't. But now I do.'

He smiled. 'So, if I search on the internet for Mario Romano's sous chef I will find ...'

Lydia raised an eyebrow. 'You won't find me. Mario, he was the executive chef. I was his head chef until ... well, until what happened.'

'What happened?'

He studied her expression, watched as her demeanour altered ever so slightly, dipping inwards. Was she going to retreat like a clam who had been disturbed when they were peeking slightly out of their shell?

'I'm ... not quite ready to share that.'

She was barely breathing, still, quiet, like one movement could set off a chain reaction of emotions and perhaps even she didn't know what kind.

'But,' Lydia continued, 'when I *am* ready, I will tell you. Because if I don't say any of it out loud I'll probably never be able to move on.'

He put a hand on her shoulder and gently, hopefully reassuringly, moved his fingers over the spot. Whatever she had been through it still hurt her.

'From the moment we met,' Thanos said. 'From the way you talked about food. To be a head chef for Mario Romano ... you are a star.'

'No,' Lydia breathed, turning a little and looking out to sea. 'To be a star you have to have charisma. I don't have that. And I don't want the limelight. I've never wanted that. All I ever wanted was to make beautiful dishes that made for happy stomachs.'

'That is what I want too,' Thanos told her. 'To make something beautiful and feel fulfilled. To be more than someone who chops tuna into steaks and cooks them the same way every Tuesday.'

'Then we need to get started on my interview for *Luxe Living*. Make sure a lot more people are introduced to your food.'

'OK,' he answered. 'Let's do it while we cook.'

'What?' Lydia exclaimed.

'Come on, Lydia, did you think we would not be cooking?'

She smiled at him. 'I've cooked more in Greece since I've been here than I've cooked at home for the past two years.'

'Good,' Thanos answered. 'That makes my stomach happy.'

Forty-Three

'This is it,' Thanos said, spreading his arms out inside the stand that would become his cooking space at the food festival. 'I have no real idea what is going to go on here and, later in the evening, I will be in the centre of the arena – wherever that will be, I do not think it is built yet – and I will be doing a *cooking performance*.'

'Wow,' Lydia answered. 'And this all begins the day after tomorrow.'

'This is a crazy idea, right? I mean, I have nothing planned. I have never performed before. I have nothing to sell.' His eyes went to other stands being set up, people measuring shelves and positioning boxes, some getting out jars and tins to make a display. It was already a hive of activity and he had never felt so poorly prepared for anything he had attempted to undertake before.

'You could sell biscuits,' Lydia told him. 'The ones you made that night at the Roman ruins.'

'You think so?' he asked.

'They were delicious. Simple perfection. And using the borage flowers was inspired.' She smiled. 'They looked so pretty and borage ... well, it's so in vogue right now. And I don't think it's likely anyone else will make something like that.'

'The biscuits,' Thanos began. 'I made them because they remind me of my mother.' He slid himself up into a sitting position on the worktop and looked out at the sea, still bubbling.

'Did you learn cooking from her?' Lydia asked, pulling herself up to settle alongside him.

'Some of the Greek dishes,' Thanos said. 'I am sure she would have taught me more but ... she passed away.'

'Oh, Thanos, I'm so sorry.'

He felt her rest a hand on his shoulder, a subtle but noticeable touch that comforted.

He nodded and before he realised it, his fingers were travelling to his tattoos. 'It is not anyone's fault.' He grazed the drawing of waves and the two hearts. 'I lost both my parents the same day. They had gone to Paxos, it is another island, about thirty miles south of Corfu. My aunt, she was very, very sick and it was to be the last time that they saw her.' He took a long, slow breath. 'There was a terrible storm, something that just came so unexpectedly when the boat was already on its journey.' He swallowed. 'The boat was lost before anyone could even raise an alarm. Many people were lost that day.'

'Oh, Thanos!'

Lydia didn't know what else to say. Here she had been talking about her own loss and both Thanos's parents had been taken at the same time. She couldn't imagine.

'It is OK,' he said.

'No, it's not OK. It's terribly, terribly sad. How long ago did this happen?'

She felt his shoulder move upwards as he took a long, slow breath in.

'I was just eighteen,' he finally answered.

'Oh, Thanos, I really don't know what to say,' Lydia breathed. 'That's way too young to lose your parents.'

As she said the words she began to think about her own parents and the fact she was fighting with them. How would she feel if she were to lose them right now, when there was animosity and they weren't speaking? She swallowed, hit by the poignancy.

'When is a good time to lose your parents?' he answered with a shrug.

'You're right. There is never a good time to lose anyone, is there?'

'And God's will, it cannot be controlled.' He smiled then. 'Like genius.'

Suddenly he jumped down and moved around the workstation. 'So, the time is now, right? You can ask your questions while we fillet the fish.'

Lydia got down too and watched as he took two large sea bream from a cool box and slapped them down onto the counter.

'These fish,' Thanos began. 'They are dedicated to the goddess Aphrodite, the goddess of love, because they are thought to be the most beautiful of all the fish.'

'I did not know that.'

'Argh!' Thanos exclaimed. 'I did not bring a knife! How could I forget this? Everything will be in place here tomorrow but now there is nothing ... and I did not fillet them. I am an idiot!'

Lydia smiled and unzipped the bag that was across her body. 'Let me.'

Thanos looked up at her as she moved behind the counter, taking a small flat plastic square from her bag. 'This was a trick that *I* taught Mario. It was actually something my mother showed me. And, if you knew my mother, it is quite bizarre that this is something she learned and passed on. My mother is usually someone who protects her manicure at all costs.'

'I have no idea what you are going to do,' Thanos said, intently watching. 'I am a little bit stressed.'

She laughed. 'Trust me. You might never use a knife to fillet a fish again.'

'Really?'

'No,' Lydia said. 'But this will work well enough.'

She drew a safety pin from the box containing plasters and a small roll of bandage and unfastened it. 'Ready?' she asked Thanos.

'I am your audience.'

'OK,' Lydia said, taking a deep breath. 'So, cutting under the fin and up to the head. And ... all the way down towards the tail.' She stopped talking. 'Sorry, I didn't mean to sound like I was telling you how to do it. You know how to do it but—'

'I have never done it with something you might use to hold trousers together if you burst a button.'

She laughed, fingers holding the fish firmly yet gently as she used the safety pin like the most precise tool. 'It's tricky to hold the central bone with just this but ... there we go, so then we finish off and ... almost ... I think ... done. We just need to remove the finer bones.'

When Thanos didn't say anything, she looked up from the sea bream and saw that he was gazing at her with an expression of something close to awe. And suddenly the cooling wind subsided and the heat from the beach began to warm up this booth …

'Do you think that was ridiculous?' Lydia asked, breaking the silence. 'It's ridiculous, isn't it? But I guess in the wilds of Sweden, if you were starving, or made to do it as a challenge for the Swedish equivalent of the Brownies then it might come in handy.'

'I do not think it is ridiculous,' Thanos said, low and quiet. 'I think it is one of the most incredible things I have ever seen.'

And then he jumped up, straight on to the top of the counter and putting his hands either side of his mouth, he yelled at the top of his voice.

'Everybody! Here, there is uncontrolled genius at work! She guts a fish with a pin! Come and see!' He then put his fingers inside his mouth and produced the loudest whistle, which had Lydia reaching for her ears.

'Thanos!' she said, laughing. 'Stop!'

'Why must I stop?' he asked, grinning. 'You tell me to show *my* talent. You need to show yours!'

But, as people did begin to gather round, possibly wondering why there was a very attractive Greek standing on a worktop with sea bream and a very rudimentary first aid kit, plus someone armed with a safety pin, Lydia knew that showing her talent again scared her.

Inner conflict was already tussling with her insides like the sharp end of the pin that had dealt with the fish skin. She wasn't a showman. That had been Mario. Instead, she had always been the quietly confident, usually unflappable creator behind the curtain. That had been the real difference between the way she had cooked and the way Patrick operated. And now she knew he hadn't just wanted her out of Maison Mario. He had wanted her out of cooking altogether and he had used her parents to achieve that.

As she thought over it all again, recalling snippets of conversations that should have made it obvious at the time, there was nothing but burning, white-hot fuel firing her cylinders. She *did* have talent. And her grief, heartbreak and fear had kept it hidden for long enough. Here on Corfu, it was safe to try again. No one was forcing her hand, there was no job to apply for, no one else's rules ... it was simply about the joy of food. It might be that she was a little rusty from being out of the game but, here with Thanos, it all felt very easy, and comfortable, almost like she had only downed tools the evening before.

She looked up at Thanos then, the safety pin still tight in her hand. 'Shout again,' she said. 'But ... do it even louder.'

He grinned back at her and called out to the people preparing. '*Ela! Ela!* Come! Watch this incredible chef!'

Forty-Four

Corfu Brewery, Arillas

'What's the difference again?' Caroline asked their tour guide. 'Between the red and the green ... and what is the name of the almost alcohol free one so I know which one not to bother with?'

'Caroline!' Lydia exclaimed. 'Low-alcohol beer is really popular at the moment. For some people, like with food, it's all about the taste not how drunk it's going to make you or how clogged your arteries will be when you've finished.'

Caroline was still annoyed that Lydia had left her to go with Thanos to Agios Stefanos earlier that day. Although when Lydia had told her she had spent most of the time with her fingers covered in essence of sea bream, she had perked up a little and decided her coffee and biscuits and the return to her pre-Retrace and Retreat lifestyle was probably preferable.

'The red beer, it is a real ale. It has a strong taste of caramelised malt and the bitterness of the hops,' their guide explained. 'The green beer, it is a pilsner. It is lighter in taste.'

They were standing under the impressive arches of the beer factory, looking at the large posters of some of the company's produce. It was a family-run business, like so many of this island, having been formed in 2006 by Spyros Kaloudis and his son, Thanasis. And, each year in September, it was also the site of the Corfu Beer Festival where the brewery's own beers were showcased along with drinks from another specific country. In 2019 it was Corfu meets Holland and later this year it was Belgium's turn to share the stage.

'Can we see some of the grindy machinery?' Caroline asked. 'And did you say one of your beers tastes like chocolate?'

'Yes,' the guide answered. 'Our Bitter Dark has notes of chocolate, caramel and coffee.'

'Some of my favourite "c" words right there,' Caroline said. 'If "chips" were in there too I'd probably invest like I'm Sara Davies.'

'Caroline,' Lydia began as they sat outside the brewery a little later, sampling the delights of the whole Corfu Beer range. 'Do you *really* think I'm good at my job?'

'Why?' Caroline asked. 'Don't tell me you're having some kind of epiphany ... Epiphany.' She laughed loudly. 'Ha! See what I did there?'

Lydia shook her head and turned back to her glass of Royal Ionian Pink Grapefruit and Bergamot – sugar-free and zero alcohol – taking a long, slow sip. Caroline wasn't the right person to ask that kind of question to. Her dad was usually the one she trusted with this sort of thing, and she had actually asked him something similar at the very beginning of this trip. She'd asked him if she was good at cooking. But now she really wanted to know if she was good at *writing*. Because, as much as she enjoyed highlighting great chefs, it wasn't the same as *being* the chef. But would being told her writing was top notch make any difference to how she felt? 'Forget it,' she breathed. 'It was a stupid question.'

'No,' Caroline said, sitting up a little straighter in her seat and lowering her sunglasses 'No question is stupid. Well, you know, unless you're Robert Peston.' She took a swig of the dark ale. 'You're not getting overwhelmed with this Greek edition, are you? Because we're in it together, remember? My pages are your pages. I don't know the Spanish for that, or the Greek, but you know, "solidarity" and "unity" and all the things Brightness said that weren't about blowing on your sexual parts like you're huffing at a dandelion clock.'

'No,' Lydia answered. 'It's just I've enjoyed cooking here and it's made me think about the future and ...' She wet her lips. 'Well, you know I told you about Patrick and the TV show ... well, he invited my parents to the preview evening and ... then I found out that they basically funded my severance package when I left Maison Mario.' She took a quick breath. 'And then they agreed to make sure I didn't work as a chef again because otherwise Patrick was going to tell everyone that I … attacked him.'

She had rushed the events all together in one long whoosh so she wouldn't feel so overwhelmed by it in this moment. She wasn't sure it had worked. Her heart was thumping like someone was using it to beat up egg whites.

'You attacked him?!'

And perhaps Lydia should have remembered that she had never told Caroline the final thing that had happened, the thing that left her no choice but to leave the restaurant. Well, it was too late now …

'It isn't as bad as it sounds,' Lydia stated quickly. She sipped at her drink and wished she had opted for the Epos barley wine …

'But it was bad enough that your parents thought you'd be crucified if it became public knowledge. Or …' Caroline's eyes widened. 'Prosecuted?'

Both Caroline's gaze and the heat of the sun were making Lydia feel nauseous all of a sudden. 'It was *his* fault really,' she tried to explain, edging her seat into the shade. 'He was throwing his weight around in *my* kitchen, which used to be *Mario's* kitchen, and he was going against everything Mario had taken years to set up, his way of working that I had always known and fully embraced.' She took a deep breath. 'Antonia, Mario's daughter, had inherited the business and she never liked me. I think because she lived in Italy with her mother and Mario had left there after his divorce and didn't get the chance to visit her very often, she resented me for being where she thought she deserved to be. And her jealousy, together with Patrick's desperate ambition, were the perfect storm to finish me.' She tried to swallow the rising hurt away. 'I tried to dig my heels in, I tried to keep everything steady, because I knew whatever they were planning would go against Mario's ethos but … Patrick, he wouldn't stop. When I was trying to carry on after Mario had died, it was just biting remark after biting remark and finally my eyes were opened to *all* of it. The relationship we'd had, the one he had instigated from the beginning, the same kind of relationship he was now fostering with Antonia, it had all been finely planned, it had all led to this. He'd *never* cared for me at all. He'd used me to get into the restaurant and then he didn't need me anymore, not for pleasure and now not for business. And Mario, poor sweet Mario, his heart attack had played right into Patrick's hands.'

Caroline was leaning over the table now, chin resting on her palms. 'Did you cut out his kidney and serve it for an *amuse-bouche*? Because that would amuse me, I can tell you.'

'They say offence is the best form of defence ... and he was shouting so loudly, so horribly—'

'Like Gordon Ramsay?'

'Worse. So much worse.' She didn't really want to think about it. She had tried *not* to think about it. But repressing it didn't make any of it go away.

'You pummelled him with a pestle?' Caroline asked, sitting forward on her chair.

Lydia swallowed, shaking her head as the hurt and anger and sadness she'd experienced at the time began to patter over her skin like persistent hard raindrops.

'Swung at him with a sushi mat?'

'No,' Lydia answered. 'I ... turned around quickly and he was right behind me, in my personal space.' She took another breath. 'And as I moved, I caught his hair with my knife and ... his ear.'

'What?!' Caroline exclaimed, hands going to her face.

'I'm not proud of it. But it wasn't an attack. It was an accident. *He* was the one doing the attacking, verbally at least. But that wasn't the way he saw it.' She sighed. 'He saw it as an opportunity, and I let him use it because I was too grief-stricken to do anything else.' And her parents had compounded everything.

'That fucking little shit!' Caroline hissed. 'Smiling to the camera and pronouncing bruschetta like bro-schetta because he thinks it makes him appeal to the people of Croydon.'

Lydia took a swig of her drink and blinked away unshed tears. She should have been stronger. She should have stood up to him and Antonia. She shouldn't have let herself be walked over, have her dreams ripped away.

'So, was it, you know … a whole lobe or …'

Lydia shook her head. 'No. It was a nick. A tiny piece of skin he had to Steri-Strip. And he shouldn't have had any of his hair out of his hat.'

'And that's why you left? Because The Griddler *made* you. *And* he basically blackmailed your parents.'

Lydia let out a heavy sigh. 'It wasn't just Patrick. It wasn't even just Patrick and Antonia. It was losing Mario.' She closed her eyes and right away her mind was conjuring up the stout, slick, smiling Italian who had hugged as furiously as he flambéed. 'When I walked back into that kitchen to work after he died, it was like someone had come in and painted death all over the walls. It felt black and tainted and terrifying. Everything I cooked took longer than it should have, because I couldn't focus. All the ingredients tasted sour. I kept seeing Mario in my peripheral vision, dropping to the floor, reliving what happened.' She shook her head. 'I don't know if I could have got over that. But Patrick and Antonia made it so I didn't have the choice.'

Caroline made the sucking through her teeth noise she sounded out whenever she was devilishly excited about something. 'You know what I'm thinking?' Caroline asked. 'I'm thinking an exposé.'

'Caroline, no,' Lydia said immediately, swiping a mosquito away from her face.

'Hear me out,' Caroline said, swigging from the bottle now. 'It could line up very nicely with this Greek edition. All this lovely food we've been eating, all the historic and New Age and kitschy things I've been finding, all the joyous Greekness of the people and the dancing and the bee man … and then, enter the Devil and his naff air-fryer range. If he said something in any of those arguments about a woman's place or women needing to take orders then it's definitely a case of #MeToo.'

'No,' Lydia said with authority. 'I don't want that.'

'But he crushed your career,' Caroline continued like an unstoppable train. 'No, worse than that, he created a relationship with you! Then he *orchestrated* your whole demise with a rolling pin as his baton.'

Lydia was wishing she hadn't started this now. 'And *I* shouldn't have given him the power to do that.'

'And who needs cooking anyway, right?' Caroline sighed, nodding. 'You're absolutely right. And, the answer to your question about whether you're good at your job is, of course, *yes*! I mean, no one writes about food the way you do and you're so … honest and … kind and—'

'Liable to be walked over. Never offered bribes for good reviews.' Lydia sighed.

Caroline pointed a finger. 'That is *not* a bad thing.'

'Today I filleted a fish with a safety pin,' Lydia informed her colleague.

Caroline almost coiled up in horror. 'Eww! TMI.'

'I hadn't done that for so long,' Lydia said giving a wistful sigh. 'And it felt good. It felt *freeing* almost.'

That was how *all* her cooking had felt here on Corfu. It had been taken right back to the roots, every recipe decision hers to make, no strict guide to follow, no diners needing to vacate a table in ninety minutes. It was making her realise exactly what she had been missing – and also what she hadn't.

'That's nice,' Caroline said, adjusting her sunglasses. 'But you obviously wouldn't want to *leave* the magazine, would you? I mean, we're a team, aren't we? Look at what we're achieving on this special edition. It's going to be fabulous, the best *Luxe Living* that's ever been produced.'

'I don't know,' Lydia answered.

The truth was she didn't know what she wanted. The only thing she *was* certain of was she'd missed creating meals. And with Thanos's help she was sure cooking needed to have some place in her life. But exactly how big that spot was still had to be determined.

'Right,' Caroline said, pulling her bag up from the ground and settling it on her knee. 'Well, we have work to do before you consider going back to channelling Romy Gill. So, let's have your thoughts on the beers. I'm sure you will think of a poetic way to say "unfiltered and unpasteurised".'

'Caroline,' Lydia began, 'I wasn't saying I was going to leave you in the lurch with this issue ... just that being here is making me think and ... now there's all this with my parents and Patrick and Patrick's need to ram his TV show down my social media throat—'

'I get it,' Caroline said with a sniff, putting her pen on her bottom lip. 'You can strike the bones out of something like Bear Grylls, while all I can do is suggest industrial table lamps and dishes for crudités that feature a live goldfish.'

'Goodness,' Lydia said. 'You do so much more than that! What about that article you wrote about the one-hundred-year-old hat lady? She sold out of hats as soon as the article went live online and she had to employ several staff to keep up with demand. You changed that woman's life.'

'Well ... I suppose there was that.'

'And then there was the eco-hotel on the edge of a cliff that people were too scared to stay in because the erosion was getting worse. Your article turned their business around and they stabilised the land slip.'

'I guess,' Caroline said.

'You're so talented at finding these places and selling their story,' Lydia reassured.

Caroline let out a low shaky breath and for once, Lydia's colleague seemed off-kilter. And then she answered: 'Yes. Yes, I am. And with you on my side, I *know* the magazine is going to flourish. I *know* it and I *feel* it. From the inside of my thighs, you know the muscles Brightness told us to expand and contract, to my in-need-of-a-Brazilian-blow-out hair.'

OK, that was slightly weird. All Lydia had in response was a nod.

'So, let's make some notes on these lovely beverages and then let's find somewhere nice for dinner.'

'Agreed,' Lydia answered, raising her glass to cheers.

'*Yammas*.'

'*Yammas*.'

Forty-Five

Benitses Beach

'People are looking at us,' Onassis said out of the corner of his mouth. 'And I am still meant to be grounded, yet I am at the beach.'

'This is business,' Ismēnē responded as Nuno padded around on her lap. 'We are supporting your brother.'

'But the dance troupe needs to practise tonight! I told Panos and the others to come to our garden at nine o'clock and to be quiet so Thanos does not know they are there but—'

'Hush,' Ismēnē ordered. 'Remember what we talked about? No secrets in the family. Everything out in the open and working together.'

'But you said that—'

'Sshh, not now, Onassis.'

They thought Thanos couldn't hear them, but the sea breeze was delivering every single word as he stood in front of his very rustic, very makeshift kitchen on the sand. There were very few tourists on sun loungers now but the ones that were still making the most of the evening sun did look like they were wondering why someone had set up a table and chairs and a terribly configured temporary kitchen by the sea. *Preparation. Repetition. Performance.* He had no qualms about selling his food at the festival, he had even baked several batches of the flower biscuits already, but he was worried about the 'show' aspect. His cooking wasn't usually the spectacle, the end result was. But now he was going to be expected to entertain, so this was what this dry run was for. He had decided what he was going to cook, so it made sense to make it in front of Onassis and Ismēnē. For them to be his guinea pigs …

'Are you ready?' Thanos called to them, fingers tightening the bandana he had tied around his head.

'We are starving!' Ismēnē heckled. 'We have paid for tickets, and we are expecting to be entertained!'

He swallowed. Of course Ismēnē would not go easy on him. He had to remember that tomorrow evening he was going to be cooking in front of an audience who were expecting great things.

'OK,' he called back. 'Tonight, I will be showing you how to make … vegetarian pakoras.'

'Pakoras?' Ismēnē shouted. 'This is not Greek!'

'I do not only make Greek food!'

'You are in Greece!'

'Hoping to one day leave!'

He didn't know why he was joining in with this shouting back and forth. It was unlikely that anyone watching at the food festival would be doing this. He knew not making something Greek was a risk in this situation, but what was life without taking risks? Ismēnē had suggested he made something different! And taking chances had basically become Ismēnē's mantra over the past few months so why was she assuming now he would go back to basics?

'Is there feta cheese in the recipe?' Onassis called.

'No,' Thanos replied.

'Can there be?' his brother shouted again.

Thanos put his hands on his hips. 'Will you stop interrupting me! I am trying to present my dish for the evening.'

'You cannot be rude!' Ismēnē said, taking a hip flask from the pocket of her dress and drinking a hearty swig. Nuno tried to lick the rim. 'This is why we are testing you. Later, no matter how it tastes, I will say it is disgusting and you must not react.'

Thanos shook his head. This was not close to reality at all. Maybe he should have simply cooked at home in his kitchen and not set up this farce. He closed his eyes and refocused. No, he was going to remember how it felt cooking the sea bream with Lydia earlier that day and how much they had laughed together and enjoyed each other's company. *She* thought he was good. She thought his cooking deserved recognition. She had only met him such a short time ago, yet she currently had more faith in him than he had in himself. And, after today, her sharing her story about working with Mario Romano and showing him her trick with the pin, he felt he was beginning to get under her surface. Discover the Lydia she had been holding back. But what rocked him the most was how he *wanted* to know even more. She was getting under his barriers and into his skin like the sweetest new tattoo …

'Ladies and gentlemen,' he said with as much confidence as he could muster. 'Prepare to be amazed! As I prepare for you, the tastiest … the best … the most succulent vegetarian pakoras you have ever tried!'

'Better!' Ismēnē called. 'But I think we might need something else on the night. Something to spice things up a bit!'

'Like cayenne pepper?' Onassis suggested.

'No,' Ismēnē said, looking as if she were musing on an idea. 'Something *hotter*. Perhaps a little dangerous.'

'Like a tiger?' Onassis responded.

'Let us begin!' Thanos cut in with volume. 'We will start, of course, with extra virgin Greek olive oil.' He grabbed up the bottle and concentrated on what he was doing. Right now, the only way forward was to block out his audience, pretend the evening sun wasn't making him sweat and to give all his attention to his ingredients. Perhaps that was all he had to do at the festival. Maybe, outwardly, the set-up might be different, but how he approached it should be exactly the same.

'Let's make taste!' he said, clapping his hands together.

Forty-Six

Coconut Bar, Arillas

'So, let me get this straight, you judge food on the four "L" words.'

Lydia smiled at Caroline who was already three Mai-Tai cocktails down. They were enjoying the night air, the humidity dropping and the mosquitos less prevalent now the sky was dark. This bar was understated perfection like most places they had found on this island. Inside there were wooden beams and green vines, the stone wall of the bar fully stocked with every spirit you could imagine and some you probably could not and there was live music entertaining patrons, a mix of guitars and a singer. Outside there were comfy chairs and lush plants and cosy lighting, it was exactly the right place for winding down before they headed back to their apartment.

'"Look",' Caroline continued, '"Lay", "Linger" and ... and ... what was the last one?'

'"Last", Lydia said. 'How could you forget it? It's the "last" one.'

'It's not me forgetting,' Caroline insisted. 'It's these cocktails.' She smacked her lips together and lay back into her chair. 'So, talk me through these "L's". I want to know how you approach a meal you're reviewing. You know, unlike the rest of us who just pick up their knife and fork and crack on.'

'It's not quite as scientific as it sounds. It's just a guide I made up so I don't forget all the important elements that make up an eating experience.'

'And why haven't you told me this before?'

'Well, I wasn't sure it would be something you're interested in.'

Caroline now wore an expression that said she was a little put out. 'You didn't think I could try it.'

'No,' Lydia said quickly. 'No, not at all.' Well, perhaps she *had* thought that, but debating with Caroline after a carafe of wine and cocktails full of aged rum wasn't ever the greatest plan.

'Well, I am going to prove you wrong,' Caroline announced. 'With … these crisps.' She pulled over the bowl of snacks they had been given and, with two fingers, she took one of the cone shapes out. 'So, talk me through it. I "look".' Caroline studied the crisp as if it was going to open up wide and shoot stardust from its wheaty core.

'Yes,' Lydia said, toying with the straw in her cocktail glass. 'Does it look appealing? Does it have a balance to the dish – colour, texture, health.' She wrinkled her nose. 'It's pretty hard to make it work with a crisp.'

'I give it marks for style. It's horn-shaped, not flat and it has ridges on it.'

'See!' Lydia told her. 'You're looking at it more closely than you would before. Now, pop it on your tongue and give me your instant reaction. But don't move your mouth.'

'I've never been asked that before,' Caroline answered with a wink. She put the crisp into her mouth then stuck out her tongue.

Lydia laughed. 'You don't need to put your tongue out. Keep it in. This is "lay". What does it feel like?'

'Like I have a weird-shaped crisp on my tongue.'

'Is it heavy or light? Are you getting any other sensations, any first flavours?'

'How long do I have to hold it on here?'

'OK, do "linger" now. So, you push the food *all* around your mouth. You need to taste *everything* about the mouthful. And your tastebuds aren't just on your tongue, you know.'

'What?' Caroline asked. 'Where else are they?'

'You have them on the roof of your mouth and also in your throat.'

'Good God!'

'I'm not sure how accurate this is going to be for you,' Lydia said. But she couldn't deny she was enjoying watching Caroline take longer to eat this one crisp than she had an entire meal in almost all the time she'd known her.

'It's dissolving! It's disappearing! What do I do? What do I do?' Caroline was waving her hand in front of her mouth now like she had swallowed someone's prize queen bee.

'It's fine,' Lydia said. 'Chew slowly, then swallow and finally tell me what the lasting sensation is.'

As she waited for Caroline to complete the 'challenge' her phone buzzed from her bag. It was going to be her dad again. She'd had more calls from him earlier, nothing further from her mother which wasn't surprising. Once her mother made an effort and was rebuked there was usually no second coming. But on looking at her phone, she saw it was an unknown number. *Scammer*, it had to be. She let it stop ringing. But then, immediately, it started again. A different number.

'Lasting sensation,' Caroline said, swinging a hand towards her cocktail. 'Dry mouth, beef flavouring, it's a bit like inhaling an Oxo cube! It's not as good as those bacon ones.'

Lydia pressed the button to connect. 'Hello.'

'Hi, is that Lydia Broom?' a female voice asked.

'Er, yes, who is calling please?'

Caroline was coughing now and Lydia got to her feet to move away from the table, heading towards the step down out of the Coconut Bar and down onto the road.

'My name's Gemma. I'm calling from *News Central London* and I just wanted to talk to you about the video and all the reaction to it so far and ask you a little bit about what your plans are for the future. Have you been flying under the radar because you have something exciting up your sleeve?'

It was all rattled out at quick speed, like rapid machine-gun fire and Lydia had no idea what the woman was talking about. But her phone was also still making noises, as more calls lined themselves up.

'Video?' she said out loud what had meant to be a thought. And it was then the cogs began to whir. 'Sorry, I have to be somewhere.'

Ending the call she headed back into the bar, all the while tapping on the screen of her phone. This was madness. It wasn't going to be this. She was simply thinking about Bonnie and her obsession with anything served up to her TikTok. This wasn't that. Except … what else could it be?

'I said it's like inhaling stock!' Caroline exclaimed as Lydia came back to the table. 'Hold on, what's wrong with your face?'

'I just need to check something.'

'Lottery numbers? Dick pic from Thanos?'

Lydia wasn't really listening, she was typing random words into the search box she had up. And then, suddenly, there it was. Or rather, there *she* was.

'Lyds! I'm right here! Talk to me!'

'I … can't,' Lydia said, struggling to catch her breath as she took in what was in front of her.

It was a video on YouTube, of her expertly stripping the sea bream with the safety pin and whoever had videoed it had added the tune of a sea shanty.

'Let me see,' Caroline said, leaning over her and putting a hand around the phone. 'Ugh! That's you with that grim fish … wait, is that really how many likes it has?'

'Twenty-five thousand,' Lydia said, her voice shaking.

'And … what?! Two hundred *thousand* views! In a couple of hours! Wait, two hundred thousand and six hundred and twenty-eight … thirty … forty-nine …'

'Reporters are phoning me,' Lydia said, passing Caroline her phone. 'This is a nightmare.'

'No,' Caroline said, almost gleeful. 'This is *brilliant*.'

Forty-Seven

The Agios Stefanos Food Festival, Agios Stefanos

It was a beautiful start to the day. The sky was cloudless and the heat was moderate, although it was expected to rise to a high of twenty-eight degrees later on. Thanos was glad he hadn't risked baking anything with cream. He had a large fridge on his stall, but he didn't like anything like that to be left too long. He'd stuck to the borage biscuits, Brookies – a cross between brownies and cookies – and cupcakes – some infused with chamomile tea and others with yellow fondant icing and the faces of emojis on them. He was also planning to cook his own vegan version of *gyros* throughout the day, using cauliflower and a marinade of mustard, paprika and cumin to give it that ultimate authentic Greek taste. There was not an oven here, but he had adapted a couple of pressure cookers to be able to do that job on the hob. He had listened to Ismēnē's suggestion about keeping something Greek, but he also wanted to showcase that it wasn't the only cuisine he could excel at.

Being here at all was fortuitous. Now he had the chance to make some money from selling his wares and have the attention on his cooking later that evening. He was also going to be giving out flyers for his next pop-up restaurant night. Again, Ismēnē's many connections had come through with a large boat that would be docked at Agni Bay and diners would be paying a lot more than they had at the ruins in Benitses for a four-course meal. Quality not quantity this time, and pre-booking was essential.

And Makis was here to help on the stall. Although the only thing his friend had done so far was drink all the coffee. He was also somehow getting under Thanos's feet no matter where he positioned himself.

'*Kalimera*.'

Thanos looked up from his cake arrangement and there was Lydia, as perfect as ever. Today her hair was tied back again in a ponytail that was sectioned off with other hairbands. It was a good look on her ... and he needed to say 'good morning'.

'Good morning,' he answered. 'You look ...' He stopped himself. What had he been going to say next? Amazing? Beautiful?

'Tired?' Lydia answered for him, a finger dragging at the bottom of her eye. 'Honestly, Caroline has been driving me crazy and keeping me awake trying to spin the viral fish video into an article for *Luxe Living*. Last night it was something along the lines of "Does social media still have a plaice". That's "plaice" as in "a-i-c-e" like the fish. And the night before it was more "Oh My Cod". It would be funny if it wasn't so tragic.'

Thanos smiled. 'I have watched the video. I like the song they used.'

'Which one? Because the remix to a Rihanna tune is picking up in views.'

He had watched the video more than a few times and he hadn't watched it for any of the background music. He had replayed it to see Lydia, making light work of the tricky job with the rustic approach, the way her fingers moved, how she explained what she was doing for those who were watching, the light hitting her hair. There were a few shots of him in the background too, and what got to him the most when he saw himself, was how relaxed he seemed, how happy he appeared, how at peace. But how much of that attitude was from being away from Baptiste and the annoying stresses of Taverna Ilios and how much of that was down to being around Lydia? Things were still uncemented between them and he felt as if they were both somehow waiting for the other. Was that a sign that neither of them were ready for anything more than the one evening they had shared at Sokraki? Did he need Lydia to say something or do something to give permission for transparency on his part? Where did this go if they both wanted it to move?

'Caroline knows all the words to the sea shanty,' Lydia continued, breaking his thoughts. 'The radio in the car isn't working so we had her singing on repeat.' She put her hands to one of his boxes, ready to pop cakes or biscuits in as soon as they opened for business. 'These look great.'

'They are too plain, maybe?' Thanos asked, handling another brown cardboard box. 'At late notice there was not a lot of choice so ...'

'Brown is good,' Lydia reassured. 'It looks expensive when it's a box and it represents the earth and people associate that with health.'

'Wow,' Thanos said, smiling. 'That is a lot of information you have got from cardboard.'

'Oh,' Lydia said. 'I remember when we began doing takeaway at Maison Mario. After Mario had got over the shock that his divine dishes were going to be put into boxes at all, he paid someone ridiculous amounts of money to make sure the packaging was exactly right.'

'And they came up with brown boxes?'

'Are you mocking the evolution of creative packaging?' Lydia asked, one eyebrow raising.

'I am glad this was all the store had and it was not that expensive.'

'You should sign them,' Lydia told him, readjusting the bag on her shoulder.

'Sign them?'

'The boxes,' she explained. 'Not now. But, whenever you make a sale, you should sign them.'

'Like an autograph?' He shook his head. It sounded crazy. That someone might think something of his name written on top of a box of his cakes.

'Like a *brand*,' Lydia told him with a nod of certainty.

A brand. Was that what his food could become? Signature dishes that might one day be made into ready meals, available in supermarkets across Greece? Across the world? Before his mind could run away with that idea, the pressure cooker on the stove shifted and he jumped, grabbing for the lid.

'That smells so good,' Lydia said, leaning into the stand and inhaling. 'What is it?'

'*Gyros*,' Thanos answered. 'But the vegan kind. Cauliflower.'

'I like it,' Lydia told him. 'Will you ... show me how you make it later?'

Was this Lydia saying she wanted to spend more time with him? Or was this simply a request from one chef to another? What did he want it to be? His insides seemed to be giving a definite pulse to the thought of spending more time with her whatever the primary reason behind it.

'I will,' he answered. 'So, what are your plans for the day?'

'Well, I am going around taking photos of all the stalls and stands and making notes, talking to people, while Caroline sunbathes and lets me get on with it.'

'It seems like you are doing all the hard work,' Thanos told her.

'Oh, no,' Lydia answered. 'Caroline, she's doing all the liaising with the office back in the UK about this edition we're creating. She's constantly getting feedback on what we've put together so far so we can tweak things and focus on the concepts they are definitely going to run with.'

'Well, please, take these Brookies and some biscuits, because it sounds like you are going to have a busy time.'

He carefully put three of each item into a box and folded over the sides to secure them. Smiling, he handed it over to her.

'Haven't you forgotten something?' Lydia asked, not taking the offering.

He didn't understand. Then: 'Oh! Would you like a drink too? I have the apple tea or there is olive water or fresh lemonade.'

'No, Thanos,' Lydia said, laughing. 'The money for one.' She unzipped the bag over her shoulder and took out the required amount of euros. Then she laid something else on the counter. A Sharpie. 'And sign the box!'

'Really?' Thanos asked. 'This will make me a brand?' He took the lid off the pen.

‘Yes,’ Lydia replied. ‘And, when everyone tastes this food, well, that’s going to make you a star.’

He held her gaze, her words spiralling around in the humid air until he allowed them to sink into him. He pressed the pen to the top of the box and signed. *Thanos*.

Forty-Eight

'I feel sick.'

'You are fine. Unless you have been eating too much. Have you been eating too much?'

'I am Greek, is there ever eating too much?'

Thanos tried to block out the conversation between Onassis and Ismēnē that was going on right beside him. Now night was beginning to fall, the attention had gone from the stalls around the perimeter of the sand to the circular kitchen in the middle. Spotlights were overhead, the chairs surrounding the cooking area were full, the air was filled with the sound of wooden spoon meets wok or blade meets chopping board and the scent was an infusion of garlic, spice and herbs. Thanos was using these last moments to try to remain calm, but also he was watching the chef who was cooking in the sand arena right now. This guy had definitely done this kind of thing before; his knife skills were off the charts, everything seemed to be going perfectly and he had the crowd in the palm of his hand. Everyone had their eyes on centre stage and no one was talking. How was Thanos going to follow this? His chest tightened and those doubts started to creep in …

'Let me make some final adjustments to your outfit,' Ismēnē said.

This recipe the chef was making was *Assam Laksa* and Thanos had only made it once when he was able to get together ingredients to substitute for the ones he wasn't able to find on Corfu. It was a dish from Malaysia. How was he going to wow the audience with vegetarian *pakoras*?

Suddenly he jumped. Ismēnē had ripped his top down one side and was cutting into the fabric with scissors. 'What are you doing?!'

'I tell you,' Ismēnē exclaimed as Thanos fought her off. 'Making some alterations to your outfit.'

He looked down at the shirt that was now half-missing, most of his body exposed. 'Ismēnē, I am meant to be a chef, not a ...'

'Stripper?'

Thanos jumped at the comment that had come from Caroline. She and Lydia had suddenly arrived next to them on the sand.

Caroline laughed, fingers pulling at Thanos's top. 'Go out there like this, I'm going to be living my *Magic Mike Live* fantasies all over again.'

Thanos swallowed, feeling bare in almost all respects as his eyes fell on Lydia. She had changed from what she was wearing earlier. Now she was dressed in a short, pale blue dress, the material swooping over her every curve. If there really was any doubt about whether he wanted to revisit their intimacy in Sokraki, it was evaporating faster than an August raindrop right now.

'*Kalispera*,' Ismēnē greeted. 'You are the writers from England, here to make notes about Thanos's performance.'

'Hello,' Caroline greeted. 'Are you his manager?'

'No,' Onassis responded. 'I am.'

Thanos watched his brother grin and then he realised he had to make this interaction stop. He hadn't told Lydia about Onassis. He had only just told her about his parents no longer being here. She thought he was free to make his own decisions and to reach for culinary stars but, the truth was, he wasn't ready. Not here when he was already feeling stressed. Not yet.

He took Lydia's hand and drew her away, stepping back over the sand to find some space and some air. When he stopped and she was right there looking at him as if he was slightly insane, he realised he was shaking.

'Thanos, are you OK?'

He shook his head. 'Have you been watching ... the other chefs?'

'You're shaking,' she whispered, still holding on to his hands.

'I ... they ... are all so good,' he said, his eyes travelling back over to the chef in the spotlight now, flames flashing from his wok.

'It's a food festival,' Lydia reminded him. 'The people here all love food to some degree. It would be very disappointing if the chefs weren't good.'

His bandana felt tight. 'But, what if I'm not good? I have never done this before. They all seem like this situation is everyday work for them.'

'Thanos, listen to me,' Lydia said firmly, squeezing his hands in hers. 'You are good. You are *excellent*. I told you the first time you cooked for me exactly *how* good you are. I don't say that lightly. Your orzo, remember? It was better than Mario's.'

He looked deep into her eyes then, as if he was searching for her expression to change, for her to take the compliment back or say that she didn't mean it. But there was nothing else there, nothing but pure, vast truth.

'Better than Mario's?' Thanos asked.

'If he can hear me up there,' Lydia said, her eyes briefly raising to the sky, 'he will be absolutely livid. But, yes, for my palate, your recipe was superior.'

He squeezed her hands back, taking a second to enjoy the rush of adrenaline the comment had given him. To look at Lydia a few seconds more ...

'And, if you want to hear some more honesty ... the chefs who have cooked tonight, well, it's all a bit showy for me. The food looks good, but they're throwing knives around and putting on a spectacle. I wonder if it's a bit smoke and mirrors. Maybe the food doesn't taste as great as it should. Or maybe it's what the crowd expect. I don't know.'

'One of them cut a watermelon with a Samurai sword,' Thanos answered.

She laughed. 'Exactly! And watermelon, it's so overdone.'

'It is easy to get here. Baptiste would carve faces into them for decoration. Such a waste.'

He felt his body loosen up a little and he shrugged his shoulders up and down, trying to flex away the tension.

'Do you feel any better?' Lydia asked him as she released his hands.

'A little ... maybe if I was not wearing something that has been carved open.' He pulled the shirt away from his torso.

'Well,' Lydia began. 'I can't say I *entirely* disapprove of the amendment to the outfit.'

'No?' he responded, the word crawling up his throat.

'No,' she said, edging towards him.

God, he wanted to hold her again, feel her lips on his, the weight of her against him. What was stopping him? What was making him think longer and act slower? She was right here, her eyes alive, a touch away ... *You love, you lose*. He blinked. A tattoo. Not one on him, but one he had come across on the internet. He had looked at that one, considered it for longer than others, wondered about the truth of it. His parents, gone. His brother, permanently angry with him. Caring about people made life difficult. And that was the difference between Lydia and the other women who had been in his life. With Lydia, he was already starting to care ... but was it time now? To trust his instincts? To trust someone else and show his fears and vulnerability?

He reached out for her, his fingers grazing her neat hair.

'Thaaanno!'

He withdrew his hand at the sound of Ismēnē's calling. 'I have to go.' He made to move.

'Listen,' Lydia said.

He stopped in the sand and held her gaze.

'I ... just wanted to say ... you are going to be brilliant. You *are* brilliant and whatever you've got cooking up, well ... I can't wait to taste it.'

Thanos swallowed, all his feelings for her spiralling up like he'd put the lid on the blender and set the controller to maximum. He took her hand and squeezed tight. 'Thank you,' he whispered.

Forty-Nine

Thanos was fidgeting, moving his feet on the sand, waiting for the clearing up of the previous chef, watching the VIP guests eating their food. They all seemed to be enjoying it, tucking in and nodding their heads as they conversed about it. Were they going to enjoy his dishes as much? What if it didn't go well? Did he have anything else he could make instead of the pakoras? Perhaps Ismēnē had been right. Maybe everyone else was thinking outside of the box and no one here was going to make anything Greek ...

'Should I go up now?' he asked Ismēnē as the crew sanitising everything seemed to be done. He was wringing his hands together. They were sweating, not the best thing for a chef who was going to be handling pans and plates in front of a live audience.

'No,' Ismēnē answered. 'Be still. Be very still. I will tell you when you can move.' She drew in a breath, her gaze somewhere between the arena and the sky. 'I think, Thano, that your mother would be very proud of you right now. Your father too.'

'I do not know,' he said, letting a breath out and adjusting his bandana. 'If they could see me right now they would be wondering why I am halfway across the island when I should be in sensible employment, looking after my brother.'

'When you say that,' Ismēnē began, turning to look at him, 'it makes me think that you believe they had no hopes for your future.'

Thanos sighed, watching the food festival's evening presenter take to the stage. 'They did not live long enough to be able to think about my future.'

'Thano,' Ismēnē said. 'You know they thought cooking was your future. It was obvious. And if they were here now they would be doing everything they could to make your dream happen. You cannot blame them for getting into an accident.'

Thanos shook his head. He needed not to be having this conversation right now. 'No, of course not.'

Ismēnē grabbed his arm and held on tight. 'What I am trying to say, Thano, is you have been a chef from the moment you made your first dish. After that it only got better! The second you found that joy in the kitchen and shared it with your mama and papa ... and then the rest of the village. No one had any doubt that you would have any other career than with food ... that you would succeed.'

He squeezed his eyes tight shut, the memories beginning to overwhelm him. *Those smells.* His mother's favourite recipe filling the kitchen space, the garlic and thyme fragrancing the air, their pleasure as he served up the hearty meal for the family. *Making taste.*

'And now, we welcome ... Chef Thanos Nicolaidis!'

Thanos dragged his mind back to the beach and put one foot forward ... until Ismēnē pulled him back.

'No,' she said. 'Not quite yet.'

Suddenly all the lights went out and Caroline grabbed Lydia's arm, making her handbag fall to the floor. 'What's going on?! It's the ruins all over again!'

'How am I supposed to know what's going on? I'm not on the organising committee,' Lydia replied, trying to adjust her eyes to the darkness.

'Well, you're practically in a relationship with one of the guys taking part!'

In a relationship. No, she wasn't. Was she? A trickle of heat oozed down her spine as she thought about Thanos. They shared so many mutual ideas about cooking and people and how they'd like the world to be, and he was so hot, but ... but what? But she couldn't because she hadn't come here prepared to meet someone? But she couldn't because she hadn't trusted anyone enough to even take up the invitation of a drink since Patrick? But she couldn't because in a week or so she would be a thousand miles away?

All Lydia's thoughts took a detour to the back row of her mind when some of the lights burst on again and in front of the arena kitchen now were six, maybe seven, teenage boys dressed in black suits with bright silver stripe embellishments.

'Jesus!' Caroline exclaimed. 'It's like the Backstreet Boys in child size. Back Beach Boys? Get it? Because they're on the sand?'

Lydia didn't reply. She couldn't take her eyes off the scene. What was going on? Thanos had just been announced and now there was something else happening? She looked for him, to try to find out how he was reacting to it. Did he know about this?

A thumping beat kicked in, and then the music began, loudly. A thrumming drum-based pop tune. Next the boys started to move, all completely in synch like they were one.

This was unexpected but they were actually *really* good. And the crowd seemed to be enjoying it as the boys backflipped and pumped their hips to the music. Breakdancing ensued, sand being kicked and spun up from the earth in a blur of sequins and trainers.

'Gosh,' Caroline remarked. 'It's gone all *Britain's Got Talent*. Where's the Golden Buzzer?'

Thanos was staring out at Onassis and his friends as they performed on the beach right in front of where he was going to be cooking. He felt disorientated by it, thrown off his game. He hadn't been expecting it and as good as it was, he didn't know when it was going to end, when it would be his turn to get into the spotlight.

'The routine is only two minutes and thirty seconds,' Ismēnē whispered, her body going up and down in time to the music. 'I got them to trim it down to a special version for tonight.'

'I do not understand what is going on,' Thanos admitted. 'This is not Onassis disobeying me again? You knew about this?'

'Of course!' Ismēnē exclaimed. 'Tonight it is show-cooking, like I told you from the very beginning. It has to have razzamatazz! Pizzazz! And the hands of jazz.' She shook her hands in the air, making her fingers quiver.

'Ismēnē,' Thanos said. 'What happened to everything being out in the open and no secrets?'

'This is not a secret,' Ismēnē stated. 'This was a *surprise*. The two things are very different.'

He did not think they were different at all. This was simply a convenient way for Ismēnē to get her way again. Except ... were the crowd now clapping along in time to the music and getting invested in the routine? Thanos paid proper attention – perhaps watching would help his nerves. There was his brother, front and centre, whining his waist, falling down onto one hand and doing something artistic with his feet, *leading* this troupe. He was so grown now. He might officially still be a child, but he was changing. He was taller and stronger and he definitely voiced his opinions. Perhaps that's where Thanos had been going wrong. Had he been stifling Onassis instead of protecting him?

As the dancers performed their final spins, Thanos knew what was coming next. Starting with Panos at the bottom, the boys began to tier themselves up, one on top of another in turn until finally Onassis was at the very pinnacle, standing on Stamatis's shoulders, arms outstretched, face to the audience, holding still for the final beat drop ...

And then they tumbled to the ground like skittles.

Fifty

'Ladies and gentlemen, the best way to cook an octopus is slowly and at an even temperature. So, if you sit back and relax for the next three or four hours, then you will be able to taste the most exquisite dish.'

There was complete and utter silence for a moment, the only sounds Thanos's boiling pan of hot water and the rushing of the waves. He clapped his hands together and felt glad he had brought the ready-to-go octopus and pasta as a back-up plan. The pakoras had suddenly felt inadequate after Ismēnē had talked about his mother.

'That is, of course, a joke! Because we do not have the time, I have pre-prepared the octopus using lemon juice, shallots, capers, oregano and parsley. So, we will start with the onion ...'

'Want some popcorn?' Caroline asked, passing a bag to Lydia as they watched.

'Ugh, no,' Lydia whispered. 'I'm saving myself for some of what Thanos makes.'

'I thought the food was only for the VIP customers. It's a crime we're not VIP customers, but I guess we were late to finding out about the party.'

'Well,' Lydia said, 'if there isn't any left then he can make me some more.'

'Perks of being so close to his grill it might roast you,' Caroline said, laughing loudly as she poured popcorn into her mouth. 'Anyway, I thought you said he was making pakoras not octopus.'

Yes, Lydia *had* said that because that was what Thanos had told her. Why the change in recipe? Not that she thought it was a bad decision. The seafood was so fresh here it was practically still swimming and it was that freshness that would make all the difference when it came to taste.

'You have ten minutes remaining.'

It was a digital voice, like something you might set to remind you of a wake-up call. But where was it coming from? It had been loud enough for them to hear in the crowd and it had also stopped Thanos from explaining his steps in the recipe.

'Ooh, that was a bit creepy. And I didn't hear that when the other chefs were on. Are they running short on time or something?' Caroline asked.

'I don't know,' Lydia answered. Focusing on the kitchen in the centre of the arena, she could see it had thrown Thanos a little. He wasn't moving with confidence, he wasn't engaging with his audience, everything seemed to be internalised – no good when you were needing to put on a display.

And then the digital voice said something else: 'Nine minutes and thirty seconds until the sprinklers are activated.'

Caroline gasped and rose up on her seat. 'Oh my! That's a game changer! Sprinklers! Gushing water all over the food if he's not done in time. It's like *Ready Steady Cook* dialled up to eleven.'

Lydia was looking directly at Thanos. He'd stopped talking, he'd stopped moving and white-hot fear seemed to be the only expression he was wearing. And then she saw it: hosepipes positioned over the galley, their spray jet heads all pointing in the direction of the cooking area. Could they move them? No, it would take too long and distract from the creation of the food. This was Thanos's moment to showcase his talent. She took a deep breath. There was only one way to solve this ...

'None of the other chefs did anything like this! This is marvellous!' Caroline continued. 'Dancing and now *danger*. I reckon we could pitch this as a format to the BBC.'

Lydia's fingers were already working on her hair. She dragged the hairbands from the ponytail and started to create something different with it. Calmly, confidently, knowing exactly what she was going to do.

'He's going to need a better name if we take him to England,' Caroline stated, bouncing in her seat, jostling popcorn. 'Thanos

Nicolaidis doesn't roll off the tongue, does it? Way too many letters and no one will know where the "I's" go.' She gasped. 'How about ... The Bull?!' She seemed to muse on it for a second and then she gasped again. 'No, not The Bull. The Ox! He could make his entrance to a paso doble, with a cape and—'

'I'm going up there,' Lydia said. She twirled a hairband into the end of her second plait and got to her feet.

'What?' Caroline said, her voice a whole less excitable now.

'This isn't some game show to fantasise about. This is Thanos's life. He's a fantastic chef, who deserves to be discovered but not like this. Not with cheap tricks and ... you talking about capes and bulls!'

'Think I settled on The Ox.'

'I'm going to help him get these dishes done and you are going to round up that troupe of dancers and anyone else you can find and stand by.' She adjusted the strap on her dress. 'Because when we're plating up, I want everything off the worktop and taken down to those VIP guests before one drop of water falls.'

Fifty-One

Thanos knew who had done this. Who else could it be? This was another 'surprise' from Ismēnē. Well, this time she had outdone herself and he was set to be the embarrassment of Corfu, here on a beach in front of hundreds of onlookers, taking photos, videoing. He tried to seek Ismēnē out amongst the audience, but the lights were so bright. He had lost his way. In all respects. He didn't know where he was with his recipe and he hadn't said a word in maybe a minute. He looked down at his worktop, attempted to work out which utensils had moved from the spaces he had set them in.

'Ladies and gentlemen! Surprise! Tonight, well, it's full of surprises, isn't it? Dancing and *danger*! Wow! Well, if you thought that was more than enough ... you're wrong!'

It was Lydia. On stage. Here with him. It took Thanos a second to realise this was really happening. She was taking charge of the situation, speaking to the crowd ...

'My name is Lydia Broom or, as YouTubers are calling me at the moment, Bream-anna. But, if you aren't one of the two million people who have watched me gut a fish with a safety pin, then you have no idea who I am and you're probably wondering why I'm stood here babbling on when there are approximately eight minutes until it gets very wet up in here.'

She looked to Thanos.

'Although,' she continued, 'we might all need a little dousing down when we've got a chef this hot. Am I right, ladies and gentlemen?'

There were some cat calls and whistles from the audience and then Lydia was right beside him, her expression firm and determined.

'Listen to me,' she whispered. 'I don't know what's going on with hosepipes and stuff but we both know what a whole lot of water is going to do to the food if this isn't done in time.'

'It is a disaster,' Thanos answered her.

'No,' Lydia said. 'Not yet, it isn't. And it won't be if I have anything to do with it. You are going to embrace this challenge like you knew it was happening and treat me like your sous chef.' She wrinkled her nose. 'Why are there bananas and avocado and dates here?'

Thanos sighed. 'I am making two courses.'

'Seven minutes remaining,' the electronic voice announced.

'OK,' Lydia said, taking a deep breath. 'OK, so, they want excitement and danger. Let's give it to them.' She smiled out at the crowd like she was used to performing this way. 'Seven minutes! Well, that would be a piece of beautifully made cake for Thanos here if I hadn't come along. But, you know, I like a thrill ride so, let's see if we can make spicy octopus and macaroni and ...'

'Chocolate avocado mousse with orange,' Thanos vocalised.

'And that ... all in seven minutes ... *tied together*.'

'What?' Thanos said only to Lydia. 'What do you mean "tied together".'

'Trust me. It's easier than you think. Mario and I did it once. Ankles not hands.'

'Why would we do that? We already have to get this food out with no time at all.'

'You're panicking. Stop panicking. You need to play to your audience,' she said. 'Sorry, everyone,' Lydia called to the people seated on the beach. 'Thanos isn't used to being tied up anywhere but the bedroom.'

There were more whoops and laughs and Thanos felt overwhelmed and out of his depth. He didn't understand what this was now.

Suddenly Lydia was winding something around his ankle. What was it? Dental floss? He moved his leg and hers came too. This was craziness.

'Thanos, this audience want good food,' Lydia carried on quietly. 'But their priority tonight is to be entertained. You want them to remember you more than anyone else. In this situation, they are *always* going to remember the spectacle first. But then, when the food is also the best they've had, they aren't even going to be *thinking* about any other chef.'

Despite feeling like he was drowning, what other choice did he have? He nodded.

'Good, now tell the crowd the next steps and I'll be here in the background, well, you know, tied to you, chopping whatever needs to be chopped.'

It was under seven minutes, but fail or succeed, this whole scenario was going to be done then and he could escape. Never before had he felt that way about cooking and he hated it.

'Ladies and gentlemen, for my next trick,' Thanos said, trying to brighten for the sake of entertainment. 'I will make this octopus and macaroni and chocolate avocado mousse while I am tied to Bream-anna ... before we need an umbrella.'

Fifty-Two

'One minute remaining.'

One minute! *One* minute! Lydia's heart felt like it was chasing around her other body parts, begging them to catch up. What if they couldn't do this? She'd feel as if she had let him down. They needed to plate up quickly! They should be plating up already. The mousse was done but she didn't want to go ahead and present it *her* way. This was Thanos's kitchen and she still wasn't sure he was going to thank her for even being here, despite the urgency of the situation. Maybe she should have stayed in her seat, *why* had she thought it was a good idea to tie them together? Her ankle was burning with the pressure of being pulled one way and the other as Thanos moved from burners to blender and back again.

'We are doing this,' Thanos whispered to her. 'Please put the mousse in ramekins, mint tips and orange slices on top.'

'OK,' Lydia answered, spinning around, momentarily forgetting she was anchored to him. She inched forward a little, reaching for the bowl, then began to serve up.

Out of the corner of her eye she could see Caroline, the dance troupe and a few other people her colleague seemed to have taken ownership of, poised at the side of the stage, hopefully ready to deliver the food. Was this going to work? She shook her head, her plaits moving, sticky at her scalp. It might be outside, but here with the humidity and the hob and the stress of a countdown, things were about as boiling as they could be …

'And here we have it!' Thanos announced to the crowd. 'Spicy octopus and macaroni. Almost exactly as my mother used to make.'

Lydia side-eyed the dish as she paused between serving up the mousse. It looked spectacular, the octopus was the star of the plate, the colour was perfect and just from observing it you could tell it was going to be moist perfection on the palate. And he had used thyme, her favourite herb … and she needed to concentrate. She didn't want to disappoint him.

'Everything is OK?' Thanos asked her softly, body close.

'Everything is fine. Two more to go.'

'Bream-anna says everything is fine,' Thanos told her audience.

'Thirty seconds remaining … twenty-nine, twenty-eight …'

'We have time to dance, I think!' Thanos announced.

'What?!' Lydia exclaimed as he turned his body and she went with him, her leg still very much part of his. What a dumb idea that was!

'Twenty-six, twenty-five …'

'Onassis!' Thanos called out. 'Two last mousses. Then get everyone to take the trays. Fast!'

One of the glittery 'Back Beach Boys' came running onto the stage as Lydia found herself whirled around to Thanos whistling the beginnings of a song she couldn't fail to recognise. It was the only Greek song she knew. 'Zorba the Greek'.

'Twenty, nineteen, eighteen …'

Thanos held her close, waltzing her around the space as the audience began to clap. 'Thank you,' he whispered. 'For being here when I really needed you.'

'You didn't really need me, Thanos,' Lydia said in reply. 'You did this all by yourself.'

'But the stage, it is different and I do not know how to entertain.'

'Neither do I,' Lydia admitted. 'I mean, all I really did was say you look sexy and tie our legs together.'

Thanos raised an eyebrow then. 'The audience seemed to like that.'

'Fifteen, fourteen …'

'We should make sure all the food makes it out from under those hosepipes. Because if we don't then—'

'Sshh,' Thanos said, drawing her closer still. 'A few more steps. A little more music.' He whistled again, the same tune.

Lydia laughed. 'You really are a terrible whistler.'

'Ten … nine … eight … seven …'

The crowd were joining in with the countdown now.

'Thanos!' Lydia exclaimed, letting him go but realising very quickly she was constrained from doing anything too much because they were attached.

'*Ela*!' he said, encouraging her to concentrate on their movement together. 'Here, the last plates, to go on this tray and ... come on, Panos, here!'

'Five ... four ... three ...'

Lydia watched the last of the food make it off the stage and get delivered to the VIP guests and the relief was immense. She felt like she had after every night when Maison Mario had been packed and she had got everything out on time with no complaints or returned dishes. It was as close to perfection as it got.

'Two ... one ...'

A loud buzzer sounded out and then the water poured. Streaming from the hosepipes came loud, hissing, hard shafts of water, hitting Lydia's skin from every single angle. And it was freezing cold! In the heat here in Corfu it was difficult to get a shower cool enough to rinse off the temperature outside but wherever this water was coming from it was Arctic level.

'Oh my God! Oh my God!' she cried, flapping her hands about and trying to move her feet.

'We did it, Lydia,' Thanos told her. 'We did it!'

It was then that Lydia realised two things. Firstly that the audience were all up on their feet, clapping their hands and cheering, and secondly that Thanos was completely soaking wet already. The ripped shirt was plastered to his body, he had taken off his bandana and that shoulder-length hair was sodden too, dripping droplets of water onto his olive-skinned, taut, inked chest. It was like a scene from *Sex/Life* and she had the opportunity to direct it ...

Suddenly it wasn't about the cooking, or the applause, it was about the two of them, here together in this moment. Perhaps they should be moving, getting off the stage and away from the water but all Lydia felt, standing here, looking into his beautiful eyes, was clarity. This bubble of a moment, *this* was what was important when everything else was muted and stripped back. It was simple, humble, pure – exactly like Thanos's cooking when it was given time to breathe. Exactly like the heart of the man she was getting to know.

She moved her left leg, the one still tied to him and in a rush of spurting water and eagerness, she was in his arms and her mouth was suddenly a glorious concoction of wet lips and hot tongue. It was like they were here at this beach kitchen entirely alone, the spotlight only on how they felt about one another.

'Lydia,' Thanos breathed, his mouth finally leaving hers.

'Yes.'

He looked like he wanted to say something important, something that was bubbling under the surface but not quite making it out.

'You are amazing,' he breathed, holding her face in his hands and kissing her again.

Fifty-Three

Arillas

'Honestly,' Caroline began. 'Are people going to start asking for your autograph soon? And are you going to sign it "Bream-anna"?'

Lydia laughed. They were back at their apartments, sat on their balcony, devouring some of Thanos's cauliflower *gyros* left over from his stall at the festival. Although she hadn't told Caroline it was cauliflower and as Caroline had sampled a lot of different gins, she was suspecting her friend wouldn't really notice. It was excellent, the marinade perfect to give it that authentic taste.

After their cooking performance, Thanos had been drawn off into the crowd of VIP guests at the festival and Lydia wasn't even able to share a proper goodbye. He was the chef of the moment on this island and she couldn't be more pleased for him.

'I didn't expect to get involved in the show-cooking but—' Caroline started.

'Caroline,' Lydia said. 'You carried some trays of plates.'

'Yes, you say that, but without me, that octopus would have been doing more than swimming in its own juice, it would have been doing the breaststroke like Adam Peaty going for gold.'

'Thank you for your help,' Lydia said, licking her fingers and reaching for her glass of water. 'I'll make you a badge.'

'You put on a good show though. It was like you'd done it before. Tying yourself up. A few pre-watershed-allowed innuendoes.' Caroline swiped away a mosquito. 'That kiss though, *that* looked a little too convincing.'

'Well,' Lydia breathed, 'that's showbiz.'

'It didn't look like showbiz. It actually looked like you'd forgotten you were on stage, in front of hundreds of people, and were lost in the moment ... almost like it was one September night in the Gulf of Mexico aboard a cruise ship called *Peregrine*.'

Lydia furrowed her brow. She hadn't heard a Caroline story featuring Mexico before. But it sounded like she was having another nostalgic moment.

'Life,' Caroline said with a heavy sigh. 'It spins on a five pence piece really, doesn't it?'

Suddenly, from inside, there was a knocking on their room door.

'Are you expecting someone?' Lydia asked, putting her glass back on the table.

'Always,' Caroline answered with a grin. 'But I suspect it's for you. One of your crazed fans from YouTube. Or Thanos, come for another show shower. I'll finish the wine, shall I?'

Caroline was already tipping the dregs into her glass as Lydia went to the door and cautiously put fingers around the handle.

'Hello?'

'Is that Miss Lydia?' came the whispered voice. It was the woman from reception.

'Yes,' Lydia whispered back. Then she realised, now she knew who it was, there was no need to hold back from opening the door. She turned the lock and revealed the receptionist wearing her dressing gown with curlers in her short dark hair.

'There is a man for you in the garden.' The woman's expression was a cross between a little bit mad but also quite a lot envious.

'Oh,' Lydia said. 'Sorry. For inconveniencing you. I know it's late. I'll tell him not to do that again. I'll come, now.' She closed the door behind her and stepped out into the corridor. It had to be Thanos. Had he come for a proper goodnight?

'Make sure he goes home after he has finished doing what he has come to do,' the receptionist said seriously. 'Otherwise I will have to charge him for a room.'

'Yes,' Lydia said, nodding. 'I will tell him that.'

Lydia was practically skipping with the anticipation as she made her way through the garden to the area outside the reception that was set up for people to wait. There were some benches under a vine-covered arbour with pots of flowers equally as beautiful as the rest of the green spaces at the apartments. She smoothed her hand over an aloe vera plant and took a moment to settle with the night-time scents and noises. Jasmine in the air, the chortle of crickets, rustling in the cypress trees made by who-knew-what. Rounding the final corner, she wondered if Thanos had managed to dry off yet or whether his ripped shirt would still be a little bit saturated ...

And then she stopped dead in her tracks, the peaceful, joyful feeling torn away like it was a wax strip suckered to her bikini line. It wasn't Thanos. She'd recognise this stature of someone not-tall-but-trying-to-be-taller anywhere. And he was currently facing away from her, rising up onto the toes of his leather shoes and then down again. She could retreat, slink back into the vegetation like a lizard seeking camouflage, pretend this wasn't happening, drift away into the darkness ...

Taking one careful step back, Lydia prepared to get out of this situation and fast. Except she didn't see the drain cover and before she knew it, she was hitting the *plaka* stone ground with a thump. *Damn, that hurt!* And it had been more audible than someone eating prawn crackers in a library.

'Ah, there you are! What are you doing down there on the floor? Come on, up you get!'

Quick footsteps and an outstretched hand Lydia was never going to take. There was no retreating now. She swallowed her pride and clambered up from the floor.

'Hello, Patrick,' she greeted.

Fifty-Four

Ismēnē's house, Benitses

It was late, past midnight now, but there was no way Thanos was going to be able to sleep with so much buzzing in his mind. It was like his brain had been taken over by happy, active bees, showcasing highlights from the night and then, in turn, reminding him of the more trying elements of it. And one of the more trying elements of it was why he was standing here again, outside Ismēnē's front door.

Thanos took a breath. She had done so much to help him. If it wasn't for her he wouldn't have had the opportunity to cook at the food festival. But everything, it *still* always ended up on *her* terms. He had to make it clear, once and for all, that it wasn't how things needed to be going forward. Raising a hand, he went to brush his knuckles against the door but, as he did so, the door creaked open and Ismēnē appeared.

He stepped back as she shuffled out into her courtyard, a bottle tucked under her arm and two small glasses in her hand. No stick, he noticed. Making her way to the little table in the corner, she put the bottle and glasses down and sank into a chair.

'You will pour.' Ismēnē finally spoke as Thanos came to join her, sitting in the seat opposite. 'I do not have the energy.'

'Maybe this can wait until the morning.' She did look so very tired and every single one of her many years …

'If it could wait until the later morning, Thano, you would not have been pacing up and down outside my door for the past ten minutes.'

Always one golden Adidas step ahead. He nodded.

'It is a beautiful night and Nuno is sleeping indoors so … why have you not poured the *raki* yet?' She smiled, her eyes closing a bit. 'I am down to my last few bottles. Spiros's cousin from Crete, he used to send to us a crate of his homemade *raki* before every summer.'

'I know,' Thanos replied as he poured them both a large measure. 'My father kept the bottles you gave him on the highest shelf like it was liquid gold.'

Ismēnē reached for her glass and held it under her nose. 'Ah, that scent. The honey, the cinnamon and cloves. It takes me back.' She swigged the liquid back in one and then put her glass down for further replenishment.

Thanos added some more liquid to her glass before he sat back in his chair and put his hand around the tumbler. He allowed himself a small sip, but he wasn't going to bolt it down like Ismēnē had.

'Why are you here, Thano?' Ismēnē asked, looking at him quizzically.

'To talk with you.'

'No,' Ismēnē said, shaking her head vigorously. 'Why are you here, in Benitses, right now? Why are you not in Arillas with Lydia?'

Why am I not with Lydia? No, this was not the conversation he wanted to have.

'You are reliving the kiss,' Ismēnē said, a throaty chuckle hitting the air.

'I was not.' He sighed. It was impossible to hide the heat creeping up his neck, the sudden need to do something with his hands, to avoid Ismēnē's scrutiny. He tipped back his glass and swallowed his *raki* in one.

'What is it you are most afraid of, Thano?' Ismēnē asked in her wise way.

'I do not know what you mean.'

'Your brother performing tonight,' Ismēnē started. 'Unworried about falling from a great height if the pyramid failed, or if the steps went wrong. That is the confidence of youth that depletes so rapidly. But no matter your age, you should never be scared to make a beginning.'

'And that was what I was doing. My first food festival. My beginning of show-cooking. Except I did not realise there was going to be timers and countdowns and tricks with hosepipes.'

'You think I made it this way,' Ismēnē said with a nod.

'Did you not?'

'No,' Ismēnē told him.

'You did not know?' He didn't believe it.

'I did know,' Ismēnē admitted. 'But there was nothing I could do about it. It was the headline slot, the end of the evening, you know the chef that was supposed to take part dropped out and there was to be no changing of the concept. That was made very clear.'

'But why did you not tell me?' Thanos demanded to know, pushing his hair back behind his ear.

'And if I had?' Ismēnē asked. 'You would have been comfortable to accept it? You would not have worried about how you would make something perfect in that short time with the threat of water? You would not have micro-managed your ingredients and your time? You would not have rehearsed everything three or four times before, until the lightness and the spontaneity were completely gone?'

He poured himself another spiced *raki*. He couldn't deny that was true. And now he didn't know what to say.

'As for Onassis and the boys ... they wanted to help. Onassis was so excited his brother was going to be cooking in front of an audience. The dance group needed a dress rehearsal before the competition. They have been practising so hard and I thought the entertainment would set the right tone before the cooking,' Ismēnē continued. 'They were exceptional, weren't they?'

'Onassis now thinks he is a teenage version of Snoop Dogg.'

'I do not know what that is,' Ismēnē said, frowning. 'I am a cat person.'

Thanos picked up his glass and looked at the liquid inside. Instead of the usual colour of *raki* – completely clear until you added water or ice to it and then it turned milky – this was brown. It looked more like a whisky liqueur.

'It should be one thing,' Ismēnē said. 'But it is entirely another.'

'What?'

'This *raki*,' Ismēnē continued, studying it exactly like he was. 'And ... Lydia.'

He sat up straighter in his seat then, stopped looking at his drink and took a sip of the liquid.

'That was what I meant,' Ismēnē began again. 'Earlier when I asked what you are most afraid of.'

Thanos was finding this conversation uncomfortable now. Because as stressful as the kitchen experience had been, talking about his feelings was over and above all the checking of Fahrenheits and Celsiuses.

'I think that you like Lydia. But you are afraid that you like her a little too much,' Ismēnē said.

'I think you should not be thinking anything about what I think.'

'I think that if I do not think anything about what you think you will be spending the next twenty-five years thinking instead of doing.'

'Ismēnē! Stop!' Thanos ordered. 'Please, just stop.'

'Because it is too difficult to hear?'

'Because all these things ... they are *my* decisions to make!'

Thanos hadn't realised how much he had raised his voice until it hit the air and seemed to echo off the night around them. He drank his *raki* down, then got to his feet, suddenly needing to pace. Although on Ismēnē's small patio there wasn't really anywhere to get to.

'You are right,' Ismēnē said. 'Of course you are right.'

'I did not mean to shout,' Thanos said, resting his hands on the back of his head and straightening his core.

'It is good to shout sometimes,' Ismēnē told him. 'It is part of a process. We think, we internalise, someone frustrates us, we shout ... and then maybe we listen.'

He came back to the table. 'Lydia feels ... more than an opportunity to me.'

Ismēnē nodded. 'I understand.'

'Do you?' Thanos asked. 'Because I do not fully understand

it myself.' He sighed. 'You know how my life has been until now. Cooking, creating, trying new things with food, that *is* my life. That is all I have focused on. It has been my work and my hobby, my only interests. Girls ... women ... they have not been significant.' He swallowed. 'And, to begin with, she was just an attractive woman who loved my food and said that she was going to write about me.'

'But something has changed, yes?'

'The more time I have spent with her ... it has been less about the food and more about wanting to talk with her, to understand the way *she* see things. How *she* feels things.' He looked directly at Ismēnē then. 'I have not had that before. I have always been closed off to knowing anything about anyone else. Because I have not had the space for it. There is me. There is cooking. There is Onassis. That was it.'

'And now?' Ismēnē asked him.

'And now,' Thanos said, re-taking his seat. 'Now, I feel like there is a tiny gap opening up. I do not know how it has happened. But, somehow, there it is. And it is growing wider and taller, a little bit every single day.' He sighed, stretching his arms out over his head. 'I am losing my focus. Right now, at this critical time, when I am out of work and I need to be thinking about ... asking the bakeries to sell my cakes or ... asking Dina if I can take over her restaurant for a night here and there ... or—'

'Or following up on the offers we have coming in after your performance tonight.'

Had he heard correctly? Had Ismēnē just said they had offers after his show-cooking tonight?

'Offers?' he asked her, his heart beginning to race. 'What offers?'

'Many offers,' Ismēnē told him, eyes shining. 'I have so many telephone numbers and business cards I could make cushion covers out of them.'

'But ...' Thanos said, his chest bursting with the idea of the possibility. 'Why did you not say anything?'

Ismēnē looked at him intently, waving her empty glass in the air. 'I did not say anything ... because you needed to shout at me first, so you would be able to listen.'

Part of him wanted to laugh. This wise old woman. Always in control of everything. How did she do it?

'Choices, Thano,' she said as he topped up her glass. 'From leading your own kitchen at restaurants, to private cooking for the rich in the villas here, many opportunities to consider.'

But there was always Onassis to think about – as he had known from the beginning, as he had still known when he cooked under a canvas canopy at the ruins and started this change. However, 'offers' such as these, where he was a commodity in demand, could perhaps be made to suit his needs. Hours he dictated? Time off to make sure his brother was still well cared for ... ?

'With this,' Ismēnē began, 'you should take time to consider what is the best next step before you make a commitment. This can wait until the morning, and the days to follow.'

He nodded. Yes, breathing space. A little time to rest, a few moments to bathe in the energy from the festival ...

'But, I think,' Ismēnē started again, 'that no more time needs to be taken in respect to your matter of the heart.'

Lydia was immediately there, a picture in his mind, her hair tied back in braids, her beautiful smile, the way she seemed to listen so intently when he talked about how food made him feel ...

'Less thinking, Thano,' Ismēnē whispered. 'More doing.' She smiled at him. 'You are not ever afraid to share the dishes you create ... do not be scared to share a piece of your heart.'

He checked his watch. It was twelve-thirty now. But was it too late? To make clear his intentions. To ensure that Lydia knew this wasn't only passion like in their kiss on the show-kitchen, that his heart was getting involved too, that he trusted her.

'Take Spiros's car,' Ismēnē urged. 'The keys are under the visor and the blanket is still in the boot.'

Thanos got to his feet in a rush, ready to depart, then he stopped and opened his mouth to speak – but Ismēnē beat him to it.

'I will check on Onassis. Nuno likes food every two hours. We will be like professional sentries. Go!'

Needing no further reassurance, he headed out of the garden.

Fifty-Five

Arillas

'You're looking ... somehow exactly like you looked the last time I saw you.'

Lydia instinctively put her fingers to the plaits she still had in. Suddenly they didn't seem so much of a new beginning but more a rehash of the old her, the her she had been when she was with Patrick. But, no, she wasn't going to let him filter through her subconscious, especially when he was standing right in front of her like waltzing into her Greek research trip was as natural as her booking a table at his restaurant.

'Is this an unhappy coincidence?' Lydia asked him, folding her arms across her chest. 'Are you over here filming a segment for your new TV show? It's very weird you've chosen the village I'm currently in. And surely I'm subject to some restraining order somewhere, aren't I?'

Patrick shook his head, smiling. His blonde hair was as stiff and coiffured as it always had been – like a human Bart Simpson.

'Right, well, I hope you have a lovely stay but it's late and I need to get to bed. Caroline and I are visiting someone who paints with yarn tomorrow.'

She went to turn around, because walking away from him, from whatever *this* was, was her only option. But Patrick put a hand to her arm and stopped her.

Immediately Lydia recoiled like she'd been branded. 'Don't touch me!' she hissed. 'After all you've done to me! After everything I'm finding out you did to threaten me and my parents!'

Patrick held his hands up, either in some show form of surrender or because he was a bit scared by her tone. How could she not be angry? He had put her through hell. And now here he was trying to sabotage her trip here, invading her space again, trying to claim some kind of ownership over it. For what purpose? Yes, he really wasn't saying enough. He was just there. *Here*.

'What are you doing here?' Lydia questioned.

'I'm here to see you, obviously,' he replied.

'What, so you thought you would just hop on a plane and scour the island for me and turn up at gone midnight at the place I'm staying ... I mean, that isn't creepy *at all*.'

'Don't be hysterical, Lydia. You know it doesn't suit you.'

'What?!' Lydia exclaimed. 'Hysterical doesn't suit me?! Well, do you know what also doesn't suit me, Griddler? You! You being here! And exactly why are you here? Because don't you have some launch party to prepare for? A launch party using *my* menu!'

He pointed a finger then, another smile taking over his slightly oversized mouth which she knew he was self-conscious about. 'So you *did* see the social media posts and the emails?'

'You *tagged* me in them! And that is a huge violation!'

'Ah, well, that wasn't entirely me. The television network handles all that stuff for the show so they were just working on the list I gave them of influencers in the business.'

Influencers in the business. Who was this person stood before her now? Someone who, when they had first met, barely knew one end of a radish from the other. Yet, he had always known how to influence, hadn't he? Mario, Antonia, everyone else at Maison Mario, her parents ...

Lydia gritted her teeth. 'Whatever it is you want, I have nothing for you.'

'Oh, but you do,' Patrick replied, still somehow oozing confidence like it was a Gucci fragrance he'd bathed in.

No matter how much she hated him being here, hated *him*, her interest was piqued. And she tried desperately to not let it show.

'I watched you on YouTube,' Patrick told her. 'Filleting that sea bream like you were creating a dress out of it.'

Bream-anna. Of course he had seen it. She shrugged. 'So?'

'So, that's what I want! That's what I need for my show! People doing extraordinary things with food.'

He waved his hands in the humid air as he said the words 'extraordinary things', like he was performing a magic trick or writing with a bonfire night sparkler.

Lydia shuddered. 'It's called *Get Chips and Grill*. It doesn't sound very aspirational.'

'Oh, you'd be surprised. I've filmed a few segments for the non-live sections. I went into this family's house in Hartlepool – they didn't even have a cooker, can you believe it? Two rings and a microwave – and I taught them how to make—'

'Chicken quesadillas,' Lydia interrupted.

Patrick frowned. 'How did you—'

'Patrick, you think chicken quesadillas are a poor person's Siberian sturgeon caviar.'

'I do not.'

'And I cannot be bothered to argue with you right now! I am here in Corfu, *working*, and it's very late and I've had quite an evening cooking at the local food festival under the most bizarre kind of time pressure and—'

'You've been cooking at a food festival?'

Patrick had said the sentence like Lydia had just revealed she had been moonlighting as a drug lord's enforcer. She wasn't sure whether it made her feel powerful or kind of dirty … but she knew what making the food tonight had meant to her. It had been exhilarating. The biggest high. Not the stage performance but simply being in a working kitchen, getting the job done, making the ingredients fit together in the best possible way.

'Well … I can … offer you more money,' Patrick stated.

'What?' Lydia questioned. 'I don't understand.'

'What's not to understand? I want people like you for my show. To supplement it, if you like. The company said "pad it out a bit", well, I want the best padding the budget can buy.'

Lydia shook her head, stuck between wanting to vent more anger on him and wanting to laugh. This TV opportunity didn't sound like a golden goose, it sounded like a very thin, poorly defrosted then burned to a crisp, festive turkey. And he wasn't about to entice anyone into working with him if he described them as 'padding'.

'Have you asked Gino D'Acampo?'

'Lydia—'

'What about Sue Perkins? Or is she still dressing up as a dragon and singing?'

'Lydia—'

'Jeremy Pang is pretty bloody excellent.'

'Lydia, I'm being serious,' Patrick said.

'So, am I! Because I still can't believe you're standing here in Corfu offering me a job when you basically faked a relationship with me and then you and Antonia systematically hounded me out of a job I loved and made sure, using my *parents*, that I would never bother you in the cooking world again.'

'You cut off my hair! And you savaged my ear!' Patrick screeched.

'You aren't bloody Vincent Van Gogh! And I apologised straight afterwards while you … you used that one mistake to ruin my life!'

Lydia was shaking now and it was only when the final words were out of her mouth that she realised how much power she had given him. And she hated that. She loathed the lava-esque feeling in her stomach. How much anger was still there. How all the memories she had of Maison Mario were stained with her horrible demise starting with the huge loss of her mentor and continuing until Patrick had gradually, subtly destroyed her. And he was here again now, to do what? Ask her to work with him again? After *everything*! Just because someone had captured her taking bones out of a fish with a safety pin and it was ruling the internet?

'What can I say?' Patrick asked, spreading his arms wide, like he thought he might be Jesus gesturing to heal the sick. 'We all make mistakes. We learn from them, right? Move on?'

'What? So, you'd be happy if I … took a job working for Hotel Creneau now? You wouldn't … I don't know … threaten my parents that you'll sell your story to a Sunday supplement?'

She saw his face tighten, his lips hardening back into the firmest of lines. She didn't need to say anything. She knew the boutique, uber-expensive hotel with its world-renowned restaurant had always been his ultimate ambition, but he had never been quite good enough to get a position there. He definitely hadn't been good enough to get a position at Maison Mario either, but somehow, in that first interview, he had manipulated her, and what had been the first rung on his masterplan ladder had come across as something *she* had ordained.

'I thought not,' Lydia breathed. She controlled that breath, holding on to it as long as she could, acknowledging its presence and the scent of night too. 'It's always been about control for you. Right from the beginning. And I should have seen that. This offer, where I'm concerned at least, isn't about you needing the best. It's about you needing the best so no one else can have it.'

Patrick waved a dismissive hand. 'Please! I said I *wanted* the best. I didn't say I *needed* it. It's a prime-time television show, Lydia. To be honest, I thought you'd be snapping my hand off seeing as your magazine's in a bit of a precarious position right now.'

An icy dart drove into the bottom of Lydia's spine and sent shockwaves up her back until she could feel them invading her brain.

'What?' she asked, lips shaking a little with the sudden change in her inner temperature.

Patrick smirked, and there was that rage building within her again, the feeling telling her that he was always going to be someone who delighted in the misfortunes of others, or, worse still, went out of his way to lead the misfortune dance himself.

'Seems Escapade Publishing is in a bit of financial difficulty right now. Seeking a bail-out I've heard. Chance of redundancies whatever happens. And the grapevine suggests *Luxe Living* will be the first publication that gets culled.'

Redundancies. A publication getting culled? No, this couldn't be right. This was simply Patrick being Patrick, trying to get in her head and mess with it to suit his own agenda. Because she was here with Caroline having been commissioned to create a Greek edition of the magazine. You didn't shell out on flights and places to stay and expenses for two writers if the publication was in financial jeopardy, did you? And her silence and the cog-whirring of her mind was playing right into Patrick's hands.

'I am not listening to this,' Lydia said firmly. 'So, if the sole purpose of your trip to Corfu was to try to get me to forgive you for being the treacherous, two-faced, backstabbing wanker that you are by offering me a "padding" segment on what I am certain will be a nauseatingly boring show that will one day have to sink to the lowly depths of inviting Miranda Hart as a guest, then you've had a wasted flight!'

Patrick smiled. 'It's not the only reason for my visit. Tomorrow I'm going to visit The Governor's oil mill. Seems they are doing innovative things with production I can make a feature of.'

'No!' Lydia exclaimed. 'You can't! Caroline and I went there! We're featuring that in *Luxe Living*. We've already written the draft copy!'

Patrick shrugged then and he did it in such a way it transmitted all the I-couldn't-care-less-I-do-what-I-want-to-do-regardless-of-whose-toes-I-tread-on vibes that Lydia could almost feel the steam building up inside her like a pressure cooker. He had effectively controlled her for so long, even when she hadn't even known about it! It was unacceptable! And she wasn't going to stand around and let it happen any longer.

'I won't let you do it,' Lydia said, taking a pace towards him up the path.

'Really, Lydia, *you* won't let *me*.'

That smug, condescending look was all over his expression now and Lydia felt that need for control oozing out of him like icing in a well-squeezed piping bag. This was how he pushed people. This was how he riled people up until they had no choice but to react. Or rather they *thought* they had no choice but to react. She was wise to it now though. And she knew exactly how to handle it. She sucked in the humid air and all those comforting scents of Greece – sea salt, sand, vegetation – remembered that imagery from Retrace and Retreat of her breath sitting like a deflated beach ball in her gut waiting to be plumped, and then she went to reply ...

'How about *I* won't let you do this again?'

Lydia closed her mouth up. It hadn't been *her* saying the words, the voice had arrived from behind her. And as familiar as it was, it was completely unexpected in this situation. She spun around, to make sure her ears weren't deceiving her ... and then Lydia gasped.

'Mum!'

Fifty-Six

'Hello, Lydia,' Ulrika greeted.

Lydia swallowed. Her mum might have addressed the greeting towards her, but her mum's gaze was one hundred per cent resting on Patrick as she strode closer to them. Dressed in effortlessly classic casual chic, trousers that were neither too tight nor too loose, her blouse the same, blonde hair set in a kind of tight, controlled nest on top of her head, she looked like she had just stepped out of a geyser, dried off and then been pampered with age-defying oils.

'Mum—' Lydia began.

'No,' Ulrika said firmly. 'You do not say another word. No more conversation will be happening until our lawyer gets here.'

'What?' This came from Patrick, but it had been on the very tip of Lydia's tongue too. Her mum was here in Corfu. She was talking about solicitors. What was going on?

'You did record everything he said, didn't you, Lydia?' Ulrika asked, facing Lydia now and nodding her head. The hair nest still didn't move. 'Like we talked about on the phone.'

'Now, hang on a second,' Patrick began, holding his hands in the air and looking quite a lot ruffled.

'Yes,' Lydia said, trying to instil a bit of confidence into her breathy tone. 'Yes, I did.'

'This is ridiculous,' Patrick said. 'I came here in good faith and—'

'You did what?' Ulrika asked, stepping closer to him and putting on the expression she used when someone was saying something that really didn't compute with her. 'I do not think you would know what good faith was if it jumped out of that sea over there and threw its tentacles around you.'

Her mum had made an octopus joke. And she was standing so

close to Patrick it had to be off-putting. Her mum had always been a master at the art of spatial warfare. It was like a game of human chess, making moves to unsettle and dislodge an adversary. It used to work particularly well at parents' evenings, Lydia remembered, when Mrs Brownley – chemistry – liked to blind parents with potions-speak. Ulrika always refused to sit down and with the deftness of a ninja, managed to transition to the teacher's side of the table.

'Mrs Broom, I—'

'Shut up, Patrick,' Ulrika ordered with utter authority. 'You made a big mistake coming over here. And whatever plan you had to mess with my daughter again, it stops now. It *all* stops now!'

Ulrika's voice reverberated around the apartment complex and Lydia held her breath, half-expecting doors to open and near-naked people to burst out and demand quiet. But nothing happened. And Patrick wasn't saying anything either.

'You will not manipulate our family again. You make any attempt to tell *anyone* what happened on Lydia's last day at Maison Mario, I will finish *your* career.' Ulrika leaned a little closer to him. 'And, believe me, I have that power. I have many friends at Channel 54. One word from me and you won't be getting your chips and grilling, you will be getting the nappy rash cream for the scorch marks on your testicles!'

Even Lydia flinched a little at the analogy. Her mother, the warrior. She suddenly felt so very protected. One look at Patrick told her he was diminishing before her very eyes. Not quite shot down in flames by the Swedish siren but battered down like an inferior meatball.

'Threats,' Patrick began with a head shake. 'And to think I was coming here to release a dove of peace.' He gave a small bow. 'Well, as you wish.'

He turned around to leave the complex, and it was only then that Lydia realised how much tension she had been holding in her body. Her shoulders rolled forward and she inhaled again, willing the bad energy to leave her.

'Stand tall, Lydia,' Ulrika ordered, poking a sharp finger into the base of her back and causing Lydia to recoil from it. 'Half of the reason we get ourselves in these positions is having a sloppy core.' She waited until Lydia was more upright before she spoke again. 'Let us take a walk on the beach.'

The dark sky was wearing a full moon and its brightness was enough to light up the sand as if the sun was already starting to rise. Lydia was carrying her shoes while her mum continued to navigate the beach in her heels – surprisingly well. They hadn't talked yet, but it was an easy silence between them, listening to the sea, breathing in the air as it finally began to cool a touch.

'I don't understand what you're doing here,' Lydia said then.

'I thought I had made that plain back at your hotel,' Ulrika answered. 'I was making sure that horrible *jakel* could no longer hurt you.'

'But … how did you know he was here?'

'I didn't,' Ulrika replied. 'I didn't plan to see him. I planned to see you. Him being here was killing the two birds with one stone.'

'But why didn't you tell me you were coming?'

'Lydia, have I ever been the kind of person to dwell on things? Seek a chance to have my mind changed?' Ulrika continued.

'No,' she answered.

'So, you did not respond to your father's messages or calls. You did not answer *my* call, so I got on a plane.'

'I thought you'd give up,' Lydia admitted. 'Realise that I am still too much hassle. That I too easily destroy your need for calm.'

Ulrika snorted. 'You do not decide to have children if you wish for your life to be calm.'

'But—'

'Lydia, I know you think of me as some kind of hybrid of a mother. Like those cars they make that are half petrol and half electric. But just because I do not behave like those mothers they write in children's stories, does not mean that I do not care and love you exactly as they do.' Ulrika sniffed. 'I may not ever have engaged in gluey crafts with you, but I have different expertise. Like threatening to roast your ex-boyfriend's private parts on a barbecue.'

Lydia couldn't help but smile.

'Of course,' Ulrika began again, stepping forward into the sand, her heels disappearing. 'A lot of mothers might use the threat to create a dramatic warning, but not so many of them would follow through if they needed to.' She looked at Lydia directly. 'I would follow through if I needed to.'

And there was absolutely no doubt in Lydia's mind that she would.

'Now,' Ulrika said, turning their direction a little towards the water. 'I know you are angry about what your father and I decided to do at the time and, perhaps we were wrong to keep it from you this long but ... well, we thought it was in the past and that you were happy with your writing.'

Lydia swallowed, trying to mentally prepare an answer but not entirely sure what that answer was going to be. 'I was,' she started. 'I mean, I am, but ...'

She let her words trail off, not really knowing what to add.

'This bloody sand!' Ulrika exclaimed, finally ripping the shoes from her feet. 'Who would make such a flooring that no one could walk on! Sorry, you were saying. About your writing.'

'I am happy with it,' Lydia began again. 'But, since I've been here in Greece, I've somehow been able to engage with cooking again.' She shook her head. 'No ... it's even more than that ... somehow, the way I used to feel about cooking, at the very beginning ... it's starting to return. And, thinking back, even when I was working alongside Mario, something fell away and got lost, somewhere between the time pressure and the always feeling like you have to stay one step ahead of trends. It never maintained that sense of wonder and that feeling that anything could happen on any given day. It got routine I guess.'

And Lydia had never really vocalised all that before. She swallowed, watching her mother's expression. They didn't really have conversations like this. Her dad was the one she always went to for comfort and advice, her mum was the one who offered practicality.

Suddenly her mum was gently rotating into the sand like a

sandworm, spiralling into a cross-legged position with a simplicity and elegance that could only have come from her years performing yoga.

'Routine?' Ulrika asked, setting her jacket straight. 'Or ritual?'

Lydia had no idea what she meant but she dropped to the beach too, far less elegantly. 'Aren't they the same?'

'No,' Ulrika said with a small laugh. 'They might have a similar meaning. But, in practice, they are so very different.' She set her eyes towards the sea. 'Look at the water,' Ulrika encouraged. 'It is "routine" that it rolls backwards and forwards. But look at the way it moves.'

Lydia relaxed her breathing and tuned into the sound of the surf's pattern of movement. Soft yet powerful, controlled yet beautiful.

'Slowly it comes up,' Ulrika said on an in breath. 'Spreading itself over the sand. Then slowly it goes back again.' She let out her breath. Then inhaled again. 'Fast it goes up now ... then waits, elongates, then drifts back into position once more.' Ulrika turned her head. 'Do you understand what I mean now?'

'It's about perception?' Lydia asked.

Ulrika shook her head. 'No, Lydia, it is about taking something you consider "routine" and changing it into a "ritual". And I don't mean you have to put on robes or chant every time you make your morning coffee but being present in the moment, adding a sense of ceremony to the everyday can change how you feel about things.' She sighed. 'Feeling the time, the space, the beauty even in what you might consider mundane.'

'Like *fika*?' Lydia said.

'Exactly like *fika*,' Ulrika answered. 'But to be honest with you, if Maja only talks about her brother who has retrained as a doctor for very much longer my ritual might be taken with another set of friends.'

Lydia laughed and then her mum took hold of her hand. It jarred at first – Ulrika wasn't a touchy-feely kind of person – but as Lydia settled with it, the more it felt comforting.

'It was your father's idea to agree to Patrick's deal,' Ulrika said. 'I think at the time I suggested something similar to the ball-braising, but your father said that might show a tendency to violence in the family.' She sighed. 'We did it with the right reasons at the heart of it, Lydia. We were worried about you. And *you* had to come before anything else.'

Lydia gave her mum's hand a squeeze. 'I know you did what you thought was right. And back then, perhaps it was the only thing to do until I got back on my feet again but ... it doesn't feel right now, to limit my options. Not when I'm beginning to have them open up for me.'

'Good!' Ulrika announced. She dropped Lydia's hand and rose from the sand in one swift action. 'So, just know that if Patrick tries to contact you again or threaten you with anything from the past, your father and I are here for you and I have absolutely no qualms about using the barbecue utensils if I need to.'

'Mum,' Lydia said when she was up from the sand and standing straight again.

'Yes?'

'Thank you for coming.' Lydia could feel the tears welling up in her eyes. It had been a very long day and all the emotions were queuing up for their chance in the spotlight on the beach.

'Don't cry, Lydia,' Ulrika said. 'It gives you lines.'

Lydia swallowed back the sentiment as normal maternal service was resumed.

'Now,' Ulrika replied. 'Let us go back to the apartments and you can show me where Room 249 is. A woman wearing a net over her hair was less than hospitable when I arrived.'

Lydia smiled. 'It's not too far from my room.'

'Tell me there is coffee in the rooms and somewhere to hang my clothes. I am finding that Greece is very rustic. The taxi that brought me here had a hole where the radio should be.'

'There is coffee,' Lydia said. 'And a wardrobe. And a bed, should you be wondering about that too.'

'Lead the way. But not too quickly, I really want to put my shoes back on.'

Fifty-Seven

Benitses

Thanos took another photo even though he had at least five different shots of the same thing on his phone already. Not that he cared. This was momentous. Maybe it was a small step compared to the other offers he had at his disposal, but this meant so much to him. This little bakery/coffee shop in Benitses was everything he admired. It was new, it was funky and cool with its light turquoise painted outside and rug-covered bench to sit on, but the traditional pastries and sweet and savoury treats were exactly like the ones he had looked at with desire when his parents had taken him to Corfu Town. Mixing modern with traditional. That was what he wanted going forward with this cooking. Spinning recipes from long ago into a fusion for the future. And that began today. With some of his creations on sale right here. The borage biscuits and Brookies by Thanos were going to be sold right here today. And, if they sold well, they might be here again tomorrow.

'Are you going to post any of those photos anywhere or just keep looking at them?' Onassis asked with a sigh.

'Post them?'

'On Insta. Or Facebook for the old people.'

'What do I say about them?' Thanos asked him.

Onassis shook his head and rolled his eyes at the same time. 'You cannot be a chef that everyone is talking about without good social media.' He snatched Thanos's phone. 'Look at your profile picture. It is at least five years old. You are wearing your favourite old shirt. Ugh! This is not good.'

'I do not know what to say on these things. Always people say everything they think they are good at and that is ... embarrassing to me.'

Onassis looked up from the phone. 'So you expect people to buy the services of a chef when his background wallpaper is ... an album cover of Bon Jovi?'

It wasn't, was it? If he was honest, he didn't remember what his social media status was because he didn't go on there very much. He mainly used it to keep in touch with old friends who all seemed to either be married with children or not be married with no intention of having children as they were partying too hard. He always somehow slipped down the crack in-between.

'Look at this!' Onassis ordered.

Thanos's phone was pushed back into his face now and he looked at the profile photo of ...

2Ryot.

The picture was sharp and the boys in the shot dressed in jeans, chains, vests, their hair styles ranging from full-on sleeked back to a mohawk, looked like they had done this a million times before. Yet, when Thanos focused – his mind as well as his eyes – he saw that it was Onassis and his friends, their dance troupe. And they had over a thousand followers?

'Our bio has only a few words,' Onassis said. 'But it says all it needs to say.'

Thanos read aloud. '"R U ready 2Ryot".'

'Cool, right?' Onassis said. 'And then it just says what we are – "musician/band" – and there's a link to our YouTube channel.'

'You have a YouTube channel?' Thanos asked.

'You should get one too.'

'Oh, I don't know, Onassis. I am not good with that kind of thing. And I have to refine my menu for my evening cooking on the boat and—'

'You need to see your girlfriend?' Onassis grinned and pursed his lips, simulating kissing with all the sound effects.

'No, I need to work.'

He swallowed, finding no humour in Onassis's teasing. He had gone to find Lydia last night, driven all the way over to Arillas like Ismēnē had suggested was necessary and when he had got there he had seen her with someone else. Another man. Blonde hair, smartly dressed, neat – the very opposite of him.

He had stood there for a brief minute, watching them talking from just outside the apartment complex, and it was then he realised, if he was one hundred per cent sure that sharing himself with Lydia was the right thing, it wouldn't have mattered who she was with, he would have had the conviction to stride right into the situation and tell her how he felt. The fact that his feet had stuck like glue to the road and nothing had propelled him forward ... did that mean something? That he needed more time to work out what he wanted?

'But she is your girlfriend, isn't she? Lydia,' Onassis continued.

Thanos sighed and moved away from the door of the coffee shop as customers edged around him to go inside. 'It is difficult, Onassis. I'm not sure this is a conversation for you and me,' he said. But then who else did Onassis have to have a conversation like this with? It hit him then that talking about matters of the heart – or perhaps matters of the lips – *was* his responsibility. But was Onassis himself at that stage?

'Sit down with me for a second,' Thanos said, leading the way to the rug-covered bench.

'Oh no!' Onassis remarked, putting his hands up. 'Whatever I said I take it back. That is your lecture voice. And you said you have much work to do to prepare for your next cooking night so you do not have time to give me a lecture.'

But Onassis gravitated to the bench and sank down onto it, folding his arms across his chest.

'You want to talk man to man?' Thanos asked him.

'I think I might need more coffee.'

Thanos took a deep breath then stretched his fingers out in front of him before recoiling them back into tight fists. 'I like Lydia,' he admitted. 'I like her a lot. But sometimes, when it comes to matters such as this, it is not always so straightforward. There are many problems to overcome.'

'Like what to cook her for a date? Because she is good at cooking too?' Onassis asked.

'No,' Thanos answered. He shook his head. 'I am trying to say that "liking" someone, it is not the same as "liking" someone.'

'What?' Onassis replied, laughing.

Thanos had tried to differentiate the tone of his voice on the word 'liking' but somehow it hadn't really worked. He tried again. 'When you are young you will "like" a lot of people but that does not mean that one day you will "like" them enough to ... you know ... move things on to another stage.'

'Oh,' Onassis said, giving an all-knowing nod as Nuno arrived at their feet and looked up as if expectant for scraps. 'You do not want to have sex with Lydia.'

'Sshh!' Thanos exclaimed in horror. 'What?! No! Not that!'

'Not sex? Or no, you *do* want to have sex? I am confused.'

'Onassis, please, stop saying the word "sex".'

Onassis whispered then, leaning his dark head of hair close to his brother's. 'So, this isn't about sex?'

'No', Thanos told him. 'It is about everything *but* that. It is about a deeper emotion, a connection between two people that changes the dynamic of things.' And he wasn't explaining this well at all. He thought back to the times he had spent with Lydia. There was an undeniable chemistry floating between them, making a frothy, creamy, sexy topping, but there was also a beautiful, firm yet sweet and sticky biscuit base in their interactions as a foundation to it all. Thanos had never had that biscuit base before. 'Sometimes it is all only ... whipped cream ... but then, you might meet someone and it is whipped cream and ... the whole cheesecake underneath.' He looked to Onassis for his reaction. 'Do you understand?'

Onassis nodded his head. 'You are talking about the kind of relationship that Mama and Papa had.' He sniffed. 'Ismēnē talks about them like they are ... romantic gods.'

It was Thanos's turn to smile then. 'They were not romantic gods. Mama used to spend half her life yelling at Papa to clean up ... or stop playing his mandolin ... or telling him to not give me extra food to make into my first bad attempts at meals.'

'Ismēnē says they were always laughing,' Onassis said softly.

'Yes,' Thanos answered. 'Yes, that is true.'

'They had the whole cheesecake together,' Onassis said.

'Yes, I think they did.'

'So, you have been through a lot of whipped cream,' Onassis said, still tickling the cat. 'But this is the first time you think you might have the whole cheesecake?'

And suddenly this conversation had turned into being solely about him. Him and Lydia. If there even *was* a him and Lydia. He didn't have a response for Onassis so now it was his turn to bend down and pet the animal at their feet.

'What does Lydia think about the cheesecake?' Onassis asked.

'I ... do not know if Lydia is more about ... the whipped cream or—'

'You have had whipped cream with Lydia already?' Onassis exclaimed in a mixture of shock and awe. 'I guess it makes sense when you think about that kiss.'

Thanos shook his head. 'No, we have not had ... the kind of whipped cream that you are referring to.'

'Oh,' Onassis began. 'So, *you* know you want whipped cream with Lydia, but you also want to make the whole cheesecake with her too. But you do not know if she wants whipped cream *or* cheesecake?'

This was a ridiculous conversation. Thanos put his head in his hands, slipping his fingers through his hair as he sighed heavily. It shouldn't be this complicated. Why was it? Or were all these difficulties of his own making? Maybe he just needed to trust how *he* felt. Perhaps it didn't matter how Lydia was feeling, he simply should be strong enough to voice his own sentiments, even if he was preparing himself for a knock-back. Maybe it would be exactly like making his biscuits and Brookies this morning, signing his boxes for them to be sold in and approaching this first shop with his goods. There were no guarantees. This place made its own pastries – great ones – why would they want to sell another chef's food? Except he had pitched the uniqueness of his recipes, sold the benefits of offering their customers the widest choice.

Was that what he should do with Lydia? Voice the merits of a cheesecake with him – someone who had no job and a brother to look after – versus whoever that had been with her in the garden last night and her luxurious magazine career ...

'You should simply ask her,' Onassis said, breaking the silence and looking up from stroking Nuno. 'You are always telling me that if you are one thing in life it should be honest.'

'And that "honesty" had you selling a pig and trying to spend the day picking fruit.'

'But you also say that you learn from your mistakes,' Onassis said quickly. 'You should perhaps learn from mine.' He placed a hand on Thanos's shoulder. 'Stop speaking to me and go and speak to the person you want to make dessert with.'

Thanos shook his head, a small smile making its way onto his lips. 'Every day you turn a little bit more Ismēnē.'

'And every day,' Onassis replied. 'I grow more envious of her gold trainers.'

Thanos lightly clipped his ear with his hand.

'Hey!' Onassis complained. 'Do not deform me. I have a social media image to keep up.'

'And homework to keep up,' Thanos added. 'Come on, let's head home. You can focus on some maths and—'

'We will take a photo for your Instagram in your chef's outfit?'

He shook his head again. 'OK, but I want final approval before you post anything.'

Fifty-Eight

Delfini Taverna, Agios Georgios Pagon

'The décor is different, very few clean lines, lots of bits broken and falling off,' Ulrika began. 'But I am finding that the Greeks are very like the Swedes when it comes to taking time, relaxing and making corners of the day for well-being.'

'Corners of the day,' Caroline remarked. 'I like that.'

Lydia sat back and sipped her glass of water with ice and took a corner of this moment to really savour the fact that her mum was here on Corfu, sitting at a table *on* the stunning sandy beach, metres away from the shimmering sea, about to eat lunch with her and Caroline. It was a scenario she would never have believed would play out.

'So, what is happening after lunch?' Ulrika wanted to know. 'I have to admit I did not find the person painting with wool very appealing.'

'Oh, did you not?' Caroline asked, swigging back her water infused ouzo. 'I could hardly tell. I thought you sucking through your teeth at the noise of her tufting gun was a compliment or something.'

And there it was. The reason that Caroline and Ulrika had never previously met was not about the distance between them but because Lydia knew it destined to be like the clash of the Titans.

'The "art" was ugly,' Ulrika stated firmly. 'Who would want strings of wool hanging off in all kinds of directions fixed to their wall? It makes no sense.'

'Exactly!' Caroline said triumphantly. 'And that is the whole definition of art. My readers are going to lap it up.'

'Ridiculous,' Ulrika countered. 'In Sweden, pleasure comes from beauty and comfort, it does not come from ... chaotic spindling.'

Lydia's phone erupted and a text message appeared. Before she could swipe it up off the table, her mum had leaned in.

'Who is Thanos?'

'That's Lydia's boyfriend,' Caroline answered.

'Lydia, you have a boyfriend?'

'I ...' She was caught between reading the text and answering the question her mum had posed. She tried to do both.

Are you free tonight? I would like to take you out.

Those three bubbles were still moving on the screen like he might be about to add more. She watched them and waited until—

'Lydia, did you hear me?' Ulrika asked.

She took her eyes away from the phone. 'Sorry, yes, I mean, yes I heard you and ... Thanos ... he's someone I've met while I've been here.'

'Met?' Ulrika asked, both her eyebrows making shapes that said 'curious' more than 'disapproval'.

'We've ... cooked together,' Lydia said. 'A few times now.'

'You've *cooked* together,' Ulrika exclaimed like 'cooking' was code for 'concealed a dead body'.

'Seriously, if the idea of a shared kitchen does that to your eyebrows, Lydia should have led with "I kissed him in front of hundreds of people at the Agios Stefanos Food Festival",' Caroline said. 'Listen, I can tell this is going to turn into one of those awkward mother/daughter interrogations that are always slightly ick when the relations concerned are in their late fifties and almost thirty, so I am going to have a little walk on the beach and catch up on office stuff while you get into it. OK?'

Caroline didn't wait for a response from either of them before she was strutting away from the table, ouzo glass in hand and heading closer to the water, sunglasses balanced on her head.

'That woman is really your friend?' Ulrika asked, tutting. 'And *min gud*, I am only fifty-four!'

Lydia's eyes went back to her phone. Still the bubbles remained, like a pot of water deciding whether to stay simmering or come to the boil …

'You like this boy.' Ulrika made it a statement. 'He is not like Patrick.'

'No,' Lydia said, shaking her head. 'He is nothing like Patrick. Thanos is … sweet and kind and …' She had been going to say 'sexy' but stopped herself. 'Handsome.'

'Does he have a Greek car that has the radio missing?'

Lydia thought back to the wonderful classic car he had driven them in to Sokraki. Did it have a radio? She hadn't really been paying attention to anything other than the tension in his muscular arms as he gripped the steering wheel …

'No matter,' Ulrika answered. 'I was teasing you. So what does this Thanos do for a job? Is he rich and successful? An heir to a feta cheese empire?'

'Well …'

'Oh, Lydia! He's another chef, isn't he?!' Ulrika said as if being a chef was tantamount to being Matt Hancock.

'That's not the only reason I like him,' Lydia insisted. 'I like … the way he looks at life, the way he seems to work things out with this calm attitude … most of the time … unless he's faced with the challenge of hosepipes, but wouldn't anyone get stressed over that?' She shivered all of a sudden, remembering their high-stakes cooking last night and the way it had ended with the most passionate of kisses.

'You lost me at "hosepipes". Is that a Greek dish?'

'No,' Lydia said. She took a breath. 'I don't know, it's like Thanos has helped to open my eyes to new possibilities or, maybe, old possibilities I thought were off limits. He's brought out a part of me I didn't know still existed. And I don't just mean with food, I mean with everything. He's shown me what matters and what doesn't matter and he's made me realise the thing that's most important.'

'Tell me,' Ulrika said, leaning a little across the table.

'Me,' Lydia said, her eyes welling with tears. '*I'm* important. And I don't know why it feels so awkward to say that out loud.'

'Of course you're important, darling. Why would you think you are not?'

'Because I've spent my whole life putting other people first. I've made decisions for other people more than I've made them for myself. Even Mario offering me that tremendous first opportunity in his kitchen ... I was so young and naïve, and the chance was so huge I *couldn't* turn it down. It wasn't really a choice.' She took a sip of her water. 'And then, with Patrick being so attentive and on paper us having so much in common, again I wondered why I was thinking so hard about it? What would *people* say if I said no to someone good-looking and successful who wanted to make us a power couple.'

'So, I think you have to decide, is this about your career? Or about Thanos?'

'That's the thing,' Lydia said, smiling now as the sunlight warmed her skin and her thoughts cosied up the rest of her. 'It's about both.' She sighed. 'It's about me putting myself first for once.'

'And you are wanting to get back working full-time in a kitchen again?'

Lydia shook her head. 'No, I don't want that. Not right now. I'm happy with *Luxe Living*. It's a great job and being here creating this summer edition has been better than I could ever have imagined. Sometimes you get stuck in that comfort zone and it's only when you're forced out of it you see how much more you actually want to embrace.'

'Ritual. Not routine,' Ulrika said with a knowing nod.

'Yes,' Lydia said. 'Whatever cooking I do, whatever form it takes ... I want to cook my way, on my terms.' She thought about how relaxed cooking had made her feel here. She didn't want to go back to the being drenched in her own sweat after a night of busy service and having to do that all over again the following day and the next and the next. 'I'm so privileged to have that luxury right now. I can take the time to *explore* food again, try new techniques. Thanos, he wants to get people to try more vegan food, to use less meat but to not lose any of the taste. I love that idea and it's not done nearly enough. I don't know.' She waved a hand as if she wasn't sure putting this next idea was worth too much thought. 'Maybe I can be some kind of food consultant in the future. You know, alongside my work on the magazine.'

'It sounds as if you have it all worked out,' Ulrika said. She picked up her glass of water and raised it as if in a toast. 'You get your practicality from me.'

'I don't know whether I have it all worked out,' Lydia admitted, her eyes going back to the screen of her phone.

'And Thanos, how does *he* feel about *you*?'

'I know he likes me ... quite a bit ... but we haven't really had the chance to have that kind of conversation.'

'Have the actions been speaking over the words?' Ulrika asked.

'Maybe,' Lydia admitted, feeling the heat pick up in her cheeks.

'Well, it was like that for your father and me at the beginning,' Ulrika said, stretching her legs out from under the table and into the sunshine. 'I think your father would still be carrying on that way if it was his choice. But, words, they are more important than actions. Always. They are what turns something from a flight of fancy to something deep and fulfilling and, possibly, if you keep talking and keep listening, they might turn things into a forever.'

Her mum's words wrapped around her heart, raising it up, making it beat to a happy rhythm. This was emotional advice from her. This was new and Lydia liked it.

'God,' Ulrika said, reaching for her glass again. 'That was intense, wasn't it? You are right about this place! It creeps into you with its slightly worn and grubby origins you can't help but embrace. It's all the smiling! Everything is done with smiling ... apart from the woman who runs the apartments we are staying in.'

The bubbles had disappeared on her phone but as Lydia glanced at it again a new message came in. A direct one on Instagram.

The Griddler Official: Lydia, I very much want to move on from what's gone on before. We both made mistakes. I will own the fact that I most probably made more. What I did back then I did out of self-preservation and a lot of jealousy and I'm not proud of that and I am still in therapy over it. And I should definitely have discussed getting on a plane to Corfu with my therapist before I went ahead and did it. But this TV show is my one chance to make a success of something I could be mildly good at. You know I've always been more about the theatre of cooking than anything else and that's what Channel 54 want. But the offer for you to film a segment for the programme was genuine. I meant it when I said I wanted the best, yes, perhaps I need the best too. And the best is you, Lydia. It always has been. In every way.

Lydia swallowed as his words sunk into her. This was an apology and Patrick wiping the slate clean. Yes, it was obviously more for his benefit now he had his TV show to keep his reputation clean for, but it felt sincere. She carried on reading:

But, Lydia, I was serious when I said there are rumours about Escapade Publishing and Luxe Living being in financial trouble. You don't have to take my word for it but, just, you know, ask the right people the right questions. Make sure you're not on the back foot …

The heat was back in Lydia's cheeks as she raised her head from the screen. This time it was fear mixed with foreboding as she recalled the slightly odd conversation she'd had with Caroline back at Gardiki Castle …

'Is everything OK?' Ulrika asked. 'You look a little uncomfortable.' She picked her handbag off the floor and undid the zipper. 'I have some angelica root in here.'

'No,' Lydia said, her voice shaking a little as she got up out of her seat. 'I need to go and have a little chat with someone.'

Fifty-Nine

Cape Drastis, Peroulades

'Do you kidnap me?' Ismēnē asked later that day. 'Is this what this is?'

Thanos was beginning to realise that perhaps this track was not in the best condition and might end up doing permanent damage to Spiros's beautiful old car if he didn't take it extra slow. He eased off the gas completely and let the vehicle take the bumps and ruts as it saw fit.

'Ismēnē, if I was kidnapping you, you would not be up front in the passenger seat, you would be in the boot. And I would not have brought food.'

Ismēnē folded her arms across her chest. 'The food could be for only you. To refresh yourself after you have dug my grave and buried me.'

'So, I am killing you now?'

'A little bit, every single day.' She sighed. 'You do not say what we are doing. That is why I am suspicious.'

'But you know where we are. Look!'

Thanos indicated the vegetation bordering the pathway they were driving. Tall trees, curving trunks leading up to wide canopies of leafage, thick bamboo rustling as the car passed close to its pointed leaves, grazing the paintwork. Out of the corner of his eye he saw Ismēnē unfold her arms a little, as if the lure of this place he was taking her to had suddenly hit more strongly and it was calling to her. Fingers of one hand at the rubber seal on the window, she used her other hand to wind down the window and let in the air.

'Spiros used to play music,' Ismēnē said. 'As I stuck my head out of the window.'

'You want me to play music?' Thanos asked, reaching for the button to turn on the radio.

'No,' she answered. 'They do not play our kind of music on the radio any longer.' She drew in a long slow breath, wisps of her grey hair coming away from the pins meant to control it. 'Spiros, he would always tell me not to put my head out of the window.' She snorted. 'For some reason he always thought a large truck full of chickens was going to meet us face on and that would be the end of me.' She shook her head. 'He was always the one to put worrying in front of enjoyment. Stupid silly man.'

Thanos heard through the words to the tone of regret they were delivered in and knew, without doubt, this was the right thing to do.

'Do not go too close to the edge!' Thanos ordered.

He had parked the car and they had walked the rest of the way, only passing a few tourists. Ismēnē's speed had been restricted by the worn track and the heat of the day but he had helped her as much as he could despite carrying a basket of ingredients and basic cooking equipment. And now the view was in sight, Ismēnē was keen to get as close as she could to it. *Too* close in his opinion.

'OK, Spirit of Spiros, I am listening to you sucking all the fun out of everything!' Ismēnē called back.

And then she let out a gasp that had Thanos looking up from his pan of food as if the sight he expected to see was his friend and neighbour tumbling over the cliff. But she wasn't moving. She was standing still, one hand to her mouth, her fingers shaking a little.

'Are you OK?' Thanos asked her.

She managed a nod. 'The view ...'

He turned down the heat on the pan and moved towards her until he was standing next to her looking over the beautiful vista that stretched out far, wide and deep. Turquoise water, so wonderfully clear, and those rock formations separated from the main coastline, layering up like pages of earth pressed together, imposing and so unusual.

'It is different?' Thanos asked her.

'No,' Ismēnē said softly. 'It is exactly the same.'

'Have you not been here ... since Spiros ...' He let the end of the sentence drift. It didn't need any added words. And perhaps he should have considered exactly how momentous this might be for Ismēnē before he had got her in the car and brought her up here.

'No,' Ismēnē answered. 'Because I thought it might make me feel sad to be here alone.'

'Ismēnē, if this is too much ... if it is not something nice then we can go again. I am stupid and unthinking and—'

'No, Thano,' Ismēnē said straightaway and she reached out for his hand, squeezing it with hers. 'It is good to be here. Very good. Because it is not making me sad and I am not here alone.' She focused a wistful gaze across the expanse of sea. 'I am here with you and my memories of Spiros are with me too.'

Thanos took a breath. 'I feel closest to my parents when I am at the marina in Benitses. Somehow being in the village but looking out at the water brings everything together.' He sighed. 'Sometimes it gives me comfort that they died together, you know. That one or other of them did not have to live on alone.'

'Like me?' Ismēnē asked.

'No! I did not mean that! See, everything I say is so insensitive! How am I going to get this right when I tell Lydia how I feel tonight?' He put his hands into his hair and gave a roar of disappointment.

'You are going to tell Lydia how you feel *tonight*?' Ismēnē asked. 'What happened to last night?'

'I ... got over to Arillas and ... I was not brave. I saw her with someone else and I got scared that I am not enough for someone like her.'

'Someone like her?' Ismēnē scoffed. 'What is this "people like this" and "people like that"? We are all the same people with skin and bones and the need to pass wind.' She moved away from the edge, towards the makeshift kitchen Thanos had set up. 'There is no "not enough", only "who we are" and the sooner the whole world realises this the better.' She plucked a baby tomato from a bowl and popped it into her mouth. 'Spiros knew he would never grow old with me.' She shrugged. 'Like somehow I always knew I would end up a widow. We went into our marriage with no expectations as to how long it would last, simply with the hope that with every passing day our love would only grow. And … it did.'

'That is all I want,' Thanos admitted, coming over to her. 'To feel that connection with someone, the intertwining of my feelings and her feelings and where that might lead us.'

'And that is what you feel with Lydia,' Ismēnē said.

'You think it is crazy. Perhaps it is crazy. She does not live in Greece. I cannot leave Greece. I do not even know for how long she is here in Corfu.'

Ismēnē laughed. 'You hear, but you do not listen!' She threw her hands up in the air, almost halting the flight of a red dragonfly on its way past. 'No expectations, Thano. Belief in your heart. That is all you need to begin. But you must be brave.'

He knew that. He had really known that the minute he had turned his back and returned to the car last night. But sleeping on it, coming down a little from the excitement and the high of their performance at the food festival, meant that today his thoughts and emotions were coming from a calm, stable place. And he felt exactly the same. That he wanted to share the closely guarded parts of him with Lydia.

'OK,' Thanos answered. 'I am being brave. I am being *very* brave because I am making three courses and I want you to test them.'

'What are you making? Will I like it? Is it eggs?'

Thanos frowned. 'You think eggs are something for a romantic meal?'

Ismēnē laughed again. 'No! This is good. So, tell me what you have.'

Sixty

Ilios Living Art, Agios Georgios Pagon

Despite making notes and taking photos, Lydia was not concentrating on their visit to this unique jewellery-making establishment. Her temperament was currently on what she would call a mid-boil. Bubbling furiously but containing the urge to rise up and flood the hob with piping hot anger. And currently Caroline was using Ulrika as a big Swedish buffer.

'So, did you hear them say they offer wedding ring seminars so the bride and groom can have full input into their own special designs.' Caroline let go of a breath that seemed to say she had never heard of anything more romantic in her entire life.

'I liked the design of the bracelet with the olive leaf,' Ulrika replied as she led the way out of the building and back into the sunshine. 'It was very Swedish in its style. Slim, neat lines, simple but beautiful. Elegant.'

'Personally,' Lydia jumped in before Caroline could, 'I liked the silver bangle. Now that's a piece of jewellery you can rely on. Solid and dependable ... weighty and substantial, exactly how a good friendship should be.'

'OK,' Ulrika exclaimed. 'What is going on with you two? Because in the lovely workshop you both seemed like you wanted to take charge of the tools for hammering and hammer out pieces of each other.'

'They do seminars for that too,' Caroline stated, looking a little uncomfortable. 'Not for people to hit each other but to learn how to work with the materials.' She smiled. 'I don't want to hit you by the way, Lydia.'

'Well, I will hit you unless you start talking to me!' Lydia replied.

'Lydia,' Ulrika said sharply. 'Remember what we talked about. Make a ritual out of maintaining calm.' She sucked in a long slow breath with all the grace of a swan, shaping her arms and elongating her neck.

'Why don't I drive us back to the apartments?' Caroline suggested, about to head off.

'No,' Lydia said. 'We are talking about this right here, right now.' She stood in the middle of the road that ran in front of the sand, her arms folded. 'I want straight answers or I'm going to phone Gina right now!'

'No!' Caroline pleaded. 'No … don't do that.'

Lydia immediately picked up the absolute fear in her colleague's voice and that quickened her heart rate even more. There *was* real substance to what Patrick had told her.

'I tell you what,' Ulrika said quietly. 'I am going to sit over on that half-broken bench over there and try not to get splinters through my clothes while I phone Per.'

Lydia was vaguely aware of her mother sliding out of her eyeline but her focus was still on Caroline who seemed to be patting down her handbag looking for something, and the movement was starting to get a little chaotic.

'What are you doing?' Lydia snapped.

'Looking for my cigarettes.'

'But you don't smoke!'

'Not ordinarily.'

'Oh, is it the same as how you don't ordinarily lie to your closest colleague?'

'I haven't told you any lies,' Caroline said, fingers still seeking the elusive cigarettes.

'Oh, really! So when you said earlier on the beach that "nothing was set in stone", you said that having had no clue this whole time we've been here *Luxe Living* is in financial difficulty.'

'Argh! Fruit fucking pastille it is then!' Caroline pulled out a roll of sweets, tore off paper and foil and shoved about five of the sweets in her mouth at once.

'Caroline! Filling your mouth with food isn't going to stop this conversation!'

'Then ... what will?' Caroline inhaled so hard she started coughing and two of the sweets flew out of her mouth and landed on the floor. There quickly followed a bout of coughing that sounded wretched. But Lydia couldn't have sympathy. This whole scenario was of Caroline's making, wasn't it? Without details, she couldn't really know anything for sure. She waited until Caroline had got her breath back before she continued.

'Tell me,' Lydia said, almost holding her breath. 'Is Escapade in trouble? Is there talk of ... redundancies?'

Caroline shook her head. But it wasn't the headshake of someone who was saying 'no' to the question that had been put forward. It was the kind of headshake you did when you wanted to get something out and remove it from your brain. And no words were following the movement.

'Caroline, I need to know! I mean, it doesn't make any sense! *Luxe Living* sent us here, to Corfu! They basically told us to write a whole edition! You don't pay for flights and accommodation and expenses for a Greek copy if you're running on empty!'

'No,' Caroline said, her head now looking too heavy for her shoulders somehow. 'You don't.'

'Then what's going on? And if *you* know, why don't *I* know?'

'Because I kept it from you,' Caroline admitted, voice quivering a little, two fingers wrapping around the packet of pastilles like it was a cigar. 'Because I wanted to show Gina and the CEO that *Luxe* could come back from this. That all it needed was something fresh, something different to what the other magazines are doing currently. With my skill at finding the alternative and your ravishing food reviews, I knew we could make it work. I *know* we can make it work!'

'So the situation isn't quite as dire as Patrick made out?'

'Patrick?' Caroline queried. 'The Griddler knows? And you know because ... *he* told you?'

Yes, Lydia had forgotten she hadn't told Caroline a thing about

Patrick's visit last night. It had been enough that her mum had shown up. Perhaps she couldn't take the moral high ground if she had been keeping things secret too ...

'He came here. Last night. My mum threatened to squash his balls into a pork patty. This is changing the subject!' Lydia yelled. 'You should have told me what was going on. You should have said how important it was we got this edition right.'

'I did keep saying that!' Caroline countered, putting the butt of the fruit pastilles between her lips and sucking. 'I'm even going to write about weddings! That's pure sacrifice right there!'

'But Gina didn't say anything either,' Lydia said, furrowing her brow as a fluffy white cloud covered the sun for an instant. 'In fact, Gina never spoke to me about Greece at all. Neither did Nigel.' There hadn't been one email from either of her bosses since she had been here. Only missives from Bonnie when she needed help ...

'Well, you know, it's difficult for everyone when the "r" word is being bandied about. "Redundancy" is never something you want Susie Dent to explain in detail, is it?'

'Caroline,' Lydia said, '*Luxe Living* do know about this Greek edition, don't they? They did agree to the idea and the trip to Corfu and they are paying for it all, right?'

Caroline made a noise like wounded almost-roadkill and Lydia then realised the true depths of her colleague's deception and the desperate situation they were in.

'You paid for the flights and the hotels and we're not getting any of this money back for food and drinks and hiring the car and ... is my time here being taken as *annual leave*!?'

'Don't look at me like that!' Caroline exclaimed, striking out her right hand, still gripping the roll of sweets. 'I know what I am and I had to come to terms with that before I settled myself with the organisation of it all.'

'Oh my God!' Lydia cried. 'How did you manage to book me annual leave without me knowing anything about it?! This is insanity!'

'I like to think that when you've had a chance to calm down

about it all you'll see that doing something like that takes a lot of nerve and a great deal of skill and I would not have done it unless I thought I had another option.' Caroline drew in a breath. 'Plus, if I manage to activate Stage Two of my plan then you are going to be glad that we have this Greek edition pre-prepared.'

'I don't believe this!' Lydia said, pacing across the road to the edge of the sand. 'Stage Two? How many stages of this frankly farcical nonsense is there?! Because I didn't even know I was a part of Stage One!'

'Because you would have panicked,' Caroline answered, dropping the sweets into her bag. 'Exactly like you are doing now. And I don't panic. I perform. Miracles, I hope. Because, if I can't get us out of this situation, I don't know what I will do. I mean, look at me, the wrong side of forty, divorced, dateless, in dire need of stability and this job ... this job ...'

It seemed that Caroline couldn't carry on talking and Lydia had never seen her this emotional before. She wasn't quite sure what to do.

'Sorry,' Caroline said. 'That was rather pathetic, wasn't it? I must never do that again. I don't want people to think I'm actually human.' She cleared her throat and a little boy tugging a kayak across the sand glanced over at them.

'This job,' Caroline said. 'It's my entire life and I know you know how that feels because that's what you said you felt like when you were a chef. Except I don't have your kind of skill. I can barely work a safety pin for traditional purposes let alone do anything fancy with it. I have clawed my way from writing meaningless articles for the local paper to being a writer people look to to provide them with a trend to jump on, things to desire. I deliver them an ideal and I love that. I really love that.' Caroline took a deep breath. 'I like writing about things I get to experience because I'm writing about them, to help other people who can actually afford them find them. It gives me this deep sense of self-satisfaction ... it makes me feel worth something again.'

'Caroline—'

'Do not say something nice ... if you were going to. I mean, not that you should because I don't deserve you saying anything remotely nice. I just want you to know that I was always acting in what I thought was *our* best interests. Because no matter what the owners decide about the brand, I'm not prepared to give it up without a fight.'

What did Lydia say to that? Suddenly, having the wool pulled over her eyes seemed secondary to Caroline unravelling a little. But being kept in the dark still wasn't on ...

'Why didn't you tell me when you first found out there was a problem?' Lydia asked.

'Because the very last thing you would have done if I told you was get on a plane to Corfu.'

'Well, yes, because now I know you've paid for all this somehow and it isn't a real project!'

'Oh, don't say that,' Caroline said at once. 'Because it *is* a real project. It's *so* real! I've not been as excited about any edition before.'

'But it might not come to anything,' Lydia said, sighing. 'All our hard work might never get read by anyone.' All those delicious meals she'd tried, all those wonderful vistas they'd gazed over, the sights and the sounds of this enigmatic island, Thanos's cooking ...

'It's going to come to something. Vernon has a meeting with Gina next week.'

What? Vernon? Caroline's ex?

'What does that mean?' Lydia asked. 'What kind of meeting?'

'Well,' Caroline said, 'if things can't be resolved in-house with a reshuffle – like getting rid of Bonnie because, well, I'm not sure what she does except stream something called Crunchyroll – or a takeover from another company, then I thought why not get new investors? Vernon knows a lot of influential people. A lot. People with more money than they know what to do with. I mean I know they might be more vulture capitalists than venture capitalists but, if it's people Vernon knows then ... I don't think he would ... sell me down the river.' She swallowed. 'I hope.'

And then Lydia began to see the bigger picture in all this. As well as Caroline pushing forth with finding extraordinary places for them to visit, behind the scenes she had also been strategising, ready to line up meetings, with this huge worry on her shoulders. Lydia looked at her friend and contemplated. Yes, she had kept the truth from her, but was Caroline right? If Lydia had known what was going on, would she have come to Corfu? And if she hadn't come to Corfu she would never have met Thanos or started to cook again ...

'You're an idiot,' Lydia told Caroline.

'You're preaching to the converted with that one.'

'But ... I know why you kept it to yourself,' Lydia said, sighing.

Caroline blew out the longest breath, like breath-blowing had just become a Commonwealth game. 'God, you do! Thank God you do! I was worried you would hold it against me forever or you would ... I don't know, stay here with Thanos or ... decide you want to be a chef again and work for Raymond Blanc or something.' Caroline gasped. 'Is Raymond Blanc still alive?'

Putting herself first. Keeping her options open. Wasn't that what she had been saying to her mum? Now the writing rug had been pulled from under her, exactly when she thought she had the time and space to deliberate over her future. What was she going to do? Try and get a grip on this sinking ship with Caroline? Or see this potential downfall as some kind of karmic sign that a change was needed?

'I don't have choices like you,' Caroline said, gazing out over the beautiful aquamarine water. 'If *Luxe Living* ceases to be then I'll be face first in the overflowing skip of life like an unwanted Groupon deal or ... Dom Joly.'

'Caroline, that's not true,' Lydia replied, moving to stand next to her. 'Your writing is—'

'Full of useless superlatives lately, according to Gina.' Caroline sniffed. '"Lacks bite and crispness", she typed in red over my article about someone who reupholsters antique furniture using vintage clothes.' She shook her head. 'I thought she was describing a limp lettuce at first, not a perfectly restored Elizabethan chair covered in Mary Quant.'

'Well, Gina's wrong,' Lydia said firmly. 'And I'm sure there has to be a way through this.'

'Vernon said he would talk to someone who once bought a football club for an extortionate amount, even when they literally didn't even have two Bovrils to rub together.'

'What's good enough for Ryan Reynolds, right?'

'So, you're not mad at me anymore?' Caroline asked, turning to face Lydia.

Was she mad anymore? Would continuing to be angry achieve anything? Somehow, being angry in Corfu didn't fit with everything surrounding them – the calming water, the beautiful weather, her new outlook on life ...

'I'm not mad,' Lydia said before she considered it further. 'But you need to pledge right now that you're not keeping any more secrets. That you're holding nothing back from me.'

'I think you saw all I had to give when we were forming sexual shapes at the retreat.'

'I mean it, Caroline,' Lydia said seriously. 'Any secrets you have. Get them out. Now.'

Caroline closed her eyes and inhaled like she was doing an exercise from Headspace. 'OK,' she said, coming to. 'OK ... so, I may have once said I was you when I was really drunk and wanted someone to deliver me a battered sausage ... and I wrote them a review ... in your name.'

'What?!'

'And I once set fire to a bin in the office and I blamed it on you.'

'Caroline, I didn't mean every secret you've ever kept. I—'

'And,' Caroline said, her voice almost getting stuck in her throat now, 'I think I might still be in love with Vernon.'

Sixty-One

Cape Drastis, Peroulades

'And now, close your eyes.'

Lydia tried not to have a flashback to the last time this trip she had been asked to close her eyes. It had involved opening them again to the face of Brightness no more than three inches away from hers with a metal ring between his teeth. She gave an involuntary shudder and Thanos put his hands on her shoulders.

'You are OK?' he asked, his body close behind her, guiding her up this pathway that was winding up and around, vegetation making it feel enclosed and, in a way, secret.

'Yes,' she answered, letting her eyes adjust to being closed. 'I'm fine. Just promise me you won't let me fall.'

'I won't let you fall,' he breathed.

This time Lydia gave a shiver rather than a shudder, all those memories of that hot, wet kiss rushing over her as she crept forward along the path.

A few moments later, with Thanos closely guiding her, she felt the earth beneath her feet alter in its composition. It had gone from a well-worn sand consistency to scrub, her steps having to be adjusted accordingly.

'Is it far?' she asked.

'It is worth the walk, I promise again,' Thanos answered. 'Only a few more steps and ... we are here. Open your eyes.'

Needing no further encouragement, Lydia let her eyelids flick up – and what a view it was! She couldn't even gasp, she was so very awestruck by the scene. Right ahead of her was a table set for two but beyond that her eyes were drawn to the ground that seemed to just drop away, showcasing the clear lustre of the bright cerulean water that seemed to go on for miles. Then, jutting out from the coast were these mounds of rock, seeming to grow up from the seabed with an almost lunar quality about them. It was like nothing else Lydia had seen in her entire life.

'Thanos,' she breathed. 'What is this?'

She stopped walking a little way from the edge, feeling the power of the height all of a sudden. She was so small, this tiny frame standing gazing at the sheer magnificence of the formation of nature. She had never felt so insignificant yet, at the same time, she also felt a part of this incredible view simply by being here.

'This is Cape Drastis,' he told her, standing slightly behind her, his breath warming her ear. 'One of my favourite views in the whole of Corfu.'

'It's so beautiful,' Lydia said, almost getting emotional.

'Do you cry?' Thanos asked as if he was sensing it. He came around her, standing next to her, his eyes seeking hers.

Lydia shook her head but her tears were betraying her now, glazing her vision, the emotion of everything spilling out.

'Hey,' Thanos said softly. '*Ela*. Come.'

He drew her into him, holding her close like they might be preparing to perform a dance across the cliff-edge. It wasn't the tight smother of someone who wanted simply to make the crying stop, it was an embrace from someone who always somehow knew exactly what she needed.

'It's so … perfect here,' she answered, holding on to him. 'It puts so much into perspective.'

She felt him nod, his face close to hers. 'The rocks, they have been here for thousands of years, yet always they are constantly changing. But no one really notices the small erosions, the minor movements. Like life, yes?'

Small erosions and minor movements. It depended on your outlook how you perceived what Fate handed you. She smiled, stepping away a little and dashing the back of her hand at her eye to whisk away the tears.

'Last night was crazy, wasn't it?' she said, smiling at him. 'We haven't had a second to even talk about it.'

'Well,' Thanos began, 'I hope we can talk about it as we eat.' He indicated the table she had almost overlooked for the vista and he gave a bow.

'You've made another outdoor kitchen?' Lydia asked, looking over her shoulder and catching the table with the burner, pots, plates and other kitchen paraphernalia in place.

'I almost cannot remember cooking any other way,' he answered with a grin.

'Do you want some help?' she asked.

'Are you going to tie us together again?' he commented with a sexy raise of one eyebrow.

'Only if you want me to,' she answered.

He placed the flat of his hand on his chest and took a breath. 'Focus, Thano. She is trying to sabotage your service.'

Lydia laughed as he pulled a chair out for her with a flourish.

'Please, take a seat,' he told her. 'The food will be ready soon and no one is booked at this table for the whole rest of the night.'

Lydia closed her eyes as she bit into the cheese flutes – *flogeres*. This was the perfection she had been expecting when she had ordered them from the menu at Baptiste Boras's taverna in Benitses. They were perfectly crisp on the outside and then the inside filling was not too gooey but equally not too firm. There was just a kick of chilli and quite the hint of thyme.

'You added more thyme than usual, didn't you?' Lydia asked, licking her fingers.

'You told me that thyme was your favourite herb.'

'It is. And these are delicious. Really.'

'Good enough for you to still write about me in your magazine?'

Lydia sighed, taking a moment to sip a mouthful of the cold white wine Thanos had poured them both. 'Believe it or not, so much has happened since last night.'

'It has?' he asked, pausing in his eating.

She wiped her mouth with a serviette. 'My mum is here on Corfu.'

'Oh,' Thanos said. 'This is unexpected?'

'You could say that,' Lydia said with a nod.

'She was not supposed to come?'

'No. And my mum isn't the type of person to do anything without a lot of planning.'

'So, this is a good visit?' Thanos asked.

Lydia thought about what he had said for a second. Despite the overall circumstances, the way it had turned out was good. She felt as if her mum had opened up to her perhaps for the first time and bared parts of her she never had before. Their relationship might have ended up being strengthened.

'Yes,' she told him. 'I think it is a good visit.'

'Is she staying for a week or ... longer?'

Thanos was holding his breath, drinking Lydia in a little. His question had been as much about how long Lydia herself was staying as it was asking about her mother.

'A few more days, I think,' Lydia said. 'She has a flexible flight booking but my dad doesn't do well at home without direction.'

He nodded. He needed to ask. 'Does that mean you will be ... going with her?'

Lydia shook her head. 'No. I don't know when I'm going back to the UK yet. But things are a little unsettled with *Luxe Living* right now.'

'Your magazine?'

Lydia nodded. 'I can't say anything too much but there's a chance I might be looking for a new job.'

'Oh, Lydia,' he said, reaching across the table for her hand. 'And all I was asking was about myself.'

'No,' she said. 'It's OK. And it might not be as bad as we're thinking yet. I'm keeping upbeat and I know, no matter what, Caroline and I have done great work here. Our Greek experiences are not going to go to waste.'

He squeezed her hand. 'If there is anything I can do. I know nothing about how magazines work but—'

'You've already done so much for me, Thanos,' she replied, wrapping her fingers around his. 'You helped me rediscover cooking and ... you showed me how to believe in myself again.'

He shook his head, hair moving. 'That was not me. You ... you are a true artist when it comes to food. You don't just have the professional training, food is part of who you are. You simply lost your muse and it made you lose your faith for a while.'

'And you helped me find it again, Thanos.'

'I do not deserve any credit. It was you who pushed me to believe I could do better than chopping up a tuna every Tuesday.'

'Perhaps we can agree that we helped each other,' Lydia suggested.

Thanos let go of her hand then and put his fingers to his hair, pushing it away from his face. 'Lydia, there is something you should know.'

She didn't say anything and he held his breath, the night air seeming to still around him.

'I came to find you, last night, after I had already driven home,' he spoke. 'Ismēnē made me see that I needed to make things clear between us. That I should tell you how I feel and how you make me feel.'

'You came back to Arillas?'

He nodded. 'I got to your apartments and I saw you talking with someone and I started to question my timing. I decided to take the night, to let *you* take the night and see if things felt the same in the morning.'

'Patrick,' Lydia said through tight lips. 'You saw me with Patrick.' It was her turn to shake her head.

'I do not want you to think I was ... jealous. I just did not want to interrupt and—'

'Patrick was the reason I left Maison Mario and one of the reasons I felt I had to give up on cooking,' Lydia told him, sitting back in her seat.

'He was?' Thanos's demeanour stiffened a little. 'Perhaps I should have interrupted after all.'

'He's also some of the reason that my mum is here.'

Now he was confused. 'I don't understand.'

'Patrick used me to get into Maison Mario. Then he pursued me, charmed me if you like, until we were in a relationship, and then he manipulated everyone and everything to ensure he took over when Mario passed away.'

'Lydia,' Thanos said, leaning towards her. 'This man hurt you and he tore away something you loved. Where is he now?'

'It doesn't matter,' Lydia said. 'He isn't important. That's what I needed to realise so that I could move on. It wasn't only about the cooking for me, it was about gaining my power back and realising that the only person who can make me feel anything is me. *I'm* in control of what I do and how I react to things, no one else.'

She looked so commanding to him in that moment, the candle on the table picking up the shades in her blonde hair and the fire in her eyes. If it was possible to fall deeper, then he was diving to the bottom of the ocean.

'He can't hurt me anymore,' Lydia concluded.

But could Thanos hurt her? What if, when he told her his full situation, she thought it was an issue that was insurmountable? He wasn't portable. He had responsibilities. He couldn't simply get on a plane and fly somewhere else.

'And I really don't want to spend another second even thinking about him. Not when we're here, in this beautiful setting, with this delicious food and the scenery could not be any better.' She grinned. 'This side of the cliff edge too.' She gave a light laugh and took another sip of wine. 'God, I'm sounding like Caroline now.'

He poured some more wine into her glass and bided his time.

'So, did you get any feedback from anyone about the show-cooking?' Lydia asked, changing the subject slightly.

He nodded, dipping a cheese flute into the dip he'd made to accompany them. 'I have many offers. Some to be a private chef for travel companies who hire people to cook for their guests at luxury villas. Others to lead their kitchens here in Corfu, another two on the mainland.'

'Oh my God, Thanos! That is fantastic! You must be so thrilled! And it's so deserved! Honestly, if I could take you back to England then I would.'

'Would you?'

And he hadn't thought for more than a millisecond before that question had passed his lips. Why had he said that?

'Sorry,' he followed up quickly. 'That was such a stupid thing to say. *Ilithios*!'

He stood up and headed across the grass towards the kitchen, away from Lydia.

Sixty-Two

Lydia watched him moving bowls and plates; clearly he was highly agitated. There was something eating at him and it was worrying her. After Patrick and her mum turning up here and Caroline's revelation about the precarious situation at *Luxe Living*, she really didn't want anything else to have to think about. But this was *Thanos*. They had been connected almost from the first moment they met. She got out of her seat and followed him.

He was tying his hair back now, eyes and mind seeming like they were focused on what he was creating in the pan. What *was* he creating in the pan? Lydia stepped a little closer and inhaled before she looked. Pork? Egg? Garlic? She looked now. Sausage, peppers of all colours and cherry tomatoes were sizzling together.

'I am making something new,' Thanos said. 'The core ingredients are what you brought to the beach in Benitses when we cooked there, but I have added a little spin on it ... some more colour and texture, a little bit of spice.'

'It smells incredible.' She picked up a spoon and scooped a pepper from the pan, popping it in her mouth.

'You know it is only the chef that should do that,' Thanos stated.

'Sorry,' Lydia answered.

'I am only teasing.' He dipped another spoon into the pot and brought it to her lips. 'Tell me, should I add more garlic?'

She held the food in her mouth, using her Rule of L technique, then shook her head. 'No, it's perfect.'

He nodded and went back to concentrating on deglazing the pan with white wine then adding sugar and some water from the bubbling pasta that was in another pan.

'Thanos,' Lydia said. 'Is there something wrong?' She paused for a second before adding: 'Have *I* done something wrong?'

'No!' he exclaimed immediately, dropping his spoon to the designated area for it. 'No, of course not.' He turned to face her, that handsome face etched with worry.

'Because I know, last night, at the food festival, I kind of took over and, maybe, you felt that wasn't what you needed and—'

'No,' Thanos answered. 'Not at all. You saved me last night, Lydia. I did not know what to do and … you were there.' He directed his beautiful eyes at her again. 'I liked that you were there with me. And you know how we chefs can be about our kitchens.' He gave a small smile. 'Well, it did not feel like it should not be. Instead, it felt like it was exactly how it *should* be.'

Lydia felt relief flood through her. Thanos was nothing like Patrick. She had known that, but it was good to have it confirmed. To have the way she felt about him clarified. Because she did feel for him. So very much.

'And that is why,' Thanos continued, 'I have to be truly honest with you.' He sighed, turning down the heat on the pan. 'I *want* to be truly honest with you.'

Oh God. Here it is. This was the moment when the sweetest, best, sexiest thing about her trip to Corfu was about to be turned on its head and ripped away from her like a prize pot on Michael McIntyre's *The Wheel*. Internally everything was beginning to react like Mexican jumping beans. Outwardly, she noticed the sky had begun to cloud over, the sun weakening as it became covered. She put a hand to the trestle table to steady herself.

'I told you about my parents passing away,' Thanos began.

'Yes,' she replied.

'Well, what I did not tell you was the full impact of that.' He took a breath.

'I can't imagine. You were so young. It must have been the hardest time.'

He nodded. 'It was. And sometimes it still is. And as young as I was when they died … there was also someone younger.'

Lydia felt her brow furrow before she even realised she was doing it. 'Someone younger?' she repeated.

Thanos nodded again. 'When my parents passed over, they didn't just leave me with the house and the bills and the responsibility to take care of myself.' He took a second before he carried on. 'They left me with my baby brother.'

'Oh!' Lydia gasped, hands going to her mouth. She needed to say something else but what should she say?

'You are shocked,' Thanos said in a matter-of-fact manner. 'It is not something you would expect, right?'

'Sorry,' she apologised. 'I just ... don't know why you didn't tell me.'

'I think because I was scared for how you would react. Because it changes things. I am not the man you think I am, I am not able to simply fly to the UK or even be away from Benitses for too long and that ... limits those options I was telling you about.' He sighed. 'Here in Benitses everyone knows I am like a single father. Girls, they are not wanting to date someone who cannot live on impulse. You coming here, the way we connect, I did not want to ruin that ... just for the moment. It was like being able to have a fresh start.'

'You thought it would change how I feel about you?' Lydia asked him.

'I thought it might change how you feel about me ... if I told you exactly how *I* feel about *you*. If I said that I did not only want to have these small days with you. That, even if you do not share the same feelings, that I want for you to know it from my side.'

'Thanos,' she breathed. 'I don't know what to say.'

'Say that I should not be afraid,' he said, the words appearing to make his lips tremble. 'Because I have nothing to offer you.'

'Oh,' Lydia said, moving a bit closer to him. 'I think we will have to disagree on that one.'

'I have Onassis. He is fourteen. He wants to be a dancer and he hates maths lessons more than he hates cleaning his room.'

'Anything else?' Lydia asked.

'I have a neighbour, Ismēnē, the one who organised the night at the Roman ruins and the spot at the food festival. She tries to also control my life.'

Lydia laughed. 'Well I have a Caroline in my life and apparently she's started smoking and become adept at subterfuge.'

'Subterfuge?'

'It means deceiving someone in order to attain your own goal,' Lydia said with a sigh.

'Like I have done? Not telling you about Onassis? To get you to keep liking me?'

'No, Thanos. Not like that.' She palmed his face then, loving the slightly rough trace of a five o'clock shadow across his jawline. 'It's nothing like that.'

'Lydia,' he said seriously, looping an arm around her waist and bringing her into his frame. 'I want to spend more time with you. I want to share everything with you. All of me.'

His voice hitched a little on the last sentence and Lydia's heart began to beat to the rhythm of a slow, sultry rumba. Her feelings exactly mirrored his. It felt so completely right even though she hadn't been looking for it, hadn't thought feeling this way would ever be in her grasp again.

'I do not know how we make this work. I do not even know if it *can* work but ... I want it,' he told her. 'I want it so much.'

'And I want it too,' Lydia gasped. 'I really do.'

There were a few seconds that somehow felt like the longest time when they were looking right at each other, drinking each other in and Lydia let herself get caught right up in Thanos's dreamy eyes. And then she didn't hold back any longer. She kissed him, hard and full of each and every tablespoon of the hot passion she felt for him as a loud rumble of thunder pierced the air.

Knocking the still-frying pan with her hip, she moved deeper into his embrace, losing herself in this moment, out in the humid air, next to the most incredible view, with this once enigmatic man, now far more understood, capturing her lips with his.

And as she tugged at his T-shirt, the dark clouds began to weep and those first sporadic drops of rain started to fall. The cooling pats on her skin were at first welcome, but as Thanos walked them backwards into the brush, the soft, fat, light patter changed to hard, driving sheets of water that took Lydia's breath for a second.

'Oh!'

'You are OK?' Thanos asked, now topless and doing a very accurate representation of a hunk from a firefighters calendar.

Lydia smiled. 'Do we make it happen, do you think? Whenever we kiss there seems to be water involved.'

'Maybe it is the Greek gods,' Thanos suggested. He pressed a smouldering kiss to her collarbone, his hair already wet.

'But is the rain a sign they are happy or angry?' She wasn't sure she could deal with tumultuous deities controlling her life's path. It sounded one step too close to subjects Brightness had talked about.

'What are your thoughts?' Thanos asked over the sound of the rain as he slipped one of the straps of her dress over her shoulder until it dropped to the crease in her elbow.

She shivered as she looked at him, the fingers of those gorgeous firm hands, making light work of her dress, as they stepped towards shrubbery privacy. Her thoughts right now were not pure enough for *any* god.

'My thoughts,' Lydia began, her hands moving to the waistband of Thanos's jeans, 'are that the cheese flutes are going to lose all the crispness I loved about them when they're floating in this rainwater.'

'They will,' he agreed as he helped the top of her dress fall down to her waist.

'And,' she said, unfastening the top of his fly, 'whatever you were making with the sausage, the eggs, and the pasta and spice ...' She kissed his mouth again, his lips wet from the rain, his tongue warming hers. She broke her mouth away, eyes heavy with lust. 'That will be ruined too.'

Thanos wrenched her dress away, discarding it on the ground, and she gasped as the rain hit her only-underwear-covered body.

'Does it make me a terrible chef?' Thanos asked her, leaving a trail of kisses from her breasts down to her belly button. 'If I think, this time, we should start with the very sweetest, sexiest dessert?'

'No,' Lydia said, closing her eyes as her skin crackled in time to the first flash of lightning over the sea. 'No ... I think innovative changes to the menu should always be an option.'

'*Poli kalo*. Very good,' he answered, spreading his hands over her soaking wet hair and pulling her closer still. 'But you should know, dessert should always be enjoyed very, *very* slowly.'

She gave out an involuntary sound that had no business making it past her lips. And as Thanos picked her up in his arms, she knew the very last thing on her mind was going to be what the Greek gods – or anyone else – might think.

Sixty-Three

Just as quickly as the thunderstorm had happened, now it had passed. The clouds had cleared away and the sun was beginning to set, turning the sky into an orange and pink, the colour of the inside of a watermelon mixed with papaya. The sun was an orb of burning amber, descending at its own pace and as Thanos drew the blanket around Lydia's shoulders he felt an inner calm he'd never experienced before.

'You brought a blanket,' Lydia said, raising her eyebrow as he moved back closer to her, wrapping them both up.

'It was not my intention that it would be used for this,' he answered.

'Really?' Lydia asked, a smile on her lips all she was wearing.

'I am a gentleman, Lydia. Do you not know this already?' He smiled back, his fingers moving through her still-wet hair. But perhaps the spirit of this blanket had something to do with the deepening of their connection here on the cliffside.

'Well,' Lydia said, turning into him, 'I appreciate manners, of course, but I'm glad you weren't too gentlemanly when you were taking my clothes off.'

'Oh, I took them off?' Thanos asked, putting on a confused look. 'I thought I looked away for one minute and they were gone. Evaporated.'

'Like the rain now,' Lydia breathed, resting her head on his shoulder, eyes fixed on that sunset view. 'Here so fast and then calm again.'

A little like their lovemaking – the quick, intense passion threatening to boil and burn up too soon and then the slower, longer, intimate learning of their bodies and each tiny reaction to a touch, or a kiss. Thanos kissed her hair and held her tight.

'This would be a fantastic place for a pop-up restaurant,' Lydia told him. 'There is more space than at the ruins in Benitses. Granted, in the half-dark, you would have to be careful no one gets too close to the edge but—'

'You know that one customer fell into the actual bath at the ruins. They were not injured but, to do something up here, I would need many licences and that would mean putting prices high and—'

'You should,' Lydia told him, taking her head from his shoulder and looking at him. 'Put prices high, I mean. The quality of your food should demand a premium. When I worked with Mario, his two-course menu was never less than one hundred and twenty pounds.'

'I know,' he breathed. 'But I do not know if I will ever feel comfortable about that.' What was he saying? It was his life's work, his only dream, to be a chef people talked about, admired, longed to be fed by, but he didn't like the world's idea of a price tag?

'People appreciate great food, Thanos. You know that.'

He nodded. 'I do know that. But to know that in my home I have to buy the cheapest of ingredients or to grow them myself to feed myself and my brother while I cook the best things for huge sums of money. It does not feel right.'

He felt Lydia slip her hand right inside his, curling her fingers around his. 'What does feel right?' she asked him.

'I do not know yet.' He sighed. 'I do not know *when* I will know or even if I will ever know. But I need a job.' He sighed again. 'Like I said before, I have nothing to offer you.'

'Please don't keep saying that,' Lydia begged, taking his face in her hands. 'I wasn't drawn to you because of material things. They really don't matter to me. The reason I started cooking was because I loved taking different things, combining and changing them and making them into something completely abstract sometimes. It wasn't about earning the most money I could and, if I had my time over again, I'm not sure I would choose working at Maison Mario.' She hesitated for a moment. 'If I could have chosen Mario and separated him from the intolerable, stressful kitchen, that would have been my ideal.'

'That is how I feel,' Thanos spoke, his fingertips brushing her arm. 'I have spent so long working for Baptiste, making recipes he does not want me to change, my creativity not even allowed to breathe, that I feel that I do not want to compromise.'

'I understand,' Lydia said. 'Because most compromises mean limited personal expression and that's what being a chef is all about.'

He looked at her, taking in her pure, natural beauty, the light freckles across her nose, her blonde hair turned darker with the weight of the rain. She might not speak Greek but she had always been speaking his language when it came to food.

'Today I sold some of my flower biscuits and Brookies to a coffee shop and bakery in Benitses.'

'Oh, Thanos, that's fantastic!' She kissed him, pure excitement in her expression.

'It was a dozen boxes.' He smiled. 'I signed them, like you told me. But I do not know if they will sell, if they will want more, or not, or if other places will take them, how far out I should try before it is not cost effective—'

'It's a wonderful first step,' Lydia reassured. 'How did it make you feel?'

'Amazing,' he told her. 'To know that a version of my mother's recipe is going to be sold in the village she lived. That people will enjoy the biscuits, something I have made, something simple to go with their Greek coffee, that means so much.'

'Simple,' Lydia whispered. 'Humble. But perfectly you.'

'And that is at the basis of my cooking. To create different styles of old favourites, bringing them into this century and changing concepts. I do not want to lose the fire I feel for food.'

'Like I did,' Lydia said.

'I am sorry, Lydia. I did not think,' he said, wrapping his arms around her tighter still.

'No, don't be sorry. I just meant I don't want you to lose that burning energy you have for cooking either. It would, in fact, be an absolute crime.' She smiled then. 'But I also don't think you should wear a cape and walk into a television studio to the tune of "Firestarter" while people chant "Ox! Ox! Ox!".'

'What?' he asked, confused.

'It was an idea Caroline had. You really don't want to know.'

'But I need to choose something. I need to contact the people who gave me their business cards and think about how this all can work for them.'

'No,' Lydia said firmly, pressing her hand to his chest. 'No, this time, in this situation, the customer does not come first.'

'No?'

'No,' Lydia said again. 'I've realised, being here, visiting these wonderful places and taking part in all these different activities, that I have spent my whole life so far being a people pleaser. And it's nice, to think of others before yourself but ... if you put yourself last *all* the time you find that people don't appreciate you at all and, actually, they can lose all respect for you and take advantage. And then you're left feeling so empty and devalued it makes you question everything.'

'That is how you felt? What that man Patrick did to you?' The alpha side of him was rearing up. He didn't want to think about anyone hurting Lydia.

She shook her head. 'No.' She took a deep breath that made his body move too. 'No, in the end, I let him hurt me because I was too weak to stand up to him.'

'Lydia, no one should make you feel afraid. Whether it is at work or anywhere.'

'I know,' she answered. 'And that's why I should have been stronger. I should have called him out on his behaviour, I should have made a formal complaint. Even if it got overlooked, I should have made that stand for myself and anyone else who came after me.'

'I very much want to hit him,' Thanos told her.

She palmed his cheek. 'Well, I'm not proud of it, at all, but I did get a little revenge with the tip of my favourite Santoku.'

'You did?' he exclaimed.

'I think it's what they call a "happy accident".'

Thanos pulled the blanket closer again as the sun started a rapid decline behind the horizon now. 'I have something I would like to ask you.'

'If it's to star in a YouTube video then I think I'm going to have to decline. I've had to turn all my social media notifications off.'

'No,' Thanos said softly. 'It is not that.' He stroked her hair and rested his hand on her shoulder. 'At the end of the week, you know I am making a restaurant on a boat in Agni Bay.'

'I am so excited for you. Cooking on a boat is something I've never done before.'

'Well,' Thanos said. 'That is what I wanted to ask.'

'I don't understand.'

'I want to make this night the biggest success. I *am* charging more money – not Mario prices, but higher prices than anything around here. Makis, he is a hard worker, but he does not understand why everything cannot be served in a pita bread with chips.'

'God, I should introduce him to Caroline. Sorry, go on.'

'I would like you in the kitchen with me,' he told her. 'If you would like to ... I can pay you ... I do not know how much, it will depend on what profit we make but—'

'You want me to work for you, Chef?' Lydia asked, smiling at him.

'No,' Thanos said at once. 'No, I really do not want you to work *for* me.' He touched her cheek with the back of his hand. 'I want you to work *with* me. Us both in charge of the kitchen. Partners.'

She wasn't saying anything and he prayed that he hadn't made a mistake in asking. She had only just started to love cooking again and he was suggesting she went straight back in to working on an event ...

'I would love to,' she answered. 'I would really love to.'

'Really?' he asked, because he still lacked so much confidence.

'Really. For two reasons. Because I want to make sure this evening is as big a success as it can be so everyone sees your talent. And because it will give me a chance to work in a kitchen again and find out whether I enjoy the challenge.'

'I need to finalise the menu. I am caught between going all in for seafood or making it a combination of seafood, meat and a vegan dessert.'

'How about a seafood dessert?'

'You are serious?' Thanos asked. 'I think I feel a little bit sick.'

'I'm serious. I once made a crab version of toad in the hole and I served it with hot spiced custard.'

'You are crazy,' he told her. 'But ... thinking about those flavours ... mmm, I can understand that it might work.'

'You know what my favourite flavour is right now?' Lydia asked, sliding up onto his lap.

'I think you will have to give me some clues,' Thanos said, holding onto her hips.

'Well,' Lydia began, leaning forward. 'The first one is pastry, right here on your fingers.' She reached for his hand and popped his index finger into her mouth. Then very, *very* slowly she removed it again and internally he was groaning with pleasure.

'The next one is—'

'Forget it,' Thanos said, pulling her into him. 'Take all the flavours! Take whatever you want!'

Laughing hard, Lydia put her arms around his neck and he kissed her as she fell back on top of him.

Sixty-Four

Agni Bay

'I literally feel like a Bond girl waiting for 007,' Caroline said, teasing her smile a little wider as more and more beautifully dressed people were welcomed on board the boat Thanos and Lydia were cooking on tonight. '007 is Vernon, by the way. I haven't decided if Gina is M and I'm hoping Reg Atkinson will be Dr. Yes not Dr. No.' Her fingers went to the diamanté necklace at her throat.

Reg Atkinson was the person who could hold the future of Escapade and *Luxe Living* in his filthy rich hands – there was so much riding on tonight.

Lydia took Caroline's hand and drew it away from the necklace. 'Breathe! Remember the techniques we learned at Retrace and Retreat.'

'I only remember how we're supposed to breathe when we're sexually admiring each other in a mirror,' Caroline answered.

'Sshh!' Lydia ordered. 'It's probably best we never repeat that out loud. Ever.'

This takeover bid had been put together quickly, but not without deep thought and an enormous amount of effort from them both over the past week. A flavour of the Greek edition of the magazine had been printed – twice, because the first time everything was upside down – and the man with too much money had bitten. Tonight Lydia was hoping Thanos's food and this idyllic location was going to wow Reg while Caroline wooed him.

'Are there chips on the menu? You haven't said,' Caroline asked with a sniff.

'No,' Lydia answered. 'But if you try everything on offer tonight, Makis is going to make you one of his legendary goat *souvlaki* and chip wraps tomorrow.'

'I'm nervous,' Caroline stated, teeth chattering together despite the heat of the night.

'I can tell.'

It was beautiful here in this cove, the luxury boat moored at one of the wooden jetties coming off the pebble beach. Guests were arriving in a mix between water taxi and car and being shown to their tables by members of the wellness centre. To strike the right high-end note, Lydia had suggested it might be better to have adults acting as waiters rather than teenage boys. The boat, acquired by someone Ismēnē knew, Thanos had told her, was large, pristine and sang luxury from its sleek exterior to the full galley they were going to be working in. Lydia had yet to properly meet Ismēnē or Thanos's brother, Onassis. She hoped he wasn't still holding back, worried about letting her into his life, and that it was more to do with them being super-busy perfecting the menu for tonight's event.

'Because it's not like my entire life's work is riding on some overinflated man with an overinflated ego and a penchant for scarves whatever the weather.' Caroline sucked air through her teeth and leaned a little against the barrier.

'I'm focusing on the fact I'm going to get to meet Vernon,' Lydia said, casting a casual eye at their servers handing out welcome prosecco. Everything had happened at lightning speed, from Vernon talking to the potential investor, to organising flights to get Reg out here to Greece to seduce him with everything Corfu had to offer and tempting him into thinking about getting around a boardroom table with the owners of Escapade.

'Not yet,' Caroline said. 'Not when he first gets here. Don't you have cooking to do?'

'Why can't I meet him when he gets here?' Lydia asked.

'Well, he's always far more entertaining after he's had a couple of glasses of wine. A bit like me.' Caroline reached out for a welcome drink and grabbed it from the tray. '*Yammas.*' She downed it like it was a shot.

'OK, well, I will head back into the kitchen and—'

Caroline suddenly grabbed hold of her arm and gripped hard. 'Don't move!'

'What? Why?' Lydia tilted her head a little, checking there wasn't a carpenter bee hovering around them like a tiny black mini-drone.

'There he is!' Caroline exclaimed. 'Oh my God, those pebbles are going to ruin those Tommy Hilfigers!'

'Is it Vernon?' Lydia asked, looking down the gangplank towards the beach and trying to pick out an individual in very nice shoes.

'No!' Caroline yelped like Lydia might be the stupidest person in Greece right now. 'Of course it's not Vernon! Vernon is ginger! And Vernon thinks that a beautiful shoe is anything other than a trainer!'

And then Caroline screamed. Properly screamed. Like someone had grabbed her by the waist and was trying to haul her overboard. Guests turned away from their light conversation and the delicate background music of the stringed instrument players from Sokraki. Lydia then noticed a grinning, six-foot-tall, red-haired man dressed immaculately in linen trousers – with no creases – and a smart, white, short-sleeved shirt, a bright Paisley patterned handkerchief in its pocket standing behind her colleague.

'Not wearing trainers tonight, darling,' he said.

'Vernon!' Caroline admonished. '*What* are you doing here?!'

'Saving your bacon, aren't I?' Vernon replied. 'Or should I say saving "*Luxe Living* – refine your life". Hello, you must be Lydia Broom. Top chef, top gastronomic reviewer. Or should I call you Bream-anna?'

'Lydia will do just fine,' Lydia replied as Vernon extended his hand and she shook it.

'Don't say that tagline so loudly, Vernon. It's supposed to be top secret,' Caroline said. She rolled her eyes. 'See, I said he was no James Bond.'

Lydia frowned. 007 was exactly what Caroline had called him only moment ago. She opened her mouth to say something but Caroline beat her to it.

'I meant, what are you doing on board the boat when Reg Atkinson is down there, ruining his shoes on the beach? Your instructions were not to leave his side from the moment you picked him up in England.'

'Reg wanted to take a short walk along the shore. He sold it as embracing Greece but I think he just wants to vape. And you are panicking, my sweet,' Vernon said, slipping an arm around Caroline's waist as if it was the most natural action in the world for a divorced couple.

'I said that,' Lydia told him with a nod.

'Of course I'm panicking! Because this is *everything*!'

'It's not everything,' Vernon said in soft, calm tones. '*Everything* is this glistening sea and the endless sky and the setting sun and—'

'Stop with the poetic talk,' Caroline ordered. 'This meeting is everything to me! I've used at least a whole yolk of my nest egg to get that man here business class and you and I need to make him realise that his life cannot go on without owning a publishing company.'

Lydia swallowed. She wanted this too. She still wasn't sure on where her future resided yet and no one liked being forced to make a change until they were ready. But she wanted it so much more for Caroline.

'And have you considered what you will do if he *does* say no?' Vernon asked, plucking a glass from a waiter.

'Which bit of "his life cannot go on without owning a magazine publishing company" was unclear?!' Caroline shot her wild eyes at Lydia. 'This chef has very sharp knives and she knows exactly what to do with a safety pin. As an *hors d'oeuvre*, she'll start with slicing up his scarf.'

'Oh no,' Lydia said, raising her hands in the air. 'Leave me out of this. I am going back to the kitchen where I am sure Thanos has got everything under control.' She smiled at Vernon. 'It's very nice to meet you.'

'And you too,' he replied.

'Make the most,' Caroline said. 'If this all goes kumquat-shaped then you'll never see each other again. Or me.'

Sixty-Five

Taste: Thanos Nicolaidis

First Act
Melon soup, ginger, mint

Second Act
Marathokeftedes– Greek fennel fritters, horseradish crème

Main Act
Stuffed leg of lamb, roasted potatoes, garlic, thyme, seasonal vegetables

Final Act
Hot crab toad in the hole, spiced custard

'We are OK. We are OK.'

Thanos was saying the words to the tune of a song Lydia had put on the speaker in the boat's kitchen. It wasn't rock music, it was something lighter but still powerful. He liked it. He also liked how they were working together in this. They had divided the small area, not so one could not cross into the other section, but so things were organised the best way to ensure smooth and timely service. But not too quick. This event was as much about letting their elite guest list soak up the beauty of the bay as it was about giving them a fine dining experience.

'Are we OK?' Makis asked, using a cloth to wipe his brow.

With his spare hand, Thanos whisked it off the counter and onto the floor, kicking it to the far corner in one swift move.

'We are OK if you do not keep putting your liquids on cloths! Hygiene, Makis.'

'Makis,' Lydia called. 'Could you pop to the supermarket for me?'

Thanos raised his head from where he was plating up the fennel fritters. 'We are short of something?'

'Those crisps that look like bacon rashers. I thought we could put them on the ... toad in the hole.'

Thanos really looked at Lydia then and she was pulling an expression – big eyes, pleading hands, two plaits whipping back and forth like they were balls on the strings of one of those children's drums.

'Yes!' Thanos exclaimed. 'Yes, this is exactly what we need, Makis. Go! Go now!'

'You are OK without me here? You will keep eyes on the lambs?'

'We are OK. Go! Hurry!' Thanos ordered.

Without washing his hands, Makis left the lower deck, scrambling up the stairs to the back of the boat.

'You are really OK?' Lydia asked, coming over to Thanos's side of the kitchen and moving his plates along to the area where their servers were collecting from.

'I am really OK,' he answered. 'But thank you for sending Makis for something we do not need.'

'Oh,' Lydia said. 'I do want the crisps. They're actually Caroline's favourites here in Corfu.'

Thanos shook his head. 'That woman is crazy.'

'Yes, she is,' Lydia said, keeping one eye on the blender she had turned on behind them. 'But she's going to be doing hard work out there tonight. I just hope she doesn't get too drunk and call him "overinflated" if he says no to getting around a table and making an offer on Escapade.'

'It is a big night,' Thanos said. He felt the nervousness in his own tone. 'It is another step forward to ... well ... maybe making a decision on what I want to do.'

'Things are still not any clearer?' She swivelled around. 'Hold that thought, let me turn off the blender and add this a second … OK … taste this.'

He watched her, moving so gracefully, multitasking from one station to the next, until finally holding out horseradish cream on a teaspoon towards him. He took the smallest taste from the end.

'Oh, no. No, don't taste it that way. Luxuriate in all of it. For me.'

He wasn't going to turn the offer down and he put the bowl of the spoon in his mouth and took it all. Suddenly his mouth was full of flavours, it was rich and creamy, it had the tart bite of the horseradish and there was something else he couldn't put his finger on, something that definitely wasn't in his usual recipe. And then …

'There is feta cheese in this,' Thanos said. 'And oregano.'

'Are you cross?' Lydia asked, looking a little apprehensive.

Was she really worried? Did she truly think she had done something wrong? He could not imagine her being made to feel that way in a kitchen.

He put a hand on her shoulder. 'I *am* mad,' he said. 'That this is better than mine.'

'Not better,' Lydia said. 'Just different. And if you don't like it, we can go back to the original recipe after this batch.'

Thanos shook his head. 'You know I would not be able to do that after I have tasted this.'

'I don't know what you mean,' Lydia said with a wry smile.

He put an arm around her shoulders as the music changed to something softer still, a warm summery tune. 'This is how I want my kitchen to be, no matter what form it takes,' he told her. 'Everyone focused, but calm, confident, collaborating. Certain that whatever decisions have to be made it is for the good of the food. To make great tastes.'

'It sounds like a kitchen I'd like to work in.'

Lydia swallowed. What was she saying? For the moment, getting his name out there, deciding what career opportunity to pursue was Thanos's vision, not hers. She still didn't know what she wanted long-term but she was also highly aware that no matter what happened with Reg Atkinson tonight, she and Caroline had a flight booked back to the UK at the end of next week.

'Would you like to cook in my kitchen?' Thanos asked her. 'My *real* kitchen. Come to my home and ... meet my brother.'

He had turned away from her to see to his fennel fritters, eyes on the pan. Lydia smiled and felt it travel from her lips and into her heart. She knew this invitation had come from the deepest part of him.

'I would love that,' she breathed, putting her arms around his waist and hugging tight.

'Really?' he asked, turning around until they were facing each other again. 'Because there is no way that I will be able to stop Ismēnē inviting herself and that cat of hers and—'

Lydia put a finger over his lips. 'You think I am going to be able to stop my mother joining? Not to mention Caroline. And possibly Vernon depending on how tonight goes.'

'If Onassis and his friends win their dance competition it could be a celebration that needs a much bigger table,' Thanos told her, smiling.

Lydia swiped up her water bottle and raised it in a toast. 'To bigger tables.'

Thanos took his bottle and knocked it gently against hers. 'To bigger tables and ... better kitchens.'

'I'll drink to that,' Lydia said, smiling.

'You realise,' Thanos spoke softly, 'if Caroline had not had the idea for you to come to Corfu then we would never have met.' He adjusted the bandana she was wearing over the top of her hair a little.

'*You* realise that she has not stopped reminding me of that fact since she had to admit what was happening with the magazine.'

'Then you might still think that the taste of Mario's orzo is superior,' Thanos teased.

'Well, you would not be signing your boxes of biscuits.'

He put his lips close to her ear. 'And I would not know that the very best taste in all the world ... is you.'

With that sexy sentiment settling on her skin, as Thanos's lips met hers, Lydia decided in their kitchen they should always make time for the moment. It was, after all, the Greek way.

Sixty-Six
A week later

Thanos and Onassis's home, Benitses

'It's so nice to meet you properly at last and I want to say that the event at the Roman ruins you masterminded was spectacular.'

The grey-haired lady wearing golden trainers wasn't saying anything in response as Lydia greeted her in the garden of Thanos's home. She did speak English, didn't she? Yes, Lydia remembered from those brief interchanges they had had. So why was she saying nothing now? *Chocolates.* Everyone loved chocolates and she had made these herself last night. No small task in their even smaller studio room here in the village. Especially when she had had Caroline and her mum 'helping'. And she needed to get them inside, out of the heat, if she wanted them to still be in their best shape.

'I made you some chocolates.' Lydia handed out the box. A smaller version of Thanos's ones she had tied with a blue ribbon.

'Do you know my allergies?' Ismēnē asked.

'There are no nuts,' Lydia answered. 'And they are dairy free.'

'What if I have an intolerance to mustard?'

'There is no mustard in them.'

'Made in a factory with mustard in it?'

'Made in a room with two single beds, a two-ring hob and a strange triangular device we haven't quite worked out what to do with yet.'

Ismēnē broke into a smile. 'You have passed the test. I have no allergies. We can kiss now.'

Lydia didn't even have time to draw breath before she was being squashed into a tight hug and kissed on both cheeks. 'I ... didn't know I was having a test. How did I pass?'

'You did not get frustrated,' Ismēnē announced, throwing out her arms. 'Well, if you did, you did not show it. Thanos, he will frustrate you in the future. He is a man. You need to prepare to initially tolerate the situation and then quietly dominate.'

'Oh,' Lydia said. 'O-K.'

She scooped up a ginger cat and sat it on her shoulder. 'I will take these chocolates inside and hide them from everybody else and I will make sure Thanos is opening wine.'

Lydia smiled to herself and felt the butterflies of nervousness recede a little. Closing her eyes she breathed in the heady scent of herbs, fruits, vegetables and beautiful *luludhia*. That was the Greek word for 'flowers'. She could see it was the most well-cared-for space, everything bright and fresh and oozing colour. The artichokes looked so vibrant Lydia almost didn't recognise them as the same vegetable she had cooked with in the UK. The from-ground-to-table time really did make all the difference and she knew Thanos was always going to source his ingredients from the best places here.

'You left me with your mother,' Thanos said, coming up behind her and dropping a kiss on her bare shoulder.

'What's happened?' Lydia asked. 'She promised me she would not offer you intestinal gas relief or talk about men with long hair. Did she say something about your hair?'

Thanos put his hands to his man-bun. 'She has an opinion on the hair of men?'

'You've been alone with her for almost twenty minutes. You must know she has an opinion on everything.'

Thanos smiled. 'She told me your father is thinking about getting a motorbike.'

'What?!' Lydia exclaimed.

'She says it would be wasted on him because he would get one with a box on the back to carry the shopping and drive it exactly at the speed limit. I think she wants him to get one so she can ride it.'

Lydia shook her head and looked through to the house where Ismēnē, the cat still on her shoulder, was conversing with Ulrika, all the hand gestures going on.

'Do not worry,' Thanos said, putting his hands on her shoulders. 'If they do not get along, we will visit them independently of each other.'

'How is that going to work if they both want to attend the opening of your restaurant?'

Thanos held his breath and felt that thrill buzz through his veins again. Along with the offers he had from the food festival, he had received another approach at Agni Bay. Reg Atkinson hadn't been the only wealthy investor aboard the boat for the pop-up night and now Thanos had to deliberate over something quite different than being head chef of a taverna on this island or cooking for private villas. This was perhaps *the* opportunity of a lifetime. Lorenzo Costa, half-Greek, half-Italian, wanted nothing more than to create a taste of Greece in Italy, *throughout* Italy. His idea was to literally buy Thanos, his skills and ideas and build a flagship restaurant around him. Then, after that, if there was success, another restaurant would follow, then another, and another. Lorenzo was sentimental about bringing Greece to Italy for his mother and he could afford to take the hit if it did not work. Thanos, on the other hand, would have to move to Italy and there was no catch net if it failed. But although there was every obstacle he had always had with regard to Onassis, it wasn't that that troubled him.

'I don't think I can take the opportunity in Italy,' he answered, sighing.

'No?' Lydia asked.

'No. And it is not simply Onassis. He is actually mad about Italy. Ever since Maneskin arrived.' He shook his head. 'It just all seems too ... easy.'

Lydia smiled, fastening her hand around his. 'Oh, Thanos, really?'

'I know you might think that is a dumb thing to say but everything worth having in life has to be earned, does it not? To think that something like that could be handed to me because I cooked things well one night when a millionaire happened to be there?' He shook his head. 'It does not feel right. It does not feel ... like me.' He sighed and put his fingers around a plump, ripe tomato on the plant ahead of them. 'To be given a restaurant, to style it and prepare it and open it with someone else's money. Despite what Lorenzo says, it would never feel like mine, it would *not* be mine. It would be exactly like working for Baptiste again, only with better ingredients.' He plucked the tomato and held it in his hands.

'I understand,' Lydia said with a nod.

'You do?'

'Of course. It is like we talked about at Cape Drastis. It's about being true to yourself and putting your own dreams above any opportunity, no matter how unmissable it sounds.' Lydia groaned. 'God, I was really looking forward to visiting Italy!'

Thanos smiled. 'It is just over seven hours on the ferry from here. Me not taking the chance does not mean we cannot go one day.' He squeezed her hand.

'Thano! I am so hungry! And so are Stamatis and Panos. The others cannot come because they are going to church!'

Lydia grinned as Thanos's brother bounded up to them, a hunk of bread in his hand and some of it already in his mouth.

'Hello,' Onassis said to Lydia, lips spilling breadcrumbs.

'Onassis, where are your manners?' Thanos reprimanded. 'Onassis, this is Lydia. Lydia, this is my brother, Onassis.'

'Hello,' Onassis repeated, this time with a low bow towards Lydia.

She laughed. 'Hello, Onassis. Or should I start with "congratulations"?'

The boy grinned from ear to ear. 'Thanos told you we won the dance competition.'

'He did and, I have to admit, I've watched the video on Instagram several times.'

Onassis shrugged. 'It does not have as many hits as you doing weird things with that fish.'

'Well, I'm going to get Caroline to share it on her story. She has choreographer friends in the UK.'

'Really?' Onassis said, eyes lighting up.

'I can't promise anything but, you know, hard work always pays off in the end.'

Lydia looked back to Thanos and gave him a smile. She was going to support any decision he made because whatever choice he opted for was going to be carefully considered and would come from the heart as well as the head.

'Well,' Onassis said, 'can you two do the hard work now? In the kitchen. We are starving. Dancers are really athletes you know and—' He stopped talking suddenly and then: 'What is for dessert, Thano? Is it ... cheesecake?'

Lydia caught an expression interchange between the two of them she didn't quite understand.

'I think it is time we went inside,' Thanos said, putting an arm around Lydia's shoulder as Onassis ran off to join his friends.

'What was that about cheesecake?' Lydia asked as they headed up the patio, bees buzzing around the lavender bushes. 'Does Onassis not like it?'

'Oh, well, he is unsure right now, how he feels about that particular dessert.'

'What?'

'Please, do not ask me any more questions about it,' Thanos said. 'It will only get complicated.'

Suddenly there was a loud popping noise, like someone had sat on a large bag of crisps. And then there was a scream.

'Lydia,' Ulrika said as Lydia and Thanos came back into the kitchen. 'What is that dreadful noise?'

'It sound like someone has shot a goat,' Ismēnē remarked.

'It's OK,' Lydia reassured everyone. 'That's the sound of a Caroline ecstatic scream. She's happy. And she's probably brought champagne.'

It was the champagne that entered the room first, spurting and shooting and spraying the entire kitchen to the delight of Onassis and his friends who began to dance like they were taking part in an exuberant music video. One person who wasn't so excited by the entrance was Ulrika.

'What are you doing?!' Ulrika exclaimed. 'Are you mad? My clothes are wet!'

'I am wet also!' Ismēnē moaned, kicking up her feet, the alcoholic drink dripping down her dress. Nuno let out a hiss.

'This is Greece!' Caroline yelled, calming the champagne shower and putting the top of the bottle to her mouth, swigging. 'You'll dry in thirty seconds tops in this heat!'

'I apologise for our unorthodox entrance,' Vernon said, deftly taking the bottle away from Caroline. 'But we are celebrating.'

Lydia felt her stomach tense. Please let it be that Reg Atkinson was going to start negotiations to save *Luxe Living*. It would be the perfect icing on the cake of their trip to Corfu if all their research and work here, all the special moments from tasting olive oil and local beer to dancing in the street of Sokraki and visiting Prince Philip's birthplace, would form the most special edition of the magazine under a new owner ...

'Tell us!' Thanos begged, fetching glasses to pour drinks.

'We're getting married!' Caroline shrieked. 'Again!'

Lydia's chest almost burst. She had not been expecting that! But she had never seen her friend look so incredibly happy. Before she said anything, as Onassis and his friends clapped their hands and Ulrika and Ismēnē looked like they didn't know what to do, Lydia ran forward and threw her arms around Caroline, crushing her tight, barrelling into her until they landed out onto the patio.

'I can't believe it!' Lydia said. 'I mean, I am so pleased for you!'

'I'm so pleased for me too,' Caroline answered, her voice sounding as emotional as it gets. 'There I was, teetering on life's Brabantia sixty-litre kitchen bin, and then, suddenly, at my very worst time, there he was ...' She sighed wistfully, holding herself away from Lydia and gazing into the kitchen at Vernon who was now pouring what was left of the champagne into glasses. He followed it up by producing a further bottle from underneath his Hawaiian shirt. 'My white knight,' Caroline breathed. 'My ginger saviour.'

Lydia took her friend's hands and drew her attention back to her. 'Are you sure this is what you want? I mean, I wouldn't be a good friend if I didn't make you take a second and think about … how you'll feel once the initial wedding excitement has dimmed a bit, or if I didn't remind you that … you've been married to Vernon before.'

'I know,' Caroline said, straightening up and seeming to lose the romantic fog from around her. 'But Vernon negotiated hard, in ways he knew I would respond favourably to. A super king bed because he's seventy per cent legs and his feet are always cold and it's like sleeping with a tarantula that's got frostbite. And … work never coming before "us".'

'What?!' Lydia exclaimed. This was new. This was something she never thought Caroline would be able to commit to.

'I know,' Caroline said, the words seeming to drag up her throat a bit. 'I know it's not going to be easy but, Corfu has rubbed off on me a bit. Not the fennel. That still makes me gag, even though those fritters on the boat were deep-fried.' She sighed, gazing around at Thanos's small but perfectly formed garden space. 'No, it's the people … though not the weird ones in robes maybe … and it's the having time and being slightly disconnected from stress somehow.'

Lydia could absolutely understand where Caroline was coming from. She felt all that and more. And she was going to miss being here when she got back to the UK. Miss being with Thanos. Her eyes went to him now, chatting with her mother – eek! – Ismēnē taking a tea towel from his arm and bustling towards the oven, three teenagers juggling with oranges, a cat licking its bum and looking pleased with itself. She was going to lap all of them up over the rest of this week. Perhaps not the cat …

'Want to know something else?' Caroline whispered like she was about to impart a secret.

'You're going to get married at Gardiki Castle?' Lydia asked.

'What?! Are you insane? I might have agreed it would be a great venue to tout in *Luxe Living* but Christ, you couldn't wear any kind of heel there and it has *no* roof!'

'O-K.'

Now Caroline was wearing a really, *really* ecstatic expression and Lydia was wondering what could be more exciting than her wedding and the promise of a giant bed in her master bedroom.

'Reggie took the bait! Negotiations start next week and I have absolutely no doubt he's going to do a bail-out!'

Now it was Lydia's time to squeal as she crushed Caroline for the second time. This was the *best* news.

'So, you know, despite your reservations about me keeping things from you and planning a whole unsanctioned trip to Corfu behind your back, I'd say it turned out pretty well in the end,' Caroline said.

'Come on,' Lydia said, grabbing Caroline's hand and dragging her back into the house.

'Ooh, OK, are the chips ready? There are chips, right?'

Lydia touched Thanos on the arm. 'Where are your shot glasses?'

'Shot glasses?' he asked, raising an eyebrow. 'We have not even had lunch.'

'I know but, I want to do a toast now. With ouzo.'

Thanos moved to one of the cupboards. 'Glasses are kept in here. Mugs in here.' He touched another door. 'Plates here.' He opened another cupboard. 'I will give you a full tour when everybody else has gone,' he said, moving to kiss her cheek.

'Including the bedroom?' Lydia asked.

'*Fisika*. Of course.' He smiled. 'Please think of my home as your home. Then, when you come back, it will not feel unfamiliar.'

Currently, Lydia couldn't imagine Corfu ever feeling anything less than somewhere that had put its arms around her. She drew Thanos closer, wrapping her arms around him and holding him tight. 'I've never felt this happy,' she whispered.

'For me too,' he answered. 'It is going to be so hard to see you leave.'

'It might be better if I stayed.'

'What?' Thanos exclaimed, stepping back from her.

Lydia put her hand to her mouth. 'I mean, I let my heart speak then and … that's what it wanted to say. I don't know how to figure it all out but—'

The rest of her words, whatever they were going to be, got lost to his mouth capturing hers with the hottest kiss.

With shot glasses filled with the famous aniseed-flavoured drink and handed out, the scent of the lamb *kleftiko* in the air and almost all her favourite people gathered around the space, Lydia raised her glass.

'I'd like to propose a toast. Several toasts, actually so take small sips!'

'This is Greece,' Ismēnē told her. 'There is much more ouzo.'

The young boys all cheered.

'But not for you,' Ulrika admonished. 'You will kill your liver before you are twelve.'

'But we are fourteen!' Onassis replied, outraged.

Thanos tapped a spoon against his glass and everyone quietened again.

'I would like to propose a toast to Caroline and Vernon. Congratulations on your engagement. I can't wait to see the ring.'

'Neither can I!' Caroline shouted.

'So, to Caroline and Vernon,' Lydia said, raising her glass.

'Caroline and Vernon,' the group parroted.

'And let's drink to Reg Atkinson and ask the financial Greek gods, if they have a set of gods for that, to help him make the right decision and save *Luxe Living*.'

'Do we raise the toast to this Reg? Or to the Greek gods?' Ismēnē wanted to know. 'The Greek god for wealth is Plutos. But the god of business is Hermes so …'

'Hermes? I thought they were the gods of shite delivery services,' Caroline remarked with a hiccup.

Lydia jumped in. 'To Reg, Plutos and Hermes!'

'Reg, Plutos and Hermes!' everyone said.

'And finally …' Lydia said, her eyes going to the man who had helped her find herself again. 'I want to raise a glass to Thanos.' She swallowed, emotion bubbling up without warning. 'Whose incredible food has nothing on his perfect soul. Gosh … I'm going to cry.'

'Do not cry,' Thanos said, stepping towards her and slipping his arm around her shoulders. 'We are not cutting onions yet.' He raised his glass to his guests. 'I think the final toast, if Lydia agrees, should be to all of you.' He sighed. 'So many different flavours, coming together into this mixing pot that we call … *ikoyenia*, family.' He smiled. 'To family.'

'To family!' everyone said with much cheer.

'That was so special,' Lydia said, hugging Thanos to her as everyone talked loudly around them.

'Family is special,' Thanos told her. 'Whatever form it takes.' He kissed her lips. 'Welcome to the family.'

Lydia beamed and held him close, eyes shutting as she recalled all the perfect memories she'd made so far in Corfu. She'd had just a taste of Greek summer and she could not wait to try much, *much* more.

Epilogue
A year later

Corfu Town

Lydia lifted her head to another blue-sky day and sucked in the mid-morning here in Corfu Town. Like it was marking this moment of reflection, a church bell rang and pigeons took flight from their nooks amid the roofs of the Venetian architecture. Washing lines crossed from balcony to balcony, towels, shirts and underpants rippling in the breeze and the hum from insects and mopeds alike dominated the sounds.

Taking a step back on the shiny cobbles, she admired the restaurant standing before her. It was called *Gefsi* which translated to 'taste, flavour, palate, zest'. As soon as Thanos had suggested they use the word that had described his menu on board the boat at Agni Bay, it had felt right. With its mix of contemporary and traditional exterior – green wooden windows with shutters, a covered seating area spilling out onto the square, window boxes of bright flowers – and the same continuing inside – intimate tables for two or long rustic wooden benches for parties and large families, booths at the back for private occasions – it was how perhaps every restaurant should be: unpretentious, welcoming, for *everybody*.

That was the real beauty of this place – the choice. The menus they had devised catered for all budgets and tastes, from people like Reg Atkinson who demanded new, adventurous and expensive, to those seeking a simple cheaper plate for lunch. Lydia was sure everyone thought they were a bit crazy but, so far, in their first few weeks, the only crazy they really were was crazy busy!

The front door of the restaurant flew open, the bell ringing and Onassis arriving in a frenzy of backpack, trainers and a lot of hair gel.

'Wait!' Lydia said, before he could dive around her.

He stopped and stood to attention. 'I am late.'

'Not yet, you're not,' Lydia said. 'The church bell just rang and we all know that chimes at least three minutes early for reasons I still do not understand.' She smiled at him. 'So, show me, one last practice.' She slipped her phone out of her pocket and pressed for some music – Warren G's 'Regulate'.

Dropping his backpack to the ground, Onassis was quickly into position, perfecting the moves he had been putting together for the past few weeks since he started dance lessons at weekends here in Corfu Town with his group. They still lived in Benitses, in their family home, but between her, Thanos and Ismēnē they managed the school run and the late nights and demands of their restaurant.

Lydia clapped her hands together. She always marvelled at Onassis's perfect popping, locking and moonwalking. He was such a fantastic dancer and the lessons Thanos had agreed to seemed to be a good carrot to keep him on track with school.

'That was the best one!' Lydia told him.

'Really?' Onassis asked, picking his bag up again.

'Honestly! Now, have you got a drink?'

He nodded.

'Did you take enough for lunch?'

'Three bread rolls, ham, cheese and the crisps that look like bacon.'

Oh no! Lydia had bought those for Caroline. But she smiled at Onassis. 'Good! Then go! Have fun! Be back by one o'clock!'

But Onassis was already halfway across the square and peeling off down one of the tiny alleyways. She smiled as she turned her face up towards the sunshine again. She couldn't deny, it had been like inheriting a son she hadn't birthed or raised; Caroline had provided her with all the 'son cuts step-mom's hair while she sleeps' articles from the internet and worse, but Onassis had been nothing but nice to her. Well, apart from the odd spat about eating leftovers in the middle of the night – leftovers that she had made plans for – and leaving wet towels on the floor of his bedroom but other than that ... she let his brother handle everything. She wasn't trying to be anything but Lydia to him. That's who she was in their unconventional family that included an eighty-year-old and a cat who had just given birth to a litter of seven! And everyone had thought Nuno was a boy!

'Lyddy!'

She needed another coffee because that voice sounded like her dad. And her parents weren't supposed to be arriving until twelve. She had arranged to pick them up from the ferry herself.

'Lyddy!'

There it was again! She sheltered her eyes from the sun and looked the opposite way across the grey paved square from where Onassis had run to and ... there they were! Looking like absolute tourists, in khaki shorts, vests, wide-brimmed hats – was that a map hanging around her dad's neck? – her mum and dad were heading her way and her heart contracted with joy. They were here again.

It had been six months since she had seen them in the depths of a Greek winter where it rained for days on end and everyone lit their fires and basically hibernated like hedgehogs. However, coming from Sweden where the winters were ordinarily very dark, they had simply made the most of walking when the weather was dry enough and enjoyed time with Lydia, Thanos and Onassis. Although Lydia had noticed her mum had a big soft spot for Ismēnē and it was their conspiring that had led to this restaurant becoming theirs.

Their restaurant. Every time Lydia said it, even in her head, it felt too good to be true.

She threw her arms out wide as they approached. 'What are you doing here? You said your ferry didn't get in until twelve.'

'She is disappointed to see us, Per,' Ulrika said. 'Come on, let us find a different *taverna* to drink ouzo in.' She took her husband's arm and turned him around.

'No, don't be silly! I love that you're here early, I just—'

'Well,' Per began, 'Paxos was delightful but there was an early boat so we thought, why not?'

Her parents were planning to tour some of the Greek islands this summer. Starting with Paxos, then here in Corfu, followed by Kefalonia and Zakynthos.

Per stepped forward and threw his arms around her. 'How are you, Lyddy?'

'I'm really good, Dad. Really good.' She squeezed him tight. 'And the sun is out for you.'

Per let her go and held his map out. 'Long may it last. We have a map of the island and we are ready to take on the Corfu Trail. Your mother has even packed sensible shoes.'

'Hi, Mum,' Lydia said embracing her mum hard, 'I've missed you.'

Ulrika hugged her close and whispered in her ear, 'I have missed you too.' Then she stepped away. 'Goodness, Lydia, we only saw each other in January. What have I told you about being sentimental?'

Lydia smiled. Spending quality time with her mum and speaking on the phone more regularly, Lydia had learned that her dad revelled in being the soft parent and her mum was keen not to impinge on his role. It was simply how they worked.

'Oh, look at this place!' Per said, admiring the outside of the restaurant and bringing his camera out of his pocket to take pictures. 'The photos do not do it justice.'

'Really?' Lydia said, a little uneasy. 'Because I want the restaurant to look good in photos for the magazine.'

'Per, it looks the same as it does in the photos except it is summer and the flowers are blooming,' Ulrika told him. 'Do not listen to him, Lydia. It looks exquisite.'

'Is Thanos inside?' Per asked, hand on the door. 'I could very much enjoy one of those big Greek beers. The Corfu Red, was it?'

'No, Thanos isn't here. He should be back any second though.

He's collecting Caroline and Vernon from the airport and getting Ismēnē from Benitses.'

'I know this,' Ulrika said. 'And Ismēnē texted me a photograph of the kittens this morning. I have tried to suggest that if she keeps all seven of them in her tiny little doll house she will have nowhere to sleep but the garden.'

'I know!' Lydia exclaimed. 'We would have one but with staying here in Corfu Town at weekends and dashing back and forth to Benitses in the week, it wouldn't be fair to have a pet.'

A car horn tooted and there was Spiros's old Mercedes gliding to a halt outside *Gefsi*. Lydia still got shivers every time she looked at Thanos and acknowledged he was her partner, in business, in love and in every corner of their lives together.

'Please,' Ulrika said as doors began to open. 'Do not let me get sprayed again.'

'Thano,' Ismēnē moaned. 'Do not help me! Do you know how many times I have got in and out of this car in my lifetime!'

'And I wish for you to be around long enough to get in and out of it many more times,' Thanos answered.

It still took Thanos's breath away to see Lydia here in Corfu, standing outside the restaurant they had created together, with the menus they had worked hard to devise together, building this business from the absolute ground up. It was so much more satisfying than walking into something constructed by a millionaire that, at any time, could turn as throwaway as a *gyros* wrap.

It was hard, incredibly hard sometimes, juggling everything they had up in the air and wanting to achieve success for this venture, but it was the most satisfying feeling. Everything he did every day wasn't only for himself, it was for his family. And it was hard to imagine that once upon a time he saw success as something other than that. When he thought about all the proposed job offers, they were all really only about him. *His* journey. *His* status. His *fame* in the cooking world. Well, he didn't want fame. He couldn't believe he ever had. All it brought was stress, tension, being pulled in too many directions. He had that already, being a guardian to

Onassis, he didn't want anything else taking his attention away from his family and dulling the passion he had for his art. Some might say he lacked ambition, but he knew he had it; he wouldn't be a part-owner of already one of the most highly rated restaurants in Corfu if he didn't have it. But home was where his heart lay. And home was Lydia and Onassis. Always.

'Oh my God!' Caroline announced, stepping out of the car. 'The photos didn't do it justice!'

'That is what I said!' Per announced.

'Look at it, Vernon! It's *gorgeous*! What flowers are they?' Caroline asked, stalking closer to the front of the restaurant. 'Do you think you can get them in Sudbury Yellow? That's the colour I want my bridal bouquet.'

'Er ... I think they just come in the colours they grow in,' Lydia said.

'Oh, you can spray anything these days!' Caroline said, turning back to the group.

'Ismēnē,' Thanos said, turning to her, 'do you have the photo of you and Spiros?'

He had reminded her before they left the house but she had been fretting so much over the kittens he had decided not to push the point. It had been Lydia's idea for the photographs. Black and white and sepia tones of the people they loved, the ones who had helped them make this restaurant a reality.

'Of course I do,' Ismēnē answered. 'I am not losing my mind yet.' She drew it out of her large bag and sighed with satisfaction as she looked at it. 'The new frame looks perfect.'

It really did and Thanos could not wait to honour these people in his restaurant. He did not know the full details, he did not *want* to know the full details, but between Ismēnē and Ulrika and Ismēnē's garage of furniture, they had ended up with money, enough money to obtain the bare bones that was this building and to renovate the way they wanted. Except his pride would not think of it as a gift. It was not quite the same as the opportunity with Lorenzo Costa, but he was determined to pay back every cent and more.

*

'Actually,' Caroline said quietly to Lydia, 'I have something for you too.' She reached back inside the back of the car and drew out a large wrapped flat parcel.

'What is it?' Lydia asked.

'Duh! Open it!'

Lydia ripped the tissue paper away, pulling it down until it tore completely and revealed its contents. It was a copy of *Luxe Living*, framed in a golden surround. And it wasn't just any old copy. It was *their* copy. Their Greek edition had been brought to fruition by Caroline and her new team at the magazine and had finally been published in the spring. Lydia had already read it cover to cover and it had made her feel so warm inside as she remembered the beautiful research. This was special. Definitely something for the wall.

'Caroline, it's brilliant. It looks incredible framed!'

'Doesn't it? And I'm so glad no one listened to Bonnie about putting a Santorini dome on the front. I mean, Corfu isn't generic Greece, is it? It's *Corfu*!'

'You kept on Bonnie?'

'She mainly makes the tea … and pops out for the occasional kebab for me. Oh, and sometimes I get her to stalk The Griddler's socials. Such a shame *Get Chips and Grill* didn't get renewed for a second season.'

'I heard,' Lydia answered with a smile. 'And Antonia has sold Maison Mario.'

At first that news had upset Lydia, thinking about all the work Mario had put into building his flagship restaurant and his glittering career and all the wonderful memories she had of working there. But then she thought about how much it had changed since his death, how it could never really have been the same without him at the helm. The new owners were Italian brothers, doing innovative things with pasta. She knew Mario would have approved.

'Well,' Ulrika began, stepping into the conversation as a moped passed them all by, zipping up the street ahead. 'If we are gifting. I have brought you something for the restaurant too.'

Out of her bag she produced a bright red horse with a very smug expression on its face.

'Ugh!' Caroline said. 'What's that? An effigy of a grumpy Trojan horse? That'll scare customers away!'

'No,' Lydia said, hugging the horse to her. 'This is Josefin. She's my Dalecarlian horse I've had since I was a child.'

'If any part of you was cool or Swedish or cool *and* Swedish then you would know,' Ulrika said to Caroline.

'It's perfect, Mum,' Lydia said, giving her a hug. 'Thank you.'

'OK, everybody,' Thanos said, clapping his hands together. 'Let us get off the street and come inside.'

Lydia watched him open the door and their slightly eclectic group began to filter into the restaurant. But before Thanos disappeared inside too and they started to prepare to open for lunchtime, Lydia stopped him at the threshold.

'Stand with me a minute,' she breathed, closing the door and facing him. She took one of his beautiful hands and held it in hers.

'A minute of calm before the storms from Greece, England and Sweden collide?' he asked, a smile on his face.

'A minute for us,' she told him. 'Here in this perfect corner of Corfu, outside our very own restaurant. Thanos, can you believe it?' She squeezed his hand and then she traced her fingers over his skin and onto the tattoo he had inked for her. It was thyme, her favourite herb. And its dual meaning was not lost on either of them. Life here would be lived, but at their own pace.

'It is our time now,' he told her, brushing her hair back from her face. 'And, I know, it is going to last forever.'

Lydia looped her arms around his neck and drew him towards her, breathing deep and feeling so grateful as his lips connected with hers. And there was absolutely no doubt in her mind that all the ingredients of this love they shared together was a recipe to be treasured.

A Note From the Author

You've reached the end! I hope Lydia and Thanos's story has left you with the biggest smile on your face and that you enjoyed your virtual trip to the Greek island of Corfu! It really is the biggest privilege to be able to write about this gorgeous destination I call home.

So, tell me, who was your favourite character? Were you rooting for Lydia? Did Caroline make you laugh? Was Ismēnē someone you would want in your corner? And what about Thanos? Did this Greek chef leave you hungry for more?

I spent four weeks in August visiting all the places featured in this book, sucking in the atmosphere as well as the ouzo, olive oil and Corfu Beer. If you have the chance to visit Corfu, why not use this book as your guide and go to some of the locations featured in the story? I can guarantee you will receive the warmest welcome!

I love to hear from my readers so if you enjoyed *A Taste of Greek Summer* why not let me know! You can connect with me here: —

Website:	www.mandybaggot.com – Sign up to my newsletter!
Twitter:	@mandybaggot
Facebook:	@mandybaggotauthor
Instagram:	@mandybaggot

And why not join The Mandy Baggot Book Club on Facebook!

Acknowledgements

As always, a huge, big thank you to my FANTASTIC agent, Tanera Simons, and the whole Darley Anderson team. No one works as hard as you do, Tanera, and I feel so incredibly lucky to have you on my team!

THANK YOU to the AMAZING Hannah Smith at Embla Books. I cannot tell you how wonderful it is to be back working with you again. I don't think any other editor has 'got' my writing the way you do and I'm so excited to begin this journey at Embla Books with you!

A massive THANK YOU to my bestie, Rachel Lyndhurst! I had no idea that our *Ready Steady Cook* appearance was going to result in me writing about a Greek chef! But our trip to Scotland to put on our aprons was, without doubt, my best lockdown memory! It's your turn to write a chef book now!

A big THANK YOU to one of my Bagg Ladies in particular! Susan Baker – you are always there proudly supporting my books and I so appreciate it!

THANKS also to these wonderful people in Greece:

Heather Skinner – for pointing me in the direction of information and groups to help with my research for Benitses before I could get there myself!

George Dafnis from The Governor Olive Oil – for his guided tour around the family business, the delicious treats his mother made for us and, of course, for the exceptional olive oil!

The fantastic chef who took time out to answer all my crazy food and cooking-related questions – even the question I asked about being tied up in the kitchen! I hope I have made Thanos and Lydia as realistic as possible, and I will be forever grateful for your help and for our friendship.

And last, but definitely not least, THANK YOU to all my readers wherever you are in the world and whatever language you're reading this story in! Without your love and support I wouldn't be able to continue to write these stories as a full-time author. Every click, every share, every comment and email from you really does mean the world to me!

Mandy Baggot

Mandy Baggot is an international bestselling and award-winning romance writer best known for her laugh-out-loud romantic comedies featuring strong heroines, gorgeous heroes and always that happy-ever-after!

Mandy loves the Greek island of Corfu, wine, cheese, Netflix, country music and handbags.

Also a singer, she has taken part in ITV1's *Who Dares Sings* and *The X-Factor*. Most recently, Mandy took part in BBC1's *Ready Steady Cook* with Greek celebrity chef, Akis Petretzikis.

Mandy is a member of the Society of Authors and lives near Salisbury, Wiltshire, UK with her husband and two children.

About Embla Books

Embla Books is a digital-first publisher of standout commercial adult fiction. Passionate about storytelling, the team at Embla publish books that will make you 'laugh, love, look over your shoulder and lose sleep'. Launched by Bonnier Books UK in 2021, the imprint is named after the first woman from the creation myth in Norse mythology, who was carved by the gods from a tree trunk found on the seashore – an image of the kind of creative work and crafting that writers do, and a symbol of how stories shape our lives.

Find out about some of our other books and stay in touch:

Twitter, Facebook, Instagram: @emblabooks
Newsletter: https://bit.ly/emblanewsletter